DOUBLE BLIND

HEIDI CULLINAN

Know when to show your hand…and when to hedge your bets.

Randy Jansen can't stand to just sit by and watch as a mysterious man throws money away on the roulette wheel, especially since Randy's got his own bet going as to the reason this guy is making every play like it's his last day on earth. The man's dark desperation hits Randy right in the gut. Half of him warns that getting involved is a sucker's bet, and the other half scrambles for a reason—any reason—to save the man's soul.

Ethan Ellison has no idea what he's going to do with himself once his last dollar is gone—until Randy whirls into his life with a heart-stealing smile and a poker player's gaze that sees too much. Randy draws Ethan into a series of wagers that leads to a scorching kiss by midnight, but he isn't the only one with an interest in Ethan's vulnerability. Soon they're both taking risks that not only play fast and loose with the law, but with the biggest prize of all: their hearts.

This book is a work of fiction. The names, characters, places, and incidents are products of the writer's imagination or have been used fictitiously and are not to be construed as real. Any resemblance to persons, living or dead, actual events, locale, or organizations is entirely coincidental.

Heidi Cullinan, POB 425, Ames, Iowa 50010

Copyright © 2017 by Heidi Cullinan
Print ISBN: 978-1-945116-14-8
Edited by Sasha Knight
Cover by Kanaxa
Proofing by Lillie's Literary Services
Formatting by BB eBooks

All Rights Are Reserved. No part of this book may be used or reproduced in any manner whatsoever without written permission, except in the case of brief quotations embodied in critical articles and reviews.

First publication 2010
www.heidicullinan.com

For Maura Peglar

ACKNOWLEDGMENTS

Thanks to Crystal Thompson for the cat-training tips, Kari Hayes for the virtual motorcycle lessons, Tom and Nina Cullinan for the Vegas mug with my name on it which I drank out of every day in November 2009, Dan Cullinan for going with me on the virtual Vegas vacation and for putting up with a house that looked like a tornado hit it for twenty-five days again, Stephen Blackmore for the ins and outs of Mary Jane, The Central Iowa Authors for being the most awesome and supportive NaNoWriMo group ever, Mary Eagan for being the most amazing municipal liaison and den mother who ever walked the earth, NaNoWriMo and Chris Baty for one hell of a ride every November, LJ Amazon Nano for support and cameo appearances, Hillari Hoerschelman for the Spanish help (again), Susan Danic for reading the alpha draft, D.W. Marchwell, Dan Cullinan, and Catherine Duthie for being the world's most awesome beta readers.

Thank you to Sasha Knight for showing me how to trim this behemoth into a lean, mean machine I'm pretty sure Crabtree would be proud of, and thanks as always to my patrons, especially Pamela Bartual, Rosie M, Marie, Kaija Kovanen, Sarah Plunkett, Tiffany Miller, Erin Sharpe, Chris Klaene, Sandy C, Sarah M, Deandre Ellerbe, Deanna Ferguson, Michele C, Jennifer Harvey, Katie M Pizzolato, Ninna, Karin Wollina, and Maija.

One of the best places to expose a person's true character is at a poker table.

—Barry Greenstein

CHAPTER ONE

T HE MAN AT roulette table number three on the main floor of Herod's Poker Room and Casino played like a fool, and it drove Randy Jansen crazy.

Randy lay sprawled across the plush leather sofa in Billy Herod's office, making occasional "Yes, I'm listening to you" noises as his employer launched into one of his monologues, but mostly Randy watched the security feed from the casino floor.

Though it was money in the bank for the house, this guy's stupid playing made Randy itch. With the grimness of someone marking out a plot for his own burial, the somber-looking and meticulously clean-cut man laid out his chips and bet on black, over and over again. He lost every single time.

A nudge to his foot startled him out of his voyeurism, and Randy glared at Billy. "What?"

"Quit scanning my floor for dates, and tell me what you think of my brilliant plan." Billy planted himself in front of Randy, his paunch rolling over the waistband of his expensive trousers. "Go on, I dare you to tell me it won't work. I *dare* you."

Randy glanced across the room to the other occupant of the office. Billy Herod's godfather, Crabtree, was round and soft and tricked out in a massive head of white hair like Santa. He even had Santa's laugh, and the sound rumbled out of him now, his blue eyes twinkling as he took in the byplay between Randy and Billy.

The fuck if Randy would give Crabtree the satisfaction. He turned to the television screen.

The man's sweat wasn't actually visible through the feed, but enough of the tells were there for Randy to read perspiration. The money, which could never have been much and was absolutely more than the guy should have been gambling with to start, was almost gone. The man's shoulders rounded, and he watched the chips go as if sending his children out to slay monsters.

This time the nudge came at Randy's shoulder. "Randy."

Randy glanced at Crabtree, whose whole body trembled with his mirth, and yes, it did look like a bowl full of jelly. Randy wondered how many people had let themselves be distracted by this image right up until the moment the knife went into their belly, Santa's eyes still dancing as he bled their life away.

"*Randy.*" Billy tried to poke again, but Randy rolled onto his back at the last second, escaping the jab.

He looked up at Billy. "It won't work."

Billy beamed and hitched his thumbs in his belt loops. "Oh, it will. See—"

"Just because you hire a bunch of twinks to walk

around shirtless, it does not automatically follow that rich gay men will come in here to gamble. It's a *possibility*, yes. But it's also a possibility there won't be enough rich men for you to make back what it's going to cost."

Billy sneered with imagined superiority. "It *will* work, because more and more of you gays are coming to Vegas, and I read a magazine that said gay men have money to burn. And it makes sense—no kids, and you're even more oversexed than regular men. Rich gay men will come in droves when they see what I offer every Tuesday night."

From the other side of the room he heard Crabtree's chuckle.

Randy covered his face with his hands and shook his head. "God, they hit you with the stupid stick way, way too hard." Randy ticked his objections off on his fingers. "First of all, Junior, you'd have to hire all these cute young men to be your sugar-daddy bait, and cute twinks willing to work for your cheap-ass wages are not as thick on the ground as you might be assuming. They can get more working on the street. Which brings me to point two—if you get anyone in here, you will get street boys, which means you will also get police. As I recall, you and Crabtree don't care for that kind of attention. Third, no matter how oversexed gay men might be, we aren't idiots, and if you treat us like fools you're generous enough to bilk every Tuesday night—"

He stopped as he realized his employer wasn't listening, already lost in his latest wild hair. Crabtree's laugh rumbled, and the old man occasionally slapped his thigh.

Randy tossed Crabtree a quick flash of his middle finger and settled into the couch. "Never mind. It's a brilliant idea, Billy. Go for it. Just make sure I work that night, so I can watch."

Billy rubbed his hands together as he stared at the faded 1960s photo of the Strip hanging above his godfather. "I'm gonna bring back the glory days, Randy. I'm going to be rich, and then—" He glanced down at Crabtree and briefly scowled. "Well. Then it will be good again."

"You're already rich." Randy found his quarry on the cam. The man was still there because he hadn't run out of money yet. He looked like somebody had beaten him about the head as once again the wheel failed to land on black. Randy threw up his hands. "Jesus, buddy. *Switch to fucking red.*"

"What?" Billy jerked himself out of his vision. He zeroed in on the screens with hawklike focus. "Is somebody cheating me?"

"God no." Randy pointed to Roulette 3. "This guy keeps betting on black, over and over again. The wheel hasn't hit black in six spins, but he just *keeps at it.*"

"Oh?" Billy smiled and leaned in closer. "Bet black again."

Randy shoved him away from the camera. "No. I want him to go to his room, get drunk, and watch some porn on pay-per-view."

"You want him to be such a good boy, why don't you tell him to call his wife?" Billy stage-winked at

Randy. "Because I'm right, aren't I? There's a wife at home."

"Shit, no. There's no wife." Randy grimaced as the man ran his thumb along the pitiful stack. "He doesn't have kids. He wanted some, maybe, but he never had any. He's sure as hell not married. There was somebody, but they're gone now." On the screen, the man's thumb slid around the top chip reverently. Randy shook his head. "And the cash went with them."

"You're full of shit." Billy shook his head. "You can't know all that."

Randy could, and he did. He'd been watching this guy for half an hour. The particulars might shift a bit, but he knew he was more right than wrong. "He's been dumped and screwed out of money, and now he's decided he'll turn his life around by betting his last dollar on the goddamned roulette wheel—by betting on black on a wheel which hasn't won black since he sat down."

Crabtree ambled over to stand behind Billy. Blue eyes flickered across the screen as they took in tells, making judgments, assessments, and predictions—all in a matter of mere seconds. Flattening his lips, Crabtree lifted his drink.

Fucking hell. Randy had really hoped he was wrong this time. Why, he didn't know. Something about this guy got to him.

He returned his focus to the screen as Roulette Man slid another five-stack forward, all on black. Again.

Billy shook his head, mystified. "Why the hell does

he keep doing that?"

"Because he's an idiot," Crabtree replied into his drink.

Randy cut a glare at the gangster. "Because he thinks the wheel owes him. He's not an idiot. He suffers from delusional thinking. It's been red too long. It's due to go black, more now than ever. He's thinking about laws of averages, and probably fate too. It *has* to fall to black. But the wheel isn't ruled by averages or fate. It's ruled by chaos. It's completely random. It doesn't owe him black. It doesn't owe him anything."

Crabtree grunted. "Which is a long way of saying he's an idiot."

Randy's fingernails bit into his palms as the dealer called a halt on bets. The ball began to slow, getting ready to bounce itself into its final resting place.

"You do realize," Crabtree said as the wheel continued to go around, "Billy Junior is not entirely wrong. The twinks will come because they will be thinking of the sugar daddies. The sugar daddies will come for the sex. And they'll do the negotiating over these tables and the machines and at the bar, and they'll finalize the arrangement upstairs in our hotel rooms."

Billy turned to his godfather, surprised. "You really think it will work?"

Randy kept tracking the ball. "It's tacky as hell, and I can't believe you're encouraging him, Crabtree." *Land on black, you fucker. Land on black.*

Crabtree snorted. "Of course it's tacky. Everything about this place is tacky now. I didn't say it was a good idea. I just pointed out it would work. Except, as you say, for the police. Which will never do. But the fact remains, idiots are idiots and make us a lot of money."

The ball landed. Randy swore, and Billy clapped his hands.

Crabtree sighed. "Ah, the dear, sweet lambs. They never disappoint."

Roulette Man shrank farther into his chair. He had one stack of five chips left in front of him, and then it would be over.

"There's got to be a way around the police." Billy stroked his chin as he walked away from the camera screens. "I'll have to work on that. Thanks for bringing it up, Randy."

"You're not welcome." Randy thought the man at roulette might seriously vomit on the table. Over five fucking dollars. Goddamn, but Randy hated this. He hated how it bugged him as much as he hated watching. He should get up and forget about it, but for some reason he couldn't.

Crabtree sat on the edge of the sofa and patted Randy's foot. "People are people. They will be the card they were dealt to be."

"This guy's smart. Normally, anyway. He's just got his head wrong."

"Oh yes," Crabtree agreed. "This one's an ace."

"You think?" Randy tilted his head and studied the man on the screen with new eyes. Then he nodded. And grimaced. "Fucking hell, he is. And stuck on playing himself low."

Billy settled in at his desk. "You two and your aces and kings. You can't figure people out just by watching them for five minutes."

"It's been half an hour," Randy corrected him, "but yes. You can. And in a lot less than five minutes. It's called a tell, Billy."

"But you were so specific with this one," Billy dogged, leaning forward now. "You think you're right? This guy's been dumped, cheated out of money, and down to his last dollar?"

"Yes," Randy snapped.

Crabtree looked amused. "And for some unknown reason you care about him."

Randy glared at him. "Not everyone is as unfeeling as you."

"No, but *you* usually aren't this involved. You've been funny, in fact, ever since Mitch got married." A smile played at the edges of Crabtree's lips. "Randy Jansen, are you going soft on me? Do you wish you could go down there and sweep this sorry little sack off his feet, then console him and live happily ever after?"

Randy rolled his eyes. "Oh yeah, that's it. I just wish I could go down there and save his poor, sorry ass. I'm dying for an excuse."

Billy leered at Randy. "Bet you can't."

Randy snorted. "You want me to go down there and seduce this guy on a bet?"

"I want you to go down there, flirt with this guy, and find out his story. See if he's what you think he is. And if you aren't one hundred percent right, and if you don't get him into bed with you, I win."

"You're a sick fuck, and I'm not taking your bet."

"Okay—go and see if you're right. I want to know."

"If he's gay?"

"If you were right about what happened to him."

Randy eyed Billy warily. "*Why?*"

"Because I'm curious." When Randy snorted, Billy waved a hand airily. "I am. I want to know if you're right or wrong, or even just close. I want to know if people can be pegged this well. It could be interesting."

Which meant he thought it might be profitable.

Randy caught Crabtree observing him with an interest that unnerved him and forced his attention to the security feed. He thought of Crabtree's blithe dismissal, of his own frustration. *Maybe I can re-screw this one's head on just a little. Send the ace to the top of the pack again. A sort of public service.*

Besides, despite being a bit morose, Roulette Man was hot, and Randy enjoyed flirting. Probably would come to nothing, but it was always fun to mess with a hot straight man.

"Not that I'm taking it," Randy said as the ball spun again, "but what would you want to bet for?"

"If I'm right, you're one of my shirtless twinks on opening night for Gay Nite."

Randy laughed. "I'm not a twink."

"Then you'll be whatever you are, but you'll be in the sexy getup. Or at least something really embarrassing for you. *But* if *you're* right, I make sure you get your *own* twink. Or whatever. Whichever one you like best gives you his full attention for the evening."

Randy considered this. On the monitor, the roulette wheel went round and round. Randy knew with soul-deep certainty he wasn't wrong.

Unfortunately Crabtree was also right. Randy had been feeling funny the past few months, and he didn't like it. He was restless, irritated, and sometimes even lonely. Were twenty dollars of drinks and several hours of conversational dirge worth potential, unspecified tail?

Would it make the restlessness and loneliness better or worse?

Crabtree sipped his drink again. "When an ace falls, he doesn't get up easily. The only way aces go high after falling as hard as this one has is under extraordinary circumstances. The odds are bad, Randy." He stroked Randy's ankle. "You can make much better use of your time and talents."

Randy paused. It'd been a while since he'd gotten kinky with Crabtree, and yeah, that'd do for a distraction.

On the video screen, the roulette ball went round and round and round, its final destination impossible to guess.

"How would you verify it?" Randy asked Billy. "How would you tell who was right or not? Would you take my word for it?"

Billy shook his head. "Has to be a witness. Someone neither of us could pay off. Who's working bar tonight?"

"Scully." Randy tracked the ball. *Land on black, goddamn it.*

"Scully will do nicely." Billy threaded his hands behind his head. "So?"

Crabtree said nothing, but his massage on Randy's ankle became more direct, his invitation quite clear.

Randy couldn't take his eyes off the ball. It started to bounce, ricocheting wildly across the spines. Why would anyone bet on this, outside of masochism?

He had to find out what this guy was about.

"I pick the guy," Randy said at last.

"That's what I said."

"No—I pick who you hire. And he understands the full-service nature of his employment."

Billy shrugged. "Sure. Is it a deal?"

"Yes." The ball had landed once more on red. "*Fuck.*"

Crabtree lifted his hand from Randy's ankle. He studied the screen for a minute then finished off his drink before setting it on the edge of Billy's desk. "Better get down there. If he really is out of money, he's going to run away."

Randy stood and slid into his shoes, wondering why he felt so disoriented and nervous.

"Remember," Billy called as Randy headed for the door, "go to Scully to verify."

"Give your fallen ace my love," Crabtree called, as Randy pulled on the doorknob.

"Fuck you," Randy replied.

"You turned me down, remember?" Crabtree called

as Randy squared his shoulders and headed for the elevator.

As the last of his chips slid across the felt, Ethan Ellison wiped his hand over his mouth, suppressing the urge to vomit.

"Bad luck again. Sorry about that." The dealer, a middle-aged man with a thin silver mustache tickling his upper lip, glanced inquiringly at Ethan. "Can I get you some more chips, sir?"

With force of will, Ethan pushed himself up. "No. Thank you—no."

He stared at the table, focusing not on the sea of numbers but on the red and black squares at the edge of the felt nestled between the words EVEN and ODD. *A fifty-fifty chance, and I still couldn't win, not even once.* The pain in his head increased, and his throat began to close.

He started to turn away from the table, but he glanced at the dealer as he left, remembering the nicety of a goodbye at the last second. His smile fell as he caught an expectant look in the dealer's eye.

Oh God. The man wanted a tip.

Ethan flushed and patted his pockets, more for a stall than because he thought to find anything there. He looked up guiltily at the dealer. "I—I'm sorry—" He searched more desperately now, in case he had something, anything left. Not so much as a dime. "I don't have anything."

The dealer's friendly, hopeful expression vanished. He rolled his eyes, shook his head, and returned to stacking his chips.

Ethan faltered, feeling like more of a loser. "I'm sorry, I didn't realize—" *Because I'm an idiot, a sorry, soppy idiot.* He dug deep into his trousers then paused as he hit the bit of metal.

It wasn't money, but once it had borne great, great value to Ethan. This little silver circle had been his everything, and now it was detritus in his pocket. The thought turned dark and bilious in Ethan's wounded soul.

Ethan swallowed hard, pulled the object out, and laid it on the table. "You can have this." At least his voice didn't break as he spoke the words.

The dealer leaned over and inspected it. "Is it real silver, or what?"

Ethan stared down at the plain gray circle with the simple engravings which had once brought him such comfort. Now they made him feel foolish. "I don't know. Whatever it is, it's yours."

A hand came down on Ethan's arm, weathered and stained with dark streaks as it closed over the discarded ring. A man stood beside Ethan, rangy and wild-looking with a head of shaggy hair and thick eyebrows. Sharp, dancing eyes met Ethan's, and the stranger winked.

The dealer glared at the newcomer. "Hey—Jansen, you prick, that's my tip."

"It isn't customary to give tips to a dealer when you do nothing but lose." The stranger scooped up the ring, held it by the bottom of the circle, and shook it once at the dealer. "Unless you're a *prick*."

The dealer's face turned stormy. "He gave it to me, you ass."

"First prick, now ass." The stranger lifted an eyebrow. "You coming on to me, Tyler?"

The confrontation made Ethan uncomfortable. "I don't mind if he takes it."

Those dark eyes pierced him, and Ethan felt as if he were being stripped right there in the middle of the casino floor, laid more completely bare than ever in his life. As if he were being measured, parceled out, and judged. And found, he suspected, very wanting.

The stranger turned to the dealer.

"Tell you what, Tyler." The man's voice was smooth as velvet but with a knife inside. "Let's play for it."

The dealer swore under his breath.

The stranger ignored him and leaned over the roulette table, his palms resting on the padded edge. "I'll let you pick the game."

The dealer stopped scowling. "Seriously?"

Ethan was done being ignored. "Excuse me, but who are you, exactly?"

"Randy Jansen. So. Tyler. You feeling lucky?"

The dealer looked hopeful. "Any game. You'll bet against me in any game on the floor?"

"Anywhere in the casino." Randy nodded at the main floor and smiled darkly. "*Any* game."

Tyler drew back. "The fuck I'm playing poker against you."

"Then name something else."

Enough was enough. "This is hardly necessary. I gave the man my ring of my own free will."

Randy still didn't look at Ethan. "And now he's going to bet against it of his own free will."

"*Any* game," Tyler repeated.

Randy stood straight and held out his hands, indicating his complete compliance.

Tyler pointed to the wheel. "Roulette."

Randy shrugged. "Fine."

He said this, but he didn't seem happy, and Tyler was beaming. "Put it down and make your call. Red or black."

Randy raised an eyebrow. "What about the zeroes?"

"We re-spin if they fall there. Or we split the odds. I get single, you get double."

"No. Even or odd. And the zeroes are even."

"You can't pick even." Tyler pointed at the table. "Not when you just gave it a two-number advantage."

Ethan frowned. "But zero *is* even. And so is double zero."

Tyler aimed a finger at him. "You stay out of this." He turned to Randy. "Zeroes are out. They're nobody's."

Randy almost looked bored, except for the focused concentration in his eyes. "They have to go somewhere because I'm only making one bet with you."

Tyler glared at Randy then flicked a glance at Ethan. "Him. He gets both zeroes. If it lands on one of them, it returns to him."

"Sounds fair to me." Randy indicated the wheel. "Spin."

Tyler hesitated, as if he suspected anything Randy readily agreed to would be an arrangement against himself.

Ethan saw a tall man in a tuxedo and an earpiece watching them carefully from a few tables over. "Are we going to get into some sort of trouble for this?"

Tyler followed Ethan's gaze and winced. "Shit. Pit boss. Hold on, Jansen. We're clearing this with Herod first."

"Trust me. Herod is watching our every move." He sat in the chair Ethan had vacated and nodded at the wheel as he let Ethan's ring fall onto the felt. "Let the ball fly, and get this over with."

Tyler spun the ball into the rotating wheel, and it traveled around and around, moving in opposition to the swirl of colors.

Randy leaned closer to Ethan. He still wasn't looking at him, but Ethan knew he wasn't speaking to anyone else when he said, "If I win, you're having a drink with me at the bar."

Ethan wanted to tell him what he could do with his drink, but something about the spinning ball stayed him. "And if the dealer wins?"

"Oh, then you're having two."

Ethan glared at him. "And what if *I* win?"

"Then I'll let you decide how many."

"What if I don't want to have a drink with you at all?"

On the wheel, the ball began to bounce. Randy had tracked it, eagle-eyed, but at Ethan's question his lips quirked, and that searing gaze was on his. "Then I suggest you think of what else you have to bargain with to win your way out of a trip to the bar."

Randy returned his focus to the wheel, but Ethan stared, rattled, at the man's arrogant head. There had been a *knowing* on Randy Jansen's face going beyond arrogance. As Ethan huffed, trying to convince himself he'd imagined it, he felt a warm, brief touch on the back of his thigh. Startled, he looked down in time to see Randy's hand falling casually to his side.

"You—" Ethan started, but there was a soft click as the ball fell into place. Randy smiled at the same moment Tyler swore.

"18." Randy turned to Ethan, his smile tilting to rueful as he added, "Red."

"You son of a bitch." Tyler glared at Randy. "You rigged this."

Randy gave him a withering look. "How, Tyler, did I rig your wheel?"

"I don't know how, but I know you did, goddamn it."

The pit boss, who'd watched the entire game from just a table away, stepped forward. "Is there a problem?"

"He's *cheating*." Tyler pointed at Randy.

Randy looked innocently at the pit boss. "I think your dealer could use a break. But ask him to place the dolly first, please."

The pit boss frowned at Ethan's ring lying on the

table, but as he opened his mouth to speak, he paused before pressing fingers to his earpiece. "Hold on," he said to the table, fixing his gaze on a random point as he listened, nodding occasionally. "Yes, Mr. Crabtree." He turned to Tyler. "The play is fair. Place the dolly, dealer."

Tyler's face was red. "He's *cheating*—"

"—and then report directly to the office. Mr. Crabtree's assistant would like a word with you."

The color drained from Tyler's face.

The pit boss nodded again at the table. "Place the dolly, please."

Hand shaking, Tyler moved the gold marker from the rail edge in front of him to the number 18.

Randy swiped the ring from the felt and stood, reaching into his pocket. He pulled out two blue-edged chips, passing one to the pit boss, flicking the other onto the table. "Have a good night, Tyler." He turned to Ethan, and in front of the now-considerable crowd watching them, slipped his arm through the crook of Ethan's own.

Too shocked to resist, Ethan let Randy maneuver him down the line of tables toward a series of archways beneath a glittering chandelier. As the crowd thinned out and they passed beneath a dark curve into a room lined with slot machines, the spell Randy had cast at the table broke, and Ethan pulled away.

"I'm not having a drink with you. I don't know who you are, but I do know I don't have to have a drink with you."

He expected Randy to fight him, or mock him, or even, given the way this was headed, try to seduce him. But as if Randy could read his mind and wanted to make sure he thwarted him, he didn't do anything Ethan expected. He held up his hands and smiled ruefully.

"You're right." He bowed and turned away.

For a second, Ethan could only stare. Randy ambled off, past the video poker machines, sauntering to the entrance of the bar attached to the casino.

Ethan could leave. He could be rid of this idiot once and for all.

The vision of his alternate future burned hot and dark and short, and Ethan went still.

Something else rose up through that bleakness, something as black as the mark on the table which had never, not even once, gone Ethan's way.

Tightening his fists, and his jaw, Ethan glared. "*Hey,*" he called, and when Randy didn't stop or glance over his shoulder, he swore under his breath and stormed after him.

CHAPTER TWO

RANDY KEPT WALKING toward the bar, but he slowed his pace so Roulette Man caught up with him at the last of the Triple Diamond slots. The bouncer near *The Wizard of Oz* machine cast a quick glance between Randy and his pursuer before raising an inquiring eyebrow. Randy gave him a wink and a grin, wiping his face clear seconds before Roulette Man grabbed his shoulder.

Though the action had been meant to communicate the tall, slight man's anger, the dominance of the act was buried in a significant sediment of nice. He gripped Randy's shoulder, yes, but his fury was checked by an apparently overwhelming urge to be polite and deferential.

Well, an *almost* overwhelming urge. Randy's lips quirked. Perhaps this evening could be salvaged after all. Randy took in a whiff of the spice and soap teasing him the whole time he'd leaned against the rail of the roulette table. At this close range it made his blood hum. At least it did until his assailant shoved away from Randy with an angry push.

"Who the *hell* are you?" The man gestured toward

the tables with a long, elegant arm and a slight flick of his wrist. "What—*why* did you do that?"

The spice tingled Randy's nostrils, mixing nicely with his appreciation for the sleek curve of the stranger's jaw. He couldn't quite see the man's angry pulse point, but he could imagine it beating visibly where his neck was exposed by his collar, which had opened an additional button since Randy had studied it through the surveillance camera.

Randy waggled his eyebrows. "Because you smell so good."

He delivered the line with just the right tone and pitch, making it impossible for Roulette Man to tell if it were a tease or the truth, and then he watched to see how it was received. The flash of shock he'd expected, but he focused on the length of the other man's pause. It hung on a bit before switching over to anger, and that was the tell. No arousal, but no revulsion, and no wall. This flustered fellow played on Randy's team.

Randy was in the game.

Winking, Randy patted him on his shoulder. "Come on, buddy. Let me buy you that drink."

The man pulled back, but not as far away this time. "I'm not your buddy."

"Then give me your name." When this only made the man's glare deepen, Randy checked a grin. God, but yanking this one's chain was so damn easy it was almost criminal. "Or I could name you, I guess. Let me buy you a drink, Mr. Black."

"Ethan," the man spat. "My name is Ethan."

With a mock bow, Randy tucked his fingers beneath Ethan's arm. "Right this way, Ethan Black."

"Ellison. My name is Ethan Ellison."

"Right this way, Mr. Ellison. You can tell me what an ass I am over a drink." Randy glanced at Ethan. "Let's see. Not beer. This isn't a beer moment."

"I don't need a drink."

Randy ignored him. "You're not quite ready for something stupid and fruity, but that might be good for a chaser. Straight alcohol isn't going to be your thing though either, so no tequila shooters. Let's see. Rum and Coke? Or—no, God, how thick am I? You're a G&T."

Ethan looked at him askance. "Have you been stalking me?"

"Just reading you, baby." Randy noted Ethan flinched but didn't withdraw at the endearment. He smiled to himself as he ducked his head, wiping his face clean as they approached the bar. "Hey, Scully. A big gin and tonic and a double Dirty Whiskey."

"Dirty Whiskey?" Ethan repeated.

"Bailey's and Jameson's." Randy slid onto a stool. "Are you going to tell me it's girly?"

"Girly? It's nothing but pure alcohol."

"Yes, but it's sweet and creamy, which is enough to damn any drink." Randy took his drink from Scully and waved impatiently at Ethan. "Sit. I can't flirt standing up, and you're freakishly tall."

Randy turned away, ostensibly looking at Scully. As the bartender had a mug that could have been improved by a run-in with a hacksaw, this wasn't a pleasant task. But it didn't matter, because all his attention was on Ethan, who hadn't sat down yet but hadn't walked away either. Randy stared at Scully's ugly mug and tipped his glass to his lips, rubbing his thumb against the cold damp of the tumbler to bleed off some of his tension.

Come on, baby. I played it perfectly. This is your cue to sit, have a drink, and try to work out what's going on.

Ethan hovered, and for a few agonizing seconds Randy realized he must have misread the man after all. The thought, while alarming, was also stirring.

Ethan perched carefully on the stool beside Randy. "What exactly is this? What are you doing? What's going on here?"

Randy gave Scully a rueful smile, but the bartender just shook his head. He stayed close though, which meant Billy had tipped him off about his role in this little play.

Randy realized he'd half-forgotten his actual mission with Ethan. Now wasn't that interesting?

He nudged Ethan's G&T toward him. "I'm buying you a drink. Don't they buy people drinks in Utah?"

Ethan's eyes went wide. "You *are* stalking me."

"No, baby, I told you. I'm reading you."

Ethan still looked spooked, and Randy decided he'd pushed right up against the limit of how much of being an asshole he could get away with. He leaned on the bar. "Utah was a guess. I just got lucky."

Ethan kept shaking his head. "But—how? Out of fifty states—"

Randy rolled his eyes. "*Please.* The list of places you *aren't* from is longer." He ticked them off on his fingers as he spoke. "You're too uptight for Hawaii, and you don't smile enough for California."

Ethan flattened his lips. "Smiling?"

"It's a light in the face, California. An aggressive sort of friendliness, something about the corners of the mouth. It's different north to south too, but none of it's you. You aren't laid-back enough for the Pacific Northwest. You don't have the accent or manners for the South. I know *damn* well you aren't from Michigan."

"But *how?*"

"Because I'm from Michigan, and you always know your own." He took a moment to enjoy Ethan's stunned expression before resuming his explanation. "You've got the wrong accent for the East Coast, and wrong demeanor. So now we're down to West and Midwest. Most people wouldn't be able to spot the difference, but again, you know your own, and you have the nice, but it's the wrong kind. Western nice is a little more distant. For all they say about cowboy chivalry, there's more of a 'oh, let me lay down my coat for you, I don't mind the mud, honestly' about the center of the country."

Ethan looked at Randy as if trying to find the two-by-four smacking him in the head. "Are you making this up as you go along?"

"Sort of. You want to know how I got Utah. I knew you weren't Nevada. You felt too out of town to be local. Odds are too good you'd at least have been to Reno before, if you were native, and you act like Vegas is about to eat you whole. You don't feel like Arizona or New Mexico. So now we're down to Colorado, Wyoming, Utah, Montana, and Idaho. I ruled out the last two for distance, because you've clearly run away from something, and traveling too far would give you enough time to come to your senses."

Wide eyes again. "How…?"

Randy waved him away impatiently. "Now we're down to three, which means I'm looking at better than a thirty percent chance. But I want better odds. So I'm making a call on Wyoming because it doesn't feel right, and really, it's also too far. Now I'm fifty-fifty, western Colorado or pretty much anywhere in Utah. Though now I know that one's right, I'm willing to get cocky and say Salt Lake City. Or Provo."

Ethan looked seriously spooked now. "I'm from American Fork, and I lived in Provo after college. But *how—*?"

"Frankly? You have this vaguely Mormon feel, but you also don't. So, you grew up steeped in it but weren't overpowered. So you're from somewhere big enough to be diverse."

Ethan stared a few seconds longer, then took a deep drink of his G&T.

Randy drank too, but just a sip. "I've been told when I read people like this, it's scary. I take it you concur?"

"I think if you lived in the Middle Ages, you'd be burned at the stake."

Randy snorted. "No. I'd never let my talent be so obvious. Unless, of course, I wanted to get someone into bed." Ethan stiffened and cast him a warning glance. Randy shrugged. "You're sitting now. I'm flirting out of relief."

Ethan took another drink. "I believe you could flirt if you were stripped naked, tied up, and dangling over a pit of snakes."

Randy's laugh became a purr of its own free will. "If you were the snake charmer, baby, I'd surely try at the very least."

Ethan put his drink down. "Don't call me *baby*."

Randy hadn't realized he had. "Is there an endearment you prefer?"

"My name is Ethan."

"*Endearment.*" Randy rubbed his jaw thoughtfully. "You certainly aren't Sunshine, and anyway, the name's taken. Black is too dismal. Baby suits you in the abstract, but it's too blasé for a nickname." He ran his gaze over Ethan in a critical scan. "Slim would fit, but it's too neutered."

"Just call me Ethan." He slid his thumb along the side of his glass as he stared into the ice. "So why did you come up to me, really? Why did you make the bet against my ring?"

"That one's complicated." Randy glanced at Scully. "I bet against your ring because Tyler is an ass. I don't care for the shitty odds in roulette, but I comforted myself with the knowledge he'd see your win as my win too, so I still had the best of it, in a way."

"But he was the one who suggested I take the zeroes," Ethan said, and Randy grinned.

"And I made sure it went down that way, baby." Randy caught himself this time and winced. "Sorry. I'm honestly not doing it on purpose." He scratched his cheek. "I came up to you at all because of a different bet, if you must know."

Randy hadn't exactly meant to come so clean, and he ran his finger around the edge of his glass, buying time as he tried to figure out how to save this.

He extended an index finger to the silvered dome in the ceiling above the bar. "See that? It's camera number seventy-two. There are three hundred of them in the casino, which actually isn't quite enough, but it's all we've got."

Ethan seemed impressed. "This is your casino?"

"No. But I work here sometimes."

Scully snorted.

"You're a security person?" Ethan's voice spiked in panic.

"I'm not security. I'm a prop. But I wasn't working earlier, just hanging out in Billy's office. He likes to watch some of the tables himself, and I saw you playing. Fantastically badly, I might add."

"I don't understand. Who's Billy? What's a prop?" Ethan frowned. "What was wrong with the way I played? I was waiting for black."

"You were waiting for fucking Godot, baby." Randy drank. "Billy is Billy Herod. It's *his* casino. A prop is harder to explain, but for now let's say I play poker." Randy drank again and then set the empty glass down. "The bet is what's important here, sweetness. I watched you play, and I read you. I declared to Billy I knew three things about you. Billy thinks I'm cocky, so he roped me into a bet, and to win I have to find out if I was right or wrong. And I have to be right on all three counts, for the record. Igor here"—he jerked his head at Scully—"is the witness."

Randy waited while Ethan sputtered, indignant. In a few seconds he'd make some outraged cry, demanding to know if that was all this had been, if everything about their encounter was about a bet.

"Do you mean," Ethan said, his consonants sharp and angry, "this whole thing, everything at the table, getting this drink, the flirting and calling me *baby* has all been about a *bet*?"

Randy sighed. Sometimes he wished people would surprise him.

"I saw your sad face in the camera, and I fell in love. I came down to propose to you. Of course it's a fucking bet. The fact that you like being flirted with and you look good when you're pissed off is just a plus."

Ethan's nostrils flared. "I do *not* enjoy being flirted with. Not by you."

Randy started to get bored. "Fine. Take my quick survey, lover, and then you can go. I say you came to Vegas—from Utah—because someone dumped you and broke your heart. They did this in part by taking a significant amount of money from you. You came here with what was left, and you pissed away your last dollar, determined if you sat there long enough, black had to come around because it owed you." He threaded his fingers behind his head and smirked. "Isn't that right?"

He saw the truth of it in Ethan Ellison's wide, pale eyes—the shock, the fear of exposure, and most of all, the pain. It hooked the edge of Randy's heart, which *was* a surprise, and he softened his expression. Ethan had been through enough. He didn't need mocking too.

Then there was a shift, a hardening of Ethan's mouth, and Randy stilled as he read something else, something troubling in Ethan's eyes.

Triumph.

"No," Ethan said.

Scully, who'd faced the TV but glanced at Ethan for his answer, now turned toward them full on.

Randy sat up. "Excuse me?" His heart beat faster. No. He could not be wrong. He'd seen it, both upstairs and here, now. He was right, he knew it.

Ethan leaned forward. "I said no. You're wrong. Yes, you were right about some of it, but not all. He took money, and yes, that was my last dollar." His chin went up, and his eyes glittered as he added, "But it was *me* who dumped *him*."

No. No, that was *not* what he had seen. But then he looked again, deeper, using the full force of what Billy liked to call his "freakish gift for reading people", using the parts of it he couldn't explain out loud even if his life depended on it. Randy read the shades he'd glossed over before, what he could never have seen from the camera and what he'd been too confident and too lazy to acknowledge in real time.

Ethan Ellison was not lying.

Randy sank into his chair, staring open-mouthed.

Then the rest of it hit him. He turned to Ethan, then to Scully, then to the camera again. "*Fuck.*"

Scully laughed, the mirth of one who'd waited a long time for this moment. "You better start doin' some sit-ups, Jansen. Otherwise your beer gut's gonna hang out over them little neon shorts Billy's gonna make you and the other twinkies wear."

"Jesus *fuck.*" Randy collapsed onto the bar, resting his head against the rail as he tried to compose himself.

"What's going on?" Ethan still sounded confused, but he was clearly enjoying Randy's discomfort as much as everyone else.

"What's going on is Randy Jansen, who is never, ever wrong about a poker face, just read yours and *lost.* Buddy, your drinks for the month are on the house. Another G&T?"

"What about me?" Randy lifted his head. "I'm the poor bastard who has to wear the shorts."

"You still owe me for the first round."

Randy glared at Scully as he sat up and dug into his pocket. "Here," he said, slamming a twenty-five-dollar chip onto the counter. "Happy?"

Scully scooped up the heavy toke. "Oh, very."

Smarting from the misread and unsettled by his own sloppiness, Randy didn't know how to finish this. Ethan wasn't gloating, wasn't reveling over how he'd just done what a healthy portion of Vegas had wanted done for years. He only regarded Randy uneasily, remaining patiently nice as he watched to see what would happen now.

Goddamn it, but it turned Randy on.

The only way out was to raise the stakes, but it was a bitch to pull off when there was only one player in the game. He slammed down another chip—a fifty this time. "You can damn well wait to buy Slick here a drink because I'm getting this one too. Another Dirty Whiskey and another G&T. Small T, and a big, big fucking G."

"Slick?" Ethan repeated.

Randy curled his lip in a snarl. "You want to go back to *baby*?"

Ethan's smile reverberated in Randy's toes as his body posture eased, and he braced one long arm against the bar. "Slick's fine."

Randy took in the tempting, tender, and smooth flesh of Ethan's exposed wrist, and his arousal heightened as he imagined the way his skin would taste. The thumb crooked once, then twice, as if calling to him, but when Randy looked up at Ethan's face, the man was too distracted watching Scully make the drinks to have done it on purpose.

Unless, of course, Randy had misread him again.

"Fuck." He slumped onto the bar.

ETHAN WASN'T ENTIRELY sure what had happened, but he understood enough to know somehow he'd bested Randy.

Good.

Ethan still worked on the first drink, but there was a second G&T sweating on a coaster. As he drank, the bartender joyfully needled Randy, who remained with his forehead on the rail.

"I hope yours are pink, you little fucker." He leered at Randy. "Really bright fucking pink."

Randy lifted his head and gave the bartender a withering glare. "Wearing pink doesn't threaten my masculinity like it does yours."

"Pink shorts, real tight. With your fat ass hanging out."

The comment brought Randy up short. "My ass is *not fat.* You, however, could supply the kitchens at Bellagio with lard for a month."

Scully continued to snicker, but Ethan's attention drifted, drawn to a subtle study of Randy's referenced anatomy, hiding his perusal behind the illusion of taking another drink. It wasn't a fat ass at all. None of Randy was fat, not really, and if anything, he was a bit muscular. He had the look of someone who worked out infrequently, just enough to keep real trouble at bay. By no means was he clean-cut. His dark, curly hair was a mess, and he had stubble on his jaw. In Hollywood he'd be *artfully tousled.* In real life he could use a bit more grooming.

In short, he wasn't Ethan's type at all.

Randy turned his head, catching Ethan staring, giving Ethan a full-on view of his eyes—dark, huge, and so sharp they made Randy shiver. It was a dramatic, foolish thought, but when Randy looked at Ethan like this, he would swear the man could steal inside his soul.

Worse, Ethan acknowledged as Randy's smile darkened, the little devil seemed to know exactly what he did to Ethan.

Ethan drained the last of the cocktail and set the glass down, still watching Randy carefully.

He's here because he made a bet about you, about what you were doing at the table, about why you're here, and he was almost completely right. But that's all he cares about, not you. The speech was meant to be a warning to himself, but the problem was Randy wasn't actively coming on to him, and it threw Ethan off.

The gin gave Ethan the liquid courage to voice aloud the question rattling inside his head. "So what happens now?"

Randy shrugged. "No idea. There's always your upside-down snake idea, I guess."

Ethan choked on his gin. "That was a metaphor, not a proposition."

Randy grinned. "There. That's what we're going to do. We're going to have a proposition." He pulled a cell phone out of his pocket. "It's eight thirty now. I say it'll happen by…" he blew his breath out in a heavy exhale, then tossed his head from side to side as he considered, "…midnight, I think."

"I don't know what you're talking about." Ethan tried to sound dismissive, but Randy's gaze made him squirm.

Randy leaned forward. "By midnight tonight I will have wooed you."

"No."

"Excellent. We have a bet. Terms?"

"I'm not betting with you. Especially not about *wooing*."

"You're right, it needs to be more specific. Hmm." He ran his fingers over his lips as he narrowed his eyes. Ethan moved his own gaze deliberately down and ended up staring at Randy's fingers. The tips of two of them were tucked inside his lips, making them part. Ethan had noticed them before, and he noted it again—Randy's fingers were stained, lined with…grease?

"Engines."

Ethan blinked. "What?"

"Engines." Randy waggled his fingers. "My fingers are stained because I work with diesel engines all day. Also motorcycles. My hands are clean, for the record. They're just stained."

"I don't care." Ethan winced at how prim he sounded.

Randy's mouth turned up at the corners, and his sharp eyes twinkled. "By midnight I'll have kissed you, Ethan. That's the bet."

Ethan's pulse raced in alarm. "You won't have, because I won't let you."

Randy's smile became dangerous. "Scratch that. By midnight, Slick, *you* will kiss *me*."

Ethan said nothing, deciding the way out of this was not to dignify Randy's idiocy with a reply.

This didn't slow Randy down. "If you manage not to, you'll get one thousand dollars."

Ethan held up his hands. "You're insane."

"The hell I am. When I win, you remember that's how badly you wanted to kiss me, enough to give up a thousand dollars."

Ethan turned to the bartender for help, but Scully held up the fifty-dollar chip Randy had given him. "I'm bettin' on you, Jansen."

Randy lifted an eyebrow. "You expect me to bet against *myself*?"

Ethan glared at Scully. "You think I *will* kiss him?"

"Come *on*, Jansen. This is a sure thing." He looked to Ethan. "*You* bet me, then."

"He doesn't have any money," Randy pointed out.

"You could put up my ring," Ethan said, even as part of his brain told him to shut up.

Randy leered. "Have you forgotten? It's *my* ring now."

Ethan felt his cheeks color, but he kept his chin level. "It hardly matters. I'm not taking this bet."

Randy held out his hands. "How can you not? All you have to do to get one thousand dollars is resist me until midnight. Easiest money you'll ever make."

Scully fished in his pocket and brought out several other chips and thrust them at Randy. "An even hundred. *Please*."

Ethan's head spun from more than just gin. There was nothing encouraging about the way Scully was so sure he would lose, but at the same time, there was no way he was kissing this arrogant asshole.

You shouldn't do this at all. You should turn on your

heel and walk away from him right now.

A deep, empty wave of cold swept in on the thought's wake. *And if I do, where will I go?*

Ethan shook off the cold. "So if I lose, do I owe you one thousand dollars?"

"No, Slick." Randy put a hand over his heart. "The pleasure of your tender lips will be enough of a payment for me."

Oh, he was an arrogant, arrogant bastard. Ethan glared at him a moment, hating him, hating all of this.

But if it weren't for him, where would you be right now?

Darkness threatening again, Ethan shut his eyes and nodded. "Fine."

When he opened his eyes, Randy's smile had faded. "Slick, you okay?"

"I'm fine." Ethan sat up straight. "And I'll take your stupid bet."

Scully pulled all the chips out of his pocket. "Somebody *please take my bet.*"

Randy studied Scully's multicolored pile. "This looks like about a hundred and fifty dollars."

Scully shoved them forward. "I'm good for more."

Randy waved an impatient hand. "I'll back him for the one-fifty, but he has to agree to the bet with you."

Ethan couldn't believe this. "You mean you're going to either end up paying me one thousand, or him one-fifty? How do you win this?"

"If you lose, I'll pay him for you. And you'll pay me." He nodded at Scully. "You'll repeat the kiss you gave me in front of him, right here at the bar."

"This is going to be *great*." Scully rubbed his hands together.

"He hasn't agreed yet," Randy pointed out.

Ethan looked between the two men, at Scully eager for his easy money, at Randy lounging against the rail, confident as all hell.

Ethan gave a brittle smile. "It's a deal, Scully."

Scully whooped.

Randy nodded at Ethan's drink. "You might want to leave that. I'd hate for you to feel you lost because I got you drunk. I'm happy to feed you too—an empty stomach makes it worse."

"I've already eaten." Ethan picked up his drink defiantly, but then he remembered Tyler at the roulette table, insisting Ethan take the zeroes. *And I made sure it went down that way, baby.* Setting the alcohol down, he pushed it away. "Water please, Scully."

Randy's lips quirked. "Good. It'd feel cheap, if I could lead you so easily."

Oh, if only Ethan could smack him. "I assume I'm obliged to be in the same room with you until midnight?"

"It'll be too hard for you to kiss me otherwise."

"Fine." Ethan drained the water Scully set down before him. "Where are we going?"

"A better question might be where *aren't* we going?" Randy slipped his arm through Ethan's and led him away from the bar. "Come on, baby. Let me show you my town."

"I'm not your baby."

"Come on, Slick. Let me show you my town."

"Stick it down his throat, Jansen," Scully called as they departed.

Randy's wicked laugh reverberated up Ethan's arm and into the center of his chest as they drifted to the exit.

CHAPTER THREE

RANDY RESTED A hand against Ethan's shoulder as they leaned against a railing. "What have you seen? What haven't you? What would you like to see?"

Such innocent questions. Yet Ethan stood there, unable to answer, his knuckles white as he gripped the metal bar and tried to process the hard left his life had taken.

When Ethan had arrived in Las Vegas that morning, he'd been in a haze. After parking his car and pawning his few remaining possessions—save the ring—he'd stepped into the first casino he'd seen. He'd lost a large chunk of his savings there. Then he'd wandered around in the heat. After being overwhelmed by a pedestrian mall, he'd ended up at Herod's. He hadn't even made it to the Strip. He hadn't cared. He'd been reeling, full of rage and pain and things he couldn't name.

Now he was back on the pedestrian mall, on Randy Jansen's arm, riding out a thousand-dollar bet for four hours. A bet to kiss him. The lights and crowd and noise dimmed in his vision, blurring into a spinning kaleidoscope.

It stopped abruptly as Randy's face filled his vision,

his dark gaze shooting through Ethan's internal fog. "Hello? You still with us, Slick?"

Ethan felt the pull between despair and—and what, he couldn't know. Between despair and Randy, as best he could tell. What a bizarre set of poles. He gripped the rail tighter. "I don't want to do this."

"We can go somewhere else. Fremont Street Experience was just the closest thing. Have you seen the Bellagio fountains at night? Even as a local, I have to tell you I never get tired of them. Or the Stratosphere tower. *That* you have to see."

"I haven't really been anywhere," Ethan confessed.

Both of Randy's eyebrows went up. "Nowhere? Only *Herod's*?"

The kaleidoscope effect returned, spinning around everything but Randy. "It doesn't matter. Forget this. Forget all of this."

"Hey. *Hey.*" Randy caught him by the arm, and when he couldn't turn Ethan around, he used his grip as an anchor to put himself in Ethan's way and forced Ethan to look at him. "Are you okay?"

No. "I'm fine." He tried to escape again.

Randy kept Ethan pinned in place. Ethan gave up and looked away so he didn't have to meet Randy's eyes, but he still felt the scrutiny.

Randy slid his hand into Ethan's, and when he spoke, his tone was light and careful. "Let's start with a walk."

"I don't want to take a walk." Ethan knew he sounded surly and possibly petulant, but he didn't care.

"I do." Randy led them toward the escalator, not letting go of Ethan's hand, not even when Ethan tugged.

"I don't want to hold hands with you."

"Baby, it's Vegas. Nobody gives a shit."

"*I* give a shit."

Randy's eyes twinkled. "Tell you what—I'll let go if you give me a kiss."

No one had ever infuriated Ethan this much this fast. "You're a real jerk, you know that, right?"

"Usually I get told I'm an asshole." Randy put his free hand over his heart and looked at Ethan with soulful eyes. "You must really love me."

Rage and indignation swept up in a rush inside Ethan, and he bore down on Randy, ready to vent his spleen. Then Randy batted his eyelashes, and as if someone had waved a magic wand, the rage shifted, and suddenly Ethan was laughing.

Randy winked. "There you go. That's better."

"You *are* an ass." Ethan couldn't stop a smile, though. "Why the hell are you doing this? Are you that bored?"

"I told you. You smell good." But Randy kept his gaze elsewhere, and Ethan felt a tiny ripple of victory, like he'd scored a blow against a tornado.

"I could give you the name of my cologne," Ethan said, then remembered he wasn't wearing any.

"Oh, but I haven't smelled all of you yet. It might not be the cologne. I'll need to make a thorough inspection of all your scents before I know what's drawing me in."

They stepped off the escalator, and Randy led them beneath the edge of a huge canopy. Ethan couldn't quite tell whether it was a building or an amphitheater or something else entirely.

Randy gestured to the sea of lights and people swarming around them, then up at the canopy overhead. "This is the Fremont Street Experience. We won't stay for it, but they have a show every night. They turn off all the lights and do scenes on the ceiling. They make it day, make it night, make it whatever. Vegas all the way."

Ethan squinted, trying to see within the space ahead of them. "Is it a stage? But there are shops on the side."

"It's four city blocks, baby. It's a street with a ceiling on it." When Ethan glared at him, Randy looked at him blankly, then laughed. "Called you baby again, did I?"

"I have a perfectly acceptable name. You don't need to belittle me all the time."

"Good God, Slick, get the stick out of your ass. Yes, your name is fine. But don't you want to be somebody else every now and again?"

The last few days in all their darkness and despair swept up like a heavy blanket kept at bay only by the sheer volume of lights and noise around him. "Yes. But you can't escape who you are."

"Jesus. I should have poured the drink down your throat." Randy stopped walking and let go of Ethan so he could turn to stare at him. "He really did a number on you, didn't he? You don't just have a rain shower over your head. You have the whole goddamn wall cloud."

Ethan's throat closed, lest the emotions clawing at it escape. "I don't want to talk about it."

"Yeah, that much I've figured out on my own. Yet every time I stop talking or get a syllable wrong, you're right back there, swimming in the shit. So how about we make a deal. Either we go sit somewhere, get you screaming fucking drunk, and you barf it all up, the drink and the story, or we go somewhere fun and distracting, and you don't think about it at all. You pick, Slick. I'm game either way."

"*Why* are you doing this? All you get if you win the bet is a kiss. You must be bored. Or insane."

Randy's smile turned enigmatic. "Interesting how you assume I'm bored, not shallow. I could just be doing this because I'm stupid and flighty, because I enjoy manipulating people, and you're quite a puzzle to put together. But you assume I'm doing this because I'm restless."

Ethan faltered, self-conscious. Then he got a better look at Randy's face and shook his head. "But you are. You're an ass, but you're also restless."

Randy tried to shutter his expression, but he couldn't quite manage it. "Do you, Mr. Ellison, by any chance play poker?"

"Never. Why?"

Randy took his arm. "Come on. You don't want shops. You don't want the Strip, either. You want a casino."

"I don't want to go to Herod's."

"God no. Herod's isn't really a casino. It used to be, but now it's sort of casino theater. Billy's a dick. Worse, he's a dick with a trust fund. Herod's is a playground for his whim of the moment. He's vacant and stupid, and all he wants to do is manipulate people."

Ethan snorted. "Unlike you."

Randy appeared genuinely offended. "I *play* with people. *With* them. Big fucking difference, Slick."

God, now he wasn't annoyed, he was tired. "Do you have a nickname I can toss at you?"

"Sure. Go ahead and give me one."

"I'd be fine with recycling one already in circulation."

"My CB handle is Skeet."

"Skeet?" Ethan wrinkled his nose. "The stuff you shoot?"

"It's a poker term." Randy aimed Ethan onto the street. "Only used in home games, but it's kind of like a straight. It ranks between three of a kind and a regular straight. Nine and five and two, and a little something in between."

Ethan had no idea what Randy was talking about. "Whatever Skeet is, it's not what I had in mind for a nickname."

"No, you wanted something embarrassing to poke at me with. Tough luck, Slick. You'll have to invent that yourself." He pointed down the street. "There—see the shitload of lights ahead? That's where we're going, the Golden Nugget."

At first Ethan had no idea how he was supposed to

distinguish between one *shitload of lights* and another, but then he saw the glittering, golden galaxy of lights at the end of their path. "This place is insane. The *energy* you must waste."

"Yeah, we're real low on yurts around here." Randy gestured to the panorama of decadence around them, of lights and shops and people, half of them drunk, all of them laughing and talking and soaking in the dizzy madness that was the city. "Isn't it gorgeous? I love to go up in the Stratosphere tower to look down on it all. So much sin wrapped up in so much pretty."

"Hedonism."

Randy patted his arm. "It's cute how you contradict everything I say, and it's nice foreplay, but be careful how you don your monk cowl. You'll only feel foolish later when you inevitably cut loose. Because you will, Slick. And it is going to be fucking glorious."

Ethan opened his mouth to argue, then deflated. "All right, I'll admit I don't really care about the environment, and no, I'm not a monk. But I still don't like it."

"Because you're jealous of the people who can cut loose when you can't. You can, Slick. It's practically bursting out of you, if you'd let it."

"Do you head-shrink all your friends? Or is it how you lost them all?"

"Most of my friends aren't as beautifully bottled as you are. They also don't bet their last dollar on black like some dogged idiot. You've captured my attention."

"You keep bringing that up." Ethan glared down at

him. "Why is it so stupid to bet on black?"

"Roulette sucks. There's no way to beat it. You never, no matter what you do, have the best of it. In fact, the bit we did with your ring was the first time I've ever had an advantage on the wheel in my life, and I only played it at all because I didn't give a shit about the outcome. I won no matter what."

"But if it had landed odd, you wouldn't have gotten the ring."

"I wouldn't have gotten it if it had landed on green, either. But I didn't want the ring, Slick. I wanted you."

Those three words unraveled Ethan's edges a little. Which, come to think of it, had probably been the real reason Randy had said them.

"For the bet, yes. But it doesn't explain why I was stupid to bet on black."

"You were stupid to play roulette. It's the same screwy thinking that brought you to the table which had you insisting it would eventually come around to you."

"The law of averages—" Ethan began, but he stopped when Randy laughed and shook his head.

"Don't, Slick. Don't quote that shit to me. You're smarter than the idiots who come to Vegas because of the fucking law of averages. The law of averages is a fancy phrase that sounds like math but actually translates to *wishful thinking*. I will admit there is such a thing as karma, but do not talk to me about the fucking law of averages. It is *not* the case that if you let a scenario play out over a period of time it will work itself out. If you spin a wheel full of red and black, it is *not* obliged by a sense of nicety to be balanced or to rotate politely between one pole and the other."

"But—"

Randy rode right over Ethan's objection. "A roulette wheel is *random*. It is designed—and regularly, rigorously tested—to be *random*. It can be red all fucking night. It can be red once in an hour full of black. It can hit the same number six times in a row. It can do anything, because it's *random*. It's a goddamned wheel. It doesn't know who you are, doesn't care that some guy was a complete asshole to you, or that you won big at craps. It's a wheel, and a ball lands in it. You can't guess where. You can't guess the color or the type of number. Well—you can *guess*. But you can't know. You can't even get into probability. You *can't*, Slick."

They'd stopped walking, and people were starting to stare at them. Ethan glanced around awkwardly. "Why are you yelling at me?"

"Because you're better than that." Randy stepped in close, those intense eyes boring into Ethan's gaze. "I watched you, and it drove me nuts. You thought, 'It's due for black.' It's not due. It's never due anything. What you were thinking, Ethan, is it *owed you*. You humanized the wheel. You made it the guy who should have treated you better. You decided this was the moment the world would do you right, and you rationalized it was fair to ask for special treatment, because all you wanted was five bucks. You wanted one win. You wanted to feel heard. You wanted someone to notice, so you asked black to give you a little loving. And it hurt like hell when even black let you down. For five bucks."

It was getting difficult for Ethan to breathe. "Stop talking."

Randy stepped so close Ethan couldn't just smell him, he could taste him. "I ride you, Slick, because you're smarter than that. Don't fucking go to roulette, where you can't get the best of it."

Ethan felt raw and turned inside out. "Where am I supposed to go then? *You?*"

Randy's grin could have corrupted a saint. "No. You go to poker, baby."

It wasn't right, the way the world melted when Randy looked at him. "I don't know how to play poker."

"By the end of the night, Mr. Ellison, you won't be able to say that anymore." Randy tucked Ethan's hand in his and nodded across the street where the Golden Nugget stood waiting. "Get your notebook, because school is in session."

"So what," Randy asked, as he led Ethan onto the Golden Nugget's casino floor, "do you know about poker already?"

Ethan couldn't reply, too busy taking in the sight before him. Randy was right—this was breathtaking. The casino was built on greed and gambling and sin, but it was the most elegant sin he'd ever seen, making him feel like a king in his palace. Lights flashed, and people shouted and laughed over the rattle and hum of slot machines all but drowning out the soft music playing overhead. Everything was posh and opulent, and every employee was slim and smiling at him, as if they were happy only because Ethan had finally arrived.

Randy took Ethan's chin in his hand and turned his face toward his own. "Poker. Tell me about it."

"It's a game." Ethan hesitated, feeling silly. "You bet on it."

"On what?"

"On…the cards. On your…" Ethan tried to think of the word, "…hands? What you're dealt. I swear, that's all I know. Something about a full house and a straight and a flush and pairs. I think aces are good."

"Never anything wrong with an ace." Randy tilted a glance at Ethan. "That's the poker you know?"

"That's what I know." Ethan readied himself for ridicule.

Randy led Ethan into the rows of slots, stopping at a brightly smiling blonde girl for change before taking them to a far wall where he sat Ethan beneath a row of slots under a sign reading VIDEO POKER. Instead of putting in money, Randy sat down beside Ethan.

"Poker is capturing the pot. You make a bet, and you try to win your money back plus the money of everyone else playing. You don't even need cards to play it. In the River with Scully—"

Ethan held up a hand. "What river?"

"The Ace on the River. The bar, where we made the kiss bet. You remember how Scully kept raising his bet? He was playing poker, but he was frustrated because he didn't have anybody else playing with him. Imagine the same game, and there was somebody else there betting just as hard in your favor, not mine. Each of them thinks they have the best of it, thinks they know the outcome. So they keep betting."

Ethan nodded slowly. "Okay, I think I get it. But how is this poker?"

"Imagine Scully and his imaginary opponent, and pretend you and I are two cards. Each time the players bet, they're tossing money between us, money they can't get back unless they're the one who is right or the one still standing when the game is over. They keep raising, higher and higher, and eventually they call, which means they stop and they see who's right and who's wrong—do you kiss me, or not—or one of them *folds*, which means it doesn't matter whether or not you were ever going to kiss me, whoever gave up lost."

"But why would they do that?" Ethan blushed, flustered by all this talk of kissing. "Why would they fold?"

"Because they can't afford to put any more money in the pot, or because the other bettor manages to convince them their hand is stronger. If it comes to a showdown, whoever wins is the one who guessed right. Except they don't just guess like roulette. They use reason, and some math, and a shitload of people reading."

Ethan was beginning to get this, he thought. Maybe. "Scully bet on you because he knows you, because he thinks there's no way I won't give in and kiss you—because guys usually do?"

Randy looked chagrined. "Between you and me,

Slick, my reputation is a little grander than my reality. But you bring up an interesting point. Scully bet on me, but he was an idiot because he didn't consider you. He acted like a guy with pocket aces and another on the board. He ignored the fact that there was a clear shot at a flush, which would beat him flat."

"You've lost me now."

"Scully only considered what he knew about me. If I were his hand of cards, he would be looking at two aces and thinking, 'Nobody can beat this.' But there are a lot of things that can beat a pair of aces. You might be a flush, or a straight." Ethan's mouth quirked in a smile, and Randy rolled his eyes. "A straight is a run of five numbers. 2-3-4-5-6. 9-10-jack-queen-king. A flush is a set of five cards of the same suit. Don't have to be in order."

"What if they *are* in order? What if it's 2-3-4-5-6, all hearts?"

"That's a straight flush, and it's a very fine hand. The best hand of all is a royal flush, which is 10-jack-queen-king-ace, all the same suit."

"So aces are high."

Randy shook his head. "They can be low too. You can run ace-2-3-4-5 for a straight."

"What about jokers?"

"No jokers in casinos, not in the cards, anyway. In a home game, jokers are usually wild. They can be whatever you want them to be." Randy held up his hand, ticking off his fingers. "Royal flush. Straight flush. Four of a kind. Full house. Flush. Straight. Three of a kind. Two pair. One pair. High card. That's the hand ranking in order from high to low. This is what you're paying attention to, all the time. You're looking for the highest-ranked cards in the highest-ranked hands."

"What's a full house?" Ethan knew he'd never remember all this.

"A full house is one pair and three of a kind together in one hand. Three 4s and two 8s. Three kings and two jacks. Three aces and two queens. Another way to say it is *aces full of queens*. That means you have three aces with two queens. The three set full of the two set."

"Okay." Ethan tried to iron it out in his head. "Except I've already forgotten half the orders of the hands."

"You'll learn by playing. But do you get the concept? You'll be dealt five cards. You want to form the best hand you can from what you're given. Now in this game"—he tapped the monitor in front of Ethan, which was flashing INSERT COIN TO PLAY—"you're only playing against the hand you're given, and you only get one discard."

"Discard?"

"You get five cards, and then you get a chance to hold or redraw however many you want, up to five. In this game, unlike at a table game, you'd need to get jacks or better. Any single pair lower than a jack is garbage, so ignore it. In a real game you could win with a pair of 2s, if you had the best hand or the best bluff or if nobody else had any other pair. But you can't bluff in video poker, and nobody's playing against you." He pulled out his wallet and rolled off a twenty, which he fed into the machine. "Just bet one at a time to start." He pushed a button. The screen immediately changed, and five cards came up. "Now. What do you have in this hand?"

Ethan blinked at the screen. 5 of diamonds, 3 of clubs, ace of hearts, 2 of clubs, king of spades. "I don't know."

"You have jack shit, is what. But don't worry about that. Look at it again, Slick, and tell me what you *could* have. What hands do you *almost* have, or what could you have if you discarded some and drew again? What possibilities are here?"

Ethan studied the cards. He still had no idea. "I have an ace. That's good, right?" Randy said nothing, so Ethan kept searching. "I have two clubs. Oh—and they're in order." He started to see it. "I have a 2, a 3 and a 5. If I had a 4 and a 6, I'd have a straight." He stopped. "Wait, no, I have the ace. I almost have a straight!"

"Very good. What else?"

Ethan squinted. "I have an ace and a king. If I had a queen, a jack, and a 10, I'd have a straight. I have two clubs, which meant if I had three more, I'd have a flush." Randy seemed to be waiting, so he looked one more time. "Oh—either the ace or king could get me a pair that would pay."

Randy nodded. "Good. Now you've got to discard and redraw. What are you going to hold on to?"

Ethan tried to remember the hand rankings. "The ace, 2, 3 and 5? To try for a straight?"

"Well, see, this is the trouble. The odds of you getting one of the 4s is not high. Of course, neither are your odds of getting anything else. You're probably going to lose this one."

"Can I fold?"

"Not with video poker. The only other thing worth trying is to hold the king or ace alone and try for a pair, if you don't go for the straight. It's about *odds*. If you go for the straight, you have one shot to draw one of the four 4s. But if you try for an ace or king pair, you have three shots of getting one of the remaining three."

"So I should try for the pair?"

"Ah." Randy pointed to the side of the screen. "This is where we talk about payouts. Check the payout for a straight versus a pair."

Ethan leaned forward and scanned the list of how many credits each hand made. His eyes went wide when he saw the straight. "Shit."

"You can get your credit back for going for a pair, or you can get eight credits for going for a 4 to complete your straight. Which would you rather have, Slick?"

"I want a fucking straight," Ethan said, and Randy laughed.

"Then you have the best of it with trying for a 4." Randy pressed several buttons below the cards, which made the word HOLD appear over the ace, 2, 3 and 5. Then he nodded at the DRAW button. "Hit it, baby."

Ethan held his breath and hit the button. The screen shifted, and where the king had been, he now had a 9 of clubs. His shoulders fell.

"Sometimes that's the way it rolls." Randy hit BET

ONE, then DRAW. "Try again."

Ethan tried again and again. He got several pairs and a few three of a kinds. He lost most of the hands, and after ten minutes of playing, he was down thirty credits overall. But he understood why Randy had sat him down here because he was starting to see how the hands played out, and he knew what to hold and what to discard. He knew, too, what hands were the better choice for odds. Sometimes Randy would stop him and point out something he'd overlooked—twice he'd missed a near straight—and sometimes he'd coach Ethan through a debate on what to hold and why. After another half hour of playing, Ethan was really starting to get into it. Two aces came up, so he held them and then hit DRAW.

Another ace and two 5s came up, and the screen exploded into light and a merry tune blared out of the speakers. Ethan started, and Randy clapped and laughed. "You did it, Slick."

"What? What did I do?"

Randy clapped him on the back. "Full house, baby. Ten credits."

"I did?" Ethan watched five dancing jesters prancing their way across the screen. Standing, he pumped his hands over his head. "I *did it*." He whooped, then turned to Randy, gripping the sides of his head and—

Ethan stopped halfway to Randy's mouth, realizing what he'd been about to do.

Randy's grin tipped. "It's only a quarter to ten, Slick. Better hold out."

Ethan let him go, embarrassed, but then he looked at the screen and felt his chest puff out from the inside. "*God.*"

Randy pressed CASH OUT. "I think you're ready for phase two."

"What's phase two?" Ethan took the receipt from Randy. Forty dollars. He'd started with twenty, and now he had *forty*. He'd *made* money—by playing a game.

"In phase two I teach you the beauty that is the game of Texas Hold 'Em." Randy clapped a hand on Ethan's shoulder. "Unless, of course, you'd like to take your forty dollars over to the roulette table?"

"No," Ethan replied, and Randy took his hand and led him off into another part of the casino.

CHAPTER FOUR

O F ALL THE poker rooms in the whole city of Las Vegas, the one at the Golden Nugget was Randy's favorite.

The room was cozy without being crowded, elegant without being ostentatious. Tables were evenly spaced with ample room to maneuver around them, and while there were plenty of hanging lamps distributed over the tables, the room itself was low lit, giving the place the same feel as Randy's uncle's kitchen where he'd learned the game. The room was done up in cream, yellow, muted orange, and brown, which when combined gave the place a golden glow appropriate to the casino's moniker. Even the felt on the tables was brown. Though Randy believed felt should always be green, even with this deficit the Golden Nugget Poker Room was perfect.

He wouldn't admit to many that half his attraction was due to the ambience, given how often he lectured people on the importance of the players in the game and the integrity of the host or casino, but the Nugget had this too. They had a reliable supply of live ones, and the dealers knew Randy. He always tipped, so they sat him down at tables he would enjoy. They knew for him the best table wasn't necessarily the one where he was most likely to win.

One of his favorite floor hosts was working tonight, and she smiled when she saw Randy. When he slipped a twenty-five-dollar chip into her hand, she kissed him on the cheek.

"Hey, Mandy," he said, touching her on the arm as he leaned in close. "Got any good tables for me, sweetheart?"

Mandy nodded at the back of the room. "Several. Number Six has a businessman from Atlanta going on tilt and two live ones, though I'll warn you Buddy's over there already and might think you're poaching. Five has good action and might be the better choice if you're in one of your moods—two little old ladies from Milwaukee. They know their poker, but they're used to playing home games for pennies and nickels. Jones is working prop there. I'll have to pull him if you go over, but I could use him on Three, to be honest." She glanced over Randy's shoulder at Ethan.

Ethan was oblivious to the both of them, trying to bluff the fact that he was intimidated. Randy saw Mandy take in Ethan's handsome face and quiet, easy stance. Her eyebrows lifted, and she looked both appreciative and hopeful.

Randy drew Ethan forward. "Slick, this is Mandy Carter, one of the prettiest, nicest floorpersons in Las Vegas."

Ethan accepted her hand. "Ethan Ellison. It's a pleasure to meet you."

"Pleasure's all mine." Mandy turned up the wattage on her smile. "What brings you to Vegas, handsome?"

Randy caught the shutter passing over Ethan's face. "Just thought it was time I saw the place for myself."

Mandy all but purred. "Let me know if you need someone to give you a tour."

"I'm teaching Ethan how to play poker. Thought I'd start him out with some nice low buy-in, no-limit Hold 'Em."

"Table Five's what you're after, then." Mandy winked at Ethan. "You're learning from the best there is, honey. If he roughs you up too much, you holler, and I'll make sure you're taken care of."

"Thank you." Ethan glanced at the tables again before frowning at Randy. "Do you really think I'm ready?"

He wasn't even close. Randy clapped him on the shoulder. "Don't worry, I won't let the little old ladies eat you."

"Little old ladies?"

Randy passed Mandy another chip as he led Ethan past, but she grabbed his hand and held him there as she jerked her head at Ethan. Randy gave her a rueful glance, then reached over and placed a bold hand against the firm, fine globe of Ethan's ass.

Ethan glanced over his shoulder and gave Randy a quelling glare.

Mandy caught it and all the undertones the look carried, and she sighed. "Do me a favor, Jansen. Next time you come, skip the toke and bring me one who looks like that and plays for my team."

Randy kissed her cheek before sliding his hand up from Ethan's butt as he led him to the tables. He didn't take them all the way to Five, though, but rather held him back a moment, letting Ethan see the tables and players clearly where they could still speak to each other without disrupting the game. Keeping his voice low, Randy did his best to explain Hold 'Em.

"There are a lot of different versions of poker. What you were playing on the computer was Five-Card Draw, which is probably what you've seen in westerns on TV. But the most fun are the community card games— Seven-Card Stud and Omaha. This one, Texas Hold 'Em, is the most popular."

He pointed to the dealer at the nearest table. "Everyone gets two cards of their own. These are your hole cards. You look at them and keep the information to yourself. You might decide to fold based on what you see there alone. Or you might look at them and know you're going to go all the way unless you get the whiff of someone with nuts. That's a hand you know statistically cannot be beat. If you get one of those, your biggest job is to keep the information off your face. But more on that later." He nodded to the center of the table. "Those cards laid out there in front of the dealer are called the board. They're public cards, five in total, dealt in three waves you'll hear people call streets. The first three are dealt at once, and they're called the flop. The fourth card is called the turn. The final card is called the river." He glanced at Ethan. "You taking all this in, Slick, or do you want a rewind?"

Ethan studied the table, his pale eyes sharp and focused. "I have it. I think. Keep going."

Randy continued. "You get your two cards, and then there's a round of betting before the flop." He pointed to the white chip with DEALER printed on it lying before one of the players. "In a home game you'd take turns dealing. In a casino or club, there's an assigned dealer. But since the blinds have to rotate, they put that chip out—it's called the button—so everyone knows who the 'dealer' for the round is. The first two players to the left of the button are the blinds."

Ethan nodded. "Okay. I'm with you."

"Hold 'Em is a double-blind system. Everybody takes turns betting blind, and two people go at a time. The first blind is the small blind, which is for slightly less money than the big blind. Those two positions have to bet no matter what, and everyone takes their turn there. After that, the players move around to the dealer, and they call, raise, or fold. To call, you place the minimum bet for the round, which is posted at the table. We'll be playing at a five-dollar table—five early, unlimited late. You raise if you think your hand is pretty good and you want to drive up the betting. The bigger the pot, the more you get. Be careful how and when you raise, or you'll drive the live ones out."

"Live ones?"

"Poker shorthand for a player who doesn't know what he's doing and whom you can probably beat. If you're out to make money, live ones are critical in a poker game. Always treat live ones well, because they're buying your dinner. Oh, and when you win, or when you leave a table, be sure to leave a toke for the dealer." When Ethan looked at him blankly, he clarified. "A toke is a tip."

"Then why didn't you just say tip?" Ethan frowned at the table. "I'm a live one, aren't I?"

"Not while I'm here with you. But you will be if we both sit down and play, because then I can't help you without getting us both in a lot of trouble. People will be thinking we're a team as it is." He saw the question in Ethan's face but rode over it. "Back to the play. If you don't call and you don't raise, you fold. You fold if your hand is garbage. Depending on the game, anything offsuit and lower than a 10 is a good benchmark for throwing away to start. You also fold if it's clear from the raises and re-raises before your turn to act that your hand isn't strong enough to compete. The later your position after the button, the better off you are."

"So sometimes you're lucky, sometimes you're not?"

"Yes, but you're always playing your position, your odds, always getting the best of it. Once everyone has called and met raises or folded, the flop is put down. Now you bet again, only this time you're looking at what is in your hand. You get to make a hand of five cards using any from your hand and anything on the board. The flop changes everything—you might fold as soon as you see it, you might suddenly have gold, you might be sorry you already folded. The one thing you need to know for sure is if you have Big Slick—an ace and a king of any suit, connected or off—you keep it and you stay in. Might come to nothing, but you don't fold with Big Slick unless it's clear someone is plowing their way toward something serious."

Ethan gave Randy a hard look. "Are you calling me Slick because of poker?"

The question took Randy off-guard. "Maybe I am."

Ethan lifted an eyebrow. "Am I a king or an ace?"

"Ace, baby." He turned to the board. "So. You've bet on the deal and the flop, and now you get the turn. This usually doesn't change much, though sometimes it makes you lucky. Same procedure—except on all the board bets you can check instead of call until someone else calls first. If you check, you don't put in money, just knock the table, and play moves on. You can't check after a call, though—you have to meet the call. So you check, call, raise, or fold through the turn, and then you get the river, the final card. If everyone stays in all the way to the end, you show your cards, and whoever has the best hand wins. That's Hold 'Em."

"How would you have a game where everyone didn't stay in until the end?"

"If the betting gets too high, if you think you're in danger of being beat, you fold. If everyone folds to you, you win, even if all the cards aren't dealt. In this case, you don't need to show your cards, although some people do. If you're the last man standing, you get the pot, which is how you can win with absolute shit for a hand. If you bluff everyone into thinking you have the best hand, you win."

Randy saw it clicking in Ethan's head. "This is why you're good at poker. You're good at bluffing, and you're good at reading other people."

"That, and I've been playing the game since I was six." He rocked on his heels. "So, Slick—you ready to give this a go?"

Ethan didn't seem too confident. "Couldn't I watch for a while?"

"Yeah, sure—grab a chair from the rail and sit off to the side of me, but be careful not to crowd the other players. I'll show you my hole cards, and you can watch how I play. Sound good?"

"Sounds good," Ethan agreed.

THE LITTLE OLD ladies were named Betty and Martha, and they were every bit as colorful as Mandy promised.

They were round and plump and gray, wearing matching neon-pink shirts with their names cross-stitched across the front in a bed of flowers and playing cards, and it was a toss-up over which had gaudier dangly earrings. As Randy approached, they were actively charming the pants off Jones and the balding man to his right. Even the uptight-looking fat man on Jones's other side, who absolutely had to be a used-car salesman, looked ready to fall for their charm. When the ladies saw Randy and Ethan, they smiled cheerfully.

Betty introduced the pair of them and then patted the chair beside her. "Have a seat."

Randy set down the tray of chips he'd picked up

before heading to the poker room. He nodded to the dealer and again to Jones. "How's it going?"

Jones tossed a salute. "Good. How's the action at Herod's tonight?"

"Didn't work the room, but I heard there's some good games at the high tables. You might want to check it out if you get off in time."

"Thanks." Jones glanced at Mandy, nodding before tossing a chip at the dealer and a smile at Betty and Martha. "Ladies, it's been a pleasure, but duty calls me to another table."

Martha caught his hand. "You take care, young man, and I hope to see you tomorrow."

"I hope so too." Jones kissed her hand and then Betty's, making both ladies giggle again. But as Jones slipped past the dealer, the used-car salesman began to sputter.

"He's a prop? I've been playing with a *prop*?"

"Oh, stop your fussing," Betty scolded him. "You didn't lose because of Jones. You lost because you're lousy."

But the salesman was standing now and huffing from indignation. "I'm going to speak to the floorman about this." He stalked off, leaving his chips in place.

Martha rolled her eyes, and Randy leaned back when Ethan tugged on his sleeve.

Randy whispered the answer before Ethan could ask the question. "A prop is a player hired by the casino to get games going or fill in tables if the action is low. They play with their own money, and the casino has no stake in them at all—in fact, if the action gets too good, they pull the prop."

"And you're the prop at Herod's?"

Randy nodded, then leaned in closer and lowered his voice even more. "Keep that quiet. You saw how our buddy here reacted to Jones. Once he starts playing against me, he's going to get pissed off enough without extra ammunition."

"How much are you going to pay me to keep the information to myself?"

The comment so surprised Randy he turned his head and stared at Ethan, which only made Slick's eyes dance even more. *Oh, you beautiful, wicked man,* Randy thought, bit back a smile, and reached for a fifty-dollar chip. He brought it slowly to his lips, kissed it, then held it out.

Ethan took it with a curt nod. "That'll do. For a start."

Desire curled in Randy's belly. *I am having this man in my bed by the end of the night.*

Ethan had been a lot better since Randy had gotten him onto poker. Randy would keep him at it all night if it continued to keep away the black hole he'd seen Slick slip in and out of between Herod's and the Nugget. It was killing Randy not knowing what the hell this ex in Provo had done to corkscrew Ethan, but he knew Ethan wasn't ready to talk about it. Randy felt lucky to have read what little he'd managed. His consolation was the more he needled Ethan, the more the man opened up. He'd gone from bristling and complaining to giving as good as he got.

If he kept it up until they hit the sheets, Randy would have no complaints whatsoever. In the meantime, he'd be just as entertained to watch Slick handle his first real game of poker.

Randy played tight once they got started, getting a feel for the other players. A few times he wanted to explain something to Ethan, but the salesman—Louis from Ohio—was still sore from the gentle but firm whipping Mandy had given him about the Nugget's use of prop players, and he didn't want to rile the man up just yet. He was a live one if ever there was one, and Randy had gotten attached to the idea of lightening the man's significant stack of chips.

After six hands, Randy had won two, folded four. On the seventh he ended up in a showdown with Betty, who surprised him by cottoning on to his bluff, and he folded before she could see he'd gone to the river with nothing more than a 2 and a 3.

"I wondered what the hell you were doing," Ethan murmured when Randy fished in his jacket for some money for drinks.

"Hush your mouth, Slick." When Randy moved, his lips grazed Ethan's hair, and he startled. "Sorry. What do you want to drink?"

Ethan didn't appear affected by the accidental kiss, which only irritated Randy more. "Diet Pepsi."

Randy handed the waitress a five. "What he said, and a bottle of water." Randy turned to Betty and Martha. "Ladies, can I get you something?"

They giggled, ordered a daiquiri each, and Randy added another five-dollar bill and a ten-dollar chip to the waitress's tray. They played two more hands while they waited for the drinks, Randy folding on both.

As the drinks arrived, Randy decided it was time he did too. Slick had seen enough safe playing. Time for him to see some poker.

"Poker is an art," Uncle Gary had told Randy. "It's about probability and statistics too, but mostly it's about art. It's combining your head and your heart and mixing them together with a little bit of magic. It's a game of people as much as it is a game of cards." At the age of six, Randy hadn't understood a word of it—he'd nodded and pretended he did so he could sit on Uncle Gary's knee, sneak sips of Pabst Blue Ribbon, and feel the warm safety of his godfather's presence.

But as he glanced around now at the table in the Golden Nugget, reading the faces of his fellow players, knowing the full range of how and when he'd bet before he even so much as lifted a single corner of his own cards, he thought of Uncle Gary and smiled.

Randy liked to win at poker, yes, and when his finances dipped a little low, he was more than happy to play around the table and pad his wallet again. But what he really loved was the game—the chance to use his skill and his smarts to make sure even when he didn't have much of a hand, he always had the best of it. It didn't always work out, which was part of the fun. But more often than not he could control a game, almost any game, and this, to his mind, was the whole point of playing.

Watch me, Slick.

Randy went to work.

Betty played aggressively, calling almost always and often past when she should have folded. She was one of those who called "to keep you honest, young man," which had been her words exactly, right before Randy had laid down pocket rockets and cleaned her out of the seventy-five dollars she'd stubbornly put into the pot. She hadn't forgotten the lesson, backing off from then on as soon as Randy raised aggressively past the flop. Martha, for all her gruff talk, folded on everything but pairs, aces, or face cards, and Kevin, the bald man, was even more conservative. Betty, Martha, and Kevin were completely oblivious to everything but their own hands, and they either folded after the draw or went doggedly to the end because in their mind they were due to win.

Then there was Louis.

Louis was a real fish. He was clearly the big winner in his home pots, where from the depth of his strategy he apparently played zombies and coma patients, but this didn't matter because in Louis's head he was a winner. Randy didn't like Louis. Even before he'd caught Louis curling his lip when Randy flirted with Ethan, he'd pegged Louis as a jerk, and Randy would bet his stack Mr. Salesman had plans to get himself a hooker with his poker winnings. He'd try a woman he didn't have to pay for first, but he'd end up with a hooker because nobody but the downtrodden carpet in Ohio unfortunate enough to be Mrs. Louis was going to bed with this asshole without a paycheck.

If Randy had his way, Louis would return to Ohio as pure as the driven snow and significantly poorer.

Randy's hole cards were a 9-10 offsuit, not that this mattered. He was the big blind, so he tossed in his chips and watched Betty call, Martha fold, and Kevin, his hands shaking, raise. Which meant Randy had been right—Kevin had his own rockets now.

Louis, unfortunately, noted Kevin's bold move too, and paused. But to Randy's relief, he met the raise.

Randy checked his cards again, tapped the rail absently with his fingers, then re-raised. Betty matched him, but she watched him carefully. Kevin matched him too, and Louis glared at him as he met the raise.

The flop came down as ace of spades, 9 of hearts, and 8 of clubs.

Randy covered his surprise by rubbing his nose as if to ward off an itch. He'd gone from jack shit to 8, 9, 10, and a pair as a spare. Huh. Well, his hand was unlikely to get better. Still, when it was his turn to act, he didn't raise as he'd planned, just called and left the raise to Kevin, who of course did.

"Didn't get what you wanted?" Betty nudged Randy with her elbow. Randy shrugged and watched to see how Louis played. Randy crowed silently as Louis, with a smug smile, re-raised.

Louis, Randy was sure, had Big Slick, and now he had what he hoped was top pair with a nuts kicker. He wasn't even considering Kevin could have triple aces, because this was his game, he'd decided, and he was due a win. He'd almost gotten his head on straight when Kevin had acted so boldly, but Kevin looking like somebody who should be cowering under him on his showroom floor helped Louis convince himself this wasn't possible. Now, with the ace on the board, he happily sailed to certain victory, and this time he wasn't going to let Randy stand in his way. In fact, it was going to give him great pleasure to beat the slimy little faggot.

Randy didn't know the *exact* wording of Louis's thoughts, but he was confident he had them pretty close.

Randy played the man, feigning a hesitation any pro would have seen through right away but this packet of live ones didn't even know how to unpack. This unfortunately drew Betty out a bit more than he preferred, but she'd confided to him after her second daiquiri she was "filthy rich", so he didn't feel too bad. She had a pair, but it wasn't high. She was smarter than Louis and suspected something was up. She folded on the turn.

Which was, of all things, a jack of hearts.

Randy didn't have to feign his discomfort this time, but it wasn't for the reason his opponents were thinking. He was trying to decide how the hell he'd gone from bluffing his way through garbage to one card away from a straight. He didn't have to bluff anymore, either. He could have mumbled "fuck me" under his breath and remained invisible as far as Louis and Kevin were concerned. Their game had taken on a life of its own, and they didn't need Randy to egg them on. Kevin led the show.

"You can't beat me, not this time." Kevin's face was flush with his victory. "I'm going to win the whole pot."

"Go ahead and think that." Louis tossed a re-raise down, smug as hell.

It was this more than anything else that prompted Randy to re-raise him right back, egging it on until it went one more go-around. Finally, the pissing contest ended, and the dealer laid the river: 7 of diamonds.

Randy had a goddamned straight.

Louis raised, and Randy re-raised him in a sort of daze. Kevin boldly re-raised again. The pot was huge for a five-dollar game, three hundred dollars, a good chunk of the money being Randy's own. The betting came around again, pushing the pot toward four hundred.

Louis only had one hundred fifty dollars left, but it hardly mattered. Kevin, full of dizzy glory, shoved his remaining chips forward, because in his idiocy Randy had accidentally over-raised him.

"I'm all-in." Kevin shook with anticipation.

Louis matched Randy's re-raise, then got ready to gloat as he started to turn over his cards.

Quick as lightning, Randy shoved his own cards forward into the muck. "I fold."

"You can't fold when we've all called." Louis turned over his cards, which as promised were ace and king, both diamonds, then pointed at Randy. "Dealer, I demand to see his hand."

"They were nothing." Randy's voice was sharp, partly from panic at being found out, partly from trying not to throw up over throwing a *fucking straight* into the muck on the river. "2 and 10 offsuit, okay? It was embarrassing."

Louis glared, clearly suspecting something, and Randy was ready to pull out the 10 and whatever card was next to it so long as it wasn't another goddamned 9, but Kevin saved him by laying down his treasured aces and whispering, "I won."

Everyone turned to him, Louis too. "What?"

"I *won*." Kevin laughed, wheezed, then fumbled in his pocket and withdrew an inhaler. After he got his air back, he slapped his hand on the rail and hooted. "Oh my God, I *won*."

They all cheered him, and Randy gave him a cha-grined smile, ducking his head to hide his real delight when Louis swore, picked up his remaining, paltry chips, and left the table.

Randy's joy was short-lived, however, because the next thing he knew, Ethan hauled him up from his chair and away from the table. Randy followed, bewildered, as he was led out of the room, down the hall, and around a corner into the shadows, where Ethan backed him to the wall and bore down on him like a sexy avenging angel.

"You had a straight. I thought at first I must have been wrong, until you said you had a 2. You didn't. You had a 9 and 10, and you had a straight. Which beats three of a kind." Ethan hesitated. "Right?"

Randy shushed him then glanced up the hall to make sure Louis hadn't been around to hear. "Keep it down, Slick. Yes, I did have a straight, and yes, it does beat three of a kind." He sighed. "Look. All I wanted was to clean out Louis, and if you must know, I wanted it to go to Kevin. I had no idea I'd pull a goddamned straight out of my ass."

"You could have cleaned Louis out by winning, but you threw the game. Why?"

Randy shrugged. "I can win anytime. Kevin's going back to Burbank to tell everybody in his cubicle how he won at the Golden Nugget. Sometimes the pot isn't the money."

Ethan stared at him with an intense, searing look for a long moment before he spoke. "What time is it?"

Randy pulled his phone out of his pocket and peeked at the time. "11:40."

"Good." Ethan grabbed Randy's face and pressed his mouth down on Randy's own.

All thoughts of thrown straights fled as the sharp taste of Ethan filled Randy's mouth, and several brain cells melted as well as Ethan drew on Randy's bottom lip before stealing deep inside. He could no more stop the groan rumbling in the back of his throat than he could keep his hands from sliding around Ethan's hips to the fine slope of his ass. He drew in a long, deep breath of Ethan, then thrust his tongue against the one claiming his mouth, giving as good as he got.

When they finally pulled apart, resting their foreheads together, both of them were gasping.

"Jesus Christ, Slick." Randy dug his fingers into Ethan's ass. "Please tell me we're fucking later."

"That depends." Ethan ran his fingers weakly down

Randy's chest as he paused for more air. "You were going to throw our bet, weren't you?"

Randy shrugged. "Already had the pot I was after. Figured I could get a cheaper kiss out of you after midnight. But you were right. This was better."

Ethan tipped Randy's face up and looked him in the eye. "Don't do it again." There was a tightness in Ethan's face, and no small amount of pain. "Don't tell me we're playing for one thing and then play for something else without telling me. I'll fuck you in bed, but not if you're fucking with my head out of it."

Randy wanted to argue he hadn't been fucking with him, that he was too caught up in enjoying Ethan's company to try and play the siren, but then he got lost in the hollow shadows of Ethan's gaze. *Jesus fuck, but that guy did a real number on you, didn't he?*

Randy held up his hands. "Was never what I meant, Slick. But I swear—I won't."

The pained edge eased in Ethan's gray eyes, and after a beat, he gave a reluctant smile and touched Randy's face, making Randy's cock swell happily in his jeans.

Oh Jesus, Randy thought, more blood rushing south as he read the heat in Ethan's expression. He fished in his pocket and pulled out a hundred-dollar chip. "I can't afford another thousand-dollar kiss unless I get to an ATM, but I'm curious to see what this will buy me."

A long, slender hand cupped Randy's balls as a hot mouth closed, featherlight and open-mouthed, over his own. It was over almost as quickly as it started, and

Randy was damn glad he was pressed against the wall as Ethan pulled away, because otherwise he'd have fallen over.

Ethan took the chip and ran it lightly down the bridge of Randy's nose. "I want to go play poker," he said in the same tone another man would use to say, "I want to fuck you."

"Then let's go play poker." Randy stayed against the wall and watched Ethan head toward the poker room. When Randy thought he could walk straight or at least come close enough to count, he pushed off the wall and followed.

Mandy took one look at him and lifted her eyebrows into her hairline. "And here I thought I was going to have to warn your boy you can be a little hard to handle."

"Oh no. He doesn't need any warnings." Randy ran a hand through his hair.

Mandy laughed. "Need a drink?"

"Several."

"I'll send Carol over with a Dirty Whiskey for you." Mandy patted his arm. "On the house."

Randy drifted over to the table, where Ethan had already seated himself in Louis's empty chair. He'd also changed in his video-poker winnings and his bribe and kiss tokens for a modest pile of ten, five, and dollar chips. He smiled when Randy sat beside him, and Randy settled in as comfortably as he could with his dick screaming in his pants.

"All right, Slick." Randy's voice was almost steady. "Let's see what you've got."

CHAPTER FIVE

I T ALL CAUGHT up with Ethan when Randy took him to the fountains.

He'd done well for his first time playing poker—even he had to admit it—and he could tell Randy's praise of his playing had not been feigned or embellished, because he'd criticized as much as he'd approved.

"You play too long," he'd told Ethan as they debriefed in the bar after. "A lot of green players do, but you're better than most green players, so stop. If your hand is bad you fold. *I know*, sometimes you fold and then find out you would have had a damn full house. Hell, look at the straight I had. But you have to play the odds, Slick, and you have to play the players. Don't go chasing fate in a card game, ever."

"You let Kevin."

Randy shrugged and focused on his beer. "Kevin's not you."

They kept talking as they left the Golden Nugget and hailed a cab to head for the Strip. "Keep your purse in mind. Not a bad start. You made two hundred dollars tonight on top of the money I gave you."

Ethan let the smile on his face creep into his voice. "I earned some of what you gave me."

Randy's hand slid across the seat and closed over Ethan's thigh. "Yeah, but you threw away the big purse, so don't get too cocky, baby."

Remembering the way he'd felt when he realized what Randy had done for Kevin, how it had swelled inside him when they were alone in the hall as he'd confirmed it had been deliberately done, Ethan knew he'd thrown away nothing. But he didn't tell Randy how it had impressed him, how hard he had fallen in that moment, and as they crawled through the snarl of traffic past the glittering, flashing lights of Vegas that turned it into a single, indistinguishable kaleidoscope, he admitted he had no intention of ever letting Randy know.

They got out in front of Bellagio, and Ethan saw the fountains.

He heard the music first—soft, almost ethereal female vocals drifted over an even more effervescent setting of strings, swelling to a crescendo as Ethan stumbled forward, lightheaded and disoriented. He stepped up to the railing as the song intensified again and a spray of water arced up in time to the swell of sound. The pool below glowed, as if there were a bright, blue-white fire within.

Ethan had a distant memory of the receptionist at his office in Provo telling everyone about how she'd seen the fountains at Bellagio on her honeymoon, saying they were so beautiful she'd cried. He'd written the story off as over-hyped garbage. Now he stood at the rail himself, raw from the day, thrown for so many loops he was almost accustomed to spinning. He watched the water shoot toward the sky as a disembodied soprano soared and a light hit every color of the spectrum at once, and he could not hold himself together anymore.

Emotion swelled inside him, and he tried to let out his breath to ease the pain inside his chest, but it wasn't enough. The next thing he knew he clutched the railing so hard his fingers hurt, and he spiraled away, overwhelmed by pain deeper than anything he had dreamed could exist. When he landed again, a steady hand anchored his arm.

"Hey—*hey*." The hand slid up to Ethan's shoulder and turned him away from the water. "Baby—Ethan, honey—"

Ethan gave up. He leaned forward against Randy's forehead. The anchor of those hands, one on each of his shoulders now, gave him strength. He drew courage from the pressure of contact and the musk and whiskey scent of Randy. Ethan let it support and center him, and the pain reduced to a dull ache, a simple pit in his stomach once again, not a hard, killing fire screaming through his veins.

The words broke out of him in jagged chunks.

"A car." He kept his eyes shut. "All I have left is a car. No credit cards. No house. No job. Just the money I won and you gave me in my pocket, and a car in the parking lot of Herod's." He fumbled in his pocket, pulling out the keys, his hand shaking as he held them out for Randy. "There's a gun. Under the driver's seat."

The music swelled again, but Ethan couldn't hear it because it was drowned out by the screaming sound of an oncoming train inside his own head—and then Randy's hands caught the sides of his face, shaking as he tipped Ethan's head back, pressing the keys into his cheek. Ethan opened his eyes enough to see Randy's face lit by the blue-white light of the fountains, his dark eyes no longer sharp and cunning, just wide with shock and a little bit of fear.

"Jesus Christ, Slick," Randy whispered, and then he kissed him.

The kiss was soft, so soft, and tender, and sweet. It was the sort of kiss which, even an hour ago, Ethan wouldn't have expected from Randy. It healed Ethan and opened him up too wide all at the same time.

They broke the kiss, both of them shaking, their noses seeking each other out, nuzzling. Ethan acknowledged how close he had come to never having this moment, that every single breath he took now was one he hadn't expected to take. He shut his eyes tighter and pressed his hands against the sides of Randy's neck.

Randy stroked his face. "So. What now, Slick?"

"I don't know," Ethan confessed. "But I know I don't want to go to my car."

Fingernails curled briefly into Ethan's cheeks. "You aren't fucking getting within ten feet of it." His fingers relaxed. "I'm thinking we're done with the sightseeing for tonight. You okay with coming to my place?"

"Please." Ethan brushed a kiss against Randy's eyebrow. "And we can—I mean, if you still—"

"Fuck yes," Randy said, and Ethan laughed.

They held hands not just all the way to the cab, but inside as well. Ethan felt slightly awkward, as if they had stumbled into a place beautiful but unfamiliar to both of them even under normal circumstances, let alone to have tumbled there in the span of a single evening. Ethan hoped it would get easier once they were at Randy's house.

Then Randy told the cab to pull over again, and they crossed a busy street to another hotel. Ethan looked up to see the word *Stratosphere* scrawled in neon red against the side of the building, and a tall, needlelike structure rising off to the side.

It was to this needle Randy dragged him, taking him through the lobby of a hotel not half as beautiful as the Golden Nugget and up an escalator to a ticket counter, pausing only to stop and get Ethan a huge strawberry daiquiri in the most ridiculously tall plastic drink cup and straw combination Ethan had ever seen. Ethan sipped it gratefully as Randy purchased them a pair of tickets and put them in the line for the elevator, and then they were going up, up, up. Ethan's ears popped as the alcohol soothed the frayed edges of his nerves, and then the doors opened. Randy took his hand again, and they walked out of the round, window-filled room onto an open-air balcony. Las Vegas, in all its hedonistic glory, glittered below.

They stood there for a long time, soaking it in.

"I come up here when I feel a little crazy." Randy paused, then added carefully, "Not that I think you're crazy."

"I'm not sure it's entirely sane to sell everything you have, drive to Vegas, and spend all your money with plans to put a bullet in your brain when it's gone."

Randy shuddered and squeezed Ethan's hand. "Don't even say that."

Ethan's gaze lingered on the Bellagio fountains when he found them on the Strip. They were huge, even from here. "If it helps, I don't think I was going to go through with it. When I lost my last five dollars at roulette, I was terrified because I'd realized I didn't want to end it, but I didn't know what else I was supposed to do." He smiled. "Then this idiot came and started betting on me."

Randy leaned into him, nudging him with his knee. "Sorry, Slick."

This time it was Ethan who squeezed his hand. "Don't be."

They stood in silence again.

"I'm a little out of my element here," Randy confessed. "I'm not normally…deep. I'm going to apologize in advance for any fuckups I make in my inexperience."

Ethan's gaze remained on the lights below. It looked like the world's largest Christmas display, and it was ten times as soothing. "I think I knew I didn't mean as much to him as he did to me, but I didn't want to admit it. All the signs were there in the way he arranged his life, in the double standard he had with everyone, but I loved him, and I told myself he might be that way with other people, but he wouldn't be like that with me. It hurt, a lot, to find out I was wrong."

"What the fuck did he do to you, Slick?"

Ethan shook his head. "Not now."

"I wish he were here right now. I'd throw him over this goddamned rail and cheer when he hit the street."

Ethan kissed Randy's temple. The gesture caught Ethan on the edge of his heart, and he held himself there a second, shutting his eyes and taking in a deep draught of Randy. "What the hell are we doing?"

"Damned if I know." Randy threaded his fingers into Ethan's hair, keeping his eyes on the Strip. "But I hope to God we're fucking."

Ethan slid a hand around Randy's waist. "How about we go to your place and do that now?"

They hid behind a crowd of Korean tourists, running their hands discreetly over one another as the elevator shot down like a bullet. Back on the street they hailed a cab, where Randy gave the driver an address. He drew Ethan against him and made maddening love to his ear as they slogged through the traffic again, moving deeper and deeper into the city.

"I'm leaving my truck at Herod's," Randy whispered between nibbles. "Don't want to fuck with it, and I'm probably too drunk to drive anyway."

"Sure." Ethan shut his eyes as Randy's mouth brushed his neck. He felt himself spinning again, the moment at the fountain but safer, more contained. He let himself hang there, suspended, until the cab pulled into a driveway, and after Randy tossed money at the driver, he led him past a sagging cactus to a front door. Then they were inside, and before the door even closed they were in each other's arms.

They stumbled through their kisses down the hallway to a bedroom. Ethan caught glimpses of a sparse but neat living room and a peek at a bathroom before he fell into the mattress of a soft, fragrant bed smelling of fabric softener and Randy Jansen.

Randy pressed his body to Ethan's, grinding his hips, and Ethan shut his eyes and opened for him, his mouth, his legs, and his soul.

They came out of their clothes in a surreal sort of symphony, reminding Ethan of the swell of the Bellagio fountains, the slide of a shirt sleeve perfectly timed with a lingering, open-mouthed kiss. Jeans fell from hips at the exact moment fingers found a nipple and took possession, tugging a gasp out of Ethan's mouth as the last of his clothes fell away. They pushed and pulled and danced between kisses and touches and disrobing, and then they were skin to skin, mouth to mouth. For one close, precious second, everything was okay.

"I'm a little afraid," Randy whispered against Ethan's collarbone when his mouth began to travel again, "I'm going to wake up in the morning and find out you were no more than a fantastic dream."

"I'd better not wake up in Provo." Ethan arched his back and gasped as Randy took a nipple into his mouth.

"How do you want it?" Randy nuzzled Ethan until he writhed. "I don't give a damn how it happens, so long as one of us is in the other somehow."

Ethan wanted badly to be inside Randy, wanted to jack Randy's cock while he took him, but he didn't think he could gather himself together right now to lead. As Randy's hand stroked him, as his mouth drifted down, ready to have a taste, Ethan knew what he wanted, and he sat up enough to reach for Randy's hip, trying to drag it up and over toward him.

Randy laughed darkly. "Oh, yes, that's a good compromise." The perfume of Randy's cock hit Ethan before he saw the thick, straining shaft rising out of the dark curls, swelling against his foreskin. Ethan closed his hand around it just as Randy took his own cock in hand. Shuddering against the wet wonder of his lover's mouth, Ethan leaned forward and offered him the same pleasure in kind.

They lay in the safety of the dark, sucking one another, each taking the other's cock deep, touching balls and thighs and quivering bellies, giving in to the wild madness of the night and to each other. Ethan let the fountain of emotions rise within him, and he came with a gasp of relief into Randy's eager mouth before helping him find release, drinking down the salty offering until Randy, too, was spent.

When they were able, they crawled to the head of the bed, and Ethan settled against the pillow as Randy tugged the blanket over them before taking Ethan into his arms. They held each other close, shutting out everything, grateful for this moment, this night, this strange miracle they had somehow found.

ETHAN WOKE WITH a heavy head as Randy stroked his hair.

"I'm going to run out and get some breakfast for us. What can I get you?"

"Coffee." Ethan's stomach gurgled. "Maybe some yogurt and granola too."

He felt a kiss against his forehead. "Done. Go to sleep, Slick."

Ethan shut his eyes. He did try to sleep, but fifteen minutes after he'd heard the front door close, he lay on his back, staring up at the ceiling.

He'd slept like the dead all night long without dreaming, his spirit for those hours as blissfully sated as his body. He'd gone to sleep with Randy's forehead pressed against his own, with their hands and legs and depleted cocks nestled with one another, and he didn't think he'd so much as moved until Randy nudged him awake to ask what he wanted at the store. It had felt good. It had *been* good.

Now that he was awake, however, doubt crept in.

He wasn't going to do much moving, that much he decided as soon as he tried to sit. He lay right down again and studied the ceiling. He doubted he'd be able to eat or drink anything Randy brought home. How much had he had to drink? Just those two G&Ts, and then a Diet Pepsi. Oh, yes, and the monster daiquiri. "A fruity, stupid drink," Randy had called it. It hadn't been enough to make him too hungover, just enough to unravel him.

He remembered the press of mouths and bodies, the

feel of teeth and tongue against his flesh, and the nausea threatening him subsided, replaced by something much more pleasant.

Sliding his hand absently over his penis, he teased the erection into half-life as he wondered what he was going to do now. Have breakfast with Randy, and then what? He had nothing but his poker winnings, which wasn't much at all. He could sell his car, he supposed, for a few thousand dollars. He had no idea what to do with the gun.

Ethan rolled over and drew the pillow around the sides of his head, wrapping himself inside its cocoon.

He must have fallen asleep again because the next thing he knew he heard footsteps coming into the room. Ethan panicked and held still, thinking Randy would leave to let him sleep if he kept quiet, and he could put off this most awkward of morning-afters a little longer. The bed sank behind him, but he held fast, willing Randy to go away and give him just ten more minutes to get his head on straight.

A hand slipped beneath the sheet and up across his back in a caress so gentle it startled him.

Ethan's eyes opened as the hand moved down, skimming his hip, sliding over his ass. His cock stirred as the hand, butterfly-soft, curled its way over his pelvis and toward his erection. Ethan's eyes fell closed again, and he shifted unconsciously toward the touch. Something jumped inside his chest, a loose ball bearing bouncing around, because this wasn't a touch he associated with Randy, so tender and yet wickedly erotic at once. It unnerved him as much as it aroused him, and he kept still, afraid to turn over and let Randy know how much his tenderness affected him.

The hand left his cock and slapped his ass.

"Wake up, lazy," a cheerful voice called. A voice which absolutely wasn't Randy's.

Ethan's eyes flew open, and he tossed away the pillow and rolled over in one motion. He looked up into the handsome, youthful face of a sandy-haired man whose smile faded and color drained as he looked down at Ethan.

"Oh—" The young man faltered, then almost fell off the bed in his haste to get off it.

Ethan sat up, confused and uncertain. The stranger stumbled for the door, only to be blocked in his escape by another man. This one was as tall as the door and almost as broad, and he caught Ethan's assailant in one hand while waving at Ethan with the other.

"Hey, Skeet—" The big man stopped, his bushy blond eyebrows rising up into the mass of his untidy blond hair. "Shit, Sunshine, that ain't Skeet."

"I *know*." The younger man buried his face in the larger man's chest.

The blond blinked at Ethan, then laughed, a good-natured sound that put Ethan unexpectedly at ease, even before the big man lifted his free hand to his hairline and tipped an imaginary hat.

"Hey there." He indicated the empty space beside Ethan. "Randy here?"

Ethan cleared his throat. "He went out. To get

breakfast."

"Hope he got extra." The man grinned. "I'm Mitch, by the way. I'm going to leave you alone now while I go soak my husband's head in the sink so he doesn't burn up from blushing. You go ahead and get dressed, and we'll meet up in the kitchen. Sound good?"

Ethan nodded, not knowing what else he was supposed to do, and then he watched in a daze as Mitch led the younger man out. The pair of them went down the hall, the younger whispering and the older laughing.

When he was able, Ethan climbed out of bed and tried to hunt down his pants. He found them laid out neatly over a chair with his shirt draped over the top of it, and he was halfway into the latter before Mitch's words fully penetrated his brain. He paused with one button partly through its hole.

Husband?

CHAPTER SIX

RANDY HAD TO ride his motorcycle all the way to Herod's before he could go and get groceries, because his truck was still at the casino. As he got to the parking lot, he saw the plain silver Mazda with Utah plates parked the next row over from his truck. He stowed the bike, pulled the keys Ethan had given him at the fountains out of his pocket, and tried them in the door. They worked.

As Slick had confessed, there was a gun and a pack of bullets beneath the driver's seat. Randy stared at them, feeling sick and slightly disconnected.

"New car, Jansen?"

Randy dropped the gun and kicked it under the seat, trying to look casual. The guy speaking to him was a new dealer, one Randy didn't know.

"Hey." Randy flashed a wide smile and leaned against the steering wheel. "Nah, this belongs to a friend of mine. Just checking something out."

"This wouldn't be your new friend from the bar, would it?" The dealer grinned. "I just got off my shift, and everybody's talking about your bet with Scully. You really bet against yourself, Jansen?"

What was this guy talking about? Bet against himself? Then Randy remembered he'd offered to spot Ethan his one-fifty against Scully. Which, technically, he'd lost. Randy grimaced, then ran his hand through his hair to try and cover it, but he didn't think it worked.

The dealer beamed. "Come on, Jansen, spill. Did he kiss you? Because I got in on the side-bet action, and I said he did. I could totally see you betting against yourself just to get a kiss."

You don't even know me, you prick. Randy supposed that was his legacy, wasn't it? Randy the fearless. Randy the big asshole. Randy the fun guy. Randy the quirky little bastard. Randy, Crabtree's piece on the side.

Randy rubbed his hand over his face, not liking any of this. He wasn't so bad, or he was deeper than what the dealer had insinuated. But everything in this guy registered yes, everybody believed Randy Jansen lived like that.

This, more than anything else, made Randy's decision for him. "I'm afraid you lost your bet, buddy."

The dealer's smile vanished, and his eyes went wide. "No way." His shock became anger. "You bastard, I didn't even *have* that hundred."

Let it be a lesson to you. Randy splayed his hand in halfhearted apology. "Sorry."

"But you can read everybody. You're *never* wrong." The dealer scowled. "You felt sorry for him or something. Because this doesn't make sense."

Randy gave him a withering look. "Yeah, that

sounds like me, doesn't it?"

It sobered Randy to see how well this worked to soothe the dealer's objection—his objection which had actually been the truth.

This got shittier every second, didn't it? He tried to recover. "Tell you what. I'll make it up to you with a poker lesson. Next time I'm playing prop, come on over, and I'll give you some tips. You'll win your money back and then some in no time."

The young man smiled. "Hey, thanks, Jansen."

Randy watched him go. When he was alone, he slipped out of his jacket and wrapped the gun and the bullets inside of it. Then he headed with the whole mess down the street to Tina's Pawn and threw it on the counter.

Tina paused mid-draw on her cigarette when she opened the jacket. She raised her eyebrows, then looked up with mild interest at Randy. "Hot, is it?"

"No idea," Randy said. "I want it gone."

Tina resumed her draw, held the smoke in for a minute, then blew it out at the ceiling from the corner of her lip. "How much you gonna pay me to take it off your hands?"

Randy gave her a withering look.

Tina didn't budge. "I ain't supposed to take guns, Skeet."

"Oh for the love of Christ." Randy dug into his pocket. He had a hundred, a fifty, a ten and a handful of chips. He passed her those. "I need the rest for groceries, so this is what you get, and you cash it in yourself."

Tina had caught the denominations on the bills in his hand. "You don't need that many groceries."

"Yeah, well I'm making breakfast for the poor bastard who was going to blow his brains out with the gun you're screwing me over, so tough."

Tina's hard edges softened. "No shit? Well, I guess I can rub the serial off and give it to Burt." She paused, giving Randy a knowing grin. "Wait a minute. This poor bastard wouldn't happen to be your new friend from Herod's last night, is it? The one who won a thousand off you because you read him wrong?"

What the fuck? Randy started to deny it, to explain the bet with Billy, then realized he would expose Ethan. He faltered, not knowing how to get out of this one.

Tina slapped the counter in victory. "There's no poor bastard at all, is there? You're just trying to get money out of me because you need to pay him back."

What? "Wait," Randy said, but Tina rode over him, waving the butt of the gun at him with one hand before putting it down to take another drag on her cigarette.

"Just tell me he kissed you by midnight and I'll take this as it stands. Otherwise you're giving me the fifty, because it's what I bet on your slippery little tongue sliding down his throat."

Glaring, Randy peeled off a fifty and headed out, Tina's laughter burning in his ears. But once he returned to the parking lot, he saw Ethan's car, remembered the gun was gone now, and he let out a breath he hadn't realized he'd been holding. Balling his jacket into his hand, he tossed it in the passenger seat of his truck, climbed inside, and headed to the store.

He felt better browsing the aisles of Albertsons, putting fresh beans for coffee good enough to impress Slick and an array of granola and yogurt choices in his cart as he trolled the aisles for further culinary inspiration. It was a little surreal to be cooking for somebody he'd slept with, because with few exceptions men he'd sleep with and cook for did not fall into the same category. Slick put a twist on the whole works by being, well, Slick. He seemed so fussy, to the point Randy picked out brand-name products instead of store, just in case. He could make a quiche or a fancy omelet, but suspected a nice cozy casserole would say *home* to the man.

Then it hit him how seriously he was taking all this, how much he wanted to impress Ethan, and Randy stared down at the bottle of fancy mustard in his hand and shook his head. Putting the mustard in the cart, he doubled back to the meat counter, where he picked up some spiced sausage before heading over to the international cheeses. He decided to compromise and make Slick a *gourmet* cozy casserole.

He felt smug as he waited in the checkout line, pleased with his choices and looking forward to Ethan's guaranteed surprise when he found out a guy with grease stains on his hands could cook like Julia Child. It pretty much impressed everybody, save the knuckle-draggers he'd left almost fifteen years ago in Detroit, and good riddance to them anyway. He liked engines and cards and cooking and cock? So the fuck what? That was what he loved about Vegas. Nobody fucking cared.

In Las Vegas Randy had cultivated a life of casual friends and favors and a reputation at the table which got him respect wherever he went. No, he was never going to be a famous poker player like Doyle Brunson, and this was fine. He'd never write a book about poker or enter the World Series of it, either. He'd play prop at Herod's, dabble at the Nugget and the MGM and Caesars and Bellagio, and when he got tired of playing poker, he'd head over to the Watering Hole and scare up a fuck or two.

He wasn't fond of everybody thinking he was a fucking gigolo, but after today his rep ought to have some significant, Ethan-shaped dents in it. And Ethan shouldn't have to pay for a drink again.

Right now, Randy decided, everything was good. He'd go home, make Slick breakfast, then talk him to bed for one more fuck before they got to the uncomfortable conversations such as "Where are you headed now?" and "Would you want to crash here for a bit?" But those would be fine too. Somehow. Because this was a good day. And because Slick was hot and fun to charm.

Yeah, he thought, his libido rising as he pulled onto his street. Yeah, it was gonna be great.

Then he saw the big, blue semi cab parked bobtail in the middle of his driveway, and he knew surprise, elation, and regret all in one strange go. Mitch and Sam were here.

This was going to make everything interesting.

Mitch came to the doorway and leaned against the frame as Randy carried the grocery bags up the sidewalk. He smiled as he sipped at a longneck. He looked good, really good, and happy, and despite the fuckery his presence was going to cause regarding Slick, Randy was glad to see him.

Of course, there was no point in letting him know that.

"What the fuck, Old Man?" Randy nodded at the beer. "Marriage driving you to drink before noon already?"

"Nope, just bucking up the courage to look at your ugly mug again." Mitch grinned and slapped Randy's ass as he passed. "Now get your butt into the kitchen and cook me up something to eat."

Randy was sharpening his retort when slim arms closed around his neck, and he had to brace against the onslaught that was Sam Keller-Tedsoe.

"Randy!" Sam planted a kiss against his cheek before hugging him once more.

"Hey there, Peaches." Randy brushed a kiss on his hair, which he noted absently was lighter than the last time they'd been through. "How's my favorite nurse?"

To his surprise, Sam blushed and withdrew. "I—I messed up, Randy. I'm sorry." He glanced over his shoulder at Ethan, who stood quietly against the archway to the hall, already dressed—in the same clothes as the night before. Sam's blush deepened. "I went to your room to say hello."

It took a second for Sam's hints to penetrate

Randy's understanding, but the slightly frazzled look on Ethan's face and the mortification on Sam's began to paint a picture. Randy didn't know whether to swear or laugh, so he shifted the grocery bags all to one hand and ruffled Sam's hair. "Don't sweat it, Peaches. I'll take care of it."

Sam kissed his cheek again, then returned to Mitch's side. Randy nodded at Ethan as he headed toward the kitchen table to deposit his load. "So, I see you met the family?"

"That I did," Ethan said, a hint of innuendo in his voice. Sam whimpered into Mitch's shirt.

Mitch grunted a laugh and patted Sam's back loudly. "Sunshine, come out and help me unload Blue, will you?" Then they were gone, and it was just Ethan and Randy and the breakfast which was likely not going to lead to hot sex on the table afterward.

"Let me guess." Randy stuck the cheese and butter into the fridge. "Sam came in to say hello and mistook you for me?"

"He had his hand on my dick and appeared ready to give me more, if I'd wanted it."

"Once he gets to know you better, he probably still will." Randy shoved the beer aside to make room for the milk. "Of course, he's going to turn red every time he sees you for a good week right now."

"But he's married."

Randy shut the door to the fridge and turned to Ethan, hiding the nerves he felt over explaining Mitch and Sam and himself. "You might as well know I've fucked him. A lot. Shit, I fucked him on his wedding night."

Ethan's brow furrowed, his mouth hung open, and he gestured toward where Mitch had stood.

Here we go. "Yeah, Mitch was there, enjoying the whole thing." Randy leaned against the fridge. "Look, it's how they are. It's who they are. And they're my friends, so if they make you uptight, I'm going to ask you not to let them know."

Say you're not uptight, Randy's heart whispered, and then he told his heart, *Shut up.*

Ethan's face was carefully blank. "Is that who *you* are?"

Oh, leave it to Slick to go right for the belly. Randy rubbed his jaw, trying to suss out how to answer this one. "I like sex. Kinky sex. I like vanilla sex too—I just plain like sex. The Old Man and I go way back. And Peaches—Sam, that is—" Randy sighed. How to explain Sam? "He's real shy, Slick, so don't tease him. He's shy, but bent too. He's this precious little fire, so hot, but so fragile. The world should have eaten him up and spit him out a long time ago, but it hasn't, and goddamn, but I'd do anything for that twerp."

Ethan relaxed against the wall. "Ah. So you're in love with him."

Randy would have been able to better guard against a bucket of ice water.

"Calm down." Ethan sounded unruffled and quietly amused, which was almost worse. "I'm not going to say anything."

"I'm not *in love with him*," Randy replied, angry at being called on it, unsettled by it being Slick who did the calling. "I'm not going to fuck up their marriage or anything."

"You'll just fuck him?" Ethan suggested, sounding more amused all the time.

Randy swore, shut his eyes, and gave up, pressing his forehead to the cupboard door. He stilled, though, when Ethan placed a hand on his back.

"Calm down." The hand drew gentle circles then slid up to Randy's neck, sending a shiver down his spine. "Actually, I think I sort of understand. Given the way he touched me, thinking it was you—well, if it helps, I was pretty much butter in his hands."

Glancing over his shoulder, Randy arched an eyebrow. "Thought it was me, though. So you would have been butter in my hands?"

Ethan's eyes darkened a moment before he lowered his hand. "Randy, is my being here going to cause a problem?"

"No." Randy caught Ethan's hand and threaded their fingers together. "No, baby. I wasn't expecting them for another week or so, but they just come and go. The worst you're going to have to put up with are Peaches's moans, because I'm not gonna lie to you—those two fuck like bunnies."

"His moans, but not yours?"

Randy recaptured Ethan's hand. "Not unless it's you making me come, Slick."

Ethan tilted his head and narrowed his eyes.

"Hmm."

Randy caught Ethan's other hand too. "Okay, so this is an unusual situation, I'll grant you. I was going to feed you and fuck you before I brought this up, but the happy couple has thrown a wrench in my plans, so we're just going to lay our cards down here and now. You got nowhere to go, Slick. I've got your keys, and I sure as fuck am not giving them to you until I know you aren't going to go find another gun or a cliff or whatever."

Ethan looked Randy in the eye. "I'm not."

Something leashed inside Randy relaxed. "You still need somewhere to stay. You don't have even enough money for a fleabag hotel. You would have had a cool grand, which could have been a stake in a poker game, but you blew that to play tonsil hockey with me, so you have only yourself to blame there." He thought about the rumors he'd just started at the casino and at Tina's, but he decided this wasn't the moment to bring it up. "I'm not going to go to bed with Mitch and Sam while you're here. Well, not unless you decide you want to come along, which for the record would, I'm sure, be an available option."

"You don't owe me that, withholding yourself from them."

For some reason this pissed Randy off. "Well, you're getting it." He pulled his hands away and opened the door to the fridge, staring into it, hoping if he stood there long enough he'd remember what he was going to reach for. "Now get out of my kitchen so I can cook."

Ethan pushed the door to the fridge shut, and when Randy turned to complain about this, his face was caught in a firm, slim hand. Then Slick's mouth was on his, taking him in a slow, sweet, grateful kiss.

Randy kissed him back, nuzzling his chin when they finished. "I'm not in love with Peaches."

"You are, but it's fine. Really."

Ethan's face was impossible to read, but beautiful and calm too, and the confident control Randy had found while food shopping dove the rest of the way into the toilet.

All this was before Ethan opened his mouth and said, his voice solid and soft and sexy as hell, "I want you to teach me more poker."

Jesus fuck, but why the *hell* did Mitch and Sam have to show up right *now*?

Randy held on to Ethan's hip. "Fucking hell, Slick, I want to push you onto the table and take you this goddamned second."

Ethan grinned and stepped between Randy's legs, taking Randy's rapidly growing erection in his hand. "I'll pay you for the lessons."

Randy let his legs open wider so he could arch into Ethan's seeking hand. "I take cash or fuck. No credit."

"I can deal with those terms." Ethan's silky tone fell away, and he looked almost sheepish as he shook his head. "I feel like I'm somebody else when I'm with you."

"Naw." Randy slid his hand up Ethan's chest to curl his fingers around his neck. "You're Slick, plain and simple."

"*Big* Slick." Ethan pressed his hips against Randy's.

"Don't I know it. I had the monster down my throat, if you recall."

"I do recall." Ethan nipped Randy's earlobe. "I'd like to put it in your ass."

"Whenever you want it, baby. Wherever, whenever, however."

He shut his eyes and tipped his head back as Ethan's tongue slipped inside his ear.

Then the front door opened, and he groaned in regret as Ethan moved deftly aside.

That was when Randy got his first good look at not just Sam's face but Mitch's. He pushed off the counter, breakfast, sex, and even poker forgotten. "What the fuck is wrong?"

"I HAVE TO make a run to Kentucky."

Randy settled in the passenger seat of his truck as Mitch drove them through the streets of Las Vegas. "But Sam's taking his first nursing job after graduation, right? I thought you were going to do short hauls here out west while Peaches got started?"

"Yeah, well, the market got tight, and jobs dried up. This isn't simply good money, it's a connection to some long-term jobs that can lead to other ones, and it will help me be able to be more flexible with what contracts I take later. We talked it over, and we decided we'd get Sam out here early, maybe make a little vacation of it before I went down to L.A. and made the run. It'd be only a week I'd miss once he actually got started, and we figured with you here it'd be easier."

"Sounds about right. So what went wrong?"

Mitch's hand tightened on the wheel. "We came on a wreck in the middle of Nebraska. Bad one. Tractor-trailer all mangled, driver shredded. It turned even my stomach, to tell you the truth. And Sam—" Mitch cut himself off.

Oh Jesus. "Sam went batshit, didn't he?"

"Like nothing I've ever seen. He was fine at first. Then all of a sudden we're in the mountains, heading for Vail, and he breaks down. I thought it was the mountains again, because you know how he gets with heights. But then he's crying so hard he throws up. *Blood*, Skeet. He threw up *blood*. I took him to the hospital, it scared me so bad."

Randy's fingers curled into the armrest. "What the *fuck*."

Mitch ran a hand through his hair. "It's some sort of repressed trauma, according to the doctors. Something to do with his mom. Makes no damned sense to me, because his mom fucking died of cancer, not a car wreck, but he's convinced now I'm going to die on the way to Kentucky, and he'll never see me again. Which is horseshit. I'm more likely to die driving around Vegas. But there's no talking to him, and the fuck if I know what to do with this, Randy. They gave him these pills to take for anxiety, and they're even worse—he stones out, and then he looks at me and cries."

"Can you get out of the run, or get somebody to

cover it?"

"No." Mitch ground out the word in a terse bite. "I've tried, but no. And the long and the short of it is, it's clear he's going to be like this if I so much as drive up to Reno. He's tearing me up, and I don't know what to do to help him."

Randy wished he had an answer, but he didn't. "Shit, Old Man."

Mitch snorted. "I don't suppose there's any chance Prince Charming there in your kitchen is a psychiatrist?"

"Fuck, he might be. I never got around to asking."

"Yet I notice he was about to get quite a fancy brunch."

Randy shrugged and nodded at the corner. "Turn here. My bike's at Herod's."

Mitch grunted. "You still working for that fuckwad?"

"He keeps me entertained."

"He's an asshole."

Randy raised his eyebrows. "So am I."

Mitch pulled into the parking lot. "Not like Billy. And I don't care for the gangster he keeps in the attic, either."

Randy undid his seat belt and turned to Mitch. "Listen, we'll figure out what to do for Sam. At any rate, yes, I'll be here for him. You don't have to worry."

Mitch frowned. "Don't want to get in the way of whatever it is you have going with Mr. Handsome."

"I don't know what I have going with Mr. Handsome, but whatever it is, it's not coming before Sam, or you." He opened the door to the truck and started to slide out.

Mitch leaned over the seat to continue the conversation. "Where'd you meet him?"

Randy grinned. "Roulette table at Herod's."

Mitch's eyes went wide. "You played *roulette*?"

"I did, and I won. But a word of warning—don't bet against Slick. He's got one hell of a poker face."

"He plays?"

"A little. I started teaching him last night, but he's got a real feel for it."

A smile played around the corners of Mitch's lips. "Match made in heaven."

Randy rolled his eyes. "You heading home, or running out to the distribution center?"

"Home, by way of the Tobacco Outlet."

"Oh good. Keep nursing your cancer, Old Man, and you can die like his mom after all."

Mitch flipped him off, and Randy shut the door. He watched Mitch pull away, thinking of everything he'd told him about Sam, letting it roll around in his head as he headed for his bike.

Halfway there he turned around, pocketing his keys as he wove his way through the cars and toward the side entrance to the casino, to the stairs leading to Crabtree's office.

Randy didn't know Crabtree's real name, and he didn't ask because he'd heard a rumor if you found out, you'd end up bones in the desert by the morning. He doubted this was actually the case, but he did know there was a strong association between Crabtree and violence as a general rule.

Crabtree was not a bad man. He'd been in the mob, a ghost all his life, never appearing in photos, never really joining society. Crabtree hung out in his office pushing paper around, doing what he could to keep the casino from going completely belly-up. Crabtree hated what Billy had done to the place, but even if he would have dared to usurp his godson, he could never own the casino outright with his history. So he stayed on the sidelines, milling around, nudging Billy into the lines when he wandered out too far.

Crabtree's office was a tiny corner of the sixth floor, a little hovel full of a desk and Crabtree and three zillion posters of cats—most of them kittens. He pointed proudly to the new one behind him on the wall as Randy walked in, a fluffy ball of orange fuzz blinking up from a bed of impossibly green leaves on a poster reminding Randy of Scholastic book orders.

Randy found the posters distasteful and borderline disturbing, but he smiled at Crabtree and nodded in approval. "Very nice."

"I found it at a flea market on the way in this morning. Isn't it precious?" He beamed at the poster for another moment before turning to Randy. "What can I do for you, Jansen?"

Randy glanced at the chair across from Crabtree's paper-strewn desk, then looked at Crabtree for permission to sit, which the older man granted with a nod.

Randy inclined his head in acknowledgment, though he didn't fully relax in his seat. One was wise to keep on his toes with Crabtree.

"You told me one of your covers for working in the Outfit was a practicing psychiatrist."

Crabtree laughed, a belly rumble that shook his whole body. "Therapist, son. But yes. I was actually licensed for that one." He arched an eyebrow. "You taking your defeat at Roulette Man's hands this badly, Skeet?"

Randy set his teeth. The bet was a bitter pill that just kept coming back to be swallowed. Or maybe it was more like one really long, rancid dick. He shifted uncomfortably on his seat. "It's Sam. He and Mitch showed up this morning. Something's wrong with Sam, and it's got Mitch all torn up. Me too." He rubbed the side of his face. "They were told he should see somebody, but I don't know anything about this shit. How do you find a good therapist? One that won't fuck him up more or lock him up?"

Crabtree looked amused. "First you try to throw a bet, then you *lie* about it, and now you're in here worrying about Sam Keller like a mother hen. Who are you, and what have you done with I-don't-give-a-shit Randy Jansen?"

Randy tried not to react, but it was like knowing somebody had just thrown a spider at you. Hard to stop thinking about so many wiggling legs. "You had us followed?" Randy gave up trying to poker face Crabtree and aimed an angry finger at him. "You have no fucking right to tail me. Yes, we've had some fun, but I am not your bitch, and you do *not* fucking put shadows on me."

"I didn't have anyone follow you. I just took a guess, and it's interesting to see I was right."

Randy remembered it wasn't generally wise to shout at a gangster and forced himself to calm the fuck down. "Okay. Yes, I tried to throw the bet. Yes, he figured it out and threw it himself before I could." Randy frowned. "No, this is too much detail for you to have guessed. Goddamn it, Crabtree, you *did* follow me."

"Not you, no. I'm looking forward to seeing your luscious little bum in a pair of hot pink twink shorts in a few weeks. If Billy gives up on his Gay Nite, I'll tell him I'll collect on the bet for him in a private performance."

"The color was not part of the bet." Randy's mind kept turning over Crabtree's confession. *Not you.* That meant he was following Slick. The knowledge threw Randy even more, and he opened his mouth a few times, trying to protest, but he couldn't seem to find his footing.

Crabtree threaded his fingers over his ample belly. "You working this evening?"

"Yes. I'm going to call in vacation to the distribution center, but Billy's got me on prop for tonight, though. Why?"

"I'll see to it you aren't working. Go home and clean your house and make something fancy for dinner, Jansen. I'll be over at seven."

Randy felt the blood drain out of his face. "Crabtree—"

"Pick up a few sealed decks downstairs on your way out. I hear your new boy is quite the up and comer at Hold 'Em."

Fuck, but this had been a big mistake. Randy held up his hand. "Crabtree, I appreciate—"

Crabtree held up a hand too, and Randy instantly fell silent.

"This is for my own curiosity. I want to meet the man you couldn't read. Besides, I'll be better able to give you a referral for Sam if I know what I'm looking at."

Randy kept quiet, but he reeled inside, kicking himself for following the instinct to come up here.

Crabtree tilted his head and gave Randy a grandfatherly look which was both reassuring and absolutely horrifying at the same time. "I'm not going to hurt him. Either one of them. If you thought I might, you wouldn't have come to me at all."

"Sam is from Iowa. Despite what he can do with his mouth, he's pretty innocent."

Crabtree nodded, still smiling. "I understand."

Randy watched Crabtree's face intently, searching for even the barest hint of licentiousness, but he really did just look like a grandfather now. Anyway, Crabtree was all about bears and otters, drifting between the two depending on his mood. Both Ethan and Sam were safe.

As safe as they could be, having dinner with the mob.

Randy's palms, suddenly sweaty, curled against his jeans.

Crabtree, of course, did not miss this. "This is purely a friendly visit. I won't be asking anyone for payment of any kind."

Randy snorted. "You're the one who told me there's no such thing as a friendly visit."

"Family is different."

Randy snorted.

Crabtree laughed. "I like you, Randy. You have the same code as I do. Yes, I regard you as family."

What code? This question was crowded out, however, by thoughts of the many twisted ways he had paid for Crabtree's services in the past.

Crabtree's laugh darkened. "Very well, incestuous family."

"Thank you?" Randy paused as another wrinkle appeared on the horizon. "Okay, normally I don't mind—"

"I'm not going to get in the middle of your blooming love life, so settle down. Unless I decide he's not worthy of putting his sausage in your cute little buns, but from what I hear he's more than adequate to the task, metaphorically and otherwise." Crabtree waved a hand at Randy in dismissal and began to sift through his papers again. "Go home and get to work. I'll see you at seven."

Randy rose, slightly dizzy. The sensation didn't abate as he headed down the stairs, and he outright ignored Billy when he hollered Randy's name as he passed. He managed to make it all the way to his bike and rode it several blocks before he had to pull over by the side of the road.

He threw up once, waited, then did it again.

At home he parked the bike in the garage and went inside, where Ethan and Sam sat in awkward silence, both not watching a home-and-garden show on television. They looked up at him as he entered, and when Randy saw their beautiful faces and thought about what he'd so foolishly done, he nearly had to run to the bathroom and have another round of dry heaves.

Swallowing them, he nodded at Sam. "Peaches, I need you to clean the house for me. *Clean.* Enough for the fucking Queen of England. When Mitch comes home, lock him in your room and do not let him make a mess. In fact, if you could fuck him into a coma, that'd be good, because he is going to try to slit my throat when he finds out what I just did, and I'd rather he didn't have the energy."

Sam's eyes went wide. "What—?"

Randy cut him off. "Slick, we're going shopping. And remind me to pick up some cards on the way home, because I forgot once already."

Ethan rose, frowning elegantly. "Randy, what's going on? You look green."

Randy glanced at his watch. "Fuck, there isn't any *time.* How the hell am I going to cook something good enough for Crabtree and get to the mall all at the same time?"

"Crabtree?" Sam, who had risen too, sank down once more. His face was white. "The gangster?"

Randy nodded. "He's coming for dinner. *Do not tell your husband.* But don't let him get drunk if he finds out, either."

Ethan raised an eyebrow. "What the hell is going on?"

"What's going on is you're going to the mall, because you aren't meeting Crabtree in clothes you're wearing for the second day in a row."

"Who is Crabtree?" Ethan asked as Randy led him toward the door.

"Santa Claus." Trembling slightly, Sam picked up the newspaper Mitch had strewn over the carpet. "With a big, bloody knife."

CHAPTER SEVEN

"**I**S THIS CRABTREE man actually a gangster?" Ethan asked as they pulled onto a busy street. "Or are you just being colorful?"

Randy rubbed his hand against the back of his neck. He looked distinctly uncomfortable. "He's a gangster of sorts. I don't know the full extent of it, and I don't want to. All I know is he's Billy Herod's godfather, and while he's not a big cog in the wheels keeping Las Vegas turning, he knows how and when to grease them. I also know he has killed people, both by order and by his own hands."

It was all so ridiculous Ethan thought it had to be a joke, but nothing about Randy's demeanor hinted this was anything but the real deal. "But why is a gangster coming to your house for dinner? And why does this mean I have to get dressed up?"

"We all have to get dressed up. I don't know what the fuck we're going to do with Mitch, but Peaches will think of something. As to why he's coming…" Randy flattened his lips into a line. "That's because I'm a big, fat idiot and drew his attention. Of course, from the sound of things, you already had his eye anyway, so I suppose I just put the inevitable in motion earlier."

This comment surprised Ethan. "Me?"

"You. I didn't read you right and lost a bet to Billy. Word has already gotten around, and Crabtree wants to meet you."

Suddenly none of this was amusing anymore. "Is he going to kill me?"

"No. But here's some advice: he loves cats. I mean, he *loves cats*. If you don't love them too, learn to fake it quick. Beyond this point, he's perfectly rational. A little perverted, but he'll leave you alone. Though you should probably get ready to watch him flirt with me."

So the Santa Claus mobster who loved cats was gay. Ethan wondered briefly how he had gone from being the only gay man he knew unless Nick was in town to being steeped in them. He stared out the windshield as he tried to process. "And where are we going right now?"

"Miracle Mile. You need some H&M. We'll swing by Whole Foods on the way home and pray the culinary gods strike me with divine inspiration."

"So this Crabtree invited himself to your house for dinner on short notice and expects you to have your house and guests scrubbed clean with a gourmet spread waiting for him?"

Randy tapped the steering wheel with his thumb for a minute before answering. When he did, his voice had the same instructive tone it had taken when he'd spoken so passionately about the law of averages.

"Here's a poker lesson for you, Slick. Crabtree

works for Billy Herod, which is to say he works for a child of the mob watching him, and you'll remember I said Billy runs casino theater, a kind of operation his father would cringe to see. Crabtree is a big, out bear in a hyper-masculine underworld. When you meet him, get a good look at his teeth and note the number of gold caps he flashes. He's never once had a cavity in his life, and he didn't cap healthy teeth for fun. He's smart as a whip, but he's weird and quirky, and it's a good thing you're not a furry man with a bit of belly and a pretty mouth."

The peek beneath Crabtree's veneer jarred Ethan. He nodded.

Randy glanced at him across the seat. "Crabtree is a powerful man who has spent a lot of time with men more powerful than he is, men who do not give him much respect. He's chosen to take on Billy of his own free will because he loved Billy Senior, and there is no question if you need something, Crabtree can get it done. Anything."

Ethan began to understand. "But the one thing fragile about him is the amount of respect he gets—honest respect."

"That, and his bizarre weakness for kittens." Randy shrugged. "I don't have to have Sam scrub the house and try to truss Mitch into something presentable. I don't have to kill myself pulling a Martha Stewart. But I'm trying to because if I pull it off, I will be making one hell of a genuflection to somebody who has saved my ass many times in the past and will do so in the future, even if I serve him frozen pizza wearing stained jeans." He paused. "Probably."

Ethan digested this, the lengths Randy was willing to go to give a nod to an emotionally vulnerable gangster just because he felt he owed him, and he knew an unexpected tug at the edge of his heart.

Then Randy said, "There is no compromising on your wardrobe, though."

"But why?"

"He's coming to scope out *you*, Slick. Unless you go courting somebody higher up on the food chain, Crabtree can either make or break you in Vegas. And you don't want to go any higher on the food chain than Crabtree."

"Do I want to be made in Vegas?"

"Fuck yeah. You sure as hell don't want to be broken."

Ethan would have thought he already was, but he didn't see the point in saying so.

They were heading onto the Strip, or rather, near it. Randy took great pains to stay off Las Vegas Boulevard itself, which given the snail crawl their cab had done even in the early hours of the morning seemed a wise move. He wove his way down the side streets until he had them entering the parking garage behind the Planet Hollywood casino, whose very existence boggled Ethan.

"Does McDonald's have a casino?" he asked as Randy led him to the mall entrance.

Randy looked thoughtful for a moment. "Well, the one at Harrah's certainly has the neon glitter down pat."

He took Ethan's hand and led him into the main body of the mall. "Come on. I'm not kidding. We're partitioning seconds now, we're so close on time."

Randy moved at light speed, and without his hand Ethan would quickly get lost in the crowd. Partially this was because Ethan had a serious rubbernecking problem.

"There's a *sky* in here." Ethan had to shout because club music was blaring from up ahead, echoing in the cavernous ceiling. At least, he thought it was a ceiling. It had to be, because in here it was dusk, despite it being blazing noon outside. Still, the buildings were—well, they were *buildings*, not storefronts. They shone in the same neon glitter as the buildings on the Strip. It was a mini-Strip within the Strip. Or something.

"Come on." Randy tugged him around a corner, and then they were at the source of the music, which was also a huge, pulsing fountain light show in the middle of a corner atrium. Ethan staggered back, caught by the sight, remembering the echo of another fountain in the dark.

"Oh fuck that, Slick. After Bellagio, this is nothing. Besides, it's just a bunch of skinny dicks shooting come."

Ethan looked again at the pulsing bursts of water then burst out laughing.

Randy got behind him and began to push him like a snowplow. "Come *on*."

The shopping expedition at H&M was the strangest thing Ethan had ever been a part of. He wasn't exactly averse to shopping, but it was usually a solitary and sober experience, not a frenzied group project where his lab partner alternated between fashion drill sergeant and the lecher who insisted on standing in the doorway watching him dress and undress.

"I never asked. What did you do for a living before you ran away to Vegas to meet me?"

"I was an investment broker." Ethan smoothed his hand over the pleats of the trousers after buttoning them, eyeing their line critically in the mirror. "Do I actually need something this fancy?"

"You need a whole wardrobe, Slick. But yeah, you'll wear these tonight." He ran a hand over Ethan's backside. "Investment broker. So you played the stock market?"

"I invested clients' money in various ways. Stocks, sometimes, but also funds and other projects as well." Ethan sifted through the pile of clothing they'd amassed on the bench. "Where's the black iridescent shirt? It would look good with this."

Randy reached into the hallway and produced the shirt. "Do you miss it? Being a broker."

Ethan shrugged and tried to focus on the shirt. "Are we done here?"

"Just a few more things. I think you're right about the shirt, which with the pants can be tonight's outfit, so as soon as we pick the jacket, you'll be set. The rest we can return if it doesn't fit." He handed Ethan a stylish gray jacket. "Did you *like* it?"

"The jacket? I haven't tried it on."

"Being a broker."

Ethan fussed with the collar of the shirt. "It was fine."

It hadn't been fine, of course, he admitted to himself as they headed to the truck, and he ruminated on his now-past life all the way to the grocery store.

He had both loved and hated being a broker. He loved watching money compound and amass, but it was never his money. His clients were grateful for his skill at reading the market, and he had been told he had a killer instinct for knowing when to switch from one type of investment account to another, but he'd had to convince himself more and more frequently this was enough. Eventually he'd begun to be more aggressive with his own savings, investing his own money, but it made him lonely. He wanted to be investing with a partner, like the husbands and wives planning their retirement futures, which was why he had gone to Nick.

Foolishly he'd thought because Nick had sworn to him it was Ethan he loved, he whom he truly felt he was married to, that he would mean it, that when push came to shove, he would choose Ethan—

The world went soft and dull, and even though there was nothing wrong with Ethan's hearing or his vision, as he stood staring into Randy's cart, the real world fell away. He sank into the cold, dark space inside his head—and then something pressed against his mouth, something soft and small and sharp. He tasted, too, the tips of Randy's fingers.

"I need cheese, and I can't decide which is better.

Help me." When Ethan did nothing, Randy pushed the cheese the rest of the way into his mouth. "Chew, Slick."

Ethan did, and the world came reluctantly into focus. He ate the cheese without tasting it. Randy handed him a bottle of water, and Ethan drank absently. But then the second piece of cheese came into his mouth, and Ethan glanced at Randy, startled as a quiet explosion took place on his palate. It was smooth, buttery, but it had a bite to it too, and something smoky—

"Second one." Randy tossed several packages into the cart. "I'll keep extra on hand too, in case you go into a coma again on me."

Ethan grimaced and drank more water. "Sorry."

Randy resumed control of the cart and aimed them toward the bakery. "You freak me out sometimes, Slick."

Ethan freaked himself out, to be honest. What was he doing in Las Vegas, playing poker and having dinner with gangsters? Why wasn't he going home to Provo, apologizing to Marion, and getting his job back? Why was he eating cheese at Whole Foods and playing dress up at H&M?

He watched Randy moving with determination through the racks of bread, pinching several and shaking his head in dismissal before picking up a large, long, crusty loaf with an almost piratical look of victory, and Ethan realized he was looking at his answer.

Because I'm following him. Because Randy is the strangest, most wonderful thing I've ever seen, and right now he's the sun I can't otherwise seem to find, even when it's right above me in the sky.

Randy waggled his eyebrows and held up a loaf of bread like the spoils of war.

I can't let him know that, Ethan thought, withholding the full warmth he felt as he returned the smile.

THE HOUSE HAD been immaculate when he and Randy had come home from the store, but Randy still went over everything, straightening pillows and wiping off the faceplates of the light switches. Once everyone had showered, he'd stood in his towel and wiped it all down again, all but getting a magnifying glass out and searching for stray hairs. For a minute Ethan had thought he was going to iron the hand towel by the sink too.

Between barking out cleaning orders and arguments with Mitch, Randy prepared a three-course gourmet meal. Ethan had already been impressed—Randy's taste in food wasn't parallel to his penchant for grease-stained fingers and shredded T-shirts. But as he watched Randy work, he saw Randy was a much better cook than Ethan was himself, and Ethan was no slouch.

Randy moved with casual skill around the kitchen, chopping and weighing and sautéing even as he aimed a butcher knife at Mitch's nose. "I didn't *mean* to do this, but it might end up being the best thing for everyone, so just *shut up and let me cook if you aren't going to help.*" After that Mitch had taken off on one of the bikes in the garage and headed for a local bar, and Randy paused his preparations long enough to console Sam. Then he sent

Sam after his husband in a cab because he didn't know how to drive Randy's stick-shift truck or the bike.

Once Sam was gone, Randy peeled out of his T-shirt, tied a bandana around his head, and got serious.

He was making, Ethan saw from the stained notes on the table, baked salmon in cucumber cream wine sauce. The first course would be mesclun salad with lemon vinaigrette, and there was some note about asparagus spears Ethan couldn't quite mentally map but looked forward to seeing. With the salmon would be new red potatoes—the notes said carved into mushroom shapes, but surely Randy didn't have time—and a julienne of fresh snow peas and carrots. The third course would be a modified tiramisu, served with fresh custard in a martini glass.

Randy's lips thinned as Ethan mentioned the dessert. "I'm cheating on the tiramisu. I've run out of oven, so the ladyfingers are from Whole Foods. I'm making the custard to go with it myself, but he's still going to know I bought the ladyfingers."

"How?"

Randy pulled an apron from behind the broom in a cupboard. "He knows what mine taste like."

They'd been talking about tiramisu, but somehow Ethan knew the double entendre wasn't an accident.

"You've cooked for him before?" Ethan asked, as mildly as he could.

Randy glanced over his shoulder—his bare shoulder, slick with sweat—and looked Ethan in the eye. "I've cooked for him. I've fucked him too, but mostly he's come here for dinner, and then we've gone to my bedroom where he's tied me up and done the sorts of things to my body that would curl your little Mormon's toes."

He resumed chopping, which was good, because Ethan needed a few seconds to recover, both from what Randy had revealed about his relationship with their imminent dinner guest and the knife cut that had been his reading of Nick.

"How did you know Nick is LDS?"

Randy shrugged. Ethan noted, helpless to do otherwise, the way it made the muscles in his back ripple. "Lucky guess." He picked up a cucumber and began to cut into it. *Slice, slice, slice.* "So he has a name now."

You had to go and open this door, didn't you? Ethan scolded himself. "He's always had a name."

Slice, slice, slice. "He a broker too?"

"He worked for Deseret Book Company. The Church of Jesus Christ of Latter-Day-Saints publishing house."

"I know what it is." *Slice, slice, slice. Chop.* "'Worked.' Past tense?"

Ethan's fingers dug into his own arms. He wore a new T-shirt, not yet washed, and it itched. "Yes. He was laid off six months ago."

Ethan didn't want to be exposed like this, and he resented being made to spill his dirty laundry. His rage spun out of reason and into wordless chaos, cycling inside him with nowhere to land because Randy wasn't saying anything. He kept cutting his vegetables, *slice,*

slice, slice, slice, chop.

Finally Randy glanced over his shoulder again. "You're gonna pass out, Slick, you keep holding your breath."

Ethan lost it.

"He's married." Ethan stormed over to him, looming over him, ignoring how fucking sexy he looked all slicked over, how he was practically oiled, how the sharp, fresh aroma of the vegetables mingled with his musk. Ethan tried to breathe through his mouth, but then he could *taste* it, and that made it worse.

It made him furious.

He grabbed Randy's wrist. "He's married, okay? *Married.* With four kids. Nick and Mary Snow, and their cherubs Jacob, Rachel, Ezra and Ruth. They look like a fucking Hallmark card in their Christmas photos."

Randy drew back, surprised. "He sends you his family's Christmas cards?"

"No, I saw them on his Facebook. Which I had to hack—" Something started to break inside him, but he pushed on, because he saw the flicker of pity in Randy's eyes. "I knew, from the moment we met. He was married then. So don't go looking at me like that."

"That's not why I was looking at you." Randy tried to school his features again, but the pity was still there, and it made Ethan all the angrier.

"I *knew* he was married, so *stop.* That's not why I left him." He waited a beat, then sneered. "This is where you ask me why, Randy."

Randy's eyebrows lifted. "Okay, sure. Why, Randy?"

The waves of fury were endless, carrying him forward, and Ethan was glad for them, because without them he was fairly certain he would go under and drown. "Oh, you're so *clever*, you little shit, aren't you? Always seeing everything, even what you shouldn't, and you're having such a *good time* picking me apart—"

"Slick?" Randy's voice cut quietly across the scream of red.

Ethan huffed, wind out of his sails. "What?"

Randy nodded discreetly toward the counter. "Would you mind putting down the knife?"

To his complete surprise, the butcher knife quivered in Ethan's hand, its tip flashing, scattering bits of cucumber and knocking over the open container of cream, sending the thick, yellow-white liquid down the drain. The knife he'd aimed at Randy's hand, which had backed up several inches and was off the cutting board entirely and now balanced carefully against the edge of the sink.

Ethan dropped the knife, let out his breath and the rage with it, and without his fury to support him, the wave crashed over. To his eternal shame, he felt the dark crush him, and he began to cry.

Sobbed, really—and why it happened then, after months of wiping away tears and sniffling and nothing more, why it was *there* he finally broke down, in Randy's kitchen, smelling of cucumber and garlic and sweaty man and lemon cleaner, why *there* he didn't know. He just knew he couldn't hold it back anymore, the pain of days—which was, of course, the pain of years, and in another view, of a lifetime. It hit him square in the center of the chest, and as if breaking down emotionally in front of Randy weren't enough, his body had to fail him too.

Randy's arms kept him from falling, and when it was clear Ethan and his pain were too much to keep upright, he eased them gently to the floor, sat Ethan between his legs and took him into his arms.

"Oh God." Ethan buried his face in Randy's neck. "Oh *God*, I'm so sorry."

"Hush." Randy's rough fingers skimmed over Ethan's shoulders before drawing him in against his bare chest with only a tiny bit of hesitation. "I'm not trying to be clever, Ethan. I'm not trying to be anything. I'm no good at this, and I'm the one who's sorry, because you deserve better than me for this."

God, it hurt all the worse, to hear the clumsy confession—from Randy, from *Randy* the poker player, the casual, don't-you-love-hedonism Randy—and to have to admit that in less than twenty-four hours Randy had given Ethan more real tenderness than Nick Snow ever had.

He figured he owed Randy at least the full story.

"He took the money," he whispered into Randy's neck.

"I know, baby."

"No." Ethan swallowed and gathered himself, because this was becoming important to say out loud. "He took the money from the account. Money we'd saved together. For later. For—" But he couldn't do it. He couldn't finish.

Randy finished for him. "For when he would leave his wife someday, and you would be together always, finally, like he'd promised." He hugged Ethan closer a little awkwardly. "Oh, Slick. Oh, baby."

It was a good thing the knife was on the counter, because Ethan wanted to put it into the middle of his own chest. "I'm so stupid. I was so stupid to think—"

"You are not stupid." Randy's hands tightened on Ethan's shoulders. "You are *not stupid*, Slick."

"It's not that he took the money." Ethan babbled now, the pain pouring out of him. "It was that he took the money for *them*, the money for *us* for *them*. And then I feel so awful, because they're kids, and she's his wife, and they're all so beautiful, and I'm—"

The hands on his arms became painful. "*Don't.* Don't you fucking finish that, not even in your head. You're beautiful too, Slick. *You.* Fine, they're cute kids, and she's a nice wife. He's the fuckwad who's gay and thought he could have it both ways."

"It's his religion, he can't—"

"Do *not* defend him. He can so fucking leave his church. Yes, it would be hard. Yes, he'd lose his family. But he'd fucking get to be himself for the first fucking time. He probably was his real self with you, or close, but he was using you, Slick. It wasn't about you. It was about him. That's why he took the money. And that's why it hurts."

Ethan felt so heavy. He thought he must be having a

heart attack, because his chest was so tight, so full of pain he kept thinking any second he would die, but it kept going on and on and on. "It hurts so much."

"I know, baby." Randy rocked Ethan gently from side to side. "I know. And I'm sorry. I'm so sorry."

For several minutes they sat there on the floor, Ethan wrapped in Randy's arms, emotionally bleeding out. Then they rose, Randy not quite carrying Ethan but lifting him and doing most of the work, and then they moved through the house to Randy's bedroom, which Ethan noted absently had only sort of been cleaned.

Randy shut the door, reached for a remote on the top of a bookshelf, and took Ethan into his arms as soft music filled the room.

"You have to cook dinner," Ethan protested, but weakly, because Randy's mouth was moving along his jaw toward his ear.

Randy pushed Ethan onto the bed. "I have to make love to you first."

What Ethan remembered most about it later, especially as he stood waiting for Crabtree tricked out in his pleated trousers and pinpoint ironed shirt and lint-free jacket, smelling like Randy's soap and aftershave—what he remembered was how much time Randy had taken with him, how thoroughly and leisurely he had kissed him, had licked him, had loved him. He remembered the maddening patience with which Randy had removed every last piece of their clothing. He remembered the smell of vegetables every time Randy's fingers had come near his face, which had been often, because though he explored every crevasse and plane of Ethan's body, he kept returning to Ethan's face, taking it tenderly in his hands before kissing him again.

Ethan remembered the way Randy had kissed him while he worked lube-slicked fingers inside, opening Ethan with an insistent but careful touch that made his insides yield along with his muscles. When Randy finally entered him, Ethan wrapped his arms around him as he opened himself, taking Randy in above as well as below, and in the middle as well, letting cock and tongue and heart pierce him. Randy lifted one of Ethan's legs and pressed it between them. Randy stretched Ethan to his erotic limits as he thrust inside, rough but loving—more loving than Ethan would have asked of him, more loving, probably, than he should receive from a lover of a single day.

This can't last. It's too fast, too improbable and, above all, too strange. But he was lonely and empty and greedy for what Randy offered him, so he hadn't resisted at all, just took him, every part of him, body and heart and soul.

Randy had stayed with him awhile after, but Ethan had told him to go. He took a long, hot shower and got dressed. He stayed in the sanctuary of Randy's room, sitting on the floor by the door with his back to the wall, staring straight ahead and breathing.

Now it was seven, and Crabtree had arrived.

He wasn't Randy's type at all. Not that Ethan was really in a position to judge, but still—this man wasn't for Randy. Big, too big—fat, frankly, and normally

Ethan wouldn't care, but it was something to judge the man on, and he took it. Because there wasn't anything else, except maybe Crabtree was too old. He looked kind, though, and handsome. Randy had been ready to see a ridiculous creature dressed in a striped suit, but no, Crabtree wore expensive but conservative clothes—gray pants and jacket with a lemon-yellow shirt, and a pink-and-blue scarf which should have been ridiculous but actually was natty. He did look like Santa Claus, not in a silly way but just in a way, and it suited him.

Ethan also caught the occasional glint of his many gold-capped teeth, and he remembered what Randy had hinted about how they'd gotten there.

Crabtree's jacket should have made him sweaty in the desert heat, but Randy had turned down the air to near arctic temperatures, and they were all quite comfortable. All except for Mitch, who had come back from the bar still agitated but calmer overall, and who now sat beside his husband, Sam, beautiful in a simple suit with a blue shirt beneath his jacket. Mitch looked like an overstuffed piece of pasta inside his tan blazer, but he was quiet, and he behaved.

Randy wore a suit as well, dark gray with a crisp white shirt, no tie, unbuttoned at the collar. He'd shaved and smoothed his hair. He looked as good as the dinner he had prepared, which he served with elegance and panache, laying down beautifully arranged salads—the asparagus spears had been blanched, and he arranged them in five points coming out of the lettuce. He did all this without so much as missing a beat in the conversation, which was almost entirely between himself and Crabtree. It ranged from business at Herod's to the elections coming up in city government to whether or not it was wise for the casinos to keep putting such deep discounts on their hotel rooms.

Ethan sipped at his wine and listened. But he noticed whenever Crabtree began to engage Ethan, prying at the edges of his past, Randy swooped in and yanked the conversation away deftly, with an edge that made him think Randy was telling his former lover to back the fuck off.

Then they reached dessert.

"What is this?" Crabtree picked up one of the ladyfingers and glared at it. "*Store-bought* cakes, just in berries?"

Randy, who had leaned over Sam to reach the next martini glass of desert, glared at his guest. "Look, you invite yourself over on short notice, you don't get the full monty." He slammed the glass in front of Mitch before placing another in front of Sam.

"Yes, but—" Crabtree snorted and scooped up some of the fluffy white from the side. "Whipped cream *from a can*?"

Randy rested his hands on Ethan's shoulders. "Yes. I gave my good stuff to somebody else this time."

For a second Ethan thought he had to have heard wrong, and then he heard a choke-snort of laughter and saw Sam, eyes watering and dancing, coughing into his napkin to hide his smile. Mitch didn't bother, just grinned what could only be called a shit-eating grin, and for the first time Ethan realized the expression came from watching someone else eat the shit.

Randy's hand slid off Ethan's shoulder, and he went to pour the rest of the coffee. Ethan dared, through what courage he couldn't say, to glance at the gangster at the other end of the table.

Crabtree stared back at him, his gaze ten times sharper and more dangerous than any scrutiny Ethan had ever borne under Randy. Ethan waited. For one brief second he thought he saw Crabtree's smile. Then it vanished.

"Hmpf." Crabtree bent his head and focused on his dessert.

Ethan reached for one of the ladyfingers himself, murmuring thanks as Randy set a cup of coffee before him and sat down again.

CHAPTER EIGHT

After dessert Randy cleared the table, and Mitch helped him. Ethan tried to help too, but Randy pushed him right back into his chair. He reappeared with a G&T for Ethan, a beer for Sam, and a scotch neat for Crabtree.

Crabtree took his drink with a nod of acknowledgment and regarded Ethan. Ethan tried to meet the stare, but he was suddenly possessed by an image of this man tying Randy up, and he had to look away.

With a quiet chuckle, Crabtree turned to Sam. "So, Mr. Keller. I hear you've graduated. Congratulations."

Mitch glared at him as he picked up a plate from the table. "Keller-Tedsoe."

"Ah, yes." Crabtree threaded his fingers over his stomach. "Graduated and married. Where are you working, son?"

"Valley Hospital." Sam sipped his beer. "I'm going to be working in pediatric oncology."

Crabtree nodded, showing thoughtful interest. "When do you start?"

"In a week and a half."

Crabtree's eyes flickered to Mitch. "And the other

Keller-Tedsoe—I understand you'll be traveling to Kentucky soon?"

There was no mistaking the cloud that came over Sam's face or the chill in Mitch's reply. "Taking a special-order piece of machinery from L.A. to Bowling Green. Should lead to some good, steady contracts in both places later."

"I see, I see. Will it be an oversized haul?"

Mitch passed a platter to Randy as he shook his head, but Ethan thought he looked slightly wary. "No, it's regulation. I'll have to take a particular route because of the weight, though."

Crabtree nodded, a glint in his eye. "What will you be bringing west?"

Now there was no mistaking the apprehension in Mitch. "I'll get a contract, probably from the company there."

"Good, good."

Randy picked up the last of the dishes. "Sam, would you take Ethan and go get the table?"

It was an odd question given they were currently sitting at one, but Sam only nodded and rose, excusing himself quietly to Crabtree, who raised his glass and continued to lounge in place, untroubled. Ethan didn't excuse himself, but he found he couldn't help but nod to the older man as he passed. It was hard not to like him, and even if he hadn't gotten the earful about his awkward position from Randy, it would have been difficult not to show respect. Though the idea he'd been Randy's lover got in his way no matter how he tried to dislodge it.

Once he was in Sam and Mitch's bedroom peering inside the closet, Ethan laughed. Of course. They were fetching the poker table.

It was essentially a regular card table, except it was an octagon, had a padded rail, and was covered in green felt. A large piece of cardboard cut from the box of a large appliance was propped carefully against the front, clearly to keep the felt from being dinged accidentally from other items in the closet—a real statement, as the front was also placed facing the wall. Ethan followed Sam's lead and bore the table out carefully into the living room, where Mitch and Randy had already moved aside the coffee table and couch and set the chairs from the dining table around the perimeter.

Mitch saw to the assembly without being asked, and while he did this, Randy brought out three collapsible trays and set them up strategically between the chairs. Crabtree remained off to the side, watching. Once everything was in place, he took a seat, and with only glances and nods for indicators, placed the rest of them. Sam on his right, Randy his left, Ethan to Randy's left, and Mitch to Sam's right. When Randy handed him a sealed deck, Crabtree inspected it, nodded in approval, and cracked it open.

"Mr. Keller." Crabtree winked at Mitch as he corrected himself. "Excuse me. Mr. Keller-Tedsoe. Have I ever told you the Parable of the Cards?"

Mitch gave a quiet grunt, and Randy smiled enigmatically.

Sam shook his head. "No, you haven't, though you did tell me I should never play poker with anyone but you and Randy." His hand slid over to his husband's leg. "Well, and Mitch."

"That's because you're practically a book of tells," Randy murmured, but Crabtree waved a hand to silence him. As he shuffled the deck with a casual and expert hand, he spoke, and Ethan knew immediately where Randy's lectures came from.

"We divide the deck into numbered and face cards, and so we divide the types of men. The numbered cards are the underlings, the parasites of the world. When you play a man who is a numbered card, he looks out only for himself with no consciousness that others are in the game with him. If you wish to be kind, you can say these men are the subordinates of the world, but they are parasites all the same. They attach themselves to someone greater, learning if they are young or inexperienced enough, leeching if they are strong or experienced enough to know better but would rather remain weak. They don't contribute to the world. They only take from it, and if a man remains in this state, he is no better than a sheep. Numbered men are as disposable and interchangeable as the animals they mimic."

Crabtree bridged the cards, shuffled them together then continued to pass them over one another between his hands as he went on with his lecture.

"The face cards are men who have seen the way the world works, who know the only way to survive is to kill or be killed. These men are the cannibals. They drive and lead the parasites, bluffing them into traps and bleeding them when necessary for their own survival or for that of the parasites they have chosen to protect. Depending on what level of face card they are, they bleed them to serve those they owe allegiance to. This is the way of the world. You may find it harsh or overly simplified. But in the end you will find these are your choices. You may be a face card, or you may be a number. The power to choose is yours."

Ethan said nothing, only watched Sam, who considered this with distaste. "Well, I guess I'm a parasite then."

Predictably, Mitch did not like this. "Ignore him, Sunshine."

Sam tapped his index finger on the table. "No, it's okay. I mean, how can I be anything else right now? I'm just out of school, just married, and starting my first job. And I'm the youngest." He looked thoughtfully at Ethan. "I don't know how old you are, but I know you're older than me. I'm always the youngest now that I'm with Mitch. And I am dependent on other people. But I don't want to stay there. I hadn't thought about it like that, but—" His lips flattened into a determined line. "No. I don't want to stay there."

"You're fine, Sunshine." Mitch ran a hand down his husband's back and glared at Crabtree. "You're fine the way you are."

Crabtree grunted. "But neither does he need to remain forever where he is."

Mitch glowered and took another drink. Randy said

nothing, his finger tracing idly around the edge of his whiskey sour.

Ethan studied him, a thought nagging at the back of his mind. "What about aces? Are they a number card or a face card?"

Crabtree seemed pleased. "Aces are unique because they can be both a face card and a numbered card. But no matter what they are, they will always be the lowest of the low or the highest of the high—and because of this, they will always be alone. An ace does not evolve, but rather he constantly explores his dual nature. When he leads, he is acutely aware of his underlings, unable to use them with the casualness that his fellow face cards will do. When he is brought low, he is equally aware of the thin veil separating him from where he is supposed to be, and he can't forget how he and his fellows in servitude should be treated. An ace is seldom at home unless he is with his own kind, and many fall into despair and find themselves wedged quite firmly in the low side of their nature. There are few aces in the world, and so most aces, no matter who they are with, feel alone."

Mitch coughed and shifted in his chair, looking unhappy.

Crabtree resumed his shuffling. "And that, my children, is the Parable of the Cards. Take it to heart, because the secret to life lies within it." He turned to Randy. "What's the game? Draw? Seven?"

Randy took a sip of his drink. "Hold 'Em. Slick needs the practice, and Seven-Card Stud is too difficult for Peaches."

Crabtree began to deal. "Would you get the chips please, Randy?"

Randy reached behind him to the drawer of an end table. "Money to the mobster, please. What's the buy-in, Crabtree?"

"Is one hundred too rich?"

Mitch plunked down a wad of twenties in front of Crabtree. "Limits?"

Randy paused with the tray of chips in his lap. "Three/six dollar open, no limit?"

Crabtree nodded. Sam seemed panicked, and Ethan empathized.

Mitch leaned toward Ethan. "It's Crabtree's home-game version of limit poker. You bet three dollars on the flop. You raise in three-dollar increments. After the turn, it's six dollars and six-dollar increments. Blind raises would be one dollar for the small and two dollars for the big."

Sam still panicked. "I'm going to screw it up. I always do."

"We'll help you, Sunshine." Mitch accepted a large stack of chips from Randy. Ethan noticed he didn't divide them evenly, favoring his husband with a significantly larger portion.

Randy tossed some bills at Crabtree then glanced at Ethan. "Slick, you spend all the money you won off me already?"

Ethan fought a blush. "Sorry—I didn't realize. My wallet is in your bedroom." He started to rise.

Randy waved him into his seat, a ghost of a smile playing on his lips. He peeled another hundred-dollar bill off his stack and tossed it at Crabtree. "I'll cover you." He handed Ethan a stack, and another to Crabtree, and finally a set to himself before flexing his fingers. "Are we ready to play, gentlemen?"

Ethan accepted his cards, prepared his blind bet and settled in for what he assumed would be a rather instructive ride. He wasn't disappointed.

He'd drawn queen-10 offsuit, and after Mitch and Sam both folded, Crabtree called and Randy raised. Ethan met the raise, deciding he'd at least stay through to see the flop. Crabtree met as well, then laid the flop—jack of clubs, king of hearts, 8 of spades.

Randy tapped his finger on the rail for a few seconds before tossing three chips into the pot. "Call."

Ethan glanced at Crabtree, who watched him intently in return. It unnerved Ethan, and he suspected he was playing into a trap, but he kept his eyes on the gangster's, glancing down only enough to count the chips. He took six.

He tossed the chips in. "Raise."

Crabtree watched him awhile longer, then picked up nine chips. "Re-raise."

Randy stared blankly into the pot, tapped his fingers again, then nodded as he tossed in his chips. "Call."

Ethan picked up nine. "Call."

Crabtree laid the turn—another jack, this time of spades.

Randy called.

Ethan called.

Crabtree raised.

This time Randy studied the gangster, searching his blank face for almost a full minute. Then he tossed his hand into the muck. "Fold."

Crabtree waited.

Ethan called, thinking he was probably a fool, but he couldn't quite bring himself to let go. He almost had a straight, and he had two ways to make it.

Crabtree laid the river. It was an ace of hearts.

Ethan had to fight not to smile. He kept his eyes on the pot as he tossed in his chips. "Raise."

Crabtree tossed in a short stack. "Re-raise."

Ethan frowned and studied the board. What could Crabtree have? Not a flush. Two pair, which Ethan would beat, or possibly four of a kind. That was it, unless he had the same spread as Ethan. Or if he had 9-10. But would he have bet aggressively if this were the case? And even then, Ethan's straight was higher. Could Crabtree be holding two jacks? Or a jack and something else, to make a full house? Possibly.

Ethan studied Crabtree, whose face still revealed absolutely nothing. He might as well have been made of stone.

No, Ethan decided. Crabtree was bluffing. He had to be.

Maybe.

What type of man is this one? Ethan looked at Crabtree.

Cannibal.

He picked up his chips. "Re-raise."

Randy hid his mouth with his hand as he stared down at the rail, but his eyes danced. Mitch sat drinking his beer, and Sam watched, wide-eyed and attentive.

Crabtree raised Ethan again.

They went through three more rounds, each raising the other, and both were rapidly running out of chips. Neither backed down.

Randy sat up, leaned forward, and looked pointedly at Crabtree. "Be nice to my guest."

Crabtree sighed. "Call." He lay down his cards.

They were a jack of hearts—and a *joker*.

Ethan stared at the cards. "What—?" He turned to Randy, mouth opening and closing for several tries as he searched for the power of speech. "What the *fuck*?"

Randy reached for his wallet as Crabtree scooped up the chips. "Jokers are wild when you play with Crabtree."

"That would have been nice to have been told." Ethan stared at the board. *A fucking joker.*

"Would it have changed how you played?" Crabtree asked, sounding almost bored, but Ethan knew better.

"Yes." The word snapped out of his mouth, but he didn't care how many men this man had killed. That hadn't been fair.

Crabtree looked interested now. "I could just have easily had the other jack, or another king, or another eight."

"No, you couldn't have. There are two jokers in the deck, which meant instead of having to have one card, you only had to have one of three. You didn't have to have a jack *and* a king or a jack *and* an 8. You had the card which would finish almost anything for you. The turn didn't matter, and neither did the river. You could use the joker to finish anything. It changed everything. So, yes. It mattered I didn't know the card was in the fucking deck."

Crabtree turned to Randy, pleased. "Well, well, my boy. He *is* an ace, and better still, he's not stuck on the bottom of the deck."

Randy peeled off another hundred and tossed it at Crabtree before reaching for the canister of chips. "Yes. So will you please be nicer to him?"

Sam leaned forward, his eyes running around the table. "Okay, I know Crabtree is a cannibal, and so is Mitch. And apparently Ethan is an ace." He smiled shyly at Ethan, then turned, curious, to Randy. "But what are you?"

Randy rolled his eyes, reached for one of the cards in front of Crabtree, and tossed it at Sam.

Crabtree looked proudly at him. "Randy is wild. He's the joker—he's every card at once, but unlike the ace, he doesn't feel the structure of the deck. In fact, he defies it, which is why he isn't allowed in formal games—or if he is, he must be clever how he hides."

"Cool." Sam grinned.

But Ethan only studied his lover, and it wasn't until Randy dealt that Ethan was able to fully form the thought brewing in the back of his mind.

Jokers might be wild, but Ethan bet they were even lonelier than the aces.

SLICK LOOKED SO fucking good in his suit it was almost criminal, and watching him move around in it drove Randy crazy.

He also looked good when he was pissed off, and Crabtree had seen to it Ethan remained in a constant state of frustration the entire evening. He gunned for Slick, making sure he always lost or only won small pots, and only then just enough to keep him in the game. Sam, as always, despite the significant lead Mitch had given him, ran out of chips first, and Mitch, who had only been marginally interested in the game anyway, quickly spent himself out. They watched for a few hands, and then Mitch excused himself and Sam so they could retire to their bedroom. But Crabtree held up a hand as they rose, reached into his jacket pocket and pulled out a card, which he passed to Mitch.

"Dr. Laura Halstrom. You won't find better in the city, and you'll only find a few superior elsewhere. I suggest you both go for the first visit because you'll feel easier about leaving, Mitch, if you meet her."

Mitch's voice was gruff when he spoke. "Thank you."

"Be sure to look me up before you leave for Los Angeles. It turns out I have some business for you myself in Kentucky."

Mitch winced but said nothing, only nodded. He glared at Randy, though, before putting a hand on Sam's back and leading him down the hall toward the bedrooms.

Then the game really got interesting.

Randy tried to protect Slick, but it was hard enough to keep his own head above water with Crabtree, and at best he could sometimes deflect some of the attacks. He knew what Crabtree was doing, and he knew why, but he didn't like it. He'd only known Ethan a day, but he'd played poker with him for a good chunk of that time, and he knew when Slick was starting to wear down. He was pretty much a frayed nerve by this point. Randy wanted to end the game, and soon, because he wanted to have some intense sex with the man, and it'd be a lot less fun with Ethan smarting from Crabtree wiping the floor with him.

Ethan tried to adapt his strategy, and he did well, all things considered. For someone playing just one day, he was a fucking savant. But with Crabtree, even this wasn't enough. You couldn't miss a beat when you played him, and he always made sure he stayed several steps ahead of you. Most pros wouldn't play with him because he was so erratic, and he was in full form tonight. Randy had to find a way to end this, but it wouldn't be easy.

The only real weakness Crabtree had at cards was he was no good at what Randy was best at—manipulating the game from the belly. Crabtree couldn't because he'd never throw a game, and it was the easiest way to manipulate one. It didn't bother Randy at all. If he wanted money, he could find some live ones and clean up. In this town you couldn't walk into a poker room without tripping over four of those games. But manipulating a game was fun, and for him the fun was usually payment enough. Winning or losing money was a highly negotiable detail.

What Randy wanted right now was to have Slick to himself. He wanted to make sure he was okay. He wanted to fuck him. He wanted to ask him what he thought of Crabtree. He wanted to find out what the tic in his jaw was about—what was he so pissed about when he did that? Was he right, and it was jealousy? Or was it something else? Was he hoping too hard it was jealousy? Whatever it was, he wouldn't know until the game was over.

So he ended it.

Randy stopped trying to save Slick and began to amass chips slowly, putting himself first even with Crabtree then moving himself slightly ahead. He went out as far as he dared to go without forcing Crabtree to try to bring him back in line to save face. Then he bided his time, never putting himself at risk, waiting for the right hand.

Then it came. Oh, sweet Jesus, did it come.

He lured them both in, and he was fucking proud of himself, because he played his tells so Ethan folded but Crabtree stayed in, and then he kept building up more and more, until Crabtree had put half his stack in.

"Really think you have something, Jansen?" Crabtree asked.

Randy kept his eyes on the pot. "You calling or raising, Crabtree?"

Crabtree stared at him awhile, but Randy didn't budge. Finally Crabtree grunted and tossed in a raise.

Randy hadn't believed he could actually do this on one hand, but he'd underestimated himself. Crabtree thought Randy had overplayed, and it was too pleasing to think of nearly cleaning him out, then eliminating him on the next hand so he could focus on Ethan. It had to be this, because it was the only reason Randy could think of for Crabtree to put himself all-in, especially with such a smug grin. "Call."

They were already at the river, so Randy laid down his cards—both jokers.

"Four of a kind or full house. However you'd care to read it."

Crabtree laid down his 9 and 2, with all the hearts on the board making his hand a high pair with an ace kicker. He gave Randy a glare, but Randy didn't let it get to him. It was Crabtree's own fault for telling him he was a joker who had found an ace.

Mine, he said with his return stare, then let his eyes slide to Ethan before he reached for the pot, just so Crabtree understood what he was claiming.

Crabtree rose, reaching for his jacket on the chair behind him. "Thank you for the dinner, Jansen, and the unexceptional dessert. I will not thank you, however, for that play."

"Good night, Crabtree." Randy made sure his reply was laconic, but his heart beat faster. *Yes, leave, so I can be with Ethan.*

Crabtree turned to Ethan. "I want to see you in my office tomorrow at noon."

Randy's head whipped around, and for the first time

in his life he didn't care what Crabtree had or hadn't done, he wasn't going to stand for this, not with Ethan—and then he got a good look at Crabtree's face, and he relaxed.

Crabtree smiled briefly in reassurance. "I have need of some advice on investments. I understand you're the man to ask about such things."

Ethan, bless him, didn't so much as glance at Randy, just stared boldly at the gangster. "I'm a fair hand, but I'm not the best."

"If our meeting goes as well as I suspect it will, I may have more work for you. And of course, I'll give you some proper instruction in poker." He nodded again at Randy and reached for his hat. "Have a good evening, gentlemen."

Randy rose, and Ethan followed suit. They took turns shaking Crabtree's hand, and they walked him to the door together. They watched at the window as Crabtree went to the shining black car which had waited all evening for him at the curb. The gangster climbed inside, and the car crawled off into the night.

Randy ran a hand down Ethan's shoulder, skimming the silky fabric of his coat and catching the cool tips of his long fingers before leading him back to the table.

Ethan balked. "No. I can't take anymore."

Randy captured his hand more firmly. "I know. That's why I'm making you keep playing. You're too good to let the old bastard ruin you. Now sit down and listen."

Ethan did, reluctantly. Randy poured him another drink, hesitated over his own, then put away the alcohol and made himself a plain Pepsi. Then he sat down and began to teach his lover the next level of poker.

"You can take or leave Crabtree's Parable of Cards, but here's something to keep hold of regardless—there's a lot to be learned from a man who will confess to you his own philosophy of life. Crabtree works to make sure everyone knows he's a king, which is the biggest flag you get that he's actually at best a jack. He tells his story, then beats your pants off, and you think, 'Shit, I'll never beat this guy.'"

Ethan grunted and drank deeply.

Randy rubbed his arm affectionately. "Mitch hates playing with him. Mitch hates him, period, but I think it's more because he sees too much of himself in the man, too much of what he could become if he crossed mental lines in his head. And to be honest, it's a valid worry. Mitch and Crabtree are both dominant men up against one hurricane of a handicap: no matter how masculine they are, the world around them— particularly the one they grew up in—has declared because of who they want to sleep with they can never be full men, can never be kings."

Ethan's gaze softened, but he still stared into his glass. "I've felt this too."

"I think Sam's generation may see things differently, maybe. Hopefully. But it's over for Mitch, and it's especially over for Crabtree. Even if the whole world changes around them, in their own minds, they'll never be able to fully be kings. Mitch deals with this by making his own rules, but until Sam came along, the cost was he was lonely. He doesn't like Crabtree calling his husband a parasite, because to Mitch, Sam isn't even in the deck of cards. He's a brilliant, perfect sun. I'm pretty sure he'd kill for him."

Ethan now had his drink cradled against his chest as he lounged in his chair. "So—what, I'm supposed to feel better because Crabtree has a bad self-image?"

"No. You're supposed to quit feeling wounded and start unpacking his strategy." Randy nodded to where the gangster had been sitting. "Crabtree plays erratically. It's his only way to assure dominance. He also only plays with people he can beat—another sign of a jack. He likes to manipulate and control—but he actually wants to help, not punish. Which is why he told you to come see him tomorrow. He wants to take you under his wing."

Ethan tensed. "I don't want—"

"Hear me out. I know he grates sometimes, but stop being wounded for a minute and think this through. You already know you're a better person than he is. You're smarter, but you think your weakness is you aren't as manipulative. Well, watch and learn from him, Slick. A manipulation skill set will take you far in life." He gathered the cards and discarded the jokers before shuffling. "He's right about you being an ace. You can be ruthless when you want to be, but you also see too much. I don't know all about your past, how you viewed yourself before Nick did a number on you, but I can guess. At any rate, I know where you're at right now, and it's not on the top. So go learn from him. In the meantime, sit here for a few minutes and make some of your money back."

He dealt a hand.

"Here's the lesson the pros will teach you, what Crabtree won't—if you want to make money, play tight. Don't bluff. Fold liberally. Play hands you have nuts on or ones you're reasonably sure you can win. Play like you're playing video poker. Bet small, bet quietly, and play to win. It takes patience, which is why Crabtree can't do it. But an investment broker ought to do all right playing tight. Seems to me that's all you do. Use whatever mental mindset you use to invest other people's money to play your own. Crabtree got you because he played you. You were trying to show him you were as big a dog as he was. You were drawing dead no matter what hand you drew."

Ethan ran a hand through his hair. He slouched, but it was a move he still managed to make elegant. "I don't have a whole lot right now. I wanted some pride in front of the guy you let tie you up."

Randy bit back his grin. So he *was* jealous. "You get pride from yourself, Ethan. I know it sounds like an after-school special, but it's true. Smartest, kindest, proudest man I ever knew told me that, and nothing I've ever seen in life has proven him wrong."

Ethan looked up sharply. "Who was that?"

Randy could read the tight, *Another goddamn lover?* query in his eyes.

Oh, Slick, I could love you.

Randy had to stare down at the table for a moment, he was so shaken.

"My uncle." Randy made a show of looking at his cards, even though he already had. "Call, raise, or fold?"

Ethan lifted the corners of his own cards and pushed them forward. "Fold." Then he paused. "Wait, shouldn't I have to ante?"

Randy waved a hand. "Yes, but not now. This is instruction, not play. You're under me for two hundred already—let's not make it any worse, shall we?"

Ethan picked up the cards to shuffle them. "I'm going to have to wash a lot of your dishes to pay you back."

"If you're working off money from me, it's not going to be by washing dishes, Slick."

They put in an hour at it, and Ethan decimated another tall G&T as well. Randy explained which hands were better statistically, and he taught him which spreads were most ideal. Slick was all about odds, he quickly learned, and he made a mental note to dig out his David Sklansky books for him, because he had a feeling Ethan and the math-minded poker genius were a natural match. Ethan was also going to have to work on his bluffs, but Crabtree would be the best man for him in that regard.

"There's sort of an unspoken code in poker," he told Ethan after they put down the last hand and started counting out their winnings. "There are rules the professionals expect you to play by, and when you break them, they get upset. Poker is people. Remember that. Cards are just props. When you learn poker from Crabtree, it's going to be how to play dirty. Really dirty. Not how to cheat. But he will teach you how to cheat on the code. That's why people won't play with him, because he makes it too hard to figure him out."

"But *you* figured him out."

Randy shrugged. "He would never have let me beat him if he hadn't been so focused on you. You weren't the only one in the pissing contest, Slick."

"But you ended it. By playing a pair of jokers."

Randy smiled. "Yeah, that was pretty sweet. It's those moments I could almost believe in Lady Luck after all." He rose and picked up a handful of twenties. He tossed two to Ethan.

"You mean fate?" Ethan glanced down at the twenties. "I can't. I already owe you."

"Fate is for pussies. But as a heads up, Crabtree believes in it. He'd bet on black with you, and he's probably going to take you down to the floor to play craps first thing tomorrow." He nodded to the money. "I'll pay you forty, then, to go and take a ride with me right now."

"Ride?" Ethan echoed.

Randy jerked his head toward the garage. "On my bike. I'll take you to see the Las Vegas sign."

Ethan frowned at Randy. "You don't have to pay me to get me to take a ride with you."

God, he looked so good when he was tousled. *How the hell did I end up with a guy who makes H&M look a little bit shabby?* Randy covered the vulnerable moment with a leer. "How about I pay you forty to feel me up while we ride?"

Ethan didn't miss a beat. "You don't have to pay me for that, either."

Oh, sweet Jesus, he should go fuck him right now. But he wanted a ride first. He reached over and took the twenties.

"All right, then. But so you know, you're developing a habit of throwing money away over me." He didn't watch to see how Ethan reacted, just grabbed his belt loop and tugged him toward the door to the garage. "Come on, Slick. You need some wind in your hair."

CHAPTER NINE

RANDY HAD ALWAYS thought there wasn't anything he loved more than driving too fast on his motorcycle down the streets of Las Vegas in the middle of the night. But Slick's long, lean body pressed up against him, his half-aroused cock nestled tight against Randy's ass through thin, expensive trousers, his strong fingers gripping Randy's waist as the bike purred beneath them both? *This* was heaven.

He took Ethan down the 592 over to I-515 before turning down toward Sunset Road, and from there he took them all the way over to Las Vegas Boulevard. They went north until they got to the 5100 block, and from there Randy drove right up underneath the *Welcome To Fabulous Las Vegas* sign. He slowed the bike and pulled over to the curb.

"It's still here?" Ethan's voice had a note of wonder in it that got to Randy, and he took his helmet off and turned around so he could get a better look at him. Through the visor, Ethan's face was lit up, not just by the electric neon of the sign but by his own sense of wonder.

"They've moved it around a lot, and it went dark

completely for a while, but yeah, it's still here. It's on the register of historic places now, I think, so it ought to be here to stay. Well, if not here, then it will stay in some form or another." He drank in Ethan's rapt expression, letting it do crazy things to his insides. "Didn't peg you for one who would go mushy at the Vegas sign, Slick."

Ethan's smile stayed soft and sweet. "Me, either."

If Ethan had taken his helmet off, or if Randy thought he could manipulate his way inside the visor without bungling the moment, he'd have kissed Slick then. But the helmet stayed on, and there was time enough for that later. He reached over and slapped Ethan's thigh instead. "Want to head up the Strip, baby?"

"Sure," Ethan said, still looking up at the sign, and Randy smiled to himself as he turned around, put on his helmet, and aimed the bike toward the street.

"Hold on." Randy allowed himself a moment to enjoy the feel of Ethan's hands closing around his middle again, then took off.

They slowed way down as soon as they hit the Strip, of course. It was just past one a.m. on a Friday night, and the place was still going strong. Randy didn't mind because it gave him the chance to point out bits of trivia to Ethan about the casinos, the Strip throughout history, and Las Vegas in general.

Plus, with the slow speed, Ethan's hands had fallen down to rest more on Randy's thighs than his waist, and sometimes his fingers teased—he was pretty sure deliberately—at Randy's crotch.

"Vegas is what it is now because of Hoover Dam. The workers needed somewhere to spend their money, and Nevada had legal gambling and prostitution. Las Vegas was thirty miles away. Perfect setup. Then the mob came in and put some organization to it all and turned the town into a machine."

"Is that the mob Crabtree is a part of?"

Randy cursed the need for helmets—if safety didn't demand them, Ethan would have whispered it against his ear instead of shouting it at plastic. Of course, if the helmets weren't there, he could be looking at their splattered brains across pavement as he drifted off to the afterlife.

"The mob isn't really here anymore. Crabtree's more of an artifact than anything. The mob was biggest in the fifties and sixties. It carried into the seventies and eighties, and it will always be around, but ever since the regulation laws and the Black Book—the official blacklist of people who can't legally so much as set foot in a casino—mostly the mob is a shadow. In the fifties and early sixties they were caretakers. People say Vegas was the safest damn place you could live back then, so long as you didn't cheat the mob. They kept their house clean, no crimes in town outside of the skim in the casinos. Killing happened out of town. But then Howard Hughes bought them out, and they got old and the Chicago Outfit took over instead, and things changed. Mostly now there are just ghosts. And guys like Crabtree."

"But you said he's killed people."

"Oh yeah." Randy waved a hand to take in the Strip. "You ever watch *Casino*? Or *The Cooler*? He was part of the old school of taking care of people who cheated the casinos. There's still some of that around."

Ethan's body shifted closer, and Randy felt a clunk as their helmets met awkwardly. Fucking safety.

"Randy?"

There was a husky quality to Ethan's voice Randy loved. "Yeah?"

Ethan's hands slid into the junction of Randy's thighs, into the crease of his pants, then over to find his cock, which was rapidly coming to attention at the thought of Ethan's hands saying hello.

"Randy, I think I'm a little drunk." The hands massaged Randy deliberately. "I want to fuck you. Now. And I don't want Crabtree to fuck you ever again. I *don't* want him to tie you up."

The lights of the Strip pulsed around Randy, as did the noise of the traffic and the crowd. His bike roared as he flexed his hand on the accelerator, and they cooled their heels at the stoplight next to Circus Circus. Randy felt drunk too. Drunk on Slick. He turned his head so Ethan could hear him.

"Then who's going to tie me up, baby?"

The helmet slammed into his again, but it didn't matter. Randy could imagine what it would have felt like to have Ethan's tongue inside his ear.

Ethan tightened his hands on Randy. "Me."

By sheer force of will alone was Randy able to keep from running the bike into the cab in front of him.

Suddenly he hated the traffic. He wanted to leap onto the sidewalk and run the pedestrians down, because the thought of putting off the sensual promise in Ethan's words and hands another minute was too much to bear.

"Hold on." When the light changed, Randy wove through cars, illegal as hell, and when he got onto the 589, he turned right and sped like a bullet toward home.

He put the bike in the garage only because he had to, but once they were off, he tossed his helmet into the corner, grabbed Ethan's, gave it the same treatment, then hauled his lover into his arms.

They made out up against the bike, because it was there and because it was sexy-dangerous. The tailpipe still burned hot, and the whole thing seemed ready to tip over any second. Ethan sent the button to Randy's pants flying off into the darkness, and he practically tore the zipper off its threads as he yanked Randy's waistband down and freed the cock he'd been teasing for the past forty-five minutes. Straddling the bike, Ethan pushed against Randy's shoulders. Randy watched, then gasped as Ethan took hold of his cock, stroked it, then slid his hand up and down the length. When Randy began to shake, Ethan leaned forward, and with his hand still on Randy's dick, kissed the divot above Randy's collarbone. Then he licked it. Then he opened his mouth, sucked the skin, and nipped, hard enough to make Randy cry out.

"I want to fuck you, Randy."

Please do, Randy thought. "Here on the bike?"

"In the house." Ethan nipped again and tightened his grip. "In your bed."

"Still going to tie me up?" Randy's body somehow seemed to have lost most of its bones. He already knew all his blood was in his crotch.

Ethan's laugh was wicked. "Oh yes."

They stumbled into the house, through the door, down the hall and into the room—Randy threw the door closed, but it banged back open, and Ethan didn't seem to give a damn about it. *Well, Sam and Mitch can just have a taste of their own.* He cried out as Ethan's mouth closed against his neck.

Slick was a biter. Who would have thought?

Ethan bit, licked, and sucked his way across Randy's shoulders, arms, chest, and thighs. Randy hoped this was something special, this Ethan Slick gave him. Maybe this was all the pain and emptiness that had been scaring the shit out of Randy all day turned on its head, pouring out in a ruthless game of poker, a ride down the Strip, and enough gin to float an oil tanker.

He hoped, at the very least, idiot Nick Snow had never had a taste of this Ethan, because he didn't fucking deserve him.

"Where?" Ethan slid up Randy's belly. "Where—? I want—" His hands closed over Randy's wrist, pinning it down.

"Box. Floor. Behind you." Randy's mind ran a swift inventory of the box's contents, and his cock hummed in anticipation. He fell onto the sheets, clutching at them. "Use whatever you want."

Ethan moved away, and Randy lay still, quiet, waiting. He worried maybe Ethan would see what was in there and freak out, but he pushed the thought aside. No. That wasn't going to happen, not tonight.

Now who's betting on black?

Randy wasn't betting on black. He bet on Slick. That was different. His hands, now sweaty, tightened on the sheets. He *hoped* it was different.

The pause went on a little too long, and Randy got nervous. Then Ethan loomed over him, his eyes wild, but with lust, not disgust. He held up a pair of shackles and a harness in his hand. "Show me how to use these on you."

Randy did.

There was some awkwardness but not much, and Ethan's enthusiasm for binding and probing Randy more than made up for it. Whispering, nudging, encouraging, they moved through the dark, Randy explaining in exquisite, erotic detail how Ethan could best spread him open, pin him down. Ethan did. It didn't take long for him to have Randy kneeling over a bench, his ankles held wide apart by a metal spreader, his hands cuffed almost painfully behind his back and attached to the chest harness. Knees braced against the cushions and his forehead pressed to the bench, Randy trembled, open and waiting as Ethan decided what he wanted to do next.

Randy knew what *he* wanted—for Ethan to pick up the paddle he'd ignored, and he wanted Slick to slap him with it. But even though he absolutely wanted it,

Randy was fine with skipping that for now. He'd only ever let Crabtree paddle him before. Well, and the one time with Sam, but it was different. It had been for Sam. This—this would be for him. This would be about letting go, about being safe with Ethan.

It was a bunch of shit, is what, because he was *not* safe with Ethan, not yet, not after one day. He was an idiot for doing this much. This was too much, too fast, for both of them.

But sweet Jesus, Randy wanted Slick. He loved kneeling here, nervous and twitching, knowing Ethan was behind him, still mostly dressed, hesitant and powerful all at once. Ethan whom twice now he'd made sweet love to, the kind he never did, not even with Sam, and now here he was with Ethan.

Oh God, he wanted this to turn loose. He wanted Ethan to slap him. Spank him. Whip him with the lash—stupid, stupid that one, because Slick didn't know how, and how fucked up was the sub teaching the Dom how to hold a whip?

But they were both switches, really, and *fucking hell* Randy wanted it, wanted it—

Thought stopped as Ethan's cool hands closed around his cheeks. Then he moaned as, with no preamble, Ethan's tongue pushed inside him.

What Randy liked about the spreader, about being restrained, about having to hold himself still while someone else took pleasure from his body, was how outside of his head and even his body the sex became. He was aroused, physically—his cock was rock hard, and he was gasping and sweating—but more restrained than his body was his mind, hyped on the experience of having Ethan—*Ethan, my God, Slick, baby*—behind him, his hands on him. Ethan, who ran so hot and cold, so reserved, who right now was so incredibly *not* reserved. Here was Ethan tongue-fucking him. Here was Ethan who had broken down two, almost three times on him now, come close several others—Ethan demanding to know how to tie Randy down so he could dominate him. Randy submitted to him, because…

Because he was Ethan.

Randy would have yielded for Ethan, would have held himself open for him, would have guided Ethan inside, but Ethan had taken that away, so Randy enjoyed being taken, especially when Ethan switched to lube-slicked fingers, thrusting as he ran his mouth over Randy's back, his butt, his thighs, biting again, nipping as he fucked him. Randy rode it, accepted it all, hoping he at least had one souvenir hickey in the morning.

Except he'd have a souvenir Slick too.

Ethan had already loosened him, but Randy relaxed further as Ethan donned a condom and began to push inside him. *Yes.* This, he wanted this—he wanted this, hard and fast, with Ethan slapping his ass, but he'd take it however it came.

All of a sudden Ethan was gone, and Randy opened his eyes, blinking as the shackles of the spreader fell away from his ankles, and then Ethan's shaking fingers fumbled at the restraints at his back.

He tried to turn his head. "Slick?"

"I want—" The wicked, possessed Slick was fading, caught in some internal storm.

"You want me on the bed, baby?" Randy kept his tone seductive, not brash. "You want to push me onto the bed and fuck me?"

The hands stilled, then clutched at Randy. "Yes. I can't—it's—I want it, but it's too—"

"Too much too fast. It's okay. I'm not going anywhere, baby. We got time. You need help undoing those straps?"

Ethan laughed, an almost mournful sound. "I'm sorry, Randy, I'm sorry—"

"Slick, honey, I hate to burst your bubble, but I've been in worse fixes than this." He kept his voice easy, reassuring as he coached Ethan through undoing the restraints, and then, because he could tell Ethan needed to put the whole box behind him, the harness too. He rose from the bench, took a second to work the kinks out of his knees—such a bitch, getting old—and led Ethan toward the bed.

Sure, people turn their noses up at somebody topping from the bottom, but that was what Randy did, lifting their hands together over his head, then turning his wrists, guiding Ethan to take control, which he did. He nudged Ethan into pinning him to the bed, pressing their bodies together, pushing Randy down. Then he stalled, so Randy lifted one leg and slid it up alongside Ethan, threading it through their arms and up, and by then Ethan had picked up on it and moved Randy's other leg up on his own. Ethan looked flustered and still slightly lost. But he was stiff, pressing up against Randy's thigh, and it was enough.

Ethan rested his forehead against Randy's calf. "I'm so fucked up."

"I like you fucked up." Randy turned his captive hands and stroked Ethan's fingers, then laced their fingers together. "I like *you*, Slick. You're weird. But you're something else, something I've never seen before. And I live in Vegas, baby. That's quite a statement."

Ethan's face was obscured by the dark, but Randy could still read the tenderness there. "I like you too, Randy."

Randy nudged against him. "Fuck me, Slick."

He did. He pushed inside Randy, bent and kissed him, soft at first, hard as he began to move. Letting go of Randy's hands, Ethan rode him. Randy took it, a rough, twisted little fuck, with so much switching he couldn't keep up.

It worked. And it was good.

It was really fucking good.

ETHAN WOKE ONCE again in Randy's bed. His head hurt four times as much as it had the day before.

He couldn't even roll over because the thought of moving hurt too much, so he pulled the pillow more completely over his head and concentrated on trying to absorb himself into sweet, soft oblivion where he might have a prayer for peace. Certainly none was going to be found inside his skull. Or his stomach. This was twice now in a row he'd had too much to drink, and he was too old for this.

Twice, too, he'd had mind-blowingly intense sex before going to sleep. Three bouts of sex total—in twenty-four hours. He'd thought he was too old for such things, but clearly not.

He opened his eyes and stared at the white nubs of cotton, remembering, or trying to. What his brain was telling him had happened could not be what actually happened. Because he would not have—

Memory flashed, sharp frames of video, and he saw Randy bent over a bench, wearing this black strap thing, his arms—his *legs*—

Ethan's head still killed, but his eyes were wide now, and he was absolutely awake. He could *not* have done that. He didn't doubt Randy would have, and yes, there was a part of him curious, but he never—he *wouldn't*—

He maneuvered himself to the edge of the bed, then over onto the floor, half-climbing, half-falling out as he made his way to the small wooden chest tucked against the wall beside the nightstand. He flicked open the catch and lifted the lid. Blinking to clear the sleep from his eyes, he took in the sight before him. The black strap thing with silver rivets and a ring. Another one which they hadn't used but he vaguely remembered Randy explaining was to help hold a plug in place. Which they hadn't used, because Ethan had wanted full access to Randy's ass. He flushed in memory, remembering feeling rough and raw as he'd said it, wanting to use Randy—*use*, not make love to, not have sex with, *use*—

and he thought he might have said so, and Randy hadn't even blinked, just continued to explain how better to strap him down.

Ethan reached into the chest, touching the dildos, the whips, the long wooden paddle. What the hell was he *thinking*? He hadn't thought. He'd been drunk, stung by Crabtree's beating, caught up in the feel of Randy and the pulse of the bike and the sensual swirl of Las Vegas at night, and like a fool, he imagined he could be as good as the gangster. That he could be what Randy wanted, what he wanted for himself—

A soft knock startled him, and he slammed the chest shut, catching the edge of his finger on the way down. "Shit." His fingers flew into his mouth as the door opened, and Sam stuck his head in.

"Ethan? Are you—?" Sam spied Ethan on the floor. "Oh, you are up."

Embarrassment colored Ethan in a wash, and he looked around for loose clothing to grab, but Randy had cleaned it all up. He tugged a pillow from the bed instead.

Sam's gaze slid over him, and he smiled briefly before putting on a pretty, paltry mask of indifference. "I thought you might be getting up soon to go to Crabtree, and I wondered if you wanted breakfast first. I've got coffee on. Would you like some?"

"Sure. I'll come and get it." He started to rise, felt his head swell and fell down with a groan.

"No, let—" Sam bit his lip. "I mean—let me bring it to you. Do you—I mean, some people need to eat when they're hung over, and then some don't—"

"Food would be a godsend. There should be—Yesterday I asked Randy to get yogurt, and granola?"

"Sure, sure. And I'll bring you some water too, because it will make you feel better than anything."

"I honestly can get myself to the kitchen," Ethan insisted.

"If you'd rather, okay. But I'll get it ready for you." He disappeared and shut the door.

Ethan did manage, but it was rougher than he would have cared to admit. He pulled on a pair of Randy's sweatpants, stopped at the bathroom, avoiding his own reflection, and then staggered into the kitchen where a canister of yogurt, a box of high-quality granola, and a bowl were waiting for him, alongside a spoon and a steaming mug of coffee and a bottle of water. Sam sat on the other side of the table, eating a bowl of Froot Loops.

"Have a seat." His smile tipped a little. "And sorry we keep meeting embarrassingly in the morning. I'm *really* sorry about yesterday."

"Don't worry about it." Ethan waved the concern away and reached for his coffee. He slurped, winced, then set it down.

"Shit, did I make it too strong?" Sam started to rise.

Ethan rubbed his temple. "No, it's my head."

"Drink the water. You need to replenish your fluids."

Ethan saluted weakly and uncapped the water. "Forty-year-old men are not supposed to behave like I've been behaving. I deserve worse than this headache."

"You're *forty*?"

"Yes." He put the bottle down. "Old enough to know better."

"Wow. I mean—it's okay. Just, you don't look it. I mean—" He blushed. "Sorry, but you were seventeen when I was born. It's bad enough Randy was eight and Mitch was twelve, but—" He reached for his coffee. "I'm going to shut up now."

Ethan couldn't help smiling. Yes, there was something about Sam Keller-Tedsoe. "It's fine."

"No, it's not. I'm always putting my foot in things." He stabbed into his cereal with his spoon. "Anyway, I'm supposed to tell you from Randy he's going to try to get off by three, but there's some big engine thing, and he has to stay. Mitch went along with him to the distribution center, but he'll be back in time to take you to Crabtree at noon."

Ethan paused as he reached for his yogurt. He'd forgotten Crabtree. Nodding curtly, he picked up the container, peeled off the top, and began to empty the contents into the bowl. It was a lovely, custard-like vanilla, and it was organic—a bit nicer, he admitted, than he'd even normally buy for himself, as was the granola. It was a quiet comfort, and he was grateful for it.

"Crabtree really is okay," Sam said.

Ethan stirred yogurt and granola together. "It's funny how you all seem to hate him, love him, and fear him all at once."

"Yeah, I guess I could see how it looks like that." Sam leaned back in his chair. "Well, I know this—Randy wouldn't let you go see him if he thought it was going to be bad."

Yes, but Randy was the worst of all of them, kowtowing to the man one minute and standing up to him the next. Maybe that was the secret? Ethan realized it was what he had tried to do too, and had failed miserably. But then, Randy knew Crabtree.

Biblically. He pursed his lips, stirring his yogurt far longer than necessary. God, Crabtree was going to make him dance a jig on coals, if he didn't figure out how to bury this by noon.

He forced himself to stop stirring and to eat.

Sam abandoned his cereal. "Well, okay. I don't blame you for being unhappy about it. I guess I'm mad at him too, and Randy, and Mitch. I guess you saw the bit with the card, for the shrink? God, I was so embarrassed. I felt like I was Mitch's *kid*." He pushed the bowl away then sagged in his chair. "But I guess I've acted like one."

Ethan had no idea what Sam was talking about, but whatever this emotion was on his face struck a chord. He considered his words carefully before speaking. "I don't know if this hurts or helps, but they don't help you out in that department. They seem to treat you as if you are their fragile egg they don't dare let break." In fact, he realized it was nearly how Randy had described Sam. He could only imagine what Mitch's analogy for his husband would be.

"We're going to go and get a car in a bit. Mitch and I." Sam sighed. "I wanted him to just teach me how to drive Randy's truck. I *want* to drive Randy's truck. I want to know how to drive a stick. I feel like an idiot, not knowing." He pursed his lips. "How am I going to *not* be their stupid egg if they don't let me grow up? I don't *want* to be their little Sunshine and their Peaches, not if it means I'm always the dumbass kid. I can't figure it out. Is it because I'm always a bottom?" He went beet red. "Sorry, TMI."

Ethan reached for a napkin from the basket at the side of the table and wiped his lips. "What time is it right now?"

Sam glanced at the microwave on the counter. "Nine."

An idea buzzed in Ethan's mind. It was ridiculous, and it probably wouldn't work, but... He tapped his index finger against the side of his mug. "I suppose they took the truck to the center?"

"They rode the bikes. They'll use any excuse to ride the bikes. Which I, of course, don't know how to drive either. Why?"

"Would you like to learn to drive a stick shift before your husband comes home?"

Sam grinned. "Can you? *Could* you? Randy says he won't teach me because I'll kill his transmission."

Oh, now they were doing this, absolutely. "You won't. And if you do, I'll take the blame. I'll tell him I insisted."

Sam's chin came up. "No. If I screw up the truck,

I'm taking the blame."

It was the Parable of Cards itching at Sam's brain, Ethan realized. He could hardly blame Sam—it itched at his too. He picked up his spoon and scraped at the sides of the bowl. "Let me finish this and grab a quick shower, and then we'll go. Try to think of somewhere with a big, empty parking lot where we can practice. Somewhere not too far away."

"Well, the distribution center would be perfect, except Randy and Mitch would come over and give us hell."

Baiting them was tempting, but Ethan nixed the idea because he wanted Sam to do well. In fact, he'd be late to Crabtree if he had to, just to make sure Sam was rock-solid in his initial foray into stick-shift driving.

There was a raunchy joke in this somewhere, two gay men and a stick-shift lesson, but Sam didn't seem in the mood for titters. He had a different light about him now, less of a cherubic glow and more of an edgy eagerness. Ethan found he had the same edginess inside himself. "It'll be a very quick shower."

"I'll have a place for us to go by the time you're dressed," Sam promised, already reaching for his iPhone.

CHAPTER TEN

A T QUARTER AFTER twelve, Sam dropped Ethan off at Herod's. Ethan was already late, but he didn't care. He was far more concerned about how green Sam looked after driving through heavy traffic. Mitch had gotten caught up at the distribution center and called Sam to tell him to have Ethan take a cab. Of course, they were out driving at that moment, so Sam delivered Ethan to the casino, but now he had to get himself home again. Ethan lingered in the cab of the truck, taking the time to reassure his protégé.

"Sam, you can do this. You drove on the interstate and down the Strip. You're actually a natural, and I'm not saying so just to build you up. You don't need me in the truck with you to keep doing well." He put his hand on Sam's hand, which clutched the ball of the stick shift in a death grip. "You'll be fine."

Sam nodded, still pale. "I know. I mean—I know it, but I don't feel it yet. I don't want to have a wreck. I don't want to mess this up when I've done so well. I want to drive to the distribution center and *show* them, not have to call them to say I've wrecked the truck."

Ethan shook his head. "Don't go to the center. They

think I came here in a cab and you're at home finishing laundry. If you go there, you *will* screw up, because you'll get nervous and lose your confidence. Go home, and you can tell them later. It doesn't look like you'll be car shopping today anyway."

Sam nodded again. Then something on the sidewalk caught his attention, and he winced. "Oh *shit*, Crabtree—I'm so sorry, Ethan. I made you so late—"

Ethan rolled down the window of the truck. The mob man waited at the curb, in a suit again, though this one was light-colored and looked to be a cooler weight than the one he'd worn the night before. He had something cradled to his side, and when the gangster came over to the truck, Ethan startled. Crabtree held a tiny, black-and-white-splotched kitten. The cool, self-possessed explanation he was going to give the man died on his lips, and he simply stared.

Sam, however, melted. "Oh my *God*, it's so *cute*." He started to slide over the seat, but Ethan's arm shot out, and he pointed to the emergency brake. Sam applied it and came over to the window. "Crabtree, where did you get her?"

It was almost surreal, the way Crabtree altered when he looked down at the animal. It practically fit into his palm, and it blinked brilliant orbs of bright blue-gray eyes at Ethan. Crabtree's face was transformed into softness and tenderness, and he stroked the kitten lovingly as he spoke.

"Behind the dumpster. I couldn't find a sign of the mother." He glanced up at Ethan. "Do you like cats?"

Crabtree's tone was gentle, but this question might as well have been asked by a fire-breathing dragon. A dragon asking Ethan if he liked baby dragons.

"I had one when I was young. I haven't since." Ethan started to reach out the window, then paused and glanced up at Crabtree. "May I?"

Crabtree beamed. "Please."

The kitten's fur was dirty, and it looked undernourished. It was not, Ethan realized, as young as he'd thought. It was only small. But it was warm and soft, and it made Ethan melt a little too.

"I apologize for being late." Ethan tickled the kitten under the chin, smiling as its eyes went shut and it began to purr. "I was teaching Sam how to drive Randy's truck."

"I drove on the Strip!" Sam tried to temper his enthusiasm. "I mean, I did okay, I think."

"He did well for his first time with a manual transmission."

"I'm sure he did." Crabtree scratched the back of the cat's head. "I'm surprised the other Mr. Keller-Tedsoe didn't insist on giving that lesson."

"He didn't offer, so I did."

"A good reason to be tardy, then. And it allowed me to find this angel, so we will cede this game to Fate, who always knows our needs better than we do." Crabtree stepped onto the curb. "But now I do have need of your services, Mr. Ellison, and I'm sure Sam has much to do as well."

Sam leaned over again. "Crabtree? If—if you see

Mitch, or Randy, don't tell them, please? I want to tell them myself."

"Of course." Crabtree inclined his head in acknowledgment, and then Ethan exited, and they stood together on the curb watching as Sam somewhat lurchingly drove away.

"That was well done," Crabtree said, when the truck had disappeared around the corner. He massaged the kitten's fur but kept his eyes on the place where Sam's truck had been. "They love him, but they do smother him. They see him as something between saint and angel, the magic boy who reunited them. And this is the trouble. He's been a man for some time now, but they keep nudging him back to boy, and after a while, he'll stay there. They think they're making life easier for him by sheltering him. But they're not thinking of him, only themselves. They're sheltering him the way they wish someone had sheltered them."

Ethan had to agree this was true. "It's not wrong to want to give someone what you didn't have."

Crabtree smiled at the kitten. "It's good to have love and protection, but at some point we need to go out into the cold world and see how we do. You did well by giving him space."

Here Ethan thought he'd been giving Sam an overdue driving lesson and rubbing Randy's nose playfully in the dirt. He didn't doubt Crabtree was right, but thinking about it like that made everything so heavy. "Are you some sort of wandering casino oracle?"

Crabtree chuckled. "Former family counselor. And

not a good one, I'm afraid. They revoked my license."

"Oh?"

"They do that when you sleep with your clients." Crabtree gave an only mildly apologetic shrug. "Emotionally vulnerable and hairy men. Every man has his Achilles' heel, and that one is mine."

"And kittens." Ethan's insides melted as the kitten lapped at his finger. "She truly is beautiful. When she's cleaned up, she'll break hearts. Will you keep her?"

The look crossing Crabtree's face was devastating. "No, it isn't possible. Perhaps one day, if I retire out of the city. But—" He stroked the cat, the very gesture a sign of his regret. "It's no secret I love cats. It's one of the jokes they make of me. And you see, when you're a man who has made as many enemies as I have, you don't keep vulnerable loved ones around you. Not unless you have a stronger stomach than I do."

"Oh." Ethan looked at the cat and at the gangster, thought about Crabtree's passion for the animals and the number he must have seen killed to put them off so far from him, and he couldn't help it. He bled for Crabtree. "I'm sorry."

"She needs a name. If I take her to a shelter unnamed, they'll name her something ridiculous like Patches. Nothing's coming to my mind, though. Care to take a stab?"

Ethan didn't have the first idea about naming cats—his as a child had, in fact, been named Spotty—but when he opened his mouth to say so, he looked down at the cat and said instead, "Salomé."

Crabtree laughed, a loud, bowl-full-of-jelly laugh. "Well done. Salomé it is." He lifted her up and kissed the top of her head. "Darling, let's go to my office, and when you're ready, we'll order up John the Baptist's head for you on a platter."

They didn't head for the main entrance, but instead entered through a side door. Nodding to security as they passed, Crabtree, cradling Salomé against his chest, led Ethan out into the casino. But they lingered along the side, almost in the shadows. There was an odd, nostalgic expression on the gangster's face as he surveyed the scene before him. Ethan waited, certain there was another speech coming up.

He wasn't disappointed.

"There was a golden age of Las Vegas. In the fifties and sixties this city was full of movie stars and singers, and people came from all over the country to see them and be seen with them. You could come to Vegas from Scranton and rub elbows with Frank Sinatra and Sammy Davis, Jr." He smiled, but it was grim. "Of course, Sammy Davis, Jr. couldn't stay at the hotel where he performed. He hung out at places like the Moulin Rouge because that was where the colored people went back then."

Ethan recoiled, then caught himself and shook his head. "You're making that up."

"Sadly, I'm not. This injustice was fixed eventually, but by then the golden age was over. By the seventies, this place was a joke. It was sleazy and cheesy, and it was a place you came to die, not be a king." He sighed.

"That's when this place was built. Oh, Billy was so sure it would bring everyone back because he would do it *right*—and I think he could have in another ten years. Herod's hit the world at the wrong time. Now he's gone, and there's just his spoiled-rotten little shit of a son. Billy Junior is never going to turn this place around. In the deck of life, Billy is a ten. He thinks he's a face card, but he isn't, and he's never going to change. Not enough to save this place."

Crabtree shifted the kitten to his elbow and reached out to pat the side of the archway they stood beneath. "Billy Senior gave it glitz and glamour, and he gave it all the old elements—a showroom doubling as a restaurant, but there hasn't been a show in there in ages. He paved the entrance to the door to the old fountain by the elevator in plush red carpet and called it the Grand Path. He added a hotel, but it hasn't been updated, and it's nothing but a fleabag now. He even, in his day, put the poker tables up front. Because he loved poker, and he wanted his place to be known as *the* poker place."

Ethan tried to imagine poker tables replacing the slots. It was hard.

Crabtree grimaced. "Billy died as the corporate cats took over, turning the Strip into a fucking Disneyland. They urged everyone to come here on their credit cards and stay in executive suites and shop and gamble with the money they refinanced from their third home mortgage. We stopped drawing the simple crowd of people with money and made everyone a king. It's a nice sentiment, but it isn't realistic. Not everyone can be a king."

Ethan would argue that was the whole of the world right now. "What should be here instead? The old days part two?"

"I don't know, but this way can't stand much longer. We need to rediscover simple pleasures. We need to love to play, not love to spend. We need to make our money in the poker rake and in the spillover of people who play the tables after. We need to draw them in with cheap entertainment and free drinks so they have more money to gamble. We need real leadership again, not teams of lawyers and corporate interests. We need to be a town, a community, not a nest of crooks and liars."

Ethan didn't know what to say, so he just looked out over the casino, really looking at it. He saw dark paneling, crystal chandeliers, and a lot of clutter. And, honestly, he saw dust. Dust and damage and decay—peeling paint, worn carpets, faded curtains. Outdated paintings on the wall. Cracked vinyl on the stools in front of the slot machines. Sagging, disinterested dealers and waitstaff. Hardly any customers at all.

Crabtree patted his shoulder. "Let's go to my office and have a chat."

There was already a litter box in Crabtree's office when they arrived, as well as a dish of food and a bowl of water, and Crabtree introduced Salomé to both stations before letting her loose on the floor. She ran immediately to the food dish and ate enthusiastically.

"Close the door please."

He gestured Ethan toward the uncomfortable-looking chair with its back to the door as he sat at in the sagging olive-green office chair behind a metal monstrosity of a desk taking up most of the room.

The office was smaller than he had thought it would be, and much shabbier, though some of this was because it was stuck in the seventies. It wasn't retrochic. It looked like it actually was seventies decor no one had ever updated. The only nods to the current millennium were the dabbles of technology—a state-of-the-art multiline phone with cordless receiver and Bluetooth headset were visible beneath a cascade of manila folders, and a sleek Dell Touchsmart desktop sat beside that. What was possibly a silver MacBook Pro sat on another pile of papers on top of a filing cabinet beneath a kitten poster Ethan tried not to notice.

Crabtree picked up a sleek black binder, regarded it with distaste for a moment then passed it over to Ethan. "This is the current financial report for Herod's. Income, expenditures, assets. There's also a tab which summarizes the history of those same three figures over the past thirty years."

Ethan took the binder and flipped through it reluctantly. Something told him there was nothing good about a gangster handing you a ledger, but he wasn't sure what else to do. Still, numbers were numbers, and he quickly lost himself in them, running his fingers down the columns, stopping only to reach down and pet Salomé absently when she tried to climb his pant leg. The casino had done fairly well in the seventies, moderately well in the eighties and hung on in the nineties. But right around 1994, a bizarre pattern of high growth, great loss, and sometimes inexplicable asset acquisition and disposal emerged.

He gave up attempting to dissuade Salomé and picked her up carefully, settling her on his lap as he propped the ledger against the edge of Crabtree's desk and tried again to make sense of the figures. Eventually, however, he had to give up. "What happened in 1994?"

"That's the year Billy Senior was killed. In a car accident," he added, an amused quirk playing at his lips. "A legitimate one, I'm quite sure. But it meant Billy Junior now owned the casino, and this wasn't a good thing. Billy has no business sense. He treats the casino as one of his playthings. Sometimes it's a toy moldering in the back of his closet, and sometimes it gets trotted out and banged a bit against the walls. It would have folded long ago, but I've kept it propped up, sometimes with my own money."

Something told Ethan Crabtree didn't spend his own money lightly. "That doesn't seem to be doing enough."

Crabtree snorted. "The current economic downturn is the greatest threat this casino has had yet. I've done my best to spur attendance and interest, but it's as challenging as it's always been to compete with the big guys on the Strip. Herod's is an out-of-the-way hole, and the few old-timers who came here just for that reason are either dying out or are sick of Billy's shit." Crabtree's lips thinned into a line, and he leaned over the desk. "I want him out. And I want you to help me do this by walking me through some investments."

Ethan winced as Salomé dug her claws a little too enthusiastically into his leg. "Crabtree—you do understand I was only a small-time broker? I invested other people's money into mutual funds. On rare occasions I helped put together some real-estate deals, but nothing like this."

"You know the business. You know how it works. And more importantly, no one here knows you—and if they look you up, it will appear just as you said. You look absolutely harmless." Crabtree pointed to a column. "I have authority to manage the income of the casino and hotel and bar. I'm responsible for paying Billy a percentage and nothing more. He owns stock, but not much, and while he is the official owner, he doesn't have the capital to start any real projects. I'm going to change that."

Ethan frowned. "You're going to give him *more* money?"

"Yes. As he notices he has some money to burn, he's going to turn to you, the man who has helped me cleverly invest my own money, to help him double it. But there is a catch, you see—he can only work with assets, and all money invested through assets remains with the casino. You will help him clean up his portfolio. You will help him make Herod's appear to shine, so a buyer might want to buy the casino, because only then will he get to have his money."

Oh, Ethan did not like the sound of this. "Mr. Crabtree, I don't have a buyer ready."

Crabtree waved this thought away with his hand. "Of course you don't. I do. But you can't divulge your sources."

"Why on earth would Billy trust me?"

Crabtree threaded his fingers over his belly. "You bluff, of course. It's poker, Mr. Ellison—just without the cards. You want him invested deeply in this game. It will be, I suspect, the finest game of poker you'll ever play, with a pot you can't see yet but will reward you for many, many years to come."

"You do understand I've only played poker for two days?"

"You've played poker a lot longer than that. You just didn't have a formal strategy. This, son, will swiftly change."

Salomé licked Ethan's thumb. He was grateful for the steady, rough brush of her tongue. He turned his palm toward her, and she eagerly gave it the same treatment. He kept his eyes on her ministrations as he spoke. "And if I tell you I wish to decline your offer?"

He waited for Crabtree to say something out of a movie—*I would advise against that,* or something with more panache, with its own ominous music trailing in its wake. Which was why he was all the more suspicious when Crabtree only shrugged and said, "Then I'll make this offer to someone else."

"But I'll find someone following me wherever I go, and some night my car will stall, and they'll discover me a week later, nothing but bones in the Mojave Desert?"

"No. If you decline, you'll return to Randy's house,

unemployed. He'll probably keep taking you to bed. He'll definitely keep teaching you poker. And you'll do all right. You'll pay him back what you owe him. Perhaps the two of you will even develop some sort of relationship, or at least an arrangement. You'll get a sedate little condo and a job investing other people's money, and you'll play conservative pots in conservative games on the weekends for fun. You'll meet Randy regularly to fuck. You might be happy. For a while."

Crabtree's gaze bore into him, and bones in the desert started to sound pretty good.

Crabtree shook his head. "I have no need to punish you if you refuse. Because I know you, Ethan Ellison. I've played poker all night with you, and I know the beast which woke inside you when you left Nick Snow. If you decline my offer and go to Randy's house, you'll punish yourself more exquisitely than I could ever hope to accomplish." He brushed imaginary lint from his sleeve. "Whichever you choose, I must ask you to please move your car. We have a policy about parking for over twenty-four hours, and if it isn't gone by five p.m. today, I'll have to have it towed."

His car—Ethan had forgotten all about it. He patted his pockets in a reflexive gesture. "I think Randy has my keys."

"I can help you around that aspect." Crabtree rose. "You'll want to think about my offer, of course. And you'll absolutely want to meet my godson first." He glanced at his watch. "I know just where he'll be."

SALOMÉ CRIED WHEN they left the office.

She tried to follow them out, and when Crabtree shooed her in, she began mewing plaintively and scratching at the door. The sound tugged at Ethan's heart, and he turned to Crabtree, waiting for him to do something.

Crabtree only looked at Ethan with amusement. "What do you propose we do with her? Bring her along?"

Salomé let out another plaintive mew, this one pitching deep and burrowing into the middle of Ethan's belly. *She was on her own outside. She'll settle down in a few minutes.* But the cries still tugged at him. He said nothing, just stood rigid, listening, getting angry at Crabtree for allowing her to cry. Crabtree regarded Ethan with quiet amusement.

The kitten yelped, a sharp, wounded-sounding cry, and though he knew it wasn't possible, Ethan swore he heard *help*.

"For God's sake." Throwing open the door, he crouched down in time to catch Salomé as she bounded up to him and scooped her into his arms. He stood, holding her close to his chest. "We can't leave her in there alone."

"Then I suppose we'll have no choice but to take her down to the floor." Crabtree rubbed beneath her chin. "Do you think you can manage her?"

Ethan paused, aware he had somehow wandered into a trap. He stammered. "I—I mean, I don't know. You mean bring her *along*? To the casino floor? And I just hold her?"

"I suspect it's either that or we'll have to put her in my office. She might as well get used to it. At the shelter she'll be in her own cage."

"Shelter?" Ethan recoiled. Salomé used her claws to climb up his shirt and lick the underside of his chin. *Shelter.*

Of course she was going to a shelter. Where else would she go?

She licked him again, purring loudly. Ethan shut his eyes in a long blink and stroked her.

Crabtree did too. "If it helps, I doubt she'll be there long. It's a good shelter. You know I wouldn't send her to her death."

Ethan nodded, but he was starting to feel unhinged. It didn't matter. It was just a cat. A kitten, yes, but—

She nuzzled her cold nose against his chin and brushed a paw along his cheek, and he had to fight to keep himself composed. For heaven's sake, what was wrong with him?

He didn't know. What he did know was he could not put her down, and he could not, not for anything, leave her in the office. He didn't even let himself think about the shelter.

Crabtree glanced at his watch. "We're going to miss Billy if we stand here much longer."

Ethan held Salomé tightly, his heart hammering against her small, filthy body. Then something snapped. He looked up at Crabtree, composed and collected, and he nodded. "We should get going, then." He tucked the kitten into the corner of his arm.

To his intense relief, Crabtree made no additional comment about leaving the cat in the office, and he reached over with a grandfatherly smile to nuzzle beneath her chin occasionally as they rode the elevator to the main floor of the casino.

Despite the shabbiness he'd noticed with Crabtree earlier, Ethan still liked the casino. It felt old and opulent but close and cozy at the same time, and he walked almost in a trance down the long, red carpet leading from the elevator to the slot machines. They headed to the craps tables closest to the door. A large crowd had gathered there, and they were cheering and whooping as a slightly overweight man dressed in white with slicked-back hair shook his hand vigorously before letting a pair of dice fly across the felt.

Another cheer went up, and a man in the center of the table wearing the casino livery boomed out, "Nine, winner in Center Field." There was more shouting, and other men moved to collect and pass out chips to players. The table was loud, and Ethan worried it would upset Salomé, but she seemed content to settle deeper into his arm.

Crabtree pointed to the man in white. "That's Billy. He always plays craps at twelve thirty before he goes to lunch. Then he takes the whole table out to eat with him in the hotel restaurant."

"I don't know how to play craps."

"Very simple. If you're rolling, don't get a seven. If you're betting, bet for or against the player to get either specific numbers, specific combinations on the dice, or that he'll roll the come-out number again before ending his roll by rolling a seven. Or that he won't. It's the casino game with the best odds for the player, and it's the most collegial. Go on. Get your feet wet." He glanced down at Salomé, then added, "Though perhaps I should watch over your young lady for the moment."

Ethan handed Salomé to Crabtree and wandered over, slightly dazed. He stood behind a lovely blonde woman at the table, but he didn't stand there long. When she noticed him, she smiled broadly and nudged over to let him in.

She leaned in close. "Hi. I'm Karen."

"Ethan." He took in the sea of words and numbers on the table—Pass, Don't Pass, 6, 8, Field, Hardways— and he wondered how the hell he was supposed to figure this out.

"I know, it made me dizzy the first time too." Karen touched his hand lightly. "Here. Let me help you." She held up her chips then passed them to a dealer. "Five on the Pass Line, please." She held up another five. "You want in?"

Ethan fumbled for his wallet. "I have—" He pulled out a twenty, then added a second one and laid them down on the felt. A dealer picked them up and looked at Ethan. "Change, please," Ethan said.

Chips were pressed into Ethan's hand. They were like the roulette chips, color tailored to him so they could easily identify him as the bettor, and each one was stamped with *BILLY'S!* He counted out five and handed them to the dealer. "Pass Line." He glanced at Karen. "Now what did I just bet?"

"You bet Billy will hit the six before he sevens out."

That made no sense to Ethan at all. "Okay."

Karen's eyes twinkled as she held up another stack. "Want to play the Field with me? Or bet on the Come?"

Sometimes Ethan wished there were a sign, some sort of dot or earring or tug of his hair he could give to quietly, gently let a woman know as much as he was flattered, she was wasting her time. He tried to communicate this with a polite, distant smile. "I think I'd best stick with the Pass, thank you."

She blushed but recovered well and placed two additional bets, one on a series of numbers marked FIELD and the long, curved box labeled COME. Then the man in the middle who did all the shouting called for Billy to roll the dice, and everyone clapped and cheered and urged *come on, six* as Billy hauled back and let the dice fly. They bounced off the side of the rail and landed before Ethan—a one and a five.

The table went wild, and Ethan rode the excitement too, though he had no idea if he'd won or not. Karen cheered as the dealer passed her chips. Then, of all things, he passed Ethan one too.

He *had* won. He beamed, laughed, and accepted Karen's enthusiastic hug.

He bet again.

Under Karen's patient tutelage and his own study, he began to understand the game. It took him some time to understand the Come bets, but he eventually managed those too. It *was* fun. It was wonderfully fun, and within four throws of the dice he was suddenly holding eighty dollars' worth of chips instead of forty.

Then a two and a five landed in the middle of the table, and there was a collective moan as most of the chips they had all placed down were collected and drawn away. Ethan, who had gotten caught up in the spirit of the game and Karen's infectious enthusiasm, was now down to twenty dollars with one cast of the dice.

"That's the show, ladies and gentlemen." Billy held out his hands in casual apology. He pulled back his jacket sleeve and glanced at his watch. "I believe my table is ready. Shall we adjourn?"

Karen tried to take Ethan's arm, but he glanced at Crabtree for guidance. Crabtree had already fallen in place with the throng, and Ethan realized he meant for the pair of them to go to lunch. Ethan moved closer to the gangster to check on Salomé, whom he found contentedly tucked in Crabtree's elbow. It seemed to be a place she liked.

Crabtree, however, handed her back when Ethan approached. "And what did you think of craps?"

"A bit compulsive. It's too easy to get caught up in the crowd."

"One could argue this is the greater payout than the chips themselves."

Ethan had a sudden vision of Randy beside him playing craps, throwing the dice, making jokes under his breath about the Come and the Field. He could see

Randy's eyes dancing, and he felt an unexpected sense of loss, because he knew that moment would never happen, not with the way Randy hated all table games but blackjack and poker.

He changed the subject. "So we're going to lunch with Billy? Are all these people going? Does he actually know them?"

"He knows some. What he mostly knows is they're all here because of him, eager to be with him, eager to feel they belong."

"What exactly will we be doing?"

"I recommend you eat. The food here is quite good."

Ethan looked down at the kitten nesting against his arm. "What about Salomé?"

Crabtree waved a careless hand. "There won't be any trouble."

Ethan still wasn't sure what he was doing or why he was carrying a kitten into a restaurant, but he couldn't seem to make himself turn around. He realized he was walking the same path through the slot machines he'd walked with Randy, and it occurred to him he'd been wandering helpless then too. He wondered how he had so completely lost control of his life it had unraveled to this strange frayed end.

At the door to the restaurant he discovered Crabtree had lied.

"What is this?" The maître d' stared in horror at Ethan and his kitten. "You can't bring *that* in here."

Ethan swung his gaze around to Crabtree, who

blinked in the worst fake surprise Ethan had ever seen, before he came forward and held out his hands. "Would you like me to take her while you eat?"

"Crabtree," Ethan called out in a harsh whisper, but the gangster had already taken Salomé from his hands and started down the row of slots. Ethan tried to follow him, but a hand on his shoulder stopped him. It wasn't a friendly hand. Ethan turned to see a man who made even Ethan look short, and he wore sunglasses and an earpiece.

"Mr. Herod wants to see you." The man herded Ethan through the restaurant. Karen waved at him as he passed, and he waved back, a little weakly, mentally cursing Crabtree all the way to the casino owner's side.

Billy was chatting up a busty woman who was a wardrobe malfunction waiting to happen, and he lingered with her for a minute before turning to address Ethan. He gave Ethan an up-and-down scan. "So you're working with Crabtree, are you?"

Goddamn you, Crabtree. "Not officially, no."

This did not have the effect Ethan was hoping for. In fact, it had quite the opposite. "Oh-ho, I see how this is going down."

"Actually, I don't think you—"

"Leave him, Arnie." Billy waved at the sunglassed monster, who released Ethan. Billy pointed to the chair beside him. "Sit, sit."

Ethan looked meaningfully at the man who was already sitting in the chair.

Billy tapped the man on the shoulder then jerked

his thumb to indicate the man should get out. Ethan took the man's seat after he vacated it.

"So what are you doing for my godfather?" Billy sipped the martini in front of him. A waiter placed a matching drink in front of Ethan.

Ethan ignored it and sipped his water. "Nothing yet."

Billy looked at him impatiently, and Ethan realized he wouldn't actually be happy with the truth. He decided he might as well continue letting Billy draw his own conclusions.

"I'm an investment broker."

Billy laughed. "Oh, *brilliant*." He picked up his knife and dinged it so hard on the glass of the man across from him Ethan expected it to shatter across the table. "Joe. Hey—Joe. This here is Crabtree's *investment broker*."

Joe, who had taken up with the busty woman when Billy had abandoned her to talk to Ethan, gave a vaguely interested smile and resumed his courtship.

Billy didn't notice, too absorbed with the idea that he really had his finger in the pudding now. "I *knew* he was up to something." He elbowed Ethan with a broad wink. "So how much you want, huh?"

Ethan couldn't check the urge to rub his bruised arm. "I beg your pardon?"

A mistake—the elbow came again, twice, and harder each time than the one before. "How *much*? Come on. You all have your price."

Oh, fucking *hell*. Ethan took a deeper drink of water. "I honestly don't know what you're talking about."

"Don't worry. I'll wear you down." Billy made a face. "Shit, you aren't a fag, are you? He banging you?"

Ethan had never had anyone be so casually bigoted to his face and in front of a tableful of people to boot. "I'm not *banging Crabtree*, nor he me."

Billy's eyes narrowed. "Say. I know you from somewhere. The fag thing made me think of it." His eyes widened, and then he laughed and slapped his leg. "You're Jansen's roulette guy." He addressed the table again. "Hey—this is the *guy*. The one with the *bet*! The one who made Randy lose his bet *twice*. I *love* this guy."

Ethan felt for Billy when he saw how not a single person at the table, despite their enthusiasm for following him around and joining him for lunch, showed interest in anything he said. Even more depressing was Billy didn't seem to realize no one here cared about him at all.

Then Billy started talking again, and Ethan quickly lost his empathy.

"Wait. Jansen made another bet to kiss you, and Scully said you didn't freak out. So you *are* a fag."

Ethan had borne quite enough of this. "I assure you, I'm happy to leave if my orientation offends you."

Billy rolled his eyes. "Jesus, fags are so touchy. Hey, I'm no bigot. I'm starting Gay Nite in three weeks. Seriously. Gay Nite at the casino. All you rich gay guys can come and spend your money, and I'll have all the hot twinkies or whatever." His grin became a leer. "And Randy will be one of them, thanks to you."

"What do I have to do with this?"

"Because he lost the bet. Those were the terms—either I gave him the twinkie of his choice if he won, or he had to be one of them if he lost." Billy slapped Ethan on the back then froze in alarm. "Hey, but *I'm* not a fag."

"Don't worry, you're quite safe." He started to reach for his water, then gave up and reached for the martini instead.

The first course was already laid before them, and Ethan tried to take refuge in his salad. It was, as Crabtree had suggested, quite good.

"That's so weird," Billy went on, between bites of salad, and sometimes during. "I never thought Crabtree would keep a secret from Randy. I mean—" He looked knowingly at Ethan. "*They* fuck."

Ethan set his teeth and took several breaths before reclaiming the bite of salad Billy had loosened and said, "I know."

"But Randy didn't know who you were. I can totally read people, and I know he didn't know you. Which means you're Crabtree's *secret* investment broker."

Ethan stared at the fork, wondering what it would feel like to drive it into the center of Crabtree's chest. Or maybe the center of his forehead.

Billy laughed wickedly. "Oh yes. I so have him now. Come on, buddy. What do you want? A million? Two?"

Ethan choked on his salad. A million *dollars*?

What sort of hell could he get into in a nest of gangsters for a million dollars?

How about two?

Ethan drained the rest of his martini.

"Look, I honestly can't go over five," Billy said. "Though the casino must be doing better than I thought, because this morning I checked my accounts, and I was sitting on quite a pile. Still, it's not *that* much more. And honestly, you can't be that good."

Ethan wiped his napkin across his mouth with a shaking hand. "I assure you, I'm not."

"Come on, man—what the fuck do you *want*?"

This was insane. He should never have agreed to come to the casino. He should have left Salomé in the office, and then Crabtree would be here to straighten this out. Except Crabtree was clearly behind all this.

A lesson in manipulation.

Ethan tightened his jaw. Fine. He'd play the cards Crabtree had given him, and then he'd be gone.

"All right, I'll tell you what I know. Crabtree has some investor lined up to buy the casino."

Billy was visibly pissed. "He can't do that. It's *mine*."

"Yes, I know." Ethan decided the only way out of this was to throw Crabtree totally under the bus. "He wants to build up the assets and invest them properly, to maximize the profit. Because—"

But Billy interrupted him. "Because he controls the *income*. The *bastard*. And then he'll come to me and tell me I have to sell for a song, and screw me out of my goddamned money when he resells for twice the amount."

Ethan frowned. "That's not—"

"Oh—three times, then? The *fucker*." Billy snapped his fingers, and another martini materialized out of nowhere. To Ethan's shock, he presented it to Ethan. "Here. Drink up. I want to hear *all about this.*"

"There isn't anything else to tell, and none of this matters because I'm turning him down." *Right after I wring his goddamned neck.*

"Oh no you aren't." Billy pressed the glass into Ethan's hand. "Drink. Eat. Order whatever you want, because it's on me. In fact, you're never paying for a drink again in this place, and you get a thousand-dollar tray of chips anytime you like. You're my man—" He paused. "What's your name?"

Oh, Jesus fucking God. "Ethan Ellison, but I don't—"

"You're my man, Ethan Ellison. *My* man." He grinned manically and toasted the glass he'd forced into Ethan's hand with his own. "And together we are going to take the old bastard down." He waved to the sunglasses man. "Arnie. Hey, Arnie, get this guy's bank account number and put a million in it for me."

Ethan was going to throw up. "Mr. Herod, you don't understand."

"Account number, Ellison," Billy demanded, then grinned, a four-year-old looking thoroughly pleased at having climbed onto the counter.

"I don't have one."

"Open my man Ethan an account, Arnie." Billy looked down at Ethan in alarm. "But you're not my man like *that.* Okay?"

Ethan didn't answer, just tossed back the martini, then gestured at the waiter for another, thinking if he drank enough of them fast enough, he might save the mob the trouble and kill himself then and there.

CHAPTER ELEVEN

I T HADN'T BEEN one of Randy's favorite days.

He'd meant to go in to work for a few hours, go home in time to shower, pick up Slick, and shake him out of whatever fuckery Crabtree had gotten away with. Then the rig he'd been working on had not just caught on fire, it had practically blown up, and of course it was a high-priority load to San Bernardino, and after two hours of trying to jerry-rig something, they'd given up and had Mitch do the run. Mitch had made the decision not to tell Sam, which Randy thought was not the best of plans, but he was too busy calling all over Vegas for parts on another rig that had to leave for Reno by seven p.m. He managed it, just, and a half hour after Mitch had gone back to the house, Randy was on his bike and heading there himself.

It was five thirty, and Slick was not home yet. He tried asking Sam what the hell was going on, but Sam was too busy shouting at Mitch for going to San Bernardino without telling him, and Mitch shouted at Sam because, apparently, Slick had taken him out to learn how to drive the truck. That had sent Randy straight out to the garage and under the hood, but no, the transmission was fine. Which was damn lucky for Slick, and he was still going to give him a piece of his mind.

If he ever fucking showed up.

He paced in front of the house for a few minutes, sweating in the late-afternoon heat, trying to decide if he should run over there now, grease and all, or if he should shower first. He'd decided to go as is when Ethan's car and a sleek black Audi pulled up.

Ethan wasn't driving. One of Crabtree's goons had apparently hot-wired it, because the keys were on his dresser along with Slick's ring. Ethan's Mazda was empty except for the driver, but as the Audi parked alongside it, three bruisers got out. While one of them went around to the trunk, the other two assisted Ethan as he appeared from the backseat. He was visibly, fantastically drunk.

He also held a kitten.

Ethan waved before pitching sideways against the car. The goon who'd pulled him out righted him. Ethan laughed and waved again. "Hi, Randy."

"Hey, Slick," Randy said carefully. The thug from the trunk came forward with a litter box and a cloth shopping bag, which Randy knew without being told held cat food and a set of dishes. "Oh *fuck*."

Ethan sobered—his expression, anyway—and tried to walk toward Randy. "Don't be angry. I can explain." His words were so slurred he almost used three whole consonants.

A small, hot fire burned in the back of Randy's brain, one he'd continue banking until he learned the extent of how fucked this was. Once he'd sorted that out, he'd bloody Crabtree to whatever degree was appropriate. He took the kitten from Ethan. "Baby, I think you'd better let me take him just for now."

"*Her*." Ethan tried to reclaim the cat but missed. "Her name is Salomé. And she's a girl." Ethan swayed again, giving his supporting goon an irritated glance. "You can quit holding me. I can stand up by myself."

"Slick, honey?" Randy winced as the cat nested against his T-shirt. "Why exactly did you bring home a cat?"

Ethan's expression turned ferocious. "Because she was *not* going to the shelter. I don't…" he paused as the alcohol temporarily washed over the speaking portion of his brain, "…care how nice it is. She can't go back there."

So far Randy knew Crabtree was going to die by stabbing, but now he thought he should do it with several small blades that hurt more than they killed. Some fingernail removal would absolutely be in order.

"Baby, she wouldn't go to a shelter. Crabtree would never take a cat to a shelter. He'd take her home."

Ethan appeared like he might cry. "He *can't*, Randy. They'll *kill* her."

Probably some toenails too. "Slick, sweetheart— Crabtree has about thirty cats at his house. They have a fucking jungle gym in the yard that they can get to from a tube in the window."

"But Crabtree said—" Ethan stopped, and the dim, drunken edge of awareness was a knife to Randy.

I'm sorry, baby. I should have known what he would do, should have known how he would try to get you, and how susceptible you would be. I should have known better. I should never have let you go there.

Ethan looked sick now. "He—You mean he—"

"Lied. Tricked you. Manipulated you."

Ethan, already fragile as glass, looked as if one more tap would make him break into shards right there in the middle of the driveway.

Randy swallowed his fury and turned to the goons, who stood silently awaiting instruction. "Leave the stuff in the garage and get the fuck out of here." He slid his free arm around Ethan and aimed him at the house. "Come on, baby. It's hot. Let's go inside."

Ethan shook, unable to walk on his own. "I'm so sorry."

"It's okay, Slick. It's okay." He caught the despair on Ethan's face and bled for him all over again. "Hey." He brushed a kiss over Ethan's cheek. "Baby, it's okay."

"It's not." Ethan stumbled as he missed the step, nearly dragging Randy and the irritated kitten down with him. "Oh God, Randy, I'm so sorry."

"We're almost inside, and then you can sit down."

Ethan looked so fucking miserable, worse than he'd looked at the fountains, or in the grocery store, or in the kitchen. Randy had let this happen by sending him to Crabtree. Because he'd been an idiot and trusted the guy.

Ethan shut his eyes tight. "I have a million dollars."

Randy stopped. "Seriously?"

"From Billy. Crabtree set me up. Wants to double bluff him. Double blind. Double something."

"Crabtree likes to get you invested two ways, get your ante in twice so you won't back out." The cat batted at Randy's chin, and Randy jerked his head away, but she reached higher. He gave in and lowered his face so she could nuzzle him. The kitten was a dirty miniature of Mirabella, one of Crabtree's favorites, but Ethan suspected this one had come directly from the shelter. That would have been more Crabtree's style. He hoped to hell the thing didn't have fleas.

Ethan looked hollow, beaten. "I tried to tell Billy. Tried all afternoon to convince him this was a setup, but he didn't care. He's made me his man." He managed a sneer. "But 'not that way'. Like I would want anything to do with his slimy little ass." The sneer fell away as he crumbled again. "I fucked it all up, didn't I? I was his live one, and he played me every step of the way."

Randy was going to take a *century* to kill Crabtree. This was going to smack so hard against Ethan's pride Randy wasn't sure even he could charm him back around this time.

Inside the house, Sam took one look at Ethan and went into nurse mode. "What happened?" He pressed a palm against Ethan's forehead.

"From the smell of him, a great deal of gin. We're going to have to get him a new liver soon." Crabtree's would do nicely. He nudged Ethan toward Sam. "Here—I have to deal with the cat."

"Cat?" Sam took in the purring kitten in the crook of Randy's arm. He softened a little. "Oh, it's the one Crabtree found in the alley, the one he had when I dropped Ethan off."

"You dropped Ethan *off?*" Mitch said from the other side of the room, and Randy peered between Sam and Ethan and gave him a hard look.

"Tedsoe, shut up."

When Mitch's nostrils started to flare like a bull's, Randy said quietly, "*Orale vato, ayudame.*"

Ethan lifted his head blearily. "You speak Spanish?"

"The barest bones of Valley Spanish, which is an animal all its own." Randy kept his eyes on Mitch. "I know just enough to beg with."

Mitch tightened his jaw then let his shoulders fall as he nodded. "*Bien.*"

Once he had surrendered Ethan to Mitch and Sam, Randy put the kitten down and went to the garage for the rest of the supplies. Ethan argued he had to take care of Salomé, but Mitch held him down and Sam refused to let him up until he'd told him how much he'd drank and how long ago he'd stopped.

"I don't know." Ethan laughed, a hollow, miserable sound. "I was trying to kill myself."

Randy dropped the bag of cat food and dishes, and the litter slid down after.

Sam pressed the back of his hand all over Ethan's forehead and face and neck. "He's clammy and he's pale, but he's not blue. Have you thrown up yet, Ethan?"

Ethan slurred when he spoke. "No, but I played

craps. And roulette. Fucking black *again*."

Picking up the supplies he'd dropped, Randy continued the task he'd set out to do before Ethan had scared the shit out of him. He took the litter box to the bathroom, where he tucked it in the space between the toilet and the sink. The kitten appeared immediately, and after demanding a stroke down her back, she climbed inside and made an inspection of it. Randy returned to the living room where he picked up the shopping bag and carried it to the kitchen. Salomé reappeared as he poured food into the dish. Randy put the bag of food in the cupboard above the washing machine, then stood there a second, gripping the edges of the appliance as he tried to center himself. It didn't work.

He gave up, pushed off the machine, and stalked through a red rage toward the door.

When Mitch caught his arm, he tried to throw him off, but Mitch tightened his grip. "I'll drive you, Skeet." He stopped, though, and looked worriedly at Sam.

Sam waved them on, one arm around Ethan. "I'm fine."

Mitch tried to linger, but Randy headed out to the garage. Mitch came out shortly thereafter, bearing the keys to Ethan's car, and Randy had to wait while Mitch moved it. His fingernails had dug indentations into his palms by the time Mitch headed for the driver's side door of the truck.

They rode in silence to the casino, and Mitch went twenty miles over the limit the whole way. He drove up to the side door and waited as Randy climbed out. "You want me to come in, Skeet?"

"No." Randy hesitated, making himself acknowledge how much trouble he could get into, going to Crabtree with this much rage. "Yes."

So he got back in and waited more while Mitch found a parking spot. Then, finally, they were going upstairs.

Crabtree was gone. So was Billy. Nobody knew where either of them were.

"We could use you for prop, though, if you want an extra shift," the floorman said, and Mitch dragged Randy out before he could vent his spleen on him.

On the way home Mitch drove a lot slower. "Do you want me to go by his house?"

"He won't be there. He won't be anywhere we can find him." Randy slammed his fist against the dashboard, cracking the plastic. Then he drew his throbbing hand against his chest and sagged into the seat.

Mitch kept his eyes on the road. "It's not your fault, Slick."

"Oh? Whose fault do you figure it is? Who the fuck went to the bastard in the first place?"

"You were trying to help Sam. I already called the lady on the card, by the way. Look—you know damn well he would have gotten himself involved as soon as he found out—" He stopped, catching himself. But Randy knew what he'd been about to say, and there wasn't any point in bandying about, not anymore.

Randy snorted. "As soon as he found out I…" he

reeled, just a second, "…was falling in love with Slick?" Jesus fuck, but it was even scarier out loud than in his head. He shuddered, then buried his face in his hands and sank deeper into the seat.

It was oddly reassuring to have Mitch reach over and ruffle his hair. "It's going to be all right."

"The fuck it will. I saw the way you looked when you showed up with Sam the first time. Your heart has been fucking walking around outside of you ever since." The words were still echoing in his head. *I'm in love with Slick.* He shouldn't have said it out loud, shouldn't have admitted it. He felt hollow now, and raw, like somebody had split him open and pinned him to the wall. "Fucking hell, Mitch. What the fuck am I supposed to do?"

"Calm the fuck down, for starters." Mitch reached into his pocket and fished out a cigarette, lighting it before continuing. "For what it's worth, I think the feeling is mutual."

Randy rolled his eyes. "Ethan's in flux. It's you and Sam all over again. I'm going to end up doing the Ethan-Randy equivalent of driving my rig back and forth between Omaha and Chicago for months while I wait for him to figure out where his life is headed. Which will head in a direction that does not include some fuck-by-night dipshit who plays poker and fixes engines for a living."

"Nice to see you have this all figured out already."

"Fuck off." Randy curled up against the door.

"Just be yourself with him. Don't be a dipshit. Be

like you are with Sam and me. Especially how you are with Sam."

Randy thought of what Ethan had figured out how he felt about Sam, and he wondered if his little secret had ever really been a secret at all. It made him feel cold and vulnerable. Could this day get any fucking worse?

Randy stared so hard at the door handle he wondered why it didn't melt. "I don't want to be in love with anybody."

Mitch grunted. "I know."

"I don't want to lose anybody else again."

There was a long silence. "You talkin' about me or your uncle?"

Good fucking question. Randy had no idea. "Both?"

Mitch's sigh was heavy. "I'm sorry, Skeet."

Randy shrugged. "You came back. Eventually." But it reminded him his uncle was never going to. And it made no sense, because it was so fucking long ago. Uncle Gary had been stupid, had known better than to go out where he did when he did. Randy knew this, but the loss of Gary even now sometimes hit him like a punch in the gut all over again. Like somebody had taken a sickle and sliced a huge crescent out of him, and when he let himself remember, he knew the pain had never gone away, that it never would. He'd felt a shade of it when Mitch had left, but it had been a different hurt because Randy had been an ass and had deserved it.

Something told him the pain of both Uncle Gary and Mitch combined wouldn't come close to what it would feel to have Slick go, and it would be eight times worse if he let him know. How? How the fuck had this happened? And in two fucking days? *Two fucking days.*

Mitch slowed the truck at the stop sign near the house. "I've circled the block twice. You want me to do another lap, or are you ready to head home?"

Randy remained fetal. "Just drive me out to the Mojave and leave me for the scorpions."

"How about I flush your idiot head in the toilet a few hundred times?"

"Whatever."

Randy didn't even move when Mitch slapped his ass.

He decided, as they pulled into the driveway, he'd make Slick dinner. They'd put in a movie, something stupid and funny, and they'd all hang out in the living room. Ethan would play with his kitten, and Randy wouldn't say anything about what was going to happen to his furniture or how the bathroom was going to smell like cat shit from this point on. If Slick perked up, they'd play some more poker, and Randy would rig it so he won but not enough that he'd figure it out. They'd have more sex, Ethan would sleep, and Randy would hold him in his arms, just as he had for the past two nights.

This night would be whatever it was. He'd enjoy it now, because it was here in front of him. Because Slick needed him. Yes, fucking hell, Randy loved him. But it would end. He'd remind himself every other fucking minute this was temporary. If he knew it was going to end, it wouldn't be so bad.

He hoped.

He prepared himself to face a drunk, dejected Ethan, but when the door opened before he could put his hand on the knob, once a-fucking-gain nothing was remotely the way he'd expected it to be. Ethan was freshly scrubbed, upright, and dressed to kill in a black button-down and stylish blue blazer over a pair of artfully faded and torn jeans.

Randy staggered. "Ethan?"

Ethan buttoned his cuff. "You might want to get a shower. The car will be by in half an hour."

"Car?" Randy looked more closely at Ethan—his eyes were still bloodshot, and occasionally he listed a little, but it was as if he'd forced some sort of sobriety on himself, and he was doing a good fucking job of it.

Mitch came up behind Randy. "Everything okay?"

"We're going out," Ethan said, his voice clear, calm, and assertive. "In half an hour."

"Out?" Randy felt like a fucking parrot.

"Yes." Ethan's eyes were hard. "We are going out. On the town. I've hired a car. Tonight is on me." His lips thinned. "Or Billy Herod, however you'd prefer to look at it."

"Slick?"

Ethan leaned forward, rested a hand on his shoulder, and brushed a kiss on his ear. "Please, Randy."

There it was—the vulnerability he'd known had to be there, shellacked under the resolve and temporary insanity that drove Ethan to hire a car and whatever else he'd been up to in the hour they were away.

Sam hurried over, half-dressed. "If one of you can redirect him, go right ahead."

Ethan's hand tightened on Randy's shoulder, and his lips pressed like a prayer at Randy's temple.

Randy closed his eyes and gave in. "All right. We'll go out on the town. All of us."

Ethan kissed him again and squeezed once more. Then he drew away and walked—mostly in a straight line—into the house. "Wear something sexy," he called over his shoulder, then collapsed onto the couch, where Salomé leapt up immediately onto his lap.

SOMEHOW IT BOTH surprised Randy and it didn't that Ethan had arranged for a babysitter for the cat. But when Mandy came out of the bathroom, Salomé curled against her chest, Randy's jaw fell open.

Mandy shrugged. "He called the Nugget, and they called me with his number—which, incidentally, is also yours. He asked if I'd come sit with his new kitten, and I said yes."

Randy folded his arms over his chest. "He's still gay."

"Yes, I know." She smiled down at the kitten as it batted at her face. "But he agreed to take me out gambling sometime and be my stud so I can catch a handsome whale."

Randy didn't like this either, but Slick appeared, looking so goddamn good it made Randy's teeth ache, and he forgot every word of the English language he'd ever learned for several seconds. Ethan seemed a lot more stable, but he still swayed a bit and constantly swilled water from a plastic bottle. He ran his eyes up and down Randy's black jeans and black button-down shirt in approval.

Still, Randy felt self-conscious. "I'm going to grab a jacket, and that'll make it look better. My outfit, I mean."

"It's fine now." Ethan got a good grope of his ass as he slid past him into the bathroom.

Mandy's eyebrows lifted. "That's a winner you've got there, Jansen."

Randy grunted and headed to his bedroom.

He'd be warm in his leather jacket now, but later he'd be glad for it. With and without it, though, he felt underdressed and slightly naked, and he dug around in the dish on his dresser for the silver choker and the shiny silver hoop earring that went with it. He found both, and then went fishing deeper for his leather-and-silver wristbands. He found them—and also Ethan's keys, and his ring. He laid the latter on the center of the dresser as he put the jewelry on, and then in a perverse impulse slipped it onto his finger. It would only fit on the pinky of his right hand, but it fit.

A knock came on the doorframe, and he turned to see Sam standing there. Randy couldn't help a wolf whistle. "Peaches, you look damn fine."

Sam grinned and turned his profile, letting Randy get a good view of his butt. "I'm wearing your favorite jeans."

These would be a pair Randy had picked out for him two years ago, which had artful slashes up and down the pant legs, two cut so high they required Sam to wear a thong or nothing at all. It went well with the smoky, tight-fitting gray-and-white-spackled T-shirt he'd put on, along with a leather necklace set with rainbow beads. He looked as good as Ethan, and for a second Randy let himself feel the regret that the playing around with Mitch and Sam was apparently over, at least until Ethan moved on.

The thought sent his head reeling again, and he gave himself a mental shake. *Quit being so fucking morose, you dumbass.*

"Shall we go?" Sam held out his arm, and Randy accepted it, waving goodbye to Mandy as he went with him out the front door.

Ethan was outside already, and so was Mitch, having a cigarette in the driveway. A huge, tricked-out, cream-colored stretch limo sat there too.

It was either a stretch or a mini-stretch. By no means was it a party bus or even a van, but it was decidedly a vehicle which said, "VIPs are inside." Expensive and elegant, but understated all at the same time—in short, the sort of vehicle high rollers would demand.

Sam looked devilish and proud at once. "I picked it out. It has a full bar, a phone to the driver, a sunroof, three lighting settings, and seating for eight." He pulled his iPhone out of his pocket and waved it as he waggled his eyebrows. "And it has a sound system we control with a remote."

It sounded fucking expensive. "How's Slick paying for this again?"

"Says he has a million dollars from Billy Herod, and it's the first down payment."

"Did you point out if he spends it all in one night, he's going to have to actually do what Billy wants or find some way to get that much money back?"

"He said he figures at this point he's screwed no matter what he does, so he might as well have fun." Sam shook his head. "He was scary after you left. He just sat there, something sucking him inside himself."

"Yeah." Randy watched Ethan pace along the edge of the driveway, weaving while Mitch chatted with the driver. "He can get that way."

"Then he switched on again, said he wanted to go out, Las Vegas style. He had me on the 'net looking stuff up—at first I was just glad to see him animated, but then I thought, maybe this isn't such a good idea. Holy shit, Randy. Then he almost got *mean*."

Randy turned in alarm. "He didn't hurt you?"

"Oh—God no. He just—" Sam's blush flared, and Randy knew where the rest of this was going, because there was only one time Sam looked like this. "He was…how you get. When."

When we're having sex. The image of Ethan filled his head: Ethan from the bike—*I want to fuck you, Randy*—Ethan turning on Sam, giving him orders, giving both of them orders—

Holy fuck, where did that come from?

Randy ran a hand over his face, pretty sure he was blushing too. "I got it, Peaches."

Sam looked guilty. "I should have said no, but it surprised me. I sort of went into a mode."

"It's okay, sweetheart." Randy put his arm around Sam and drew him close, kissing him briefly on the top of his head. "So, should we go paint the town red?"

"I think we're gonna paint it a little rainbow, but yeah."

Ethan lingered in the driveway until the rest of them were in the car. Randy wanted to make sure he was okay, but Ethan waved him away, and Randy caught a flash of what Sam had been talking about. It was a different Ethan, a sharper Ethan.

Yeah, it was a pretty arousing Ethan, even with all things considered.

It was that Ethan, Randy acknowledged as he climbed in after Mitch, who had drawn him from the start. Even in the shell of the man he'd watched on closed-circuit TV, this iron-coated man had been in there too. Crabtree would go on about how this was because Ethan was an ace, and though Randy only tangentially subscribed to the gangster's home-brewed philosophy, it was hard to argue against it, at least as it presented in Slick. And, yes, he was drawn to it. Like a fucking moth to a flame.

Sam explored the car, whispering *fuck yeah* as he discovered the mahogany-inlaid bar, the heavy crystal flutes for champagne, the mirrored walls, the fairy-dusted lights on the mirrored ceiling, the buttery leather seats, the thick carpet on the floors, and yes, the state-of-the-art sound system, complete, as the salesperson had promised Sam, with iPod/iPhone attachment. It was all done in varying but elegant shades of brown, reminding Randy a little bit of the Golden Nugget.

Ethan climbed in at last, and as Randy was only halfway into the vehicle, he leaned over his shoulder and spoke quietly into his ear. "What do you think?"

His breath still stank of alcohol, but he smelled of cologne too. The cologne was—just to fuck with Randy's already fucked-up head—Sam's. So he smelled of drunk man, Sam, and the spicy scent that was Ethan all at once, and it scrambled his remaining senses. "It's good."

Ethan chuckled and put his hand on Randy's hip, urging him onto a seat as Kylie Minogue, Sam's favorite artist, began to sing "I Should Be So Lucky".

Randy forced himself to get a grip and studied Ethan as they settled in together on the long seat across from the bar. "Are you okay?" He didn't look okay. He looked pale and wan, dancing between complete despair and crazy wild man.

Ethan reached for a pair of glasses and a bottle from the bar. "No, I'm not. But I can climb on top of it if you don't bring it up."

What are you doing, Slick? What are we doing? But asking that wouldn't help either of them. So he went for the nag. "Are you sure you should be drinking?"

A wry smile played at his lips as he handed the

glasses to Randy. "I'm sure I shouldn't." He unwrapped the foil and removed the wire cage from the cork deftly, revealing he was a man who knew his way around expensive champagne. Randy tried to think of the last time he'd indulged. He couldn't remember the occasion, but he'd been fairly sure it had been a five-dollar bottle of André. This wasn't Ethan's first time with the good stuff. Which meant he'd probably had it with fucking Nick. Up in some goddamned fancy fucking cabin in the fucking romantic fucking mountains.

What the fuck is wrong with me?

He tipped the flute toward Ethan, hand shaking. "Hand me that bucket when you're done, will you? I think I need to stick my head in it."

"You're nervous." Ethan filled the glasses as Randy held them out. "Why?"

"I don't fucking know." Randy passed the glasses to Mitch, who grinned at Sam as he continued to enthuse over every minute detail of the limousine. When Randy reached for two more glasses, Ethan shook his head and selected only one. He poured it, handed it to Randy then pulled his bottle of water out of his pocket.

Randy gave him a quelling glance. "Oh, so *I* will drink and get hammered, while you sober up?"

"I'm several layovers away from sober." Ethan worked the cap of the water off and took a careful drink. "I'm actually constantly fighting off the urge to stick my head out the door and vomit. Though it's difficult to say if it's nerves or alcohol. I don't think I was half as drunk before as I was hysterical." He tightened the lid then tightened it again. "Randy, I'm so goddamned scared."

And it's my fault. He put the glass down. "Ethan—"

"No. It's—" Ethan stopped, shut his eyes, and Randy could see him fighting the nausea. "I hate Crabtree. I swear, I could kill him right now, gangster or not. Hell, I think I'm half-mob myself, after this afternoon." He opened his eyes and stared unseeing into the glittering lights of the bar. "But the thing is, I'm scared because I think he might be right. I think I might actually need this. It's… I don't know. I don't quite understand it. All I know is when I came here to Vegas, I felt like I was dead already."

Now Randy was going to throw up. "Don't, Slick."

Ethan put a hand on Randy's, but kept his eyes on the bar. "I felt like that until you. And then Crabtree messed with me, and then Billy—and I was angry. And scared." His hand tightened on Randy's. "And alive."

He looked down at the water bottle, working it open with one hand, not letting go of Randy's. He took a drink, shut the bottle again, and stared down at it.

Ethan's hand felt good in his. He liked the spark he saw in him, terrified as it made Ethan. Randy didn't care for how prominently Billy and Crabtree played in this, but there didn't seem to be much to do about it now. He would have apologized for his part, but Ethan seemed more focused on whether or not he was stupid for wanting to play this batshit hand.

It made Randy wonder if he would do the same, were their situations reversed. He didn't think so. And he didn't know what to think about that.

He should say something, but everything that came to mind felt ridiculous and syrupy. He went for the least inane and saccharine comment he could muster. "You don't have to do this alone, you know."

Ethan grimaced. "I think it's ridiculous when people tell other people they need them, like it's some sort of weight they put in someone's lap. Nick used to say it, and it made me angry, though I suppose it's as you said. He actually did need me. Because he needed me to be able to be himself. I don't want to put that on anyone, because—because I don't. I've always been independent. Maybe too much so, I don't know. I have always taken care of myself. But right now—" He broke off, slightly tortured, and gripped Randy's hand so hard it hurt.

Randy ignored the pain. "Slick, don't be a dipshit. You can need somebody."

"I don't need somebody." Ethan stared right at Randy, fierce again. "I need you."

The words slammed into Randy, wrapping around him, lifting him up, making his heart rise ridiculously high in his chest.

Ethan gentled, relaxing his grip and turning his hand over in Randy's. "For now."

Another slam—this one into the wall, with a spike in it.

It must have shown on Randy's face, *goddamn it*, because Ethan flushed, then captured Randy's hand tight, even though Randy had been too stung to pull away. "I meant—"

"I know what you meant." Randy tried to be magnanimous, but those words kept ringing in his head. *For now.* He downed his champagne in one go, not really tasting it.

"I meant I don't want to burden you."

"It's okay." The lie came out a little better this time.

Ethan didn't say anything else. Which, actually, was another knife. Randy poured himself some more champagne, and soon he'd done some decent damage on the bottle, nursing his stupid inner drama as he sat awkwardly beside Ethan, watching Sam and Mitch enjoying each other at the other end of the car.

You knew this. You knew it was temporary. You've been thinking this the whole time. There's no cause to act like a fucking drama queen.

Except I didn't want it to be for now. I was hoping it was different, with him.

In short, betting on fucking black. He grunted, picked up the bottle, and finished it off.

When the car stopped, they were in the Fruit Loop on Paradise Boulevard, outside Firefly, which Randy knew right away was Sam's doing. They'd gone here the last time Sam and Mitch were in town. Of course, they always went everywhere when Sam and Mitch were here.

He'd waited so long for them to come. He'd made his peace with how he'd get them once or twice a year, and it would be fine. He'd lost Mitch completely for years. Wasn't this better, having him even just a little? Sam too? Now they were here early, and he had Ethan. His life was so fucking full it overflowed, nothing but one crisis after another—sheer chaos. Randy loved it. He knew what Slick meant about being alive. He felt alive when Sam and Mitch were here. Slick, in two days, had opened up a whole new definition of living, somehow.

For now.

He pushed past the three of them, ignored the hostess and headed straight for the bar where he peeled off a twenty and ordered two shots of whiskey. He downed one right away, then glared at the second, pouring all his crazy into it before he tipped it back too. When he slammed the glass down, the world spun nicely, and Mitch stood next to him.

"Skeet, what the fuck are you doing?"

"I'm getting drunk, Old Man." He ordered another.

Mitch put a hand on his arm to keep him from picking up the shot. "What happened in the car, Randy?"

Randy laughed. "Nothing."

I love him. I love him.

You. Stupid. Fuck.

Rage climbed over his sorrow. "Let go of my fucking drink."

Mitch moved his hand, but he was pissed. *Good,* Randy thought. He certainly didn't want to have this pity party by himself.

For now.

"You two are quite a fucking pair, you know that?" Mitch jerked his head toward the door. "Sam's back there with Ethan, who, by the way, looks worse than he did when he came home from the casino."

"I don't care." Except he did. Cursing under his breath, Randy waved at the bartender for another.

"What the fuck happened?"

Randy smiled a drunken, sarcastic grin. "He told me he needed me. For now."

Mitch threw another twenty on the bar, grabbed Randy's collar and hauled him bodily out of the restaurant, ignoring Randy's drunken cries of outrage. When he came to Sam, who was speaking earnestly to Ethan whom he'd backed up against a wall, Mitch gently brushed his husband aside and collected Ethan with his other hand.

He dragged them both outside and stuffed them into the limo, Ethan first, Randy second. Leaning through the doorway, he glared at them both.

"You will both fucking stay in here until you sort this out." He aimed a finger at Ethan. "You, get your head out of your ass." He turned the finger on Randy. "You, quit being clever and fucking let him see who you really are."

"I *did*," Randy snarled. "That's the problem—"

The door slammed shut, and the two of them were left alone.

CHAPTER TWELVE

H OW, RANDY WONDERED, as he sat there awkwardly with Ethan, had it come to this? It had been so good, and then Slick had said "for now," and it was over. For Randy the worst part was realizing how fucked up his thinking had become. It wasn't about Slick but about him and what he wanted. The lump in his throat returned, starting to feel permanent.

He'd wanted this thing with Ethan to be something real. He wanted what Sam and Mitch had, and he hadn't acknowledged it until Slick showed up. Somehow his heart was set on having Mitch and Sam's kind of relationship with Slick. He didn't know how to turn the feeling off. He tried to push it away, but despite the seating for eight, there wasn't room enough in the limo, not for the loneliness he had tried so hard not to feel.

Randy had played the wrong game, gone on tilt, taken his mind off the odds and the pot. He'd imagined being with Ethan would make things okay.

God, the fucking irony. Everyone was always on him to stop being such an ass—here was Mitch, too, saying show him who you are—and he already had, and look how it had turned out. *That's why I'm fucking alone,* he wanted to shout out the window.

But he didn't want to be alone, not anymore. Even right now, in the middle of this.

He was so fucked.

Ethan shifted again. "I'm sorry, I—" His voice was rough. Every hurt, and it showed. It was hell, just looking at him. "I wanted to have a night with you… I wanted—I didn't mean—" The tower of Ethan started to crumble. "I'm sorry, Randy, so sorry—"

"Just shut up, Slick." Randy wearily rolled his heart over and handed Ethan the knife, because what the hell else was he supposed to do? Drive it in himself? "Stop talking and get over here."

"This is what I meant. I don't want to need you, don't want to—but I can't—"

Randy moved over to the seat beside Ethan and took him in his arms. "I know, baby. I know."

"I didn't mean—I don't—I don't—"

Randy shut him up by taking his mouth in a kiss, pushing him onto the seat, then onto the floor. He kissed him deep, and he held him, and that was all. They just lay there, mouths pressed together, alternating between kissing and breathing. Randy could smell the cleaner they'd used on the carpet, the richness of the leather, gin, and Slick. Mostly Slick.

If you put all your chips in, you might win it all.

He didn't want to. But he started to think he'd already put himself all-in. He had to see it through to the river now. He'd been committed since the blind, which in hindsight was too fucking huge. Bad odds.

But fucking hell, what a sweet pot.

Ethan pressed his forehead against Randy's. "I wanted to take you out. I wanted to have a night out with you, a good one where I was strong. I didn't want to break down."

Just lay down the cards. "I haven't been fucking you and putting you up in my house and making myself sick worrying I've fucked you over by getting you involved with my stupid gangster friends because I hoped you'd stop breaking down." He paused, then corrected himself. "Okay, I didn't mean I want you to be upset. I mean you just do that, Slick. Being with you is like riding a tiger, but hey."

Ethan pulled back and regarded Randy, slightly scared, as if they'd finally come to something that had been bothering him but he'd also hoped to avoid.

Randy felt a little better. This game did have a double blind, after all.

Ethan didn't look any happier about it than he was. "Why *are* you doing this? Is it..." he grimaced, "...pity?"

"No." *Oh fuck, oh fuck, oh fuck. Stop talking, right now.*

Ethan leaned in. "Why, then?"

Make a joke. Make a smart remark. Distract him. Kiss him. Fuck him. Just do not answer the question, do not fucking answer the question. Because that is so fucking all-in, and this is not the time for it, you idiot.

But Randy was tired. He'd had two glasses of good champagne and enough whiskey to loosen his tongue.

As a compromise, he shut his eyes and said the stupid, deadly words, sick and light and beautifully free, all at once, like he was jumping off the top of the Stratosphere.

"Because I love you."

He went sailing over the edge, and the world expanded before him, and he embraced the fleeting moment then prepared himself for the fall—

A cool, shaking hand grabbed his chin, and when he didn't open his eyes, a finger pulled his eyelid back forcibly, and Ethan was looking down at him, shocked and wild. "If you're making a joke…"

Randy snorted and pulled his head down to try to free himself. But Ethan held him fast, his voice stronger as he spoke again, though he did let Randy's eye close.

"We've known each other *two days*."

"I think it took about two minutes." This actually wasn't so bad. Once you jumped, you could just keep going over the edge, no problem.

"*Randy*."

Randy gave up and opened his eyes. "Look. You don't have the corner on the market for feeling wounded."

Ethan's hand tightened on Randy's chin. "But I am *so fucked up*."

Randy didn't dignify that one with a response. He waited as Slick caught up.

"You don't pity me." Ethan looked like he was waiting for the rug to be pulled out from under him. "You— you…"

He couldn't finish. Randy sighed. Jesus, this bitch was work. "Love you." He decided to take another trip over the edge, to see if he still had the bungee cord on. "And, incidentally, those feelings are probably for more than just now."

"Shit." Ethan went pale. "*Shit.*"

Randy was sadistic enough to enjoy himself, but not for too long. "It's okay." This time he meant it.

"I didn't mean—I didn't know—"

Randy touched Ethan's face. "Shut up, Slick. You fuck it up when you talk."

"What do we do, then?"

"Go eat dinner. Go clubbing. Go gambling. Go make you cry at the fountains again. Go home and fuck like rabbits. Then tomorrow, I guess, you go work for Billy Herod, and we wait for our shot to break Crabtree's kneecaps."

Ethan stroked Randy's cheek. It was a tender gesture, but Randy could tell he was looking for a loophole, a catch, something to prove this to be the farce he knew it had to be. *Can't pull back the blind, baby.*

Randy grabbed Ethan's fingers and kissed them. "Come on. Let's go party."

Then Randy took the hand of the man he loved, the fucked-up, disbelieving man he loved, and led him off gently toward the restaurant.

ETHAN SPENT THE better part of dinner trying to decide if what he thought had happened in the limo on the floor with Randy actually had happened, or if he'd imagined it.

He'd gone into the restaurant in a sort of shock, feeling as he had that first night when Randy had led him to the bar at Herod's. He couldn't find his footing, and in lieu of any other real option, he followed the others along. Mitch and Sam had already claimed a table and were working their way through appetizers and a pitcher of sangria, and they greeted Ethan and Randy warmly, as if Mitch hadn't hauled them both bodily out to the limo half an hour before. Mitch poured a glass of wine for Randy and water for Ethan, and Sam chatted animatedly about the appetizers.

Ethan had no real idea what he ordered—there was shrimp, he thought, but he remembered chicken too. He spent most of the time reeling quietly. Randy could not be in love with him. Not only did it not make any sense, it didn't fit. Randy would never admit he loved him, not after the idiot he'd been so many damn times—

He kept seeing Randy's face, eyes shut as he said the words, a man laying down his sword. Except with Randy it wouldn't be the metaphor. He was laying down his cards.

Ethan didn't know what he was supposed to *do* with them.

Randy didn't seem nervous anymore. He talked with Mitch about trucking and asked Sam about the tour of the hospital he was due to have on Wednesday. Sam tried to include Ethan, but every conversation was a landmine, and between this and *I love you* still ringing in his head, he kept faltering. Randy rescued him every time, deflecting with a joke and change of subject, giving Ethan space. He put a hand on Ethan's back when they finished and headed to the car.

"It's really bugging you, isn't it? God, I'm glad I said it, then. It's about damn time you had the angst over it."

Ethan glared at him. "You *are* making it up, aren't you? You're pulling my leg. You just said—" But he couldn't come up with a reason why Randy would say such a thing. Ever.

Randy held up his hands. "Baby, I would not fucking joke about that."

"But we've only known each other two days. This isn't *rational*."

Randy pointed at Mitch and Sam, who stood with their arms threaded around one another, Sam's at Mitch's neck, Mitch's at Sam's waist as they nuzzled noses beneath the streetlight. "When they arrived in Vegas two years ago, they had only been together two nights, since Mitch had picked Sam up on a lark in Iowa. Prior to that they'd had one fuck in the alley behind Sam's aunt and uncle's pharmacy and one date over Mexican food. It was more accurate to measure their relationship in hours. They were so far fucking gone by the time they got to me, it was scary. It's not a rational subject area."

Ethan had nothing to say to that, so he followed the others into a car. This time the music was Lady Gaga's "Bad Romance", and Sam danced on his seat as Ethan shut the door.

"We should have gotten a van." Sam lifted his arms and moved his whole upper body to the beat. "Then we could dance while we rode around."

Randy looked up at the ceiling and grinned as he pushed the button on the moonroof. "Come over here, Peaches."

Sam slid up Randy's body before they began to dance together, only half their bodies visible as they stood in the narrow square of space. Randy dipped down, his black shirt gaping open as he crouched and told Mitch to crank the music. He braced against Ethan as the car went around the corner and made *up, up* motions at Mitch as he turned the system up louder and louder. As Ethan thought his eardrums would surely split open, Randy gave the *okay* sign, and rose.

The car shifted again, though, and he gripped Ethan's knee to catch himself from falling. He grinned and gave Ethan's leg a quick feel before sliding to his feet to join Sam in dancing in the desert night.

Ethan saw the glint of silver on his finger.

Nick's ring. Randy wore Nick's ring.

It was a silver circle, but it had a specific thickness and width to it, some simple markings on the band that shimmered when they caught the light. Nick's ring. And Randy had put it on with the rest of his outfit. As a trophy? A taunt? A warning? To himself, or to Ethan?

Randy crouched down again and looked at Ethan. He shouted to be heard over the music. "Where are we headed, Slick?"

"I don't know." Ethan's gaze fell to Randy's hand.

Randy met Ethan's gaze, holding it. Ethan waited to see what he would say, what he would do, what excuse he would give. But he only picked up the phone that called the driver and cupped his hand around the mouthpiece as he shouted some instruction. Then he put the phone in its cradle, his gaze grazing Ethan once more as he returned to the moonroof. Seconds later his hands reappeared and his leather jacket fell in a heap on the floor. His arms rose through the hole, and he began to dance.

It could have been a Vegas attraction, sitting in a limo full of pounding music as Sam and Randy undulated through the moonroof, only their bottom halves visible, their hips swinging and thrusting in time to the beat, their laughter filtering down. Gaga sang, the music swelled. Ethan took in Sam's slender, swaying body. Randy's muscles were more formed, but when the pair of them stood there, you realized they were not dissimilar. Randy had a few inches in height on Sam and more hours of heavy labor and at the gym, but beyond this they were a study in masculine beauty from the waist down.

The music was raunchy and strong and proud and perfect, and it set something free inside Ethan, something dark and primal but pure too. The Ethan who managed other people's money, waiting patiently while his lover lived another life he did not share with him— that Ethan fell away, and a new Ethan came forward. It was a man who had always been there, who liked hard sex, money, and games with gangsters. An Ethan who enjoyed men dancing before him, for him, in the car he had hired with money given to him by the mob. As the music banged around him, he gave in to it, to all of it.

I'm a free bitch, baby.

Mitch also enjoyed the sight his husband and friend made. Ethan hadn't spoken much to Mitch, but he'd pegged him as a gruff, quiet man of uncomplicated pleasures. He didn't doubt Mitch and Sam did fine in the bedroom, but Ethan hadn't thought much about it until now. He'd assumed Mitch was a rather vanilla sort of man, as simple in his sexual tastes as he was everything else.

He wouldn't assume that now. Even in his jeans and cream-colored button-down, Mitch looked like the highest of high rollers, the king of Crabtree's deck of men, arms extended over the back of his seat, leg kicked up over his knee, his body open and relaxed as he watched Sam and Randy dance. He enjoyed it, a lot. His face made it clear he planned to enjoy more than just dancing, a primal sort of hunger emanating from him.

"I would rather have taught Sam to drive stick myself." Mitch spoke loudly because of the music, and he kept his eyes on the dancing.

Ethan didn't know what he was supposed to say to that. Then he remembered what Crabtree had said. "Why haven't you taught him before now, then?"

Mitch drew a beer he'd rested against his thigh up to his lips and took a swig. "Because it didn't seem like a big deal."

"He can't drive while you're here in Vegas, not without knowing how to drive a stick."

"I would have bought him a car."

But there was a testiness about the way he said it that gave Ethan a strange window into the man, and he realized Randy was right. Poker wasn't cards. Poker was reading people.

"How many times have you said it—that this time, while you're here, you'll buy a car he can drive?" He saw the truth of it in Mitch's wince. Ethan pushed on gently. "He didn't want a car. He just wanted to know how to drive the truck." *Like you and Randy.*

Mitch flattened his lips but said nothing more, just watched his husband and his friend dance.

Sam dipped down, face flushed and hair wind-blown, smiling, but when he saw Mitch's face, he paused. His smile didn't die, but it changed, his expression soft and sultry at once. It was as if they were speaking a silent language, sliding into the roles of a game Ethan didn't understand but was drawn to all the same.

Sam kept his eyes on Mitch, putting an open, splayed hand on Randy's hip, his fingers resting on Randy's waistband, his thumb reaching all the way toward the line of Randy's fly. Randy's dancing stopped. His hand came down and landed on Sam's hair, fingers curling into it as his hips began to sway again.

He moved Sam's hand closer to the growing outline of his cock in his jeans.

The two gestures were so naturally erotic they froze

Ethan in place, and he waited for the rest. But nothing else happened because the music ended, and as the song changed, Sam woke from his trance, turned to Ethan, and froze. "I'm sorry." He hurriedly pulled his hand away from Randy.

The thoughts came at him not in a sequence but in clusters, clouds blooming in his mind, whole truths and images and choices. Whatever this was between the three of them, it was more than just friendship. It was mostly between Sam and Mitch. Randy played along because it was fun and because he loved them both, each in their own way, and loved the two of them as a couple.

The hint of pleasure Sam gave Randy was nothing compared to the show he gave his spouse, a show he had clearly given before and would be happy to—maybe even needed to give—again. Mitch really enjoyed Sam with another man. Probably some of it was that the man was Randy, but somehow Ethan was pretty sure a total stranger could fondle Sam or offer himself for fondling, and Mitch would find it just as erotic. Maybe more so.

Ethan knew Randy liked it. As Randy's fingers kneaded Sam's hair, Ethan understood that Randy missed it. Knowing Randy, this was another way he remained outside, with them but not of them, loving them and loved by them, but he was not of them, not completely. He was Crabtree's joker, blending in anywhere, never belonging, always alone.

How had Ethan been blind to it? Randy wasn't a joker. He only pretended to be one. He wasn't happy-go-lucky. He wasn't a court jester.

Randy was an ace. Which meant Randy, too, was alone.

Except with me.

Ethan thought about what Randy had confessed, about his wearing the ring, and then he remembered the way Randy had pushed into Sam's hand, the way he'd looked naked and tied down over the bench. How raw and vulnerable he was when he said *I love you.*

Sliding forward on the seat, Ethan took Sam's hand and placed it on Randy—right on the long, hard shape of Randy's cock.

For a moment they stayed frozen in place. Sam tracked Ethan, wide-eyed but with banked lust, his countenance soft and sultry. Randy's hand kneaded gently against Sam's hair, and Ethan could suddenly see him, standing above, looking out at Las Vegas as his lover and his friend knelt beneath him. He imagined Randy's surprise and confusion warring with desire.

Ethan released Sam's hand and freed the button of Randy's fly, then took Sam's hand and used it to tug down the zipper. The dark blue of Randy's briefs appeared, and Ethan let go of Sam again to pull the waistband of Randy's jeans and then his briefs down. Desire pooled in Sam's eyes as Randy's thick cock came into view. The smell of it surrounded Ethan, sweat and sex and the lingering scent of his soap. Sam's lips parted, wet, plump, eager, and Ethan kept his eyes on them as he closed his hand over Randy's on Sam's head and pushed him forward, kneeling and using his other hand to guide Randy's penis into the young man's open mouth.

The whimper Sam made as his lips slid down Randy's foreskin was as erotic as the sight. It was wickedly beautiful to guide Randy's cock into another man's mouth, but half the turn-on was Sam. He sucked the organ with deep pleasure, face twisted into subtle expressions of pleasure, lust, and, most subtle of all, submission. He drew Randy in to the root and pressed slim hands to Randy's hips with more joy than Ethan had ever witnessed in anything. Guiding Sam into a rhythm with one hand, Ethan curled Sam's other hand against Randy's balls, urging him to stroke. As Sam drew Randy down, Ethan leaned forward and opened his mouth over the bump of Randy's pelvis, licking and sucking the point as he urged Sam's fingers to Randy's entrance.

There was a brief gasp, then a cry from above— Ethan pushed the tip of Sam's finger into Randy's sphincter and held it there, then opened his own mouth over Randy's pelvic bone, sliding his tongue all the way down to the base of his cock, brushing briefly against Sam's lips as he drew back.

Randy reached down with his other hand and took a great fistful of Ethan's hair as his hips bucked three times roughly into Sam. His balls tightened in Sam's and Ethan's hands as he came into Sam's mouth, and Sam's throat worked as he sucked Randy down. Lips wet, swollen and rimmed with white, Sam smiled shyly at Ethan before he withdrew onto Mitch's lap. Ethan caught one steamy glimpse of Mitch pulling Sam toward him for a carnal, open-mouthed kiss, and then Randy collapsed into the car and into Ethan, pushing him to the floor, falling on top of him as he took hold of Ethan by both ears and kissed him hard.

It wasn't actually a kiss—he fucked Ethan's mouth with his tongue, grinding his fading erection against Ethan's rigid one. His pants were now above his knees, but he didn't seem to care, just undulated his bare ass as he thrust his tongue over and over again into Ethan's throat. Then he rested his forehead on Ethan's cheek.

"Slick." His hands tightened on Ethan's ears. "Slick, why—? Why did you—?"

"Because I wanted to." Ethan reached around and took firm hold of the flesh of Randy's ass. "That okay?"

"Fuck yes."

Randy shivered as Ethan started to massage his naked skin. "You seemed to need it. All of you."

Randy's hands shifted to the carpet on either side of Ethan's head as he continued the massage. In the background, just above the music, Ethan could hear Sam's gasps and tortured whimpers, and his cock hummed at the thought of what Mitch must be doing.

Breathing hard, Randy twitched as Ethan nudged a fingertip against his entrance. "Sam likes to be told what to do. A lot."

"I could tell." Ethan pushed the tip of his finger inside. Randy turned his face into Ethan's neck. "You do too, sometimes."

"When it's you." Randy hissed as Ethan pushed in

deeper. But he shook his head when Ethan started to withdraw. "No. Don't."

"You need lube."

"I need you, baby. Push it in me."

Ethan held his finger in place. "You're wearing Nick's ring."

Randy lifted an eyebrow. "I'm wearing *your* ring."

"You're wearing the ring Nick gave me. Why?"

"Push your finger into me, Slick."

Aroused almost to the point of pain, Ethan fucked gently inside as Randy's eyes closed and his face melted into a tortured ecstasy. He was tight and hot, and this had to burn, but Randy flexed his muscles and took Ethan in deeper, into the furnace of him, his mouth parting and his breath coming on a gasp as he humped Ethan lightly.

Ethan continued to gently finger him. "Why are you wearing it?"

Randy bent to rest on Ethan's shoulders. "I don't know. But I can make up a reason, if you want."

Ethan didn't care about the ring anymore. He bit back a moan at how tight and hot Randy felt. He wanted to pull down his trousers and thrust his cock inside Randy instead, to watch him take it in. He was just about ready to do it when the car stopped, and Randy groaned and sank onto Ethan's neck. "We're here, unfortunately."

"Where's here?" Ethan started to withdraw his finger, but Randy kept it trapped inside, clenching around it.

"The Mirage." He laughed. "I thought we could do with a distraction."

"Hmm." Ethan pushed into Randy.

Randy hummed and rolled his hips. "You want to fuck me first, baby? I've got lube and condoms in my jacket pocket. You want to roll me over and fuck me on the floor, let Mitch and Sam watch you take me?"

"I'd like to fuck you while we stood in the moon-roof."

"I like your finger in my ass. Your tongue would be good too. I like the way you look when you find your-self, when you get all elegant and strong and in control."

Ethan nipped at him. "You want me to tell you what to do? You want me to take control?"

"You already have all the control, baby. You've had it all along. You just need to find your footing, and you'll have the whole world by the balls, same as you do me."

As Ethan lay there, he could see the truth of what Randy said, but he knew he wasn't ready, not yet. He saw the shape of that self, but he didn't know quite how to use it.

Randy hadn't been lying. He did love him. In a strange, beautifully Randy way.

Ethan wished he could say he loved him back. He thought maybe he might. But the Ethan who could do that was as nebulous at this moment as the Ethan who could take control. It would take time to discover both.

Ethan let out a heavy breath. "I want to see the Mi-rage."

Randy smiled a sideways grin and brushed a kiss across Ethan's lips before pulling up his jeans.

The Mirage was full of people as usual, but Randy didn't care—he loved showing it off to someone for the first time, and he loved showing Slick best of all.

Ethan didn't say anything, but Randy read his face, and he could tell Ethan was enchanted. The fountains were beautiful, the walkways romantic. Slick was even impressed by the volcano.

When Ethan readily agreed to sit down for a few hands of poker, Randy suspected he did so mostly because he enjoyed the atmosphere.

They played for an hour, because Sam and Mitch would be bored if they took much longer. Mitch only did slots and blackjack, and Sam didn't do anything at all. He hated throwing money away and could not get the hang of poker for the life of him. So they waited at the bar while Ethan sat at a mid-level table with five hundred dollars' worth of chips. Randy wanted to see Slick at one of the no-limit, high-end tables, because that was where the real players were. But Ethan wasn't ready yet.

Ethan did fairly well. He still stayed in too long, and when they finally stood to leave, he was sixty dollars lighter than he'd been when he'd started, largely because of overplaying his hand.

"Half the hands I lost were to you," he complained when they went to cash in.

"What, you want me to throw the hands for you? You've got to learn to bluff. You need to learn to read tells too, but at the very least you need to start putting on a better face."

Ethan gave him a look, part frustration, part irritation. "I *am* bluffing."

Randy sighed. "You sit there and you go stone-faced, sure. But that's not bluffing. Bluffing is when you pretend you have a decent hand and you have shit. Or you pretend you have a shit hand or a medium hand when you have pocket aces. Decide what it is you want, and then act like you already have it. You play the table, Slick, or it will play you."

"There's so much to remember."

"You'll get better. You're already ridiculously better than you should be a couple days in. Remember, poker is people with cards put in. Don't worry. You'll be taking over the town within a few weeks, I'm sure." He patted Ethan's back then let his hand slide down to his butt. "I'm just hoping you still want me on your arm once you're a big shot."

Ethan dislodged his arm and took hold of Randy's own ass. "That depends, Ace, on how good you are."

It didn't hit him until they were almost at the bar. "Ace. Did you just give me a nickname?"

Ethan feigned indifference. "What if I did?"

"If you did, you took your damn time about it." He gave Ethan a dubious look. "*Ace*, though."

Ethan smiled, a wicked, knowing little gesture that sent a shiver down Randy's spine. "What, you don't want the word to get out?"

"I thought I was a joker." Randy couldn't maintain his usual sass.

Ethan leaned in close. "You're an ace, pretending to be a joker in self-defense." He brushed a kiss across Randy's lips. He had a few chips in his hand and turned them over idly between his fingers, glancing down at them thoughtfully. "You know, these seem heavier than the ones at Herod's."

"That's because Billy is cheap. He doesn't use professional weight. Drives Crabtree crazy, and I have to say, I'm not fond of it much myself. The logo is stupid too."

Ethan studied them. "It's the exclamation point that puts it over the top. *Herod's* would be better."

Randy threaded their hands together over the chips. "Let's go find Sam and Mitch."

As soon as they got to the bar, Sam jumped them. "*Oh my God,* Randy—Madame Tussauds has *Kylie.* And Lady Gaga, but—*Kylie.*"

"Well, we have to go then." Randy laughed as Sam squealed and pelted his forehead and cheeks with kisses. He glanced at Ethan. "Unless we have other plans?"

"Sounds fine to me," Ethan said, but he watched Sam's hands on Randy's shoulders, and Randy suspected he was flashing back to the scene in the limo.

Randy was too.

The ride to the wax museum was G-rated, Sam effusing and shaking as if he were about to meet the *real* Kylie. Once at the museum, they ambled about trying to figure out where the hell she was, and then they rounded the corner and she appeared, petite and blonde and swathed in white fabric and silver glitter, her left hand reaching for the stars as her right hand drew the microphone closer to her mouth. Sam made incoherent sounds for several minutes, and then Mitch nudged him up beside the statue to take pictures of Sam hugging and kissing Ms. Minogue. The same treatment was given to Lady Gaga and Madonna, and then they simply wandered around, taking it all in.

Ethan surprised Randy by having Sam take a photo of himself next to Lady Diana and Johnny Depp as Captain Jack Sparrow.

Randy raised an eyebrow. "You have a thing for princesses and pirates?"

Ethan put his arm around Sam. "I'm developing a taste for them, yes."

Mitch fell in beside Randy as they walked to the car and admired the fine set of backsides ahead of them. "Where to now?"

Randy beamed. "Stratosphere?"

"No." Sam looked over Ethan's shoulder to give Randy a glare.

Randy sighed. "Sam, you don't have to go out in the open-air observation. You can stay in the interior room."

Sam set his jaw. "No. It shakes. I don't want to ever go up there again."

Randy shrugged. "Krave? Or we could shoot pool or scare up trouble at the Watering Hole."

"We're going to Herod's." Ethan slid his hand down Sam's back before letting it rest on his hip.

Randy raised his eyebrows but said nothing, just glanced at Mitch, who showed no real reaction outside of enjoying the way Ethan's thumb kept sneaking beneath the waistband of Sam's jeans.

When Randy asked Ethan what this was about as they climbed into the limo, Ethan refused to answer. "Have a drink. I'd hate for you to sober up."

Randy reached for the whiskey. "You seem to have made all your layovers to sober-land."

Ethan touched his temple. "I have a bit of a headache, so I think so."

Randy handed him another bottle of water which Ethan sipped as they rode to Herod's. Ethan led them through the front doors, nodding at the floor manager who smiled at him warmly. He nodded again at the attendant who came over with, of all things, a massive tray of chips. And wasn't it slick how Slick pulled out a hundred-dollar toke and passed it to the attendant?

"Come on." Ethan motioned them toward the table games. "I want to play."

"Poker?" Randy asked, totally on board with this.

"Craps."

Randy made a face. "You can't be serious."

But Ethan was serious, and he couldn't be dissuaded, either. He handed chips to everyone, tucking Randy's into his pocket when he wouldn't take them.

Sam accepted his share, but he didn't seem happy about it. "I don't like gambling. It makes me feel bad when I lose."

"The chips were free." Ethan passed a toke to the dealer before he placed fifty dollars on the Pass Line and twenty-five on the Field. "Think of it as a big board game."

Randy glared at Ethan. "What the hell is this? The roulette wheel speech applies to craps, you know. Exchange the wheel for dice, and it's the same damn thing."

"Better odds in craps." Ethan cheered as the roller reared back to throw.

"Still a house advantage."

Randy scowled when the roller hit a nine and everyone cheered again, especially those who had played the Field.

Ethan collected his winnings and placed another bet.

Sam and Mitch, the traitors, played too, and soon everyone but Randy was having a great time. He was merciless when, five rolls later, the roller sevened-out.

Ethan waved him away. "We're up fifty overall."

"You know this damn table here, Billy's table, used to be a beautiful fountain? Had a statue of a horned demon in it, made of marble. Or something. The water came out of his nostrils." Randy crossed his arms over his chest. "They tore it down so they could get more goddamned slots and craps tables in."

Ethan looked intrigued, not chastised. "Do they still have the fountain?"

"Just the demon statue, I think, and maybe not even

that. The demon wasn't wearing pants, so you know. They gave him a fig leaf, but if you stood to the side, you got quite a view. From behind, you got a fine full monty. And it's gone, all for craps."

"Excellent. I'll get Billy to put it back."

Randy snorted. "You won't get Billy to put it back."

Ethan's smile turned wicked. "You want to make a bet, Ace?"

Okay, the nickname still caught him unawares and undid him more than he'd like. He shifted uneasily. "You're getting pretty cocky here, Slick."

Ethan's eyes danced. "You have objections to my cockiness?"

"Oh, I love every cocky bit of you," Randy replied, but it was more of an endearment than a rejoinder. Ethan took his hand, knowing he had won. Goddamn it.

Ethan redeemed himself when he led them to the poker room. "I want to know about the other games. How do you play them?"

Randy pointed to the tables as he spoke. "They're all different. Pai Gow, Seven-Card Stud, Omaha Hi/Lo— that's about it. Mostly it's Hold 'Em, limit or no-limit."

"And what's the room back there?" Ethan indicated an ornate set of doors beneath a stained-glass window depicting men with cards.

"Billy's Room. Billy Senior, mind you. Invite-only in there, Crabtree issuing. The rake alone can bring in more than the rest of the casino some nights. Big, big games happen there. Thousands of dollars a hand."

Ethan stared thoughtfully at the door. "Billy didn't mention it this afternoon. Have you been there?"

"God, no."

Ethan raised an eyebrow at him. "You don't want to?"

"If I had that much money, I wouldn't play poker with it."

Ethan elbowed him gently. "You haven't answered me about the bet."

"You mean about the statue?" Randy rolled his eyes. "Sure. What's the bet?"

"That I can get the fountain back."

"By when?"

Ethan considered. "A month."

It wasn't going to happen, ever, but Randy was feeling particularly sadistic. "Two weeks."

Ethan smiled. "Done."

Why was the smile getting to him so much tonight? "Terms, Slick. What are we betting to win?"

Ethan frowned. "I don't know. Money?"

"Money is so boring. How about a lap dance for the winner, from the loser?"

Ethan's gaze hooded. "That sounds acceptable."

Yeah, because we both win no matter what. Talk about getting the best of it. Randy held out his hand, Ethan shook it, and the bet was made.

"Where did Mitch and Sam go?" Ethan glanced around. "I thought they were with us."

"We headed toward poker, and they figured it was time to entertain themselves. My guess would be the

River."

"The bar." Ethan stuck his hands in his pockets and rolled on his heels for a second, thinking. Then he looked at Randy. "Well. Do you want to go find them?"

Randy shrugged. "I'm just following you around, Slick, waiting for orders."

Ethan's eyebrows lifted. "Oh, is that how it is? Why didn't you say so?" He took Randy's arm and led him through the tables.

"Where are we going, Ethan?" Randy asked, his voice full of warning.

"To play a game, Ace."

"I'm not playing craps."

"No, you're playing roulette."

"The fuck I am." Randy tried to pull away.

Ethan didn't let him go. "You're playing. I'm buying the chips. And you're playing."

Why the hell did Ethan have to get all dominant over *this*? Why couldn't he be ordering them back to the house for something interesting? But no, they had to play *roulette*.

Adding insult to injury, they sat at Tyler's table— the same dealer who had taken Ethan's last five dollars. Ethan didn't seem to care as he placed two hundred stacks on the table and ordered, with an authority that made Randy sit up straighter, two colors. Tyler even added a "Yes, sir," as he scooped up the regular casino chips and traded them out for blue and yellow roulette tokens.

Randy took up the yellow. "I want it noted I'm here

under duress."

Ethan patted his hand. "Yes, dear."

Randy had to work not to shudder. There was no fucking way he could let Slick know how those little endearments got to him.

He clinked the chips in his stack for a few seconds before pulling off a third of them. Ten dollars on the third twelve, ten on odd, and then in afterthought tucked the rest of what was in his hand on the six line of 19 and 22.

Ethan, who had put twenty dollars on the first twelve and twenty on black, raised his eyebrows at Randy's choices. "You just bet against yourself. Either 19-24 or 25-36 is going to lose."

"Oh, they'll probably both lose. It'll be 14 red. You'll be out, and so will I. And there goes the better portion of two hundred dollars."

"Yes, but it's Billy's money." Ethan leaned on the rail and looked curiously at Randy as Tyler let the ball fly. "It's that you hate to lose, isn't it?"

"I don't like anything where you can't get the best of it."

"In other words, a game you don't control."

Randy had to admit it was the truth. He shrugged and stared at the wheel, clinking his chips again as he waited for the ball to land.

Ethan paid the wheel no attention. He spoke quietly into Randy's ear. "So when you told me what you told me earlier—was it to gain control?"

Randy's nervous fingers stopped. The whole room

seemed to stop. His chest felt heavy, like someone was sitting on it. Fucking hell, *this* question was the trap. He scrambled to come up with a safe answer, but mostly his thoughts banged around, a dozen ostriches fighting for the same hole to stick their heads in. *This isn't a game* was the best he could come up with, but it would buy him a few seconds while Ethan rephrased. He knew what Ethan asked, and why. And he knew he couldn't let Ethan think he'd said the words to try to control him.

The ball bounced around the wheel as the wheel spun on and on and on.

Randy ran his thumb along the silver ring, and then, because he didn't trust himself to speak, simply shook his head.

The ball landed.

"32 red." Tyler placed the dolly.

Ethan leaned closer and brushed a kiss against Randy's ear. It was the barest of touches, but it made Randy's whole body tingle, and he had to briefly shut his eyes.

Ethan slid onto his chair. "You won."

Randy snorted. "Yeah. One bet, at two to one. I lost the five to one and the even odds. I made twenty but lost twenty-five. And you lost forty. No black again, either, I might point out."

"It'll come around."

"It *doesn't have to.*"

Ethan gave him an enigmatic smile. "But I'm fairly sure it will. Eventually." He nodded to Tyler and rose from the table.

Randy followed. "And in the meantime, how much money are you going to lose for even odds?"

"How much fun are you going to deny yourself because you hate to lose?"

Randy waved an irritated hand at him and stormed away.

It was a stupid, dramatic exit, and he knew it was stupid the second he did it, but the hell if he was going to sit there and let Tyler gloat. It didn't help that Ethan's little jibe had caught. It had caught and torn, and it felt like every step he took away from Ethan exposed the raw panic he'd been denying ever since the limo. It was still there, buried under irritation and denial, and he couldn't run from it, not even inside the casino.

So he stopped next to a line of video poker machines and waited. It didn't take long. Ethan didn't say anything as he came up behind him, simply put a hand on his arm.

Randy glowered at the blinking lights of the machine in front of him. "You know, just because Crabtree's run off doesn't mean you need to take his place as the resident manipulator." Ethan still didn't say anything, which was all the more annoying. Randy nodded over his shoulder at the tables. "You look pretty stupid sitting there championing fate and risk at the very table where you bet your last dollar before you were going to go out to your car and blow your brains out."

The thought, as always, made him feel sick and cold,

and he stopped talking.

Ethan stroked his arm. "I didn't know what I was supposed to do, having figured out I wanted to live after all but with nothing left except the car and the gun."

Randy twitched, shaking Ethan off. "Don't. Don't even talk about it, Slick. I shouldn't have brought it up. I'm sorry I did."

"I'm not." Ethan reclaimed his hand. "I was sitting there wishing—praying, even—that something would happen, so I wouldn't have to go through with it."

Randy let out a shuddering breath and tipped his head up toward the ceiling, which was suddenly blurry. He didn't say anything, but when Ethan's hand squeezed his, he squeezed back. "Let's go home."

Ethan led him to the River, where they collected Mitch and Sam and headed to the limo. Mitch and Sam seemed to have picked up on the shift in the tenor of the evening—Sam played quieter music, and they sat in the same seats they'd begun in, Sam snuggling next to Mitch, Randy sitting rigid next to Ethan, softening when Ethan began rubbing gentle circles in the small of his back. He didn't linger at the curb, though, when the limo stopped—and after saying hello and goodbye to Mandy—he headed for the bathroom.

He washed his face and brushed his teeth, the usual before-bed rituals, avoiding his own reflection while he did it all. When he was done, he shut off the light and went into his room, peeled off his clothes, put on a pair of knit pants, and climbed into bed, where he drew the covers to his waist and stared up at the ceiling. He didn't know what everyone else was doing or what they'd think of his absence, and he didn't care.

Much.

He didn't know how much time had passed. All he knew was that the door, which he hadn't fully shut, opened, and he turned, defensive and ready to face whoever it was. But no one stuck their head in. Randy was frowning and trying to decide what the hell that had been about when there was a soft *rip, rip* beside his bed, and he turned in time to see Salomé appear beside his head.

She mewed in inquiry, then came forward, purring.

Randy turned on his side to stroke her head. "Hey, sweetheart. What are you doing in here?"

She mewed again, purring louder as she nuzzled his hand. When he stopped petting, she reached out and nudged his nose with her paw, then, in afterthought, came forward and licked it too.

Unable to help himself, Randy laughed and held still, enjoying it in a weird little way.

They held a quiet communion for a while, Randy petting, Salomé purring and licking, and then she began to nest on his pillow before curling up right next to Randy's face. She tucked her nose into his neck and her legs on his chest and went to sleep.

Randy petted her for a few minutes before following suit.

He woke briefly to find the room fully dark, no light coming in from the hall, the house silent. The bed behind him dipped, and Ethan's long, warm body slid in against his. He tried to give Slick some room, but at the same time he murmured, "Don't wake the kitten."

Ethan stroked his shoulder. "Go to sleep, Ace."

Randy did, a part of him he didn't even know was tense easing as Ethan wrapped first his arm and then his leg around Randy. He fell, easily and deeply, into the sleep of kings.

CHAPTER THIRTEEN

O N MONDAY RANDY came into the kitchen to find a Sam he'd never met before.

His normally sunny and affable friend looked jagged and unsteady—his hands shook around his coffee cup, and when Randy tried to comfort him, he only shook his head, refusing to engage. But what really unnerved Randy was how still Sam was. He had it all packed away, but it was clear Sam was a floodwall holding back a tide that hadn't even come close to cresting.

Eventually he gave up trying to crack Sam back open and hunted down Mitch, who wasn't a whole lot better. He sat on his bed with a cell phone in hand, staring unseeing at the wall in front of him.

"I have to leave for Kentucky tomorrow. I'm going to miss Sam's therapy. And I can't get out of it."

Randy eased onto the bed beside him and rubbed Mitch's back. "It'll be okay. We'll make it work."

Mitch put a heavy hand on Randy's leg. "Skeet—will you take him? He has his first appointment today, and I can't go and get ready for the run too."

"No problem. I'll take off work a few days, to be

sure I'm around."

Mitch kept his eyes downcast. "This isn't the way I wanted it to happen. Any of it."

"I know." Randy squeezed Mitch's shoulder. "I'll take care of him, Old Man."

Sam, however, wasn't mollified. When Randy told him he'd be going along, Sam broke out of his trance, but only to be angry. "So you're my *babysitter*?"

"Yeah. And it's not negotiable, Peaches, so just accept it."

Ethan came into the kitchen, showered and fully dressed in some of his nicer clothes, Salomé trotting along beside him as he headed to the coffeepot. Randy frowned at him. "Where are you going so dressed up?"

Ethan sipped at his coffee before answering. "Herod's. I thought I should get started." He glanced at his wrist, which was bare, and grimaced. "I should go shopping later today too. I need a few things, and I wanted to pick up a book about cat training."

Randy snorted. "You can't train a cat."

Sam straightened in his chair. "I'll look up some websites for you, Ethan."

"That would be lovely, Sam, thank you." Ethan squeezed Sam's shoulder as he addressed Randy. "You said you had some books on poker I could read. Do you have some on Las Vegas as well? On casinos? Or should I pick them up when I go for the cat-training book?"

Randy felt dizzy. "I've got some stuff. But let me take you shopping."

Ethan smiled, making Randy a little dizzier. "Sure.

What time do you want to meet up to go?"

Randy pulled his cell phone out of his pocket and handed it to Ethan. "I'll call you when we know more. We'll get you your own phone this afternoon. In the meantime call me at Sam's number."

"Thanks." Ethan pocketed the phone, put down the coffee cup and reached for his keys. "I'll see you later."

"What, you're going *now*? You haven't eaten."

"I'll grab something on the way." Ethan patted his pants and gave Randy a rueful look. "Could I borrow a bit more cash? Last time, I promise. I spent the little I had the other night."

"Doesn't have to be the last time." Randy pulled a wad of twenties out of his wallet. "That do?"

"More than enough. Thank you." He leaned forward and kissed Randy's cheek, hesitating before catching his lips too.

Randy had to keep himself from leaning into the kiss as Ethan drew away. "What about your cat? You're ready to leave her alone now?"

"No." Ethan scooped her up. "I'm taking her with me."

Randy was going to make all kinds of noise about the kitten in the casino, and then he realized with Crabtree's history, nobody would blink. "Hold on a minute." He took a travel mug from the cupboard, poured Ethan's coffee into it and passed it to him. "For you." He grabbed a Rubbermaid container, put some of the kitten's food inside and tucked it into Ethan's pocket. "For her."

That earned him one more kiss and a smile, and he watched them go, feeling all jumbled up inside, and he didn't know why. He turned to Sam to vent some of his agitation, saw the look on his face and gave up. "Tell you what, sweetheart. You finish eating, and we'll take a bike ride before your appointment."

Sam perked up despite himself. "Where to? Zion?"

"Don't have time enough to get there and back before your appointment. But…" Randy glanced at his watch, "…if we hustle, we could swing around on 147 past Lake Las Vegas and come in on the 564. What about that?"

Sam grinned, pushed aside his bowl and stood in one motion before kissing Randy squarely on the cheek. Randy grunted and headed to the garage, calling, "Rinse your damn bowl out," over his shoulder as he departed.

They went down Carey Avenue and into the desert. The sun was bright and hot, and the land opened up before them. Randy needed the speed, the wind and the peace, the strange comfort that was Sam's arms around him. He didn't often have anyone riding with him, and now he'd had both Ethan and Sam in the same week. It was funny how different it was to drive them. With Sam behind him, he was a shelter, the man who blocked the wind and Sam held on to, the protector. With Ethan he felt different. An equal, even when Slick was weird and quiet.

An anchor. With Ethan on the bike, he was an anchor.

The drive was beautiful. Sam always grumbled

about how ugly the desert was, how he missed trees, but Randy loved it. It wasn't barren but full of life, most of it rough and wicked and tough as shit. Las Vegas was an oasis too, always had been. Vegas meant *meadow* in Spanish. Vegas had lakes and little creeks and rivers. Even Sam, who missed his green grass and rolling fields, would admit those parts were beautiful.

It was so much better to take this ride with someone along. He thought of how full the house had been this morning, everyone wandering in and out for breakfast, and how tomorrow there would be one less, with Mitch leaving. The thought was like a cloud passing overhead.

He frowned and gunned the engine, willing speed to slough off the pang of loss.

Sam's counselor was on Paradise Road, almost literally in the shadow of the Stratosphere Tower, which seemed a good omen to Randy. He parked the bike and smiled up at the tower, wondering if it would at all be possible to sneak over there and have a look-see off the observation deck, when Sam grabbed his hand.

"Randy, I want you to come with me."

"Sure, Peaches. I'll be right there in the waiting room." He could go up the tower anytime.

But Sam's hand tightened. "*No.* I want you to come in *with* me. To the therapist. Into her office with me."

Whoa. "Sam, listen—"

"Mitch said he would. He said he'd go with me the first time, and now he's not here. He said he was sorry, and I understand, but I still don't want to go alone. I want you to go with me, Randy. *Please.*"

Oh, fuck. Mitch, you fucking bastard. Randy wiped his mouth with his free hand. "Sure, Peaches. Sure."

Sam relaxed visibly, but he kept his hand in Randy's all the way until the door. They checked Sam in and settled into a pair of chairs along the far wall, and as they waited, Randy indulged in some panic.

Randy did not like therapists. They were fine for other people, but he did not care for them himself. He had seen exactly one, once, when he was ten, and while he would admit the woman had been nice, even kind, he'd left swearing he would never, ever go again. He'd managed to keep that vow all the way up until this moment. It didn't matter this was for Sam, not him. He was in the fucking office. He was going to go *sit in the fucking room.*

Jesus God, but the woman had better not try to talk to him.

He would have hung back when the therapist came out, but Sam dragged him forward, introducing him as *my good friend.* The woman, petite and pretty in a quiet, nonthreatening way, reached out and took his hand. "Hello, I'm Laura. It's a pleasure to meet you, Sam. Randy."

Randy nodded curtly, and if Sam hadn't gripped his elbow, he was fairly sure he'd have bolted.

They meandered through an office hallway, Laura gently chatting Sam up about the weather, which was a real feat in a city that got over three hundred days of sun a year. When Laura welcomed them into her cozy, plant-and-book-filled office, he steered them to the love seat and plunked them both down in it. He wouldn't even let go once they were sitting.

Randy wanted to know who was going to hold *his* fucking hand.

Nesting in the corner of the sofa, Randy ran his thumb over Sam's knuckles, a gesture that soothed him as well as Sam. He watched the therapist to see what she made of this, but she didn't seem fazed by it in the slightest.

"So." She smiled as she crossed her legs. "What is it you'd like to talk about with me, Sam?"

On anybody else the smile would seem fake, but on her it even made Randy relax. It didn't work on Sam, because the next thing Randy knew, he was losing the circulation in his fingers. That was when he realized Sam wasn't talking. He turned, took one look at Sam's face, and sat bolt upright.

"Peaches." He pried his hand out of Sam's and rubbed his shoulders. Fuck, he'd never seen anybody go so white. "*Sam.*" When Sam stayed quiet, Randy turned to the therapist for help.

She simply sat there, patient, but her smile faded in wattage, a bulb politely dimming for someone with a migraine. "Take your time."

Sam drew a slow, deep breath. "I got upset last week, and I scared my husband." His chin came up, and he looked at the therapist directly as he added, "I'm married. To a man. And it's legal, because I'm from Iowa."

"What's his name? How long have you been married?"

"His name is Mitch, and we've been married for a little under two years now. Our anniversary is February 14. That was Mitch's idea. He was supposed to be here today, but he got called in to work."

"Peaches, he was really upset about it." Randy winced and glanced at the therapist. "Sorry. I'll be quiet."

Sam shook his head. "No, it's okay. I know he wanted to be here. But I'm still mad. I'm mad he has to go at all." His eyes were wild for a moment, and when he said the rest, the words were jagged. "That's why I'm here."

Laura leaned forward. "Where is he going?"

"He—he's a trucker. He has a run to—and I—" Sam shut his eyes, turned his head slightly toward Randy and whispered, "Please tell her—so I don't have to."

God, it was almost a relief.

He explained how Mitch was a long-distance trucker, about how he'd worked the Midwest while Sam was in school but now they were stationed in Vegas. He explained about the run to Kentucky.

He wasn't sure how to talk about why they were in the office.

"There was a bad accident on the way here, and it stirred up something in Sam. He got upset, bad, in the mountains, and Mitch had to admit him for the night to the hospital. He's been edgy since, and now Mitch is leaving tomorrow." Randy looked at Sam and folded, because tears were running down Sam's cheeks, and Randy pulled Sam to him.

Randy held him, uncomfortable and helpless and frustrated. He hated how the woman sat there. Shouldn't she be doing something? But she only waited and watched, empathetic but quiet. Weirdest, though, was how the longer she sat there, the calmer Randy felt, and eventually the quiet bled into Sam too.

Sam straightened and wiped at his eyes. "Sorry."

Laura passed him the box of tissues in front of her. "You don't need to apologize. It's okay to be upset, especially in here. Is what Randy says accurate, or would you care to add or change anything?"

"I know I overreacted, and I'm sorry I upset Mitch. Really sorry, because now I have to come here. I'm embarrassed. I'm a lot younger than Mitch, and he treats me like a kid. And I'm mad because now he *really* treats me that way. I guess I deserve it, because I acted like one."

Randy took offense. "Sam, you've had a lot going on in your life. It's okay to lean on your husband. And me too."

"And what do I do if he has"—his voice hitched, but this time he pressed on—"an accident? What happens when he leaves and doesn't come back?"

"He's not—"

"*You don't know.*" Sam let go of Randy's hand so he could wave both his hands around, at Randy, at Laura, at the world in general. "How the *fuck* do you know he's coming back? How do you know he's not going to die *right now* on the way home from the distribution center? How do you know he won't have a heart attack or lung cancer because he smokes so damn much? He might die, Randy, *because you don't know.* I can't take it anymore. Not again."

"What do you mean, again?" the therapist asked.

Like a spent balloon, Sam sank into a slouch. "My mom died of cancer when I was seventeen. She had multiple sclerosis too, but that wasn't what killed her. She was doing really well, in fact. Then, *boom.*" Sam leaned on Randy as he stared down at the coffee table full of stones and bowls and soothing objects. "Nobody fought like my mom. It was just the two of us ever since I was born. My dad was a deadbeat, some dick who knocked up my mom and left her alone. But it didn't matter, because we were great. We lived in a shitty trailer, and I had one pair of shoes and three outfits and slept in my underwear, but I didn't care. I helped her, but I didn't mind. She was tired, but it was okay. We still did stuff. And she was *totally* great about my being gay. I wish she could have met Mitch. I wish she could have seen me get married. She would have loved that."

Laura smiled. "She sounds like a wonderful woman. You must miss her a great deal."

Sam nodded and wept silently, a man visiting the grave.

Randy rose to his feet, his throat full, his vision blurring, his stomach turning. Because with no warning, he was at a grave too.

Cold, windy day, the whole world gray inside and out, a weird sucking sound in his ears as he watched them lower the casket into the ground, and it was real, he knew it then, Uncle Gary wasn't coming back, not ever. Oh God, it hurt. It hurt, it hurt, it hurt, it hurt, and he couldn't take it anymore—

A hand, small and slight and familiar, pressed on his shoulder, drawing him down to the couch again. Randy blinked, almost surprised to find where he was. "Sorry." He shifted uncomfortably and tried to rise again. "Sam, sorry, but I really got to get out of here."

Sam held him fast and with surprising strength. "Randy—what just happened to you?"

Randy glanced at the therapist and saw the patient smile was now aimed at him, sending him back to panic. *Jesus fuck, get me fucking out of here.*

But he couldn't leave Sam. So he did the last thing in the world he wanted to do.

He stared up at the ceiling as he spoke. "You talking about your mom made me think of my uncle. He died when I was ten. But it's fine."

Sam's hand stroked his. "I didn't know you had an uncle."

"I had six uncles and five aunts. This was Uncle Gary. He was different." He forced a laugh. "Seriously, Sam, we'll talk about this later. It's no big deal. This is your time, not mine." *And I do not ever want a time for talking about this.*

Peaches had an iron look about him. "I want to hear about your uncle."

Randy turned to Laura for help. She just smiled at him, and Randy got pissed. "This is *no big deal.*"

Sam closed his other hand over their joined ones.

"Randy—would you tell me? Right now? Please?"

Randy looked at Sam's face, tried to find the strength to shut him down and found he couldn't do it, not to Sam, not even for this.

Fuck.

"He was just my uncle." Okay, except that wasn't fair. He forced himself to elaborate. "All right, he was my favorite uncle. So it was a little rough to lose him."

Fucking understatement of the year.

"He's the uncle who taught me poker. He was gay, which I didn't fully figure out until later, but it meant a lot to me because I was starting to think I was too." He let out a breath. "There. That's Uncle Gary. Now why don't you talk about yourself, Peaches?"

Sam went right for the jugular. "How did he die?"

Why the ceiling was so fucking safe Randy didn't know, but he didn't question it, just accepted its solace as he stared at it. "He was killed."

There. He'd said it. Wasn't so bad.

Sam's hand squeezed on his, and fucking hell if Randy didn't start talking again.

"Murdered. Knife in an alley, and it was not pretty. Never found out who, but they didn't really look. Some gay guy killed down by the tracks. Nobody cared."

I cared.

He glared at the therapist. "Why the hell are we talking about me? I did not come here to get fucking therapy."

Sam kept staring, full of empathy. "Randy, I had no idea. I'm so sorry."

"Yeah, well." Randy wiped his hand over his mouth and swallowed several times. "Me too."

He stared down at the carpet, not sure what the fuck he was going to do if they kept pressing on him.

They didn't, though. Laura gently led the conversation back to Sam, who seemed calmer now—sad, but less jagged. Which was funny because Randy felt like he had six-foot spikes coming out of him. Fuck, but he didn't know the last time he'd been this rattled.

Goddamn Tedsoe for bailing on them.

When it was finally over, he stood and waited over by the door, ready to run.

"I think we might meet later this week," Laura said to Sam. "Would you rather tomorrow, or the day after?"

"Tomorrow Mitch leaves. So maybe not then. But…" he grimaced, "…I don't know if I can afford to come a whole lot of times."

"Your bill is paid for already. There's no worry on that account."

Sam blinked in surprise, then sighed. "Oh. Crabtree."

"Go ahead and make an appointment out front. It's been good to meet you, Sam, and I look forward to working with you." She turned to Randy. "It was good to meet you too, Randy."

Randy grunted and herded Sam through the door.

His agitation didn't leave him even when they got out of the building. It followed him onto the bike as well, and not in a way he cared to drive with. So he turned left instead of right, and went like a homing beacon to the Stratosphere Hotel.

"I'll just be a minute." He worked to keep himself level so Sam wouldn't realize how raw he was. "Wait in the bar?"

Sam took his hand. "I'll go with you."

"I'm going *up*, Sam. I need some head space." He glanced at his watch. "Maybe Mitch is free and can come meet you."

Sam laced his fingers through Randy's. "No. I'm going with you."

Randy didn't have it in him to argue. He wove through the familiar hallways to the ticket counter for the tower. He felt better with every foot they went up, welcoming the rush of the high-speed lift and the popping in his ears. His heart raced in anticipation as he stepped out and saw the sun glaring in through the round windows of the observation room. He turned to Sam, knowing he needed to reassure Sam I-hate-heights Keller, but Sam, white-faced, shook his head.

"I'm coming with you."

Now Randy was impatient. "I seriously will not be long."

Sam had the bit between his teeth now though, and Randy gave up and headed for the doors, Sam still clutching his hand.

He stepped out, felt the open space and the rush of wind sweep around him, and took his first clear breath since the therapist's office. For a full minute he simply stared out over the Strip, soaking it in.

Sam had his eyes shut tight, breathing a little fast,

but considering how he usually acted when they came up here, this was a real personal triumph. Still, Randy was confused. "Peaches, why did you come up here?"

"Because you went into the appointment with me." He opened his eyes and looked up at Randy. "Thank you."

Randy nodded gruffly. "Sure."

"I want you to come again. Please."

Randy stiffened, losing everything coming up to the observation tower had given him. "Sam—"

"I want to hear more about your uncle. It helped me. A lot." He squeezed Randy's hand. "Why didn't you tell me you understood?"

Randy looked out over the Strip, trying to let himself sail away. "Because I don't want to talk about it."

"Please do this for me, Randy." Sam squeezed again. "And for you."

Randy shut his eyes.

"I won't go if you don't go with me."

Randy glared at him. "Dirty pool, Peaches."

Sam gave him a wry smile. "You're the one who taught me how to play."

"Sam, I don't go there. I talked about him once—drunk—with Mitch. And that's it."

"So that's how you think I should be with my mom?"

Randy looked up at the bright blue endless sky above his head. The Big Shot ride rushed up the pole, and he heard the distant screams of the riders as they shot up a thousand feet into the air. "You play really fucking dirty pool."

"So you'll come with me?"

The Big Shot slid the rest of the way down the pole, leaving it empty and alone against the bright blue. He sighed, lowered his head and nodded.

Sam hugged him and kissed his cheek, daring a furtive glance over the edge before shutting his eyes again and waiting until Randy was done.

Randy took his time, not leaving until Sam was twitching and shuddering from all the swaying and wind. Because Randy *had* been the one to teach him dirty pool.

CHAPTER FOURTEEN

Ethan went to the chain pet store on Rainbow Boulevard, hoping to find something to help him keep Salomé at the casino.

Logic said she would get used to it and comfort herself, but all Ethan could think about was her sitting in Randy's house, mewing plaintively. He reasoned if people could carry around those tiny little dogs in purses, couldn't he take a cat around in a casino? Of course, at some point he would have to leave her alone.

Ethan wandered the aisles of the store, trying to find something, but nothing leapt out at him. All he saw were toys and bags of food and cozy places to sleep. Salomé, as if sensing his distress, leaned up to nuzzle his chin.

"Can I help you?" A pretty young woman with long blonde hair wearing the blue smock marking her as an employee looked expectantly at him. When she saw Salomé, her expression melted into adoration. "Oh, she's *precious*. What's her name?"

"Salomé." Ethan glanced at her name badge. *Crystal.* She fawned over his kitten for a moment, and he tried to read her, but all he could tell was she really liked kittens. "I'm looking for some way to carry her around with me. She doesn't want to be left alone."

Crystal gave him a stern glare. "You can't take her everywhere. Most places aren't going to allow kittens inside, however cute they are. And you absolutely cannot, ever, not even for a few minutes, leave her in your car. *Never.*"

Ethan blinked at the force of Crystal's scolding. "I won't."

"She's going to have to learn how to stay alone, unless you plan on only ever going to the pet store and the park. But you can make it easier for her by having things she enjoys. Cats don't need a lot of toys, but cozy places to sleep are good. She seems pretty affectionate, so she might prefer blankets that smell like you. Consider a pet bed, something that makes her feel secure. Cats like to hide in places that are closed-in and secluded. You can make her one with the right setup. Do you have a scratching post?"

"I didn't think she'd need one when she was so little."

This earned him another quelling look. "She needs it now especially, so you can train her."

Ethan brightened. "So you *can* train cats?"

"Oh, absolutely. Not as easily as dogs because cats aren't pack animals, but they still respond to rewards and stimuli. I suggest you only use positive-reinforcement training." She reached up into a display and pulled down a blue plastic object the size of a fat clothespin. When she pinched the yellow button on the top, it made a sharp *click*. "This is a clicker. Use it to signal she's done something you like—get her to associate it with good things. When you click it and she does what you want her to do, she gets a treat. Work with a target too—not your hand because it's too big. The end of a wand or something small she can touch with her nose. Start there, and it won't be long before she gets the association. Just *never* call her with the clicker to punish her."

Ethan felt more than a little overwhelmed, but he nodded.

Crystal reached up on the shelf again. "This book can get you started, but what you want is one of the online communities. I can give you the names of some good ones."

"That would be great." Ethan looked down at Salomé, at her precious tiny face, and remembered his present dilemma. "But I honestly can't bear to leave her alone. She cries, and it breaks my heart."

Crystal smiled wryly, but Ethan could tell she secretly approved of his devotion. "Well, there's one other way. I assume, since you already have one cat, you either own your home or rent somewhere allowing pets?"

Ethan paused. "Actually, I'm living with someone for now."

"Someone who likes you?"

Ethan paused. What was he supposed to call Randy? "He's my boyfriend." He knew a ridiculous thrill at the admission.

"Does your boyfriend like cats?" Crystal's smile was wicked. "Or does he love you so much it doesn't matter?"

Ethan grinned back. "Both, maybe. I think. I hope."

"Then what you really want is this."

She led Ethan around the corner to a wall display of nine windows. Each and every one was full of cats.

Ethan balked. "I don't think—" He stopped as he spied the adult calico with a bent ear looking out at him. Her shoulders were hunched, and her whole existence seemed lost and forlorn.

"*Oh.*" Ethan started toward her. She blinked then hesitantly pawed at the glass. Ethan's heart clenched.

"That's Daisy. Would you like to meet her?"

Ethan knew then it was already over. He just hoped Randy truly did love him because otherwise he'd probably kill him.

ETHAN PRETENDED HE wasn't adopting Daisy by declaring he was "thinking about it." Of course, he'd also left Salomé at the store's boarding department for the afternoon, where the indomitable Crystal had arranged to have Daisy and Salomé housed in the same cage. When Ethan left, they'd been curled up together in the ultra-soft plush pink cat bed he'd purchased, grooming one another contentedly.

He hoped Randy loved him *a lot*.

With Salomé properly settled, Ethan headed over to the casino, where he confronted the real demon of the day: Billy Herod.

He had a vague memory Billy had told him to "stop by the office sometime," but this was the best sense of instruction he had, and even this he couldn't say for certain had actually happened, so he decided he would start by doing that. If Billy wasn't there, he'd figure out a new plan. But before he could start searching for the owner's office, a vaguely familiar man came up to him, mouth set in a grim line before he dug into his pocket and pulled out a stack of chips, thrusting them at Ethan. "Your money from the bet."

Bet? Ethan turned the top chip over in his hand, watching the *Billy's!* logo rotate.

The man seemed nervous. "Tell Mr. Crabtree too, yeah? Tell him I was honest by his man."

At last Ethan placed him. "You're the bartender from the first night."

"Scully's my name, sir. If I'd known you were with Crabtree, I'd never have bet against you. Nothing personal, okay?" Mumbling a goodbye, Scully hurried into the casino. It was then, finally, Ethan realized this was all about the kiss bet, which he had lost. Which this man thought he had won.

Which meant Randy had lied.

Grimacing, Ethan pocketed the chips and resumed his hunt for Billy's office.

With some trial and error Ethan made his way up through the maze of offices on the sixth floor—he stopped by Crabtree's, but the gangster was still not around. Eventually he found an efficient-looking woman at a desk. She was of an indeterminate age, professionally and elegantly dressed in a plum-colored suit coat and skirt, hair swept up in a tidy bun. She looked like a less siren-version of Joan Harris from *Mad Men*. When Ethan approached, she glanced at him severely over the top of her glasses. "May I help you?"

"Ethan Ellison. I'm looking for Mr. Herod."

The woman's expression changed from severe to glowing. "Mr. Ellison." She stood and held out her hand. "My name is Sarah Reynolds. I'm the office manager for the casino. It's a pleasure to meet you, sir. I've heard so much about you."

"From Billy?"

Sarah laughed. "No. From Mr. Crabtree, of course." She stepped away from her desk and led him to a potted silk plant covering a large portion of the wall beside her desk. "Right this way, Mr. Ellison."

"Please, call me Ethan." Ethan frowned as the office manager struggled with the plant. "Can I help you?"

She beamed at him. "Please. Just shift it about a foot, would you?" She waited until Ethan rose then inclined her head in thanks before pushing against a panel in the wall. It swung open.

"A secret room?" Ethan felt foolish when the door only revealed a narrow closet with shelves full of, of all things, towels.

"It was, once. But Billy Jr. wanted a bathroom in his office, and since we don't do the skim anymore, the actual room wasn't necessary. Once upon a time, though, this is where Herod's kept the cooked books and the cash that hadn't yet been sent out for laundering." She shifted several of the towels to a lower shelf, reaching far into the back. "Now it's mostly real laundry. We still keep the safe in here, though, and some things from the old days, because Mr. Crabtree likes to remember."

"Where is Crabtree?"

Sarah only gave him an enigmatic smile. She leaned in a little farther before withdrawing a large envelope and handing it to Ethan. "He wanted you to have this. I think you'll find everything you need in there. The keys are to your office, which is on the seventh floor. I'll warn you the air conditioning is a bit dodgy, but I have a maintenance order in. If you use the box fan and keep your door open, you should be fine."

"My office?" Ethan peeked into the envelope and immediately dropped it on the floor. Several thousand dollars and an array of credit cards fell out, as well as a folder welcoming him to Bank of Nevada Checking.

Sarah gathered the loose items together and handed them over with a stern look. "Really, Mr. Ellison, you should be more careful."

"Why are you giving me all this?"

"You are the new casino manager, Mr. Ellison. Crabtree said you'd had a little bit of trouble, and so he's set up these accounts for you. He said you didn't need to be bothered with that sort of thing because you have a lot of work to do. Which is true. I've laid it all out for you on your desk."

Casino manager? Ethan blinked for several seconds

then gave up. No, nothing was going to make sense. "Mr. Herod also opened an account for me. I made a few purchases on the promise of it last night. Which reminds me I need to write some checks. Would it be all right to use this one, since they're ready?"

"Oh, you mean the limo? I took care of it already. Crabtree instructed me to combine Billy's account with the one he opened for you. You'll find everything to be in order, I'm sure, and if not, please don't hesitate to call me. I'm extension number one on the casino line. Would you like me to show you upstairs now?"

"I can find it, thank you, if you give me the number."

"Oh, it's the only office up there. This elevator goes to the corporate areas. Get out on seven and head three doors down, just past the closet and the bathroom. Can't miss it. Welcome aboard, Mr. Ellison."

"Thank you, Ms. Reynolds." Ethan tried to sound professional and not bewildered.

He wandered down the hall to find the elevator, clutching his envelope. The elevator was slow in coming, so he took the stairs instead.

His office was the approximate size of a postage stamp, and every available surface was full of ledgers.

There were three tall empty bookcases along the walls, leaving just enough space for the door and the small, depressing window looking into the back alley. There was, as Sarah had promised, a box fan against the wall. It was, also as promised, fantastically stuffy inside the tiny room.

Ethan sat down at the desk and took in the tower of ledgers. Then, almost as an afterthought, he opened the envelope again, nudged aside the cash—there had to be at least three thousand there, as every bill was a hundred—and opened the folder for the checking account. He scanned through until he found a listed balance. When he did, he stared at it for a few minutes, then closed the folder and put it in the middle desk drawer.

Bending over, he put his head between his knees for some time.

When he was fairly certain he could sit up without vomiting, he opened the first ledger with a shaking hand. He read. Then he opened another ledger, and another, and another. When a knock sounded on the door, it startled him, and he glanced up at the nervous-looking young man standing in the doorway holding a paper sack.

"Ms. Reynolds said you might want this, sir?" He held out the sack a little farther but didn't step into the room. He seemed afraid to. "It's lunch, Mr. Ellison."

"Oh." Ethan glanced at his naked wrist. He pulled out Randy's phone instead and blinked again when he saw the time. "Oh. Yes. Thank you."

The boy scuttled in, left the bag on top of a stack of ledgers before bolting into the hallway. Ethan ate the sandwich absently, not even aware of what he was eating. He'd finished most of it and a good bit of the accompanying cup of lemonade when Billy Herod let himself into Ethan's office.

"God, it's stuffy in here." Billy leaned over and

turned on the fan, aiming it at himself as he sat opposite Ethan. He sprawled out as best he could in the uncomfortable chair. "Well?"

Well, what? Ethan took another sip of lemonade, swept his eyes over the ledgers again and decided, fuck it. "Your finances are a mess."

Billy shrugged. "Yeah."

"The casino isn't making any money. It is *bleeding* money. If things go on the way they are, you'll be bankrupt by the end of the year. It's October right now, if you recall."

"That's why I want to sell it." Billy nudged a ledger with his foot. "So. Can you move stuff around, so it looks okay?"

"*No*, Billy, I can't. No one can. You can't sell the casino until it's making a profit, or until it appears to someone it possibly could."

"So make it look like it could. Honestly, you're a little disappointing for being Crabtree's whiz kid." He snorted a laugh. "Well, you're not really a kid, are you? Make it work. Because I have a plan."

"Do you now."

Billy either missed Ethan's derision or ignored it. "I'm going to get out of this goddamned casino, that's what I'm going to do. This place is going down, and I don't want to be here when it crashes. The whole town is in the shitter. Vegas isn't any fun anymore. It's worse than when they had this being a 'family destination'. It's dead and done. I'm going to get my money, and I'm going to get out of here. I'll leave the country if I have to. Just so long as I don't have this albatross around my neck."

Ethan stared at Billy in disbelief. It was amazing to believe someone could live so far outside of reality, but Billy managed it. "You must have quite a trust fund already. Why not let it go bankrupt? Why all this work?"

"Yeah, I've got a trust fund. Three hundred million. Except it's all tied up in this fucking place. I can do whatever I want with the money, so long as Herod's Poker Room and Casino is up and running."

Three hundred million? "Then why don't you in-vest—"

"Because it's *my money*. It should be, anyway. It's not fair it's all tied up in this shit hole. I'm not spending a single dime on it out of my trust fund."

Three hundred million. The number kept echoing in Ethan's head. "What happens to the money if the casino goes bankrupt?"

"It goes to some cat sanctuary outside of Boulder City. But it isn't going to go there, because you're going to help me *sell it*. If I *sell it*, then I get to keep the money. So. Work your magic or whatever, and let me know when it's ready."

Ethan flipped through the ledger in front of him. "Billy, this place hasn't turned a profit since 1992. If you had reserves, that would be a different story, but you don't. I'm sorry, but you're going to have to invest some of your funds into the casino, or you will lose it all. I'm an *investment broker*. This means I *invest*. I do not conjure money out of thin air. To make money grow, I have to have something to start with."

"What do you need, then? A million?"

"Ten." Ethan looked down at the figures. "At least. And that's just to even out the debt. If you want to actually start turning a profit, you're going to have to bring in customers again. Many of them. For a *sustained* amount of time."

"No." Billy leaned over the desk. "I want to sell this place by the middle of November. Sell it as a bargain, I don't care. It just has to be at a profit, even of a dollar. If you do that, then I don't care what else happens. You're my man now, Ethan Ellison. I paid you. I bought your ass, and now it's mine. And I want your ass to sell my casino."

It would have been a powerful, almost frightening speech, except Billy always managed to look and sound like a spoiled child. "I can do it, Billy—if you give me access to thirty million dollars."

"Thirty?" Billy's cheeks were red. "You just said ten."

"Ten to break even. If you want the kind of miracle you're talking about, I need thirty. To make a profit right now, you'd need to sell this place for twenty-five million dollars. That means to get this place up to the mark, in addition to a miracle, I'm going to need that much money as padding in the assets, or no one will bite."

"What the fuck is the other five for?"

"The miracle. We're going to need at least a million

dollars' worth of sequins to start. I'm going to need an assistant too. And is there some reason the casino manager is located up here in the dust in the smallest office in the building?"

"The casino manager is my best friend Mark Simmons, and his office is on the sixth floor, next to mine. But he's on vacation until the end of November." Billy gave him a funny look. "Why did you think his office was up here? This is the *only* office up here."

Ethan kept his face carefully blank. "I assumed all these ledgers would be in the casino manager's office."

"You're funny, Ellison. Anyway, I gotta go—told this chick I met downstairs I'd show her my suite. She probably thinks I forgot her by now." He shrugged. "Okay. You win. Your thirty million will be moved over to the assets account by tomorrow morning. But I warn you, that's the last you're getting. You *will* deliver. You won't like what will happen if you don't."

Ethan tried to make sense of the chaos. Crabtree had authored this scheme. Sarah Reynolds had called him the casino manager. Sarah Reynolds, who knew about the secret door and who dismissed Billy and who knew all about Crabtree—*she* had handled all this. But when he asked Billy about Sarah, he laughed.

"She's nothing. Nobody. She's Crabtree's daft old secretary. Thinks this place is still run by the Chicago Outfit." He patted the doorway. "Do me proud, Ellison. Remember—you're my man." He paused, looking like he wanted to qualify that, then shrugged and went down the hall to the elevator.

The conversation rolled like a loose marble in Ethan's head. Finally, he picked up the phone and dialed extension one.

"Yes, Mr. Ellison?" Sarah answered. "May I help you?"

"Would it be possible, Ms. Reynolds, for me to get a laptop up here with a wireless connection?"

"Absolutely, sir. I'll send Fitz up with one right away."

Less than five minutes later the same gangly, nervous youth from before hovered in the doorway, this time bearing a gleaming MacBook.

"Thank you, Fitz." Though Ethan could have crossed the room to take it from him, he waited for the young man to bring the computer over.

Sarah Reynolds, who was clearly the exact opposite of what Billy had painted her as, had named him the casino manager. He thought it was probably best to act like one.

After opening the laptop, Ethan pulled up the internet and began to surf, his focus on one thing—the presence of organized crime in Las Vegas. He got far more on the past than the present, but this was an education within itself. As Randy and Crabtree had hinted, there'd been two distinct mob presences here. First was an Italian/Jewish organization based out of New York who had first monitored sports races but fell into the casinos like fish into lakes. Then the Chicago Outfit had arrived in the sixties and stayed through the eighties. Some said there was a third mob starting now.

The current mob was considered base and crass, especially compared to those before.

There was no question which mob was the most dangerous, the most brutal and the most brash—the Chicago Outfit. Of course, that was Crabtree's.

Ethan looked for a reference to the gangster, but he couldn't find any. He found William Herod Sr., but nothing on Crabtree. There were pages and pages on Spilotro, whose brutality was not comforting. Rosenthal had somehow come semi-clean and died in his bed of natural causes. Evelyn Carter—he was hard to pin down, but he didn't seem terribly pleasant. His reports were shadowy, mostly cloaked in rumor, but he was nasty. He'd also died in 1991, gunned down in the desert. Before that, however, he was the manager of Herod's.

He was also one of the last men to oversee the mob's skimming a take off the casino's income pre-taxes, and millions and millions of dollars from the casino vanished with him. Most assumed this was why he'd been killed.

Billy Senior had died in a car accident, like Crabtree had said. He'd spent most of the nineties in a mountain cabin. No foul play at all, but then Billy Senior hadn't been much for that sort of thing. He just liked to play poker and hang out in his casino.

Nothing on Crabtree, though. Which was frustrating, because Ethan was certain the gangster—or alleged gangster—was the key to everything.

Ethan was almost relieved when his cell phone rang.

It was, of course, Randy. "You still want to go shopping, or what?"

"I want to go shopping, but there had better be some poker first."

"Well." He could hear Randy relax. "I suppose it could be arranged, if you insist. Have you been to Bellagio's tables yet, Slick?"

Ethan smiled. "I can't say I have."

"Get your ass downstairs. I'll be by on my bike in ten minutes."

"I'll be waiting." Ethan didn't bother hiding his eagerness. Sometimes he didn't want to bluff. He just wanted to enjoy the game.

CHAPTER FIFTEEN

RANDY TRIED NOT to feel relieved when he saw Slick, an emotion he realized he'd suffered since his blurted confession of love. *This is what therapy fucking does to you.* And he had another dose of it coming in two days. He revved the bike a few times, making the bell captain glare at him, but he just gave him a smirk and did it again, louder.

Ethan slid on behind him, grinning. "Hello, hot shot." He kissed the side of Randy's helmet before reaching behind him for the spare.

"You're a bit overdressed for a motorcycle." Jesus fuck, but Slick did look good in a suit.

Ethan settled in, pushing forward as much as possible so their bodies pressed together. Resting his hands on Randy's thighs, he splayed his long fingers. "Want me to get undressed?"

Randy's body responded in a low-level hum. *Fuck yes, get undressed.* "You want to skip Bellagio and go home?" Then he remembered Sam and Mitch would be there, fucking but with a pile of angst. "Shit, we can't. Never mind. Let's go play poker."

"Whatever you want, Ace." Ethan squeezed Randy's

thigh.

Randy shut his eyes for a moment, enjoying it, then wrenched his focus back and took them off toward Las Vegas Boulevard.

There was no disputing the poker rooms at Bellagio were the best in Vegas. Crabtree hated them for it, because he said back in the day there was nothing finer than Herod's. Randy loved Bellagio. He loved the Nugget for friendliness and ambience and because of Mandy, but Bellagio had the best, toughest games. Their rake was the best deal going too.

Of course, you could die trying to get a drink in the place.

This was about Slick right now, not drinks, about putting Ethan up against some of the best players in the world. It would also be about losing a lot of money, which meant Randy also needed to play, to get some back.

Or so he thought.

When Randy tried to hand him cash, Ethan reached into his jacket and withdrew five Benjamins of his own. Then he took out another five.

Then another.

"Holy shit. You rob a bank?"

"Sarah gave it to me in an envelope today. Though it's not half as interesting as this." He pulled out a balance sheet from a bank account, which Randy scanned, then read again more slowly. Ethan helped him to a nearby stool, which was good because his knees had stopped working.

Ethan had an account in his name with ten million dollars.

"So," Randy said, when his voice would work. "You aren't just *playing* at gangster now."

Ethan remained oddly calm. "Do you know Sarah Reynolds?"

"Shit, yeah, I know Sarah. She runs the place when Crabtree isn't there. Why?"

"She called me the casino manager. Except Billy still thinks some other guy is. Which is understandable, since I'm a casino manager on the seventh floor in a non-air-conditioned office."

Randy wanted to protest that Ethan was fucking with forces he didn't even begin to understand, but he couldn't, because he could see Ethan was enjoying himself. He had a light about him that grew brighter with every step he took further into this shitstorm.

"Oh, and did I mention I'm supposed to make the casino profitable by the middle of November?"

"You didn't, no." Randy watched Ethan's face carefully. "That's going to be a bit of a trick, is it?"

"Just a bit." His eyes were practically dancing.

Randy gave Ethan's leg a friendly slap. "You and your wad of hundreds are going to cop a squat at the big-boy table. Time to play with the high rollers, Slick."

Ethan balked. "Randy, I can't possibly be ready for that."

"Oh, fuck no. They're going to wipe the floor with you. This isn't going to be about winning. It's about learning. Your pot today is knowledge."

Ethan didn't seem happy, but he made no further protest as Randy led him across the floor to the poker room.

The Bellagio poker room was not hidden away in some remote part of the hotel—it was proudly displayed up front. The tables were too close together, though. So Randy did his instruction on the way across the main floor, after they'd hit the cashier but before they went into the room.

"The best poker players come here daily for tournaments, but we're not getting into them now. This is the big league. They will beat you most of the time. Play tight. Do not become their fish. Play your blinds and use most of the hands as opportunities to study. We'll play for an hour, and then we'll meet up at Snacks and debrief."

"Snacks?"

Randy pointed to the small restaurant just off the poker room. "There. The name of the café is Snacks. Direct and to the point. Which reminds me, get a drink now. It will likely be the only one you see."

Randy got a Pepsi, and Ethan got mineral water. He was girding himself, Randy could tell, which was cute, but the sharks would be able to tell.

Randy rubbed Ethan's neck. "Be cool, Slick."

"I don't want to do this."

"Then you'd better dump all the money back at Crabtree and Billy and borrow what you're missing from me. Buck up, baby. You can do this. Stop making it so hard. It's just poker. Same as ever. Just for more money and worse odds. Come on." He patted Ethan on the back. "Time for school."

Randy approved of the seat Ethan chose, though it had to have been accidental. He was between Vic Tabor, one of the worst sharks in Vegas, and a cunning woman named Cate whom Randy didn't know well except she was vegan and from Canada. She played straight and fair—but to win.

He predicted Cate was going to make a lot of money off Ethan in the next sixty minutes. He was right.

"The woman beside me keeps winning," Ethan complained as he sat down across from Randy at Snacks. "I'm down to three hundred dollars because of her."

"You're down to three hundred because you're not paying attention to her. You're her fish, Slick, because you're too focused on Vic."

"That's because Vic is an *animal*."

"Vic plays loose and wild. You'll notice he hasn't won many pots, and that's because Cate is at his table, feeding off you. Vic bluffs like crazy. But he knows how to play. He's probably relieved you left because now he can focus on Cate again. Though he won't get far."

Ethan swore and reached for his G&T.

Randy smiled behind his hand. "What did you learn, Slick?"

Ethan considered. "I learned it makes me nervous to play with so much money."

"Yes. But the game is still the same. You get that, right?"

"It's hard to implement the knowledge."

"Which is why you need to keep practicing. Because you've got bigger games coming, Secret Casino Manager."

Ethan stirred his drink. "I'm not really a gangster, Randy." He looked up. "Am I?"

Randy thought about lying then decided it wasn't going to help anything. "Gangsters aren't like you see in the movies. Most of the mob is accountants."

Ethan held Randy's gaze. "Who is Crabtree? I can't find anything on him. Nothing at all."

Randy sobered, not bothering to hide his panic. "Don't look. Don't try to find out who he is, Ethan. I'm not shitting you. *Don't.*"

"But how can I—?"

Randy held up a hand. "There are games you see through to the end without really knowing what the other guy has. This is one of those. If Crabtree wants to let you know who he is, he'll tell you. If he doesn't, don't go looking."

Ethan pursed his lips. "*You* know."

"No, I don't. Swear to God, Slick. I have no fucking clue. You've been Googling, I can see. Let me give you a little more education. The best mobsters are not the Al Capones. The best ones never get named."

"You're saying Crabtree is one of those?"

"Ethan Ellison, you are further into the nest than I have ever been. You can believe it or deny it, but you know more about Crabtree than I do. Unless you want to know what he likes in bed." Ethan glared, and Randy raised his eyebrows. "That bothering you, Slick?"

"I don't care for being reminded you've fucked him."

Fucking hell, but Slick was hot when he was possessive. "I can't change the fact that I have."

"Well, you're done, so stop talking about it."

Oh, just a little more. "Who are you to say I'm done with it?"

Ethan came around to Randy's side of the table slowly. Randy held still, waiting. *Come on, baby. Give it to me. Right here in fucking Bellagio.*

When Ethan's hand came down on his shoulder, Randy jumped. Ethan bent down and spoke directly into his ear, and Randy shut his eyes, waiting for whatever masterful naughtiness Slick dished up.

"I adopted another cat."

Randy opened his eyes, blinking. "What the hell? Oh, come on. You were supposed to say something sexy, Slick, not make some stupid joke." Then he got a good look at Ethan's face, and his eyes went wide. "Fucking hell, *you did not.*"

"I fucking did." Ethan pulled out Randy's cell phone and glanced at the time. "In fact, I need to go and get them soon. Crystal said she was off at five, and I wanted to ask her a few more questions." He waved the phone at Randy. "I really need to get my own phone, but I think we've run out of time to shop. Sam texted you while I was playing—Mitch is making dinner, and he'd like us home by six."

"You adopted another cat." Randy was still processing. "What the fuck, Slick?"

Ethan's hand moved from Randy's shoulder to his chin. He held Randy's face loosely, but his thumbnail dug in enough to get Randy's attention. Randy stilled, enjoying a delicious rush of heat and the do-not-fuck-with-me look in Ethan's eyes.

"You're done with Crabtree because I don't fucking want you to have anything else to do with him. Not in bed. Have I made myself clear, or do you need additional persuasion?"

Oh, fuck yes. Randy did his best to play it cool. "I might."

Ethan's expression didn't change, but his fingers tightened. It was fucking glorious.

"We need to get going so I can pick up Salomé and Daisy." His thumb brushed Randy's lips, but it wasn't exactly a caress. "We'll deal with your persuasion once we're at home."

It was a cool play. It didn't matter that Randy could see it, that he knew Ethan had deliberately wrapped the bombshell of the kittens up in the game. It was a good move. "Well played, baby."

Ethan bent and kissed Randy's lips. "I'm serious. We need to get going."

They cashed in, Ethan leading, looking like he belonged. Because he did. The man had fucking come home.

"Were you like this before?" *With Nick?*

"No, I wasn't." Turning to Randy, he smiled wickedly. "This is all because of you, Ace."

It wasn't, Randy knew. This was Slick, coming into his own. But he didn't tell him, just squeezed his ass and led him to the bike.

RANDY HAD TO admit Daisy was seriously cute. So was watching Slick with Crystal the cat-training lady. Randy held the kitten while Ethan nodded at her, absorbing everything she said. They kept doing something with this annoying clicking piece of plastic, a pink stick, a bag of treats, and Daisy. For some reason if the cat touched the stick with her nose, they gave her a click and a treat, regarding the act as her personal triumph. When Randy left Ethan and his new family at the Mazda, in fact, Ethan looked very much the king of his realm.

Of course, when they got to the house, he was glad they had the cats. They sure as fuck needed a distraction.

The whole place smelled of good Mexican food, *real* Mexican, because Mitch did the cooking. Tamales, Sam's favorite, which Mitch made most often when he wanted to show his partner how much he loved him. When Randy got a good look at husband and husband, he knew the big love gesture was certainly called for. Sam was a wreck, and so was Mitch.

Randy launched into high court jester mode. He made loud noises about how good the food smelled, and so many rude comments about Sam's body and what he wanted to do with it that Ethan started to look at him askance. He was saved from having to explain that one by Sam finally noticing the second cat, and then Randy made snark about cat litter and scratches, and when Ethan explained the clicker to Sam, Randy zeroed in on Mitch, poking until Mitch snapped at him. Randy teased back, anything he could think of to dispel all the damn spiky energy.

Of course, Slick was starting to get a little too smart for his own good, because he cottoned on.

"I didn't realize I should have stopped by the hardware store. Or do you have a trowel in the garage? Because if you're going to lay it on this thick, Ace, you might want to smooth it out."

"They're about to turn into the movie *Beaches* over there, and I've had enough therapy for one day, thank you." When Ethan gave him a confused look, Randy pursed his lips. "Sam roped me into going to his therapist with him. I didn't like it."

Ethan kissed his forehead. "Poor baby."

Randy grunted. "So are you going to help me or what?"

"I don't think pissing them off constantly is helping much."

It wasn't, but Randy didn't know what else to do. "Nobody can give them what they need. Mitch can't get a guarantee Sam will be okay while he's gone, and Sam can't know nothing will happen to Mitch. You got any ideas on how to make them forget about that?"

Ethan tapped his fingers against his thigh. "Give me a few minutes. In the meantime, dial it down to medium-high."

"Yes, sir."

Slick gave him another kiss, this time on his lips with a tiny bite at the end. *Mmm-hmm.*

Randy returned to the kitchen, where Mitch threatened him with a spatula. Holding up his hands in mock surrender, he bent, offering him his ass, which Mitch swatted several times while Randy made high-pitched squeals of mock protest until Sam laughed. Then Mitch swatted him hard enough to hurt, and Randy yelped for real, and everyone laughed. He set the table, keeping one eye on Ethan, who was seated there, Salomé in his lap and Daisy settled at his feet as he studied them all.

Dinner was good, and so was dessert—*sopaipillas* with real whipped cream. Randy kept up his chatter, not even sure what he was talking about anymore, just waiting to see what Slick was up to.

Once all the dishes were cleared, Ethan rose. He walked around the table to where Sam sat, stood behind him and put a hand on his shoulder. Everyone watched, surprised, confused, and then simply interested as Ethan kept his hand there, massaging slowly.

"So." Ethan glanced at Mitch. "When are you leaving tomorrow?"

Ethan might as well have turned the air temperature down five degrees. "Ten."

Randy glared at Ethan, but Ethan ignored him and kept talking to Mitch. "You'll be back when?"

"Two weeks, give or take. Depends how things go."

Ethan massaged Sam's shoulder a little more.

"When do you start work at the hospital?"

Sam kept his eyes on the table. "I'm not due to start until the first of November, but they'd probably let me start early."

"Do you *want* to start early?"

Sam shrugged and didn't answer.

Ethan resumed his massaging. Randy wondered what the fuck he was doing, but didn't say anything, just waited.

When he finally spoke, Randy about fell over.

"The other night, in the limo—" Ethan looked at Mitch. "I take it everyone enjoyed themselves?"

Mitch, who had been stiff and unhappy, was a camera lens coming into focus. "Can't say I saw anything to complain about."

"What about you, Sam?" Ethan's fingers slid farther down, dipping inside the neckline of Sam's T-shirt. "Did you enjoy the limo? I was thinking in particular of when you and Randy were dancing out the moonroof. You seemed to enjoy that part."

Sam's sorrow bled away into submission. His voice, soft and quiet, went straight to Randy's dick. "I liked it a lot."

"Hmm." Ethan kneaded, keeping his eyes on the top of Sam's head. He was beautifully disinterested and alert at the same time. Randy felt unfocused and yet fantastically engaged. Fucking hell, Randy was already halfway under Ethan without being touched.

Ethan spoke again. "It seems to me there's a lot of emotion built up over this parting. Which is understandable. But I'm thinking it might be a little too much. More, say, than two people could handle alone."

Ho, shit, Randy thought, his heart pounding. Dick too.

Ethan looked at Mitch, who Randy thought was probably in much the same condition as himself, only in a Mitch way. He didn't know, because he couldn't turn away from Ethan to check. He could clearly see Sam was putty from the way he slouched into Ethan's massage.

"I thought, though, perhaps four could deal with it. What do you think, Mitch? Have I read this situation right?"

Now Randy had to look at Mitch too, and he was glad he did, because the lust there told him everything he needed to know. What it told him was they were all getting laid. Together.

So Slick's idea is to distract them with an orgy. Good idea, Slick.

Ethan bent to kiss the side of Sam's head. "Sam, sweetheart? Take off your shirt."

And away we go.

CHAPTER SIXTEEN

R ANDY HADN'T KNOWN quite what to think when
Ethan directed Sam's blow job in the limo, writing
it off as something Ethan was trying out. Randy had the
feeling if he hadn't been overwhelmed they'd have done
more that night. He admitted he'd put on the brakes,
that it was he who hadn't been ready for a foursome
with Ethan in it.

Even though Randy hadn't admitted it, Ethan had
probably figured it out and was watching him closely
now to make sure Randy wanted this.

He did. Randy wasn't sure exactly why the other
night had been too much and now it was cool, but that's
the way it went down. This was for Sam and Mitch. And
hell, for him. Watching Ethan peel Sam's T-shirt off his
body, watching Sam go from the edge of despair to
quiet and submissive and ready to be fucked was hot.
This was what he loved most about Sam, how he
managed to be so sweet and innocent and absolutely
depraved all at once. Not just in sex, but in life. He
hated that Sam was so upset. And yes, he would keep
going to therapy with him, goddamn it.

But right now…well, this was Randy's kind of therapy.

Except having Slick a part of it changed things, and not just because they were four instead of three. As Ethan drew Sam's hands up and looped them around the back of Ethan's head, making Sam gasp and moan, Randy realized all the other times it had been Randy the outsider coming into Sam and Mitch's relationship. It was a role he excelled at, and he liked it fine. Now—well, now he didn't know what this was. He and Slick coming in, but as what? Another couple?

Yes, damn it. Slick is mine.

But was he? What the hell were they doing, anyway? Randy had gone and told him he loved him because he was an idiot, but Ethan hadn't said it back. Which Randy didn't expect, since he wasn't a twelve-year-old girl or the heroine of a teen vampire novel. Still. What were they? What was this?

Ethan's fingers trailed down Sam's naked, quivering chest, and the low-grade hum in Randy's blood shut off as something more aggressive—and, goddamn it, vulnerable—took its place. Seriously—what the fuck *was* this?

Lifting his head, Ethan caught and held Randy's gaze.

He didn't take his eyes off Randy as his lips parted and his tongue stole out to tease the rim of Sam's ear. Sam shuddered, and the heat came back in a rush. But Randy's confusion remained, and he stayed rigid, watching, irritated he was being so stupid about this. Goddamn, it was an orgy with Slick and Sam in it, and he was objecting?

Ethan seemed to understand him better than he did himself. Still making an after-dinner mint of Sam's ear and grazing his fingers across the young man's chest, Ethan nodded at Randy.

"Take your shirt off too, Ace." His fingers circled Sam's nipple but didn't touch it. He glanced at Mitch. "Maybe we should take this somewhere with more room? A bedroom?"

"Living room." Mitch pushed off the counter. "I'll move the coffee table and get a blanket."

They usually did this in the living room. That was Mitch's way of being able to take Sam off if it got too heated or if he got the clue Sam was done having group sex. Because this was the way it ran. Sam drove. Sam was the submissive, and so it was always centered on Sam.

Except while Sam was exceptionally submissive tonight, the scene wasn't just centered on Sam somehow. Ethan led, deferring to Mitch. Probably because Sam was his husband. Where did Randy land in all this? It kept coming back to that, and it made him feel odd. Why did he care? Why wasn't he all over this?

Because I don't want to be on the outside this time. Which was trouble. Real fucking trouble. This was worse than just loving Ethan. This was—he didn't know, but he could feel the trap closing around him. This was truly shitty odds. There was no best of it here.

Randy's poker face must have taken the night off because Ethan whispered something into Sam's ear, and

Sam nodded and went after Mitch. Ethan came around the table to Randy. He looked down at him, still in that sexy, quiet, commander mode, but then he bent down, and it was Randy's ear he was kissing, soft, sweet, and tender. "Did I misread you? Do you not want to do this?"

Randy shut his eyes. He might have leaned into Ethan's lips, nudging them back on his ear. He hoped he didn't, though. "I don't know."

Another kiss, just as sweet. "Do you want this to stop?"

No. "I don't know." He drew a breath then forced the answer out. "No."

Ethan's hand had fallen onto Randy's shoulder, and now it slid down his arm. "Is it me? Do you want me to step out and let—"

"*No.*" Jesus fuck, what the fucking hell was wrong with him? When the *hell* did he turn into the vulnerable one? What the shit was this?

This time Ethan's kiss at his ear was slower and had a bit of tongue to it. "Tell me what you want, Ace. Let me give it to you."

How many times had they said this to Sam? How many times had Randy bent over Sam, acutely aware of Mitch watching, and asked what he wanted? That was when he realized for Slick, it wasn't for Sam.

For Ethan, it was about Randy.

He's mine after all, then. Randy sat there a minute, reeling in the discovery. Then Ethan kissed his ear again.

"You can't kiss Sam," Randy said at last. "That's not my rule. I kind of want to kiss him myself, probably because it's forbidden. That's Mitch's line in the sand. He's happy to watch anybody do anything to Sam, or hear it happened when he wasn't there, but kissing is a no-no. Also, Sam's safe word is Violet."

"That's a lot about Sam." Ethan kneaded Randy's biceps. "I was hoping to hear about you."

Me too. Randy had no idea. Okay, he knew what he wanted, but—with Mitch and Sam?

It would be okay with Slick. It was…well, he hadn't ever quite let go with anybody like that. Not outside of Crabtree.

Where else are you going to let go, if not here? With Ethan? With all of them?

Ethan brushed a kiss on his hairline. "I think I know what you want, but I'd rather you told me. It's not something I want to be wrong about."

Randy nodded. That was the first rule of these games. You had to be honest about what it was you wanted. "You ever heard the term switch?"

"I'm not sure, so probably not."

"How about dominant and submissive?"

Ethan raised his eyebrows. "Are we talking about BDSM?"

Randy waved an impatient hand. "We're talking about roles. Dominant versus submissive. You don't have to be talking about spanking or whips or anything to get into roles—though, actually, we've been into it in the past. But later for that. Do you know dominant and submissive? The idea of it?"

"One partner is in charge?"

Randy winced. Oh fuck, this was never going to work. "Never mind. Let's just go play."

Ethan held him in place. "I said something wrong. Correct me."

"It's too complicated." Randy thought for a minute, trying to find an angle. "Okay. You get dominant and submissive—the definition of the words? It's like that."

"I know you enjoy it when I take control of sex. But you're telling me the dominant is not in charge?"

Randy looked up at him, irritated. "I don't know, Slick. You feel very in charge right now?"

He should have known. Really, when had Ethan ever missed more than one beat in a row?

Ethan stroked Randy's cheek. "Okay, so I understand that part. The submissive is in charge. So tell me about switch."

"Sam is only submissive. It's what he likes. He's the fucking best I've ever seen. Mitch is dominant only. He always takes that role, and even when it's the three of us, he's the top Dom. A switch is someone who is both, or can be both."

"Hmm. That might be me. And you, when it's us." He tilted his head to the side. "What about with them, Ace?"

"That's the thing. With Mitch and Sam, I always end up dominant. But only with Sam, and there's a sort of hierarchy where I submit to Mitch, just not in sex. Mitch and I were together a long time ago, and I tried to sub for him, but I'd get freaked out. Which is how we got into threesomes. I get freaked out with most people, to be honest."

He realized where this was heading and tried to stop, but Ethan drove the train on anyway. "But you can go there with Crabtree."

"I've been there with you, if you care to remember." He bit his lip and forced the rest out. "I really want to go there with you again. Now. With them."

"So this is your long way of saying you want to switch and take the submissive role. Which means you want me to be dominant. And you want to do this with Mitch and Sam."

So nice and simple when Ethan said it, yet still terrifying. "Yes."

Ethan's fingers tightened on Randy's chin and tipped it back so he either had to look at Slick or shut his eyes. Randy didn't shut his eyes. "What's your safe word?"

"Cactus, but—"

"Take off your shirt, Randy, and go into the living room."

This was the part Randy could not have explained if his life depended on it. Not out loud. Because what tripped him up was this—the Look. Mitch always fucked it up. Mitch could never quite get rid of his dad telling him he was a fat little faggot, could never sweep all his guilt and shame aside and take control. With Sam he could, or Sam just wasn't aware of all the complexities. Or didn't care. It was possible Sam was too in love with sliding under, with surrendering, being done to. So did Randy, actually, but he could so rarely get there because every time he got hung up on this part.

The Look.

Crabtree had it. Shit, Crabtree had the Look from across a room. Complete self-possession, complete control. He looked at you, told you he wanted you, and there was this huge space, his great big arms extended, and you could go in there and let it all out. That was why it was hot. That was why Randy was always happy to be the gangster's piece on the side. It was the only real place he could surrender.

He wanted it with Slick. They'd stumbled into it a few times, but it might have been an accident. Could they do it now? Here? With Mitch and Sam? Was this absolutely stupid, to start with a group? Randy didn't know.

Randy's gaze met Ethan's, and he went still.

Ethan had it. He absolutely, totally had it.

He had the control. The conviction. Randy tried to push at it, because how, *how* could he have it when Ethan had been the guy with a gun under his front seat just a few days ago, who kept melting down? But actually, yeah. The guy who could so single-mindedly lose all his money and then gird his loins to go out and blow his brains out *was* in control. He was in control now too. He barely knew what the roles were, but he was an ace, the ace of aces. He had Randy's chin in his hand, figuring it out, waiting for Randy to catch up.

Holy shit.

Ethan's eyes were dark and dangerous. "Take off your shirt, Randy, and go to the living room. *Now.*"

Like a bolt of lightning finding its way in through a crack in the walls, the word ran through Randy, hitting the magic spot, and he went soft, almost as soft as Sam. He unhooked, and panic tried to take him over, but then Ethan led him to his feet. Randy panicked as Ethan drew the shirt over his face, but it was only there a moment and then it was gone, Ethan looking at him. Randy stared back, arms closed around him, not Ethan's arms but the arms of his control. They expanded, forming space—bigger, closer, warmer, and stronger than anything else had ever been with anyone.

Ethan brushed a kiss over Randy's mouth and drew down the hands still hovering over Randy's head. "Come."

Because he'd been commanded, Randy went.

It got harder when they joined the others.

Sam sat on the blanket, fly unzipped, and because Randy and Ethan had taken so long, Mitch kept his husband warmed up, toying with Sam's cock a little. Mitch looked up when Randy and Ethan came over, and Randy lost some of his sensual spell when he saw Mitch take in his shirtless state. He realized he might end up being submissive to Mitch too, and he wasn't sure he wanted to try it again after so long.

Ethan, who had no idea any of this was of concern, led Randy forward. When Mitch withdrew and sat on the couch to watch, Ethan accepted it, stepping into role of ringmaster as if he'd been born to it. He arranged

Randy across from Sam on the floor. Sam seemed surprised but didn't say anything, especially when Ethan put a hand on top of his head. With that touch, Sam shut his eyes and went pliant.

Salomé bounded out from between the couch and the chair onto Sam's legs, looking up at Randy, ready to play.

Mood. Killer.

Ethan laughed and scooped up the kitten. "Daisy," he called, and Randy watched man and two cats disappear down the hall. Mitch followed.

Sam and Randy were alone.

Sam smiled sleepily. "I didn't expect this."

"Slick's full of surprises."

"You like him."

Randy nodded.

"Me too."

They sat there, waiting. Because that was the game, and Sam, no dummy, had already figured it out. Other nights it would have been Randy talking dirty to him. But not tonight. Not unless Ethan directed them to.

Sam's foot turned sideways and his sock rubbed against Randy's hip. "I've missed you, Randy."

Randy reached over and massaged Sam's foot. "Missed you too, Peaches."

This was the thing about being a switch, at least for Randy—let go of the control he'd handed over for more than a minute, and he picked it up again. He kept up his massage, absently at first, but soon his finger teased the edge of his sock. Peeling it off, he took Sam's bare foot in hand. Sam's eyes went dark and soft as he fell into subspace. Randy made love to Sam's foot with his hands, drawing him into pleasure, making him gasp, making his pink, semihard cock lengthen and darken until it was red and swollen and bobbing as blood filled it. His own dick responded in kind. He just sat there, loving the feel of the control he had over Sam, loving the way Sam gave it so easily. Loving Sam.

Cool, firm hands came down on Randy's shoulders, and he stopped. He recognized the invitation to move into the arms open for him, literal and metaphorical. When he paused, unsure, Ethan embraced him from behind and whispered in his ear. "Lean forward and take him in your mouth."

The space didn't just open for him, it swallowed him up. It took the space he'd made for Sam too. It took it all. And Randy went. Fuck yes, he went.

Like a dream, he slid up Sam's legs, guided first by Ethan's hands and then moving on his own. His gaze met Sam's, but as he lifted onto his knees and shifted over Sam's erection, he bent his head to swirl his tongue around the tip. Sam gasped. Smiling, Randy took him in deeper, bracing his hands on the insides of Sam's thighs, holding him open. *Yes.* He sucked Sam deep inside his mouth, into his throat, and he hummed, making Sam gasp and moan, letting pleasuring Sam consume him.

Randy shivered when Ethan's hands reached around him and undid his fly, he whose rhythm stuttered when those same hands pulled his waistband down until it nudged his knees. When the short slap came against his ass, he lifted first one knee and then the other until Ethan had gotten his jeans all the way to his ankles, where they remained. He nudged apart Randy's knees so far Randy almost lost his balance—until those hands left him and drew Sam's bare foot and his stocking foot against each side. Randy paused, uncertain.

A hand came down—Ethan's, he knew by the touch, by the way he pressed—and pushed Randy back to his task. Randy shut his eyes and let himself be led.

He imagined what a fucking glorious sight they must be, Sam half-dressed, Randy's mouth on him, Randy spread open and moaning, bucking helplessly into Ethan's elegant, gorgeous mouth as he made love to Randy's ass. He had the picture of it in his head, and that more than anything sent him headlong into lust. He sucked greedily at Sam, who gasped in great, high-pitched sighs and breathy moans, pushing his hips off the floor, driving himself deeper into Randy's throat. Ethan let go of his ass with one hand and took hold of his balls, gently milking them as he first breathed hard against Randy's hole, then began to worm his tongue inside, forcing it open. Randy purred his pleasure as he opened himself even farther for Ethan, letting him in, urging him deeper, begging him with his body to claim him more, do more, anything, just more.

Abruptly, Ethan drew him off Sam, making him kneel. Mitch was there, hauling Sam up in the way he had that was almost rough. Then Sam was naked and kneeling and coming at Randy's cock with his mouth as

Mitch lubed his fingers. Mitch slipped a finger inside of his husband as Sam closed his lips around Randy, his moan reverberating against Randy's cock.

"Holy shit," Randy whispered as Ethan kissed him.

It was in every way an orgy—excess in its purest form. Sex. Touch. Thrusts. Mouths. Hands, fucking hell, it felt like there were thirty of them. Sam's hands. Ethan's hands. Randy's hands. Mitch, behind him. Mitch touching his stomach, Mitch bending down to breathe hot and lusty in Randy's ear. How the hell Mitch and Ethan had switched places Randy had no idea, but they had, and it was Mitch's fingers coming at him, slick and insistent, his other hand sliding down to take Randy's cock in hand.

Randy flipped out. "Wait, you just had—"

"I wiped my hands off, and I'm wearin' a glove. A new one. We both are. Hush now. Calm down." *So gentle.* Jesus, it was as if they'd gone back twelve years, to that first night. Randy shivered. Mitch stroked his cock again. "Don't worry, Skeet. Got your back, same as always."

Randy glanced across the blanket to Sam, who returned the gaze, molten with lust as one of Ethan's hands pinched his nipple and the other disappeared into the dark space between their bodies. Randy watched Sam jerk, then ease into the thrust of Ethan's hand.

Still, Randy couldn't let go, not yet. "We don't play like this, Old Man. Not anymore."

"Wasn't because I didn't want to." Mitch placed an

open-mouthed kiss on Randy's neck, making his vision blur. "I remember your word. You gonna use it?"

It was his out. One word would end this. One word and it was over. One word and this admittedly enticing but highly scary door would stay closed.

Randy couldn't do it.

"No." He melted into Mitch, terrified but trusting, and whether it was the magic of Ethan, or their own magic, or just dumb luck, this time it worked.

"Then I'm gonna fuck you, Skeet. I'm gonna finger-fuck you in front of my husband and your boyfriend. Right here. And you're gonna open up and take it. You got that?"

Randy's insides melted. Mitch knew he loved dirty talk. Really fucking dirty. "Yeah."

"Tell me how many fingers you want."

Randy looked at Ethan, right in the eye and let him see it, let him see he enjoyed this. Probably let him see the terror too. Ethan smiled, pinched Sam's nipple again and let his eyes wander down to Randy's cock.

"Three."

Mitch growled his approval against Randy's neck and pushed one finger inside.

But that was a tease. Lifting Randy's leg so he was only kneeling one-sided, Mitch spread him farther, putting him on the edge of his sense of balance. Mitch's hand left and came back lubricated. Randy hitched a breath as fingers pushed up inside him, thick, insistent. Randy looked Ethan in the eye and took Mitch in because Ethan liked watching. Because it felt good.

Because it felt dangerous and safe at once.

Mitch finished, Randy panting and pliant. He went where Mitch aimed him, which was, weirdly enough, into Sam's arms. Mitch and Ethan worked together, pressing Sam and Randy into one another. Kneeling, their aching cocks sliding together, Randy's long and thick and uncut, a big boorish thing, and Sam's slim and sleek and naked. Ethan behind Sam, Mitch behind Randy, and that was how Randy ended up with his hands on Ethan's shoulders and Sam's on his husband's. But it was Mitch's dick nudging between Randy's cheeks, not entering him, just poking him, and he assumed Ethan played the mirror of this behind Sam. Sam undulated, and so did Randy, their mouths at each other's ears, and they stayed that way until they began to gasp almost in concert, matching their rhythms, rubbing their faces against one another, caressing each other.

Mitch's hands came down, one on Randy's head, one on Sam's, and turned their faces together. Randy stared at Sam and Sam stared back, sloe-eyed and heavy lidded, his gaze on Randy's mouth. Randy took in Sam's fat, parted lips, and he felt a deep, thick pang of desire. He tried to turn away.

Ethan pushed him forward, trapping him between his and Mitch's hands.

Mitch bent to Randy's ear. "Kiss him, Skeet."

Randy and Sam went still, eyes wide.

Mitch squeezed his shoulder. "I know how you feel about Sam, and I don't care. I know how you love him, know why, what it means to you, and it makes me feel good. Makes me feel I can leave him with you, like he won't be so lonely." Mitch nudged Sam's cheek. "Show him, Skeet. Show Sam. He's the only one who doesn't know. Show him. Please."

For about five seconds, Randy couldn't do it. *This is the most fucked-up thing I've ever heard.* But then Ethan stroked his other cheek, and Sam looked up at him. Randy saw the fear in Sam. As much as Sam hated being told this, he was still too young to really know how to handle everything. Hell, maybe Randy wasn't ready either. But he juggled it better than Sam, and so, in a move that Randy chalked up to *never fucking thought I would see the fucking day, fucking ever*, Randy let himself slide even further under, not just under Ethan and Mitch, but under Sam too.

Bending forward, he pressed his lips to Sam's, to the mouth of the beautiful young man who had turned his life upside down two years ago, the man he loved in a way not about marriage or partnership, but instead was about sex and play, and above all, about protection. Under the watchful eye of Mitch and Ethan, Randy told it all to Sam. He told him with his mouth, with his hands, with a tenderness he wasn't sure he could give to anyone else, not even to Slick. Randy gave it to Sam, gave him the little boy that Sam drew out in him, the boy nobody had seen since the day Uncle Gary had gone into the ground. Randy brought him out for Sam. For Mitch and Ethan.

For himself.

Sam returned the kiss, understanding the message—*I love you*—and sending it right back.

Sam and Randy embraced, kissing like lovers, like children. They were youth inside still, boys who needed love too. This moment, this kiss, was not about sex. This moment wasn't about anything but comfort, and it wasn't about anybody but Sam and Randy and the lovers who knew how to give it to them.

Their partners switched, and the tone switched again. When Ethan nudged himself inside of Randy and Mitch inside of Sam, it was making love. They thrust, they touched, they kissed. Four bodies, eight hands, four mouths, four erections all blurring into one body, for this one time. They didn't all come at once, but Randy would be damned if he knew who started and who finished. They all found release. There was one more confused, indistinguishable round of kisses, and then it was over, everyone going to their respective bedrooms.

Randy and Ethan, flanked by a cat and a kitten, lay twined together and stared up at the ceiling.

"Wow," Randy said at last.

Ethan stroked Randy's head, and Randy could almost feel his smile. "So I did okay?"

Randy kissed him. "Thank you."

Ethan touched his nose. He was softer now, all his command sliding away. *Ace moving high to low.* "I've never done anything like that. Ever."

"I've always said you were a quick study."

Ethan went softer, then softer yet, then closed his

eyes. When he opened them, he could lift his gaze no higher than Randy's chin. His fingers rested hesitantly on Randy's cheeks. "I love you too, Randy."

Joy rose up from deep inside him—a sunrise, a balloon, a bright white light. He kissed Ethan's forehead.

Ethan nuzzled him back, a little shaky. "What do we do?"

"It's Vegas. We could run off and get married." When Ethan went white, he laughed and kissed him. "I'm teasing you, Slick."

"It's when everything slows down I lose it. I can do anything when I'm moving. It's when I stop and think and feel, and realize how fucking out of my element I am, that I fall over. You, that out there, the casino, Crabtree, Billy, Vegas—it's all easy, until I stop. And then I have no idea how a guy like me got here." He sighed and stroked Randy's cheek. "Sorry. I'm not being very dominant, am I?"

"I told you. I'm a switch. That means…" he nuzzled Randy's nose, then stole a slow, bone-melting kiss, "…I like to switch."

Ethan shivered. "Me too."

Randy watched him go under, sliding before Randy even had the space ready for him. Opening his arms, he took Ethan in. His body was spent, but his heart, still hungry, led his spirit on, and they lay there in the dark, flanked by Salomé and Daisy, two members of an orgy of four now content to do nothing more exotic than kiss.

Of course, as Mitch had always warned him, kissing was the most intimate act of all.

CHAPTER SEVENTEEN

Ethan was surprised how much Mitch and Sam's parting affected him. He'd yearned for similar goodbyes with Nick, ones he'd never received. This, compounded by the connection they shared because of the night before, meant Ethan knew a pang of loss when Mitch caught him in a bear hug, gruffly holding back tears. It was hard to watch Mitch climb into his bright blue cab and drive away. Ethan didn't even want to think of what Sam must be feeling.

To Ethan's surprise, Sam managed himself pretty well. He was quiet, and he leaned on Randy as he drove them through town, but he didn't melt down.

Randy sighed. "What shall we do with our day? Still want to go to Zion, Sam?"

Sam shook his head.

Ethan's gaze fell to the phone in Sam's hand. "I still need to go shopping."

Randy seized on the idea. "*Yes.* Shopping. I forgot. Okay. So. Where are we going? Forum Shops? Miracle Mile again?"

Another shake of Sam's head. "I don't want to go to the Forum Shops."

"Sure. No problem. We can go anywhere. What about Fashion Show?"

Sam considered this. "The Apple Store is there, right?"

From the look on Randy's face, Ethan suspected if there wasn't, he'd try to get one built while Sam used the restroom.

Sam did a search. "Yes, it is. That okay, Ethan? Fashion Show?"

"Sure." He nodded at Sam's iPhone. "May I see that? Because a phone is one of the first things I need to get."

"Sure." Sam passed it over. "I love it. Mitch has one too."

Ethan turned the device over a few times in his hand. "I had a BlackBerry before, but maybe it's time for something flashier."

"The games are great. Here. You need Sheep Launcher."

"Sheep Launcher?"

"Yeah. It's a free app, though I splurged and spent the money to get the full version. See this sheep?" He pointed to an animated fluffy white beast in an aviator cap sitting at the bottom of a carnival game, the type where a mallet slams something toward a bell. "Hit the button, and he'll fly up. Keep tapping on him so he doesn't fall, and he'll just keep going and going and going."

Ethan seriously doubted the utility of this action, but he decided he would play along for Sam's sake. So he hit the sheep, watched him fly then failed to tap him before the screen announced his game was over.

"Try again," Sam urged.

Ethan did. And then tried again, and then again, and then his sheep was seriously airborne. Eventually it went into outer space. When the truck stopped, Randy's call of "All right" distracted him, otherwise he would have made it all the way to the moon, he was sure of it. Ethan looked up at Sam, a little surprised to find he was not animated and bouncing on a white pillow.

"I'm getting an iPhone," he said, and Sam beamed at him.

Fashion Show was a mall, a high-end one. It was as Vegas as everything else, full of lights and displays and a show on every corner, though Ethan noticed the thing it was not full of was people. They practically had the place to themselves.

"This is bad." Randy grimaced as he scanned the empty concourse. "Of course, as usual, this city is a metaphor for the country. We didn't just bring everybody in to gamble—we brought them in to eat in fancy restaurants and shop in fancy malls and go to expensive shows. Now we're the playground of kings and queens in a country full of overnight paupers and those who are afraid—and probably rightly so—that they're next."

I'm going to resurrect a casino in the middle of this. "Thanks for the pep talk, Ace."

"Anytime, Slick. You want your iPhone first, or are we hungry? Because I haven't had sushi in a while, and RA is just around the corner."

"Apple Store." Sam pointed down the concourse. "This way."

Ethan ended up getting himself a laptop as well as an iPhone, and since he was already spending so much money, he tossed on a set of casino and card games as well. They hung out in the store, Sam gushing over everything Mac. He also sent several texts to Mitch, and at Randy's urging, they sent him video of them stuffing sushi into one another's faces. Then they trolled for some more clothes for Ethan, some casual, some extraordinarily fancy, but at Ethan's insistence, they were all highly conservative.

"When I'm at work, I like to be inconspicuous," he said when Randy tried to push him toward wilder shirts and ties.

"But you want to stand out a little too." Randy handed Ethan a traditionally structured shirt tinted lavender, and up close the pattern hinted slightly at subtle stripes. "You aren't an investment broker any-more. You're a mob man. Dress the part."

"I thought you said the best mobsters were invisi-ble."

"I said they were anonymous. I didn't say their fash-ion sense put nuns to sleep. Here." He handed him a stack of shirts. "Go put these on under your suit and tell me I'm not right."

Ethan arched his eyebrow as he took the clothes from him. "What, you aren't going to come ogle me while I change?"

That made Sam smile, and Randy held up his hands

in mock surrender. "Well, if you're going to *insist*, I suppose I must."

Randy was right. The suits were good, but carefully selected shirts and ties made them somehow even better. It wasn't about being flashy. It was about…something. When he voiced the thought out loud, Randy immediately had the answer.

"It's a bluff. You go in wearing a smart suit, and people assume your hand. Fact of life." Ethan cast a critical eye over Randy's threadbare T-shirt and ratty jeans, and Randy grinned. "Bluffs go both ways, baby."

They went to a discount store where Ethan picked up things he'd borrowed for days now—shaving cream, shampoo, conditioner, hair product, and razor blades. He also picked up a pillow that, unlike Randy's, couldn't double as a piece of notebook paper. He bought his favorite snacks, a few CDs he was already starting to miss, and pretty much everything catching his attention as he passed through the aisles.

Randy shook his head as it went by on the conveyor belt. "You're kind of high-maintenance."

Ethan thought about pointing out that the night they'd met everything he'd owned had fit in his pockets, but this would upset Randy, so he said nothing.

Sam picked up a CD from the pile of stuff. Then he grinned. "Olivia Newton-John. My mom loved her."

"Mine too. And look, this one's for you—a song with your name in it." Ethan turned the album over and pointed to track number seven. "See? 'Sam'."

Sam's expression became nostalgic. "Yeah. Mom

liked to sing that to me. She stopped when I was in junior high because it drove me nuts." He bit his lip.

Ethan put it back on the belt. "We'll play it in the truck."

At the house, Randy pulled Ethan aside when Sam went to the bathroom.

"I have to work prop tonight. Late. Would you—?" He jerked his head toward the bathroom.

"Absolutely." Ethan scooped Salomé into his arms and stroked her absently.

Randy aimed a warning finger at him. "Just don't teach him to drive the motorcycles or anything."

Ethan gave him a wry smile. "I don't know how to ride a motorcycle."

"Oh? We'll take care of that later, then." Randy leaned in and brushed a kiss against his mouth. "Thanks, Slick."

"Anytime, Ace."

Ethan and Sam did okay for the first few hours, which were composed mostly of Sam enthusiastically helping Ethan navigate his new iPhone and computer. Then his own phone rang, a breathless female vocal Ethan suspected to be Sam's beloved Kylie declaring all she saw was *you*, and from the look on Sam's face, Ethan knew this had to be Mitch.

Sam drifted to his bedroom as he spoke to his husband, and he stayed there for a long, long time. Ethan played poker with the casino games program until he thought it might be wise to check on his friend. When he went to find Sam, he heard no one talking, quiet music from a small radio in the corner of the room. Sam lay on the bed, stroking Daisy and Salomé.

Sam smiled weakly. "I'm fine. You don't have to check up on me, even if Randy told you to."

Ethan leaned on the doorframe. "How's Mitch doing?"

Sam shrugged. "He's trying to get as far across California as he can before he pulls in for the night. He'll text me before bed, so I'll know he's okay." But it was clear, too, these hours were going to be long and hard for Sam.

Ethan realized he had the perfect solution for them both. "Actually, I was wondering if you could help me. Though I'll have to do some explaining first."

Sam sat up, curious. "What is it?"

Ethan glanced at the other side of the bed. "Mind if I sit?"

Sam nodded, and Ethan did, telling him about the casino, about the money, about Sarah Reynolds, and even about the mob. He explained his research and his burning need to know who Crabtree really was, even though Randy had warned him not to try and find out.

When he finished, Sam stared at him for a minute, then said simply, "Wow."

Ethan let out a frustrated sigh. "Yes."

"So what are you going to do? How are you going to bring it back?"

"I don't know, but it's going to take more than Billy's ridiculous Gay Nite."

Sam looked at him oddly, so Ethan explained that

too. Sam laughed.

"Actually, it's not an *awful* idea. I mean, it'd be nice to be able to hang all over Mitch without having to deliberately ignore someone giving me a dirty look. The thing is, you have to be careful not to ghettoize us, either. You could get around it by not making it gay exclusive—hire drag queens, drag kings, showgirls—everyone. Make it a bonanza. Give it a racy name so you get everyone's attention, but make it about inclusion. Or better yet, make it a theme. Costume party. Let people dress up. That always goes over well."

"Okay, but what theme?"

"Something good. Something LGBT people will know is code for acceptance, but doesn't scare everybody off. Something showy. Something Vegas." He stared up at the ceiling, fingers tapping in time to the music still playing, something with a techno beat—Kylie again, crooning, singing love gave her everything, gave her wings. Sam turned to Ethan, grinning in triumph. "Butterfly."

Ethan arched an eyebrow. "Butterfly what?"

"That's your theme. 'Butterfly'. Don't call it gay night. Call it 'Butterfly'. Or 'Butterfly Night'. Get dancers. Get *gay* dancers, and lesbian dancers, and straight dancers. Get glitz and glamour. Theme the place. Have some sort of contest or award or something, and have a big, big show."

"A tournament." Ethan was getting into this now. "A poker tournament. And a slot tournament."

"Big winnings, everywhere. And great food."

"*Cheap* food. In price but not quality. Glitz and glamour and everything Vegas is, but have it be cheap. They pay to dress up, and they come to gamble, but they pay hardly anything. Just like the old days." He frowned. "But how do we get them in here? And how do we get them to return, so it's sustained?"

"Spread it out. Have it take place over several days, ending in a big event. *Lots* of shows. *Lots* of tournaments. You need a headliner too." He sighed. "I wish you *could* get Kylie."

"We could try. Can't hurt to try."

"I'd probably pass out and die." Sam stilled a moment, caught up in the fantasy. "But—oh, hey, that could be it. Impersonators *and* regular acts. Get everything in here. And—okay, I don't know how good of an idea this is, but what if you said some of the events are for charity? I know that doesn't bring in money, but if it's about how the place *looks*—"

"Yes. If it seems like we can give money away, we must not need it. Billy gave me enough money to make the place appear completely solvent—*yes*." He laughed, then grabbed Sam by the shoulders and kissed him hard on the mouth.

Then he stopped, realizing how that seemed after the night before.

Sam blushed. "I should—I should probably tell you. I don't... I only do that when Mitch is with me. He says he doesn't care, but—well, I do."

"Sorry. I didn't mean anything by it." Then he blushed too. "I haven't done anything like that before, last night—if it helps. I wasn't exactly sure I could face you all at the breakfast table."

Sam grinned. "Well, you're pretty good at it. If *that* helps."

"It does." Ethan sat back, looking around. "Well. It seems we have a plan. Now how do we get it started?"

Sam considered this. "What about this Sarah person?"

"Sounds like a good place to start to me." He scratched the cats under the chin, then rose. "Want to come with me to the casino, Sam?"

"Can I drive?" Sam cringed. "Oh God, I just sounded like a teenager."

"It's okay. If you really want to gross yourself out, you're technically young enough to be my son."

When Sam made a strangled sound, likely thinking of the many sexual positions they'd shared the night before, Ethan laughed and tugged him off the bed.

"Come on, Sam. Let's go play. And yes, you can drive."

CRABTREE'S SECRETARY SENT them to the Duffy Talent Agency off Sahara Avenue, which was, amazingly, still open. They were greeted by a warm, friendly looking woman who came up to them as they walked in. "How may I help you?"

"Yes—" Ethan looked down at her name badge and faltered as he saw the word C-A-R-Y-L-E spelled out. "Yes—Karl, I—"

"*Carol*," the woman corrected, still smiling. "It's an alternate spelling."

"Absolutely. Caryle, we were wondering if you could help us plan an event for Herod's Casino. Do you have a few minutes to discuss it, or should we come another time?"

Caryle did have time, and she settled them in her office, where she made them tea and gave them cookies while they talked. Ethan told her the goal for the casino's sale and the plan for the "Butterfly" event, which Sam helped explain. Ethan waited for her to tell him it was a terrible idea. But she didn't. She said it sounded brilliant, and she couldn't wait to get started.

Ethan figured he needed to be up front with her. "My budget is abysmal. I haven't even started considering what repairs and upgrades need to be done."

"To be honest with *you*, I could use the work and the publicity of this kind of thing." Caryle sighed. "I've been hanging on, but it just keeps getting worse." She tapped her finger against her desk. "You know, I have a friend who might be able to help you with putting a good face on the casino for a budget. Do you want me to give you his card?"

"Please."

Caryle searched in her drawer while she went on. "What you want for this, Mr. Ellison, is mystique. Where you don't want to scrimp is in advertising, and you want to start as soon as possible. Get yourself a logo, something sort of *Cirque du Soleil*, something that says fun and club and sexy—and androgynous—and gets your theme in there. Someone in a butterfly costume, maybe. I'll send some things over to your office tomorrow. I'll have a list for possible acts sent over too, and times available. Ignore the rates—we'll work them out."

They shook hands, exchanged numbers, and then Sam was driving them again. "Where to now? Home?"

"No. Back to the casino." Ethan paused. "Wait—the house, then the casino. I want to change my clothes first."

Sam glanced at his khaki pants and button-down shirt. "You look fine."

"I don't want to look fine, Sam. I want to bluff."

Sam grinned. "Gotcha. I suppose I should change too, huh?"

"Whatever you want."

Sam did change, but just into a button-down blue shirt and dark jeans. He fussed with his hair a bit too, brushed his teeth then declared himself ready.

"Whoa," he said when he saw Ethan.

Ethan wore all black. Black suit, black shirt, even a black tie and black shoes. The only hint of color was in his watch, which was polished silver and slipped out occasionally from his cuff when he lifted his arm. It was a nice suit, well cut, and he knew he looked good in it. As Sam stared at him, Ethan smiled and held out his arm.

"Ready to go?"

Ethan drove this time, but he parked a little ways away so they walked up the street, gathering attention, not climbing out of a Mazda and coming around from the back. He nodded at the doorman and smiled at the floor manager as he went in. Then he stood in the entrance with Sam and studied the casino. He saw the beauty of it beneath the neglect. But he saw, too, how few people were there.

Sam, seeing it too, winced. "If you get a lot of decorations, wings and things, that might help."

"The trouble is whoever buys this won't make an offer without a proper inspection. And they aren't going to buy it because we have a great party."

"You said Crabtree had a buyer in mind."

"That doesn't mean there actually is one." Ethan stared at Billy's craps table, remembering. He took Sam's hand. "Come on."

He went upstairs to Sarah's office, but of course she was gone for the day. He poked around in closets, even ended up down in the basement, but he didn't find anything.

"What are we looking for?" Sam asked, after half an hour of searching.

"A demon."

Sam's eyes went wide. "Any in particular?"

"A marble one. With horns. And a big fig leaf." He paused. "I think it was gold."

"Huh. Have you asked Randy? Because he's downstairs in the poker room—"

"Randy is not a part of this. In fact, don't even tell him I searched for it, please."

In the end they got Sarah's number by bribing several waitresses and a janitor, who went to a bellhop who sent yet another waitress to a high roller who knew it and gave it to them. Sarah didn't seem bothered by their call at all. "I'm sorry, Mr. Ellison. I should have given you my home number myself. How can I help you?"

"Do you know where the statue of the demon is?"

She laughed. "I do. It's in that cupboard I showed you, behind the towels. Did you need it for something?"

"Yes. I need to get it installed right away, right in the place where it was." He held his breath and waited for her to tell him that was impossible.

"Of course. I've always missed the fountain. Would you like me to make some calls for you?"

Ethan smiled. "That would be lovely." Once they hung up, he grinned triumphantly at the ceiling.

Sam smiled too. "Find it?"

"I think so. Come on."

They went up the stairs again, moved the plant, and opened the secret door. They moved the towels. Then they moved some more towels.

There were a lot of towels.

"How far back does this thing go?" Sam asked, once twenty-five or so teetered on Sarah's desk.

"It used to be a room. I don't see any statue, though. Unless it's really small?"

Sam crawled inside. "There's a light switch in here." Ethan heard a click. Sam gasped.

Ethan leaned in, worried. "You okay?"

"Holy. Shit."

"Sam?" Ethan moved in deeper, saw the light and

the room, and his jaw went slack.

Sam stood in the middle of a small but significant storage space, in the middle of which was a ten-foot-tall golden demon with three-foot-long horns and—

Yes. A fig leaf.

A big, big fig leaf.

Sam lifted it up and whistled. "He's happy to see us."

The demon had no pupils in its eyes, just golden sockets. It had a snout too, making it look almost like a cow, and it even had a ring in its nose. But beyond this, he was all male—broad chest, huge, sculpted muscles, and a flat stomach that tapered to his fig leaf. He was terrifying and beautiful at once.

Ethan studied the fig leaf a moment. "Let me see it."

Sam grinned and slid the green silk covering aside, revealing the full majesty and slight grotesqueness of the beast's huge, half-erect, and gleaming golden cock.

Ethan leaned over the edge of the shelf and into the room that shouldn't have been there, staring at the statue which had been taken away. He could see it, could see how it could all work, could see even Sam's Butterfly working. A Butterfly extravaganza with drag queens and a raging horndog of a demon in a fountain. *Touch his cock and you'll win big.* It would be a crock of shit, but people would buy it. And once they bought it, they'd believe it. It wouldn't always work, but neither did craps or roulette. It would be part of the story. Part of the mystique.

As would be Butterfly, and Herod's. They'd come to

see it, if the bluff was good enough. And if enough of them came, so long as no one asked to see his hand, he'd win.

He could see it. He could totally see it.

Ethan grinned. And then he laughed.

"Come on, Sam. Let's go downstairs, and I'll buy you a drink."

ETHAN DELIBERATELY KEPT them away from the poker room. It wasn't that he didn't want to see Randy, but rather he didn't want to see him just yet.

"Would you be willing to help me this week?" Ethan asked Sam as they sat together, Sam with a strawberry margarita and he with his gin and tonic. "I don't want to pull you away from starting at the hospital early, though, if that's what you want to do."

"No, I want to help. I do need to do orientation, and it'd be a good idea to do a few shifts next week to sort of wade in, but I'm loving this. It's like planning a huge party. I'm totally in." Sam stirred his drink and studied Ethan. "I've been meaning to ask you—how exactly did you and Randy hook up? I mean, I know you're living with him, but you seem like you're kind of just getting started."

Ethan considered how to answer and decided he would give Sam the edited truth. He didn't want Sam to know quite how dark he'd been. Though thinking that made him pause even more. He wasn't dark anymore, was he? He was more of a gray, and sometimes…sometimes he was whatever color normal was.

Randy did that to you. Randy's the one who helped lead you back to normal. Maybe even closer to normal than you've ever been.

Sam's cheeks pinked. "Sorry. I don't mean to butt in."

"No, it's fine. Just…complicated. He picked me up at the roulette table, over there, after I lost my last five dollars on black."

Sam paused, straw still in his mouth, eyes wide. "Your last *at all*?"

"The only thing I had left was my car," Ethan admitted. *And a gun.* He wondered what had happened to that. "I didn't have a tip, so I left a ring, and somehow Randy got the dealer to bet against it, and the next thing I knew we were in here, at the River. It took off on its own after that."

"Why did you do it, though?"

Now it was Ethan's turn to stir his drink and stare into it as the ice swirled around. "Because a long-term affair of mine ended badly."

"Love affair? A guy?"

"Yes. We were together for a long time. But he's married. I realized he was never truly going to be with me, not in the way I wanted, how much of my life I'd thrown away for him, all so I could be with him a few times a month." He stirred the drink more aggressively. "It made me a little upset."

"You mean, he was married to a woman, right? Like a beard?"

"Still is married. And yes, to a woman. Because in the olden days we didn't even dream of marrying each other."

Sam looked downright grim. "Sometimes I want to go up to all the assholes who want to take my marriage away and make them say it to my face. They carry on like it's going to change something, and it *hasn't*, and it *won't*. It just means I get to be married to Mitch." He glared at the margarita. "Sorry. You were telling me about you?"

But Ethan had to soak in Sam's passion, his anger. The insistence he, Sam, should have every right his peers did. Ethan wondered when it was he'd lost that self-respect for himself, when and where and why he had given it away, trading it for stolen moments with Nick.

He didn't know. He wasn't sure he wanted to know.

Ethan reached over and took Sam's hand. "I've enjoyed getting to know you, Sam. Both you and Mitch."

Sam gave him a wry look. "Even though I molested you before I even said hello?"

Ethan chuckled. "Maybe especially because of that."

They sat in companionable silence until a woman who sounded very much like Kylie sighed in Sam's pocket.

"It's Mitch." Sam pulled his iPhone out, and his face lit up when he saw the screen. "He's at Blythe."

He looked so relieved. So bright. So happy.

I want that. I want exactly that. Feeling brave, he added, *I deserve that.*

A loud feedback screech drew their attention across the room, where a woman stood on a small stage with a microphone. "Hello, everyone. I'm Jess, your happy host. Who's ready for some karaoke?"

Sam turned to Ethan, eyebrows in his hair, grin a mile wide. Laughing, Ethan rose from the table and went with him to the stage.

RANDY HEARD THE singing as he rounded the corner and headed to the River, and he cringed. Goddamn it, it had been a sucky night. He'd gotten three bad beats in his games and had to deal with the sleazy asshole who alternated between racial slurs, sexist remarks, and blatant homophobia. All he wanted was a drink and some peace and quiet, but fuck no, not on karaoke night.

"Boys, boys, boys!" someone shouted over the music.

Someone kind of familiar.

"Boys, boys, boys!" It came again, and this time Randy heard someone trying to sing something after that, something about drinks in bars. As one, two voices warbled badly, "Whoah-oh-uhaoah," and then there was even more laughter.

Randy moved faster. He'd known it was them just from their voices, but when he saw—*Whoah-oh-uhoah* was right.

There they were, the beautiful pair of them, Slick living up to his name, all in black, his shirt undone and a black tie dangling loose around his neck. Sweating and laughing, singing Lady Gaga at the top of their lungs, they were clearly having a wonderful time. So was everyone else in the bar, all of them crowded at the edge of the stage, cheering them on.

They saw Randy, fumbled their line as they cheered him forward then picked up the song in time to chant, "We love them! We love them!" in eager, off-key chorus.

Randy waved at them, then went up to the bar, ordered a beer, and settled in to watch. When they called out once again at the chorus, he saluted them with his longneck. "Love you too."

CHAPTER EIGHTEEN

I F THE THERAPY was why Sam was so much better, Randy was all for it. Especially since in the second session they didn't talk about him at all, just Sam's mom.

The session still upset Randy, though, and later that afternoon while Ethan and Sam clicker-trained the kittens, he took a ride in the desert to clear his head. When it didn't work, he headed to the Stratosphere. He lucked out because the woman working the ticket counter knew him, so she let him go up for free. Partly because of that and partly because he thought maybe some thrill would get rid of his agitation, he bought tickets for the rides.

He liked the Big Shot, where hydraulics shot riders up a tower like a rocket before stopping them from going off the top and bringing them gently back down. It was a ride popular in a lot of amusement parks, but this one was on top of a sixteen-hundred-feet-high tower above the Strip. X-Scream was billed as a giant teeter-totter on the edge of the observatory—essentially you sat in a small car and tried not to lose either your lunch or your mind as it shot you over the edge. Insanity basically strapped you in, tilted you sideways, and spun you over the Strip.

Randy saved that one for last, because it was the best. While he spun above the world and his fellow riders screamed and threatened to throw up, Randy let his mind go.

It bothered him that Sam had lost his mom. Right now it bothered him a lot. He'd empathized when he'd first heard the story, but today he'd listened to Sam talk about how great she was. The woman had been nothing short of amazing. Battling a debilitating disease, she still managed to raise an intelligent, competent young man *and* beat off, from the sounds of it, any homophobia that came his way. She'd been so strong, so supportive, so—shit, she was a fucking list of superlatives. It got way under Randy's skin that she worked so hard and then got picked off by cancer. If this had been a movie, he'd have walked out and demanded his money back. It *sucked.* Even when he finished on the tower, even after he stood on the edge and tried to let the wind take his thoughts away, they clung to him. What happened to Sam and his mom was wrong. It made him itch just thinking about it.

What was fucking weird was how Sam didn't seem to see that.

He teared up sometimes when the therapist pushed on the wrong spot, but it was nothing huge to him. After he wiped a few tears, he tended to go stony until Laura redirected to a more comfortable subject. Randy didn't want to tell her how to do her job, but the more he watched Sam not break down, the more agitated he got.

During the second week of sessions, he couldn't stand it anymore. "Look, why don't you let it out, Sam, and be done with it?" He turned to the therapist. "With all respect to your training or whatever—I mean, shit, it can't be good for him to keep all that in. When are you going to tell him to spill it?"

Sam regarded him in total confusion. "Let what out?"

Randy had to choke back a laugh. "Seriously? *Seriously?*" He turned to the therapist. "Don't tell me you can't see it."

She gave him a thoughtful but otherwise unreadable look for a few seconds. The woman would be dangerous at a poker table. "I'm not sure. What is it you see, Randy?"

There was a trap there, Randy was sure of it, and he regretted saying anything at all—until he looked at Sam. There it was, so close to the surface he couldn't bear it, and he gave up. "Sam, just be sad already."

The words might as well have been a switch, the way they made the walls go up. "Sad about what?"

"Your mom. Her dying like that. You having to be alone."

"You don't think I've been sad? You think I didn't *feel* that?"

Randy glanced at the therapist, but one of the plants would have given him more feedback. *Shut up and don't say anything. Don't say another damn word.* It was smart advice. He wished he could take it.

"I don't think you've *truly* been sad over it, no. You're weird when you talk about it, Sam. You talk almost like it happened to somebody else, like it's just facts. You're all wooden about it. Like if you turn to stone, it won't hurt you. But every night until your phone says Mitch is going to bed, no matter what time it is or where you are or what you're doing, you can't sleep. I don't know what the hell that has to do with your mom, but I swear to God it's something. You and Slick both do that, whenever you brush up against your demons. You just go all funny, and it creeps me out."

Laura held up a hand. "Who is Slick?"

Randy had almost forgotten she was there. "My— boyfriend. His ex was a jerk. Married, which he knew. They had a long-term affair, but the dickwad cashed in their joint savings to save his 'real' family."

Sam startled. "I didn't know that."

Randy probably shouldn't have said it. But goddamn it, he wanted this sorted out. "He came down to Vegas to gamble away all his money, and then he was going to go out to his car and blow his brains out." Sam gasped, but Randy ignored him. "Except I met him first. But God help you if you bring up the past. With either of these two. *Why* do they do that? Why do they go all stony? I just want to help them, but they don't let me. Why? Do you know? Because it's clear they aren't fucking going to tell me."

The therapist regarded Randy a moment. When she leaned forward, Randy could feel the danger coming even before she spoke.

"I don't know, Randy. How do you handle your demons? Maybe—to help Sam—you could tell him about how you dealt with your uncle's passing?"

If she'd been a man, he'd have hit her. Except that was a lie. He wouldn't have been able to then, either.

Because the Look wasn't just during sex. This bitch was good. Because there it was. Right there. Space. Safe, huge, protective space.

Twenty-two years is probably enough time to spend running. Don't you think?

Randy gave his inner voice the finger and surrendered.

"You have to understand my family was all in the auto industry. Everyone. My dad, mom, aunts, uncles. We were so blue-collar it was practically a tattoo. Not so much with the smarts, either—not book smarts, anyway. When everyone lost their jobs, it hurt everybody's pride more than anything, and it was like this cloud everybody pushed around. This big, black, fucking awful cloud. A lot of it ended up on Uncle Gary."

He shut his eyes, seeing it again all too clearly.

"He was quiet, see. Big bear of a man, so he looked mean, but he couldn't kill a cricket. Big spiders he'd have me go after, but he felt bad even for them. And he was gay. I didn't know it at the time. I assume he was having sex, but I never knew about it. That wasn't something he would have considered appropriate for us to talk about. I liked to think, later, he'd have helped me out when the time was right, that he knew how I was going to end up before I did, but maybe not."

Sam squeezed his hand. Randy squeezed back and kept going.

"All I knew then was he really seemed to understand me, and he was kind. If my mom was on the warpath or my dad was drunk, I could go to Gary's house, and he'd make me dinner and play poker with me or help me with my homework. Made me finish before we could play poker. Told me math was the most important thing I'd ever learn. He taught me about people, how to read them. How to 'turn them your way', he said, but that was just a nice way of saying how to manipulate them. He was good at it. Really good at it. He was a goddamn charmer, which was how he survived being a gay man in a working-class town full of unemployed assholes looking for someone to hit."

Randy shut his eyes, swimming in it now.

"Sometimes he'd have a friend or two over, and we'd all play together. Those were the best nights. There I was, this skinny, ugly piece of shit at the table with big, tough-as-shit men. Which, of course, they weren't. Bunch of bears, tame as all hell. Same as Gary, couldn't hurt anybody. But there I was, playing Black Maria. They gave me my nickname, which I loved. Made everybody call me Skeet, because I was a poker hand. I was cool like Gary. I was going to be just like Gary when I grew up. Mom would get so freaked out when I said that, and I'd get mad at her. 'What the hell's wrong with Uncle Gary?' Finally one day my brother said, 'Because he's a fag, that's why.' I had no idea what that meant, but I could tell it was bad, so I punched my brother in the face."

Randy stared at the ceiling for a while.

"He was probably cruising when they killed him. For a while I worried—when I was old enough to get it, to understand he was gay and who all those men were and what they were giving up to play poker with a snot-nosed kid—I worried I'd gone over too much and he'd had to go out to get laid, and if I'd just stayed away, he'd still be alive."

He had to stop there for a minute, and he caught himself going to stone. *Fuck it. Peaches, watch this, because this is how it's fucking done.* He exhaled and let the tears roll down his cheeks.

"He took a risk for sex, maybe even for love, and he got a bad beat. I've known that for a long time. But it hurt, thinking I might have sent him to his death. I can't shake it completely. Probably because I always think I could have stopped it. I would have done anything to keep that from happening. Somebody should have stopped it. People should have cared more than they did, shouldn't have fucking said he deserved it. That was almost as hard as losing him—nobody stood up for him, so I lost everybody else too. It sucked. I was only ten years old, and everything stopped. Every fucking thing."

Randy took a breath. He was mad now, really fucking mad.

"It's just wrong, so fucking, fucking wrong, as wrong as Sam's mom dying, as wrong as Ethan's stupid lover stealing the money, as wrong as so many god-damned things—but this is my wrong, and when I think about it, it fucking hurts."

He sat there a moment, reeling until his pain faded back into his personal darkness. When he glanced up, Laura was smiling.

"I never had a dad."

Randy turned to Sam, surprised, because he didn't sound like himself. He sounded like a little boy.

Sam wiped at his eyes. "I never had a dad. I never had an Uncle Gary. I never had anybody like that." He bit his lip, but the tears were coming out now, just rolling, and he kept looking at Randy—at his cheeks, Randy realized. Where he hadn't wiped his own tears away yet.

Randy didn't let himself touch them.

Sam stared at the floor as he spoke. "Mom was great. She was everything to me, and I know how hard she tried. But no matter what she did, she could never be a dad. We did the big-brother programs, but they were always run through churches. The ones in Middleton that did those programs were all anti-gay, and later she told me they kept telling me stuff she could tell made me feel sad, so she pulled me. She was like your uncle, protecting me before I even knew I needed it. But it meant I never got to have a guy around outside of *my* uncle. Who, if you remember, is nothing at all like yours."

Randy made a face. "That man is a fish if ever there was one."

"Yeah. But I used to ache for him to say something to me." He looked at the therapist. "I don't know why my mom couldn't be enough for me, but no matter how she tried, it wasn't the same. I needed a guy to tell me I was okay. Somebody to look at, somebody to copy, like you did with your uncle. Somebody. *Anybody.* But there wasn't one, not even a best friend." He turned to Randy again, his eyes so full of longing it made Randy hurt to look at him. "I couldn't wish away my mother. But if I could have had an Uncle Gary, even for a long afternoon—"

He shut his eyes and tucked his head down, going quiet again.

Randy had this weird fissure of awareness, this momentary sense that he had it, that he understood—it wasn't his mom, it wasn't that at all, it was…it was—

But it was gone before he could name it. Was it…guys? Male attention? He turned to the therapist, ready to tell her to start doing her damn job here, but she focused on Sam. "Would you tell me about your husband? You've spoken about him in passing, and it's clear you love him—but if you wouldn't mind telling me, I would be honored to hear what Mitch means to you. I would love to hear you talk about what a gift it must have been to find the person you knew you wanted to spend your whole life with."

When Sam spoke, he was surprisingly defensive. "Are you trying to tell me I married Mitch for a father figure?"

She shook her head. "No. I'm sorry if that's what

you heard me say, Sam. I sincerely meant to ask. It seemed a natural extension to me, because after wanting to find a male role model for so long, you have not a model but a partner. I would love to hear about him."

Sam relaxed and began to talk about Mitch, hesitantly at first, but the therapist was encouraging, and Sam quickly warmed to his task. He skipped the X-rated bits, Randy noted with a wry smile. Sam told her about Mitch's proposal and their life in Iowa as they waited for Sam to finish school. With or without the gay porn, it was quite a romantic tale. Yeah, there was an age difference. Yeah, Mitch liked to cocoon Sam. But he was not his dad, or his brother, or his uncle. He was his friend and his lover. His life partner.

The real kicker was, Mitch was *better* with Sam. Mitch might coddle Sam, but Sam carried Mitch too, probably more than he knew. Sam was Mitch's rudder. He'd calmed down. He'd settled down. He still had kinky fantasies, but loving Sam and living with him had made Mitch better and stronger. Sam hadn't changed, not that much. But Mitch had been transformed. Sam wouldn't know the difference, because he hadn't known him before.

That was when Randy got it. It was right there, so obvious. He stared at Sam a minute, basking in it. So *fucking* obvious. So brilliant.

"You didn't need a role model, Sam."

Sam turned to Randy, disoriented and even a little irritated at being interrupted. But Randy couldn't seem to make himself stop.

"You didn't need one. You want one, yeah, I get it. You should have had one, and it's as bad as losing your mom."

"I don't know what you're talking about." Sam was freezing up again, or trying to.

Randy'd fucking had enough of this.

"Sam, can't you see it? That great guy? The amazing brother, the perfect dad, uncle, best friend—you had the best of all, the most amazing one you ever could have had. Because only somebody who had one that perfect, that great, could turn out like you. And you had him. You had him all along."

Sam shook his head. "I don't understand."

Randy leaned forward, taking his hand. "You had you. You had that guy because you had you. Your model was *you*. Because you are *amazing*, absolutely amazing. You can't see it, because you're standing in it, but I see it. I see what you are to Mitch. I know what you are to me. He calls you Sunshine because you are a fucking sun to him, and honestly? You are to everybody who meets you. You are so gentle, so kind, and so *strong*, and so much has happened to you, so much is against you in so many ways, and yet you're always there, shining. You're great not because somebody showed you how to be a man. You're a man because you showed yourself. You made yourself great. *You*, Sam. *You*."

Sam was crying. Fuck, Randy was crying. The therapist wasn't, but she looked like she was working to keep herself even and professional. Which was good, because Randy had no fucking idea what anybody was supposed to say now.

But he tried anyway.

"Peaches, you are the best guy I know. I swear to fucking God. You're a better guy even than Ethan. The best I've ever met. I'm glad you brought Mitch back to me, but I look forward to you *both* coming now. I love you so much. So many people do." He squeezed his hand. "Remember that, okay? I know it doesn't give you the dad you should have had. I know you still wanted to have somebody, a guy, some guy, even a half-rotten guy, to have him tell you what a good job you were doing when it mattered. I know. But—shit, I'm telling you now. You're great. You're fucking, fucking great."

He was a big, fat, slobbery mess by the end of that soliloquy, and Sam was too, so when he ran out of air and then words, Randy gave up and pulled Sam across the couch and into his arms.

As they sat there, rocking from side to side, he let himself remember. He let himself remember the days he'd come home from school and somebody had hit him, when someone had made fun of him or he'd screwed up and hurt somebody else, every time when the world had been wrong and he'd gone to Uncle Gary to make it right. He replayed those moments as he held Sam.

There had been a lot of rough spots, and a lot of mistakes. His life was a lot harder without his uncle, that much he knew. He did okay, though, in the end. He liked who he was, who he'd become, overall.

But while he rocked Sam and wandered down memory lane, he wrote in a few more memories too. The times when he'd wished for Gary—it hurt to do it, but he was already a fucking mess, he was already so fucking exposed, how could it get worse? So he wrote them in, as if his life were a movie he could fix in the editing room. He pretended Gary hadn't been killed. He pretended Gary had explained sex to him, had told him how to not make it hurt. He pretended Gary had told him that first fuckwad he let have him was an asshole and not to give himself away so cheaply.

He pretended Gary had been there to take him in when his dad kicked him out, that he hadn't had to run away and sell himself. Eventually things had worked out okay, and his experiences had made him tough and smart and lean—but he pretended for a minute he hadn't had to do it. He pretended he'd finished school and gone to college and taken science and math classes like Gary had told him he should. He didn't know how to pretend after that, because it would have been a different life. But he played those parts he knew damn well had been bad over, and made them better. It hurt, but it was a good hurt.

He held Sam while he did it, and Sam really was a sun. He was warm and full of life—and he was here. He was alive.

Ethan. He didn't know what to do with Slick yet, didn't know how to think about him.

He's here right now. And he loves you right now. You have to count it, for now.

Randy shut his eyes, let the hurt come, and then let the sun burn it away with warmth and love.

"He's going to come home, Peaches. Mitch is going to come home, this time, and a lot of other times."

"You can't promise that."

"No, I can't guarantee you no more stupid shit is going to happen to your life." Randy pulled Sam's chin up so he had no choice but to look at Randy. "But I can tell you that you have the best of it, kid, and you know I always have a corner on the odds. Mitch is more likely to come home than he isn't. And even if you get a bad beat and something happens, even if it does, you have me. And I think Ethan, probably. And Crabtree, weird as he is. You have lots of people, and you're going to meet more at work. You never get one hundred percent odds, Sam. But your cards are fucking aces."

Sam's tears spilled out, but he smiled. "I love you, Randy."

Out of the corner of his eye, Randy saw the therapist move, and he turned toward her. "Sorry. I didn't mean to take over."

"That's quite all right." Her kind, understanding smile was very much like his uncle's.

Which was likely his imagination, him making it up or wanting to see it. But in that moment, in the nice, delicate little bird-egg moment? He didn't fucking care what it was. He was taking it.

SAM AND RANDY took their time getting home after the

appointment.

Randy wanted to go up to the top of the Strato-sphere again, but Sam asked if they could take another ride on the bike, so they did that instead. They rode all the way out to Lake Mead, and then stopped for dinner on the way home.

"I want to learn to ride a motorcycle," Sam said as they left the restaurant.

"Your husband would gut me if he found out I taught you how to ride." When Sam gave him an angry look, he held up his hands. "Hey. I'm not saying he's right or he's wrong. I'm telling you the truth. You should have him teach you."

"That would never work. He'd be too scared." Sam kicked at the bike's front tire. "I hate it when people point out the age difference, but you know, sometimes it *is* like he's my dad. Which seriously messes with my head, I'll tell you. I don't want that. But I don't know how to stop it."

Randy leaned on the bike. "He's scared, Peaches. He's as scared of losing you as you are of losing him. He hates that he has to be gone. Don't think he didn't try six different ways to make this work without his having to leave. Hell, he took a job for Crabtree so you could go see this therapy lady."

"I know. But I want… I want…" His jaw set in determination. "I want to learn how to ride a motorcycle. Because I want to know how, and because I don't need his permission to do it. Because he's not my dad. *I'm* my dad, like you said. I say I get to learn."

Me and my goddamned fucking mouth. Randy thought frantically, trying to figure out how to get out of this one. Then he decided there wasn't any way out but through.

"Okay, but you're telling him, and trust me, I'll know that you've done it. Not ask—tell. If you're not man enough for that, you're not man enough to ride."

"Okay," Sam agreed, but his tone told Randy he had at least a few days' reprieve before he had to give Sam a lesson.

He still spent the whole ride into town trying to decide how and when and under what conditions he could do this, or whether he should hire some sort of professional. He could see the argument both ways, and he could tell he was going to go back and forth on it for a while.

He wondered if it would be worth asking Slick what he thought. Actually, that wasn't a bad idea. He hurried home a little faster, both to ask him and because after the big raw day of digging up the past, he was looking forward to sparring with him.

But when they got home, Randy found a note on the kitchen table.

For a moment his heart stopped. *He's gone.*

The world tipped sideways until his eyes fell on the actual words.

Meet me at the casino.

Sam picked up the notepad and frowned at it. "Meet him at the casino? Okay, sure, but why didn't he call? Or text?"

"Probably for dramatic effect," Randy replied, his heart still pounding. *It worked.* "He must be planning something."

Sam brightened. "Oh, I hope it's something for Butterfly."

Randy resisted the urge to roll his eyes or wince. The fact that he was still shaken helped. *He didn't leave, you dumbass. Where's he going to go? The mob will kill him if he goes. Or Crabtree, or something. He's here for a while yet. Calm the fuck down.* "I still don't like the name."

"That's because you have no taste." Sam punched a text into his phone. Then he paused and pursed his lips. "He won't tell me anything. He just says to get there because he's been waiting for two hours."

"He's definitely planning something." Randy felt a little better. Plans were good.

They took the truck over to the casino, and continuing the theme of the day, Sam drove. Randy couldn't say he minded. It gave him the space to think.

Slick had gone balls-deep into this casino thing, and he'd been pretty good at it, actually. Well, not the casino itself so much. But Randy had seen some of Ethan's spreadsheets, and yeah, he was a fair hand with investments and money organization. The books were looking fairly decent, probably for the first time since the early nineties. And even though Randy still thought it was a disappointment waiting to happen, he and Sam were having a heyday planning *Butterfly Nights: Let your soul fly free* or whatever the tagline was. Randy hoped to hell they got a better one before the flyers went to press.

But they were having a good time. A great time. Slick was lit up. And happy. And here. Randy wasn't going to complain—too much.

They came around to the front, because Sam said Ethan had been adamant about it in his text, and Randy could tell from the way the staff jumped as they approached that Ethan had given orders to watch for them. Which was another funny thing. Ethan really was running the place, all from his little office on the seventh floor.

He wasn't on the seventh floor now. When Sam and Randy came in the door, the first thing they saw—or that Randy did anyway—was Ethan. Ethan in his black suit, which had become his signature: black suit and black tie, but tonight he had on a purple paisley shirt, one of Randy's favorites. He looked like a fucking king, so sleek and smooth he didn't have to advertise. He was cool. He was fucking sex on a fucking set of sex sticks. He was glowing, gorgeous, and so fuckable Randy wanted to do him right there.

He was also standing in front of a goddamned fountain. The fountain, in the place where Billy's craps table had been.

With the goddamned fucking demon statue in the middle of it.

"You did it." Sam rushed forward to high-five Ethan. Ethan didn't look at him, though. He was watching Randy.

He was going to have to keep watching too, because Randy could not stop staring at the damn statue. He had never seen it, just heard about it, and now here it was. All ten feet of it, water pouring out of its nostrils.

Finally Randy shook his head. "Holy. Shit."

"Isn't it *great*?" Sam regarded the golden face. "We found it in a secret room inside a closet. Sarah had the workmen take it out. I knew this was going to happen, and I knew it was a secret, but wow, I didn't know you were getting it done so fast. You had all the way until the end of the month before Butterfly."

"No." Ethan stared right at Randy. "I only had two weeks."

The bet. Fuck, Randy had forgotten about it. He looked at the fountain again, and because Sam had moved, this time he could see the whole thing—including the part where the fig leaf decidedly wasn't.

Hello, demon.

Randy rubbed his chin for a minute and kept his eyes on the leafless aspect of the statue. "So. It seems I'm now dancing for Billy *and* for you."

"Oh, you aren't dancing for Billy."

Randy cocked his eyebrow. "I'm not, you say? Because I remember losing a bet—over you, I might add—to be his floozy-rent-boy ad campaign for the night."

"Yes. We've rethought the strategy behind 'Gay Nite' and don't think it's quite the image we want. Billy's agreed to accept instead you'll work that night, probably as a dealer. Or you'll perform. I promised him your costume would be at least slightly embarrassing for you." Ethan nodded at the demon. "It's not marble, by the way. It's gold. Though technically I think it's brass."

"I can see I was misinformed."

Ethan smiled wryly. "You lose a lot of bets to me, Ace."

"Yeah, about that. You've been a little busy with your casino projects, Slick—we haven't played poker in a while."

"I was thinking that too. Actually, there was one game I know you didn't teach me." Ethan tilted his head. "What about strip poker?"

"Oh, I would be *happy* to teach you that one."

Sam's phone sounded Mitch's ringtone. He greeted his husband happily, but his joy quickly faded. He stepped away from the fountain to have an intense conversation, and he returned flushed and dejected. "There was a problem with the delivery. He won't be coming back on schedule like he planned."

Randy winced. "When's he due now?"

"He doesn't know for sure. Maybe two weeks. Or maybe even three. Not until the first of November, at any rate."

All Randy's plans for strip poker and hot sex went up in smoke, but he didn't complain, just went forward and put his arm around Sam and kissed his hair.

CHAPTER NINETEEN

I T WAS JUST as well Mitch's phone call rerouted Ethan's plans for the evening, because the truth was, if Randy looked too deeply, he'd have discovered that outside of the fountain and a little juggling of the financial columns, this was all Ethan had actually done.

He didn't want Randy telling him he couldn't do this, didn't want that look that said he thought this was a bad idea. He hated it, because it fed his own self-doubt. He wanted to do this by himself, to be cool and chic and amazing, to have Randy look at him all the time as he looked at him and at this fountain now. Or how he had been until Sam had gotten his call.

He didn't want Randy to look at him like he looked at Sam, either, a child who needed protection.

Ethan drove them home in his car, listening as Randy soothed Sam. Something had happened today at the therapist, because they were treating each other with kid gloves. "You've still got you, Sam, and me," Randy kept saying.

To be honest, the two of them were being so emotionally intimate that Ethan felt a little jealous. No, he didn't want what Randy and Sam had. But in his own drive to make the casino work, to prove whatever it was he was proving, he'd let some things go slack. For the first time since he'd known Randy, he worried he had let whatever this magical ride was slow down too much.

He worried he'd lost Randy back to Sam and Mitch again, which was where he probably belonged.

Ethan reminded himself Randy was comforting Sam about Sam's husband's unexpected prolonged absence, and tried to remember the three men had been sharing themselves with each other for some time now. But the last one didn't help and started him back down the road of worry.

Did he want Randy to involve him with the three of them? Leave space for him to be involved? Be mad he wasn't making that space himself? Did he want Randy to lean on him after? Not do it at all? Ethan had no idea. Because panic was uncomfortable, he became irritated.

This was why people didn't generally run around in unconventional three-and-four-way pairings. The politics never ended.

Yet he couldn't deny he liked Sam and Mitch. And yes, he enjoyed sex with them too, for more than physical stimulation.

Ethan studied the two men huddled on the couch, Sam spiraling endlessly into misery, Randy drowning in frustrated empathy and love. Politically tricky or not, it was clear the two of them needed comforting, and as soon as Ethan realized it, comforting them was exactly what he wanted to do.

He turned to the end table from which Randy had

withdrawn the poker chips and pulled out a deck of cards and a tray of chips. "I think what we need here is a distraction."

Sam held up a hand. "I don't want to play poker. I don't want to think."

"You won't have to. We won't play poker proper, just leave things up to fate."

This predictably got Randy's attention. "Hey."

"We're playing draw poker." Ethan put the chips on the coffee table. "No discards. Losing hand loses an article of clothing." He arched an eyebrow at Randy. "That's how the game goes, yes?"

Randy grimaced. "It won't be any fun at all. None of the hands will be any good. It'll be nothing but high card over and over again. There's no skill at all. And there will be two losers, you might notice."

Ethan thought it was telling that Randy had the chance to get the three of them naked together and he was more fixated on the fact that he'd have to rely on fate. But he also had to admit he had a point about the two losers, and even the inevitable lackluster quality of the hands.

"We'll play Hold 'Em. But there's no betting and no folding, and no ante. As for how to decide who is disrobing…" He took a plastic cup from the cupboard, brought it back to the table and set it down before picking up three chips from the tray—one green, one blue, one red. "The winner draws the loser. Sam is green, Randy is red and I'm blue."

"What if the winner draws himself?" Randy asked,

his tone silently adding, *wiseass.*

Ethan looked at the two of them sitting there, so close, so intimate, knowing so much about each other, and he grinned.

"The winner draws the loser, and he decides whether or not the loser removes an article of clothing or answers a question. And if he draws himself, he can either choose to remove an article of clothing or ask a question of himself."

Randy was still derisive. "Truth or dare and strip poker in one? Truth poker?"

"I like it." Sam scooted forward on the couch. "I don't have to think, and I might get to embarrass Randy. Or learn more about Ethan. I'm in."

"Peaches," Randy said, half plea, half warning.

"Randy, I'm tired of being soppy. Mitch feels rotten. I feel rotten. But I feel good when we do stuff like this." Sam picked up a few of the chips and shuffled them inexpertly inside his palm, watching them slide over one another. "I'd rather do it with Mitch here. But if I called him up, he'd tell me to do it. Well, he'd tell me to leave the speakerphone on or get video set up."

There was something forced about that little speech, and for a minute Ethan worried he'd made a mistake, opening this door. But before he could question it further, Randy headed for the kitchen.

"Fine. We'll do this, but I'm not doing this straight." Randy reached up above the refrigerator, Ethan assumed for a fifth of whiskey or some other hard liquor. But Randy only drew something small from inside of a canister far in the back of the cupboard, then took something else out of a drawer.

He returned to the couch with an ashtray, a lighter, and a joint.

"*Whoa.*" Sam held up his hands and slid to the opposite end of the couch. "No way, Randy."

"Fine." Randy put the joint to his lips. "I'll smoke by myself."

They stared at him while he inhaled, held his breath for several seconds then blew the smoke rather expertly at the ceiling. He gave them both a withering look.

"Oh, don't go all goody-goody on me. Jesus H., it's been a fuck of a day, and now you want this. Fine. I'll play. But I'm getting high."

"It's illegal, Randy," Sam said, before Ethan could. "What about work? What if they drug test? Even if I don't smoke, it could register."

Randy crossed his foot over his knee and looked Sam in the eye. "You don't start work until the first of November. Plenty of time."

Ethan didn't care for this, and he didn't know why. He'd lost control, for one, which was probably enough. He'd never smoked anything before, either, cigarettes or otherwise. Somehow it didn't surprise him that Randy did, but it disappointed him a little too. He just couldn't figure out why.

Or maybe it was the defiant way he was acting. Maybe it was because he was mad that all he was asking Randy to do was get naked and talk to him, and he had to try and scare everyone off.

Fine.

Ethan picked up the cat food dishes and headed back to his bedroom. Once he set the food down, he used the clicker, and the cats came bounding in. He petted them both, brought the litter pan in from the bathroom, and shut the door.

Sam met him in the hallway, which was good. He looked a little wild-eyed.

"You don't have to do this," Ethan said to him. "But I think I'm going to."

Sam bit his lip before answering. "He hasn't done drugs ever around me before, outside of alcohol. I think he's upset." He rubbed his arms. "Me too."

"You don't have to."

"It really is a big deal with my job. But at the same time, I know other nurses who use. I don't know. I knew a guy once who was a total pothead, and I don't like it, period." He tapped his fingers on his arm. "I'm not going to do it."

Ethan approved of his moral standing but knew he wouldn't follow. This once, he'd try. "Do you want to go with the cats? Or move them to your room?"

Sam's reply was almost silky. "I'm staying in the game. I'm just not smoking. And we're opening a window."

They came back to the living room, Ethan sat down, and Randy, already slightly stoned, grinned at them.

"Joining my party, are you?" He inhaled again.

"Ethan is." Sam opened a window before taking a seat in the chair between Ethan and Randy.

Randy glanced at the window, then leaned his head to the side and stuck his lip out in a little pout at Sam. "Come on, Peaches."

Sam remained lounged in his chair and looked Randy straight in the eye. "No."

Randy sighed, sat up, and passed the joint to Ethan.

Ethan's hand trembled as he took the joint. He thought about asking what he should do but didn't want to seem stupid. He brought it—carefully—to his lips, wondering with every inch if he should give up and fold.

No. Putting it between his lips, he shut his eyes and sucked.

It tasted acrid and sweet, both at once. And strong. Like a tree was burning and he was sucking it inside his body. Why the hell was he doing this again?

Randy critiqued his form. "Hold it in, Slick. Five seconds or so."

Ethan tried, but he let it out early because the buzzy feeling started almost right away. Just a jolt, humming through him. *I don't want to pass out.* He huffed the smoke out of his body. But once he did, the buzzy feeling began to slide away.

Reclaiming the joint with a wry smile, Randy drew on the cigarette and settled into the couch.

Ethan picked up the cards and shuffled them. "Shall we play?"

Sam leaned forward in his chair. "Yes."

Randy blew out another drag. "Why the fuck not?"

As Ethan dealt, Sam leaned over to the stereo and

fiddled with some music. As a male singer crooned softly, Randy took another hit, and Ethan checked his cards—jack of spades, 5 of spades. He glanced at the board—4 of hearts, queen of hearts, 4 of spades, 8 of clubs, 8 of diamonds. He had two pair, but then, so did everyone else.

Randy passed the joint to Ethan as he laid down his cards, face up—9 of clubs, king of diamonds. "Turn 'em over, boys. If there's no bidding and no folding, there's no point in hiding. Let's see what you're packing."

Sam flipped his cards over while Ethan took another hit, holding the smoke in longer. This time the buzz continued as he exhaled and looked down at Sam's cards—ace of clubs, 9 of diamonds. Sam had won.

Randy, tired of waiting for Ethan to wake up and turn over his own cards, reached over and did it for him. "Three fucking chances for a full house and we all blew it. And goddamn, but that would have been a sweet bluff." He sighed, picked up the cup, and jangled it before holding it up to Sam. "Pick your loser, Peaches."

Sam dug in, clinked the chips around for a few seconds, then withdrew a red one and grinned at Randy. "Let me see some skin." He tossed the chip back in.

Randy set it down with a snort, then reached for the hem of his T-shirt and pulled it over his head.

Ethan stared at the tanned, sculpted planes of Randy's chest, absently taking another drag from the joint.

After shuffling and dealing, Randy drew another hit

too before peeking at his cards. The board read 3 of diamonds, 7 of spades, 6 of diamonds, 6 of clubs, jack of diamonds. Ethan had 3 of spades, 10 of spades. In other words, one low pair and a kicker that might roll over and groan, but nothing else.

Randy had 3 of clubs, 7 of hearts—two pair.

Sam had 5 of hearts, 4 of diamonds.

"Peaches wins again, this time with a straight," Randy said around the butt of the joint.

"*I love this game.*" Sam chose another chip. This time he chose a green chip—himself. "Hmm." He flicked it back and forth between his fingers and grinned. "'What is your favorite food, Sam?' 'Ah. That's a hard one, Sam, but rules are the rules. My favorite food is Mitch's tamales.'" He tossed the chip in and beamed. "My deal?"

Sam laid down 9 of clubs, 9 of hearts, 9 of spades, 6 of hearts, queen of hearts. Nobody made anything off the board at all, which meant it came down to high card, which Ethan won with the jack of diamonds.

He drew a red chip.

"Fucking hell." But he'd been smoking heavily, so Randy laughed and took another hit before he held out his hands and leered at Ethan. "You want my pants, baby? Because I'll give them to you."

Ethan didn't want the pants. He wanted a question. But it was like someone demanding you say something in a foreign language—the minute you were called to do it, your mind was blank. Ethan would never, ever be able to explain why he asked the question that finally floated to the surface.

"Is the gun still under the seat of my car?" The question felt heavy, even with the marijuana, but it was funny how lightly it came out of his mouth.

Randy's leer faded, replaced with an open display of shock, then sorrow, then fear, then pain. He had, Ethan realized, no poker face at all when he was high.

"Sorry." Ethan wanted a drink. He reached for the joint instead.

Randy leaned forward and picked it up, keeping it from him. "No." Looking directly into Ethan's eyes, he passed the joint over, turning it carefully in his hand and pressing it up against Ethan's lips, waiting as he inhaled. "The gun is gone. I gave it to a friend to get rid of. No one will find it, and if they do, they'll never know it had anything to do with you."

Unexpected tears pricked the back of Ethan's eyes, and he blinked them away as he exhaled. "Thanks."

"No problem." Randy sat down.

It took Ethan a while to gather the cards and deal them, but no one rushed him.

Sam won again, with a pair of 6s. He drew himself once more, and Randy snorted and got up to go to the fridge. He returned with two beers, one he tossed to Ethan, who was glad to have it because he found he was quite thirsty and a little hungry. They watched Sam, who was clearly considering his options.

Then he grinned, reached down, and pulled off a sock.

He won the next hand, too, with a pair of queens.

When he drew himself a third time in a row, he shook his head.

"This doesn't work. I say we make a rule change."

Randy lifted his eyebrows at this. "Let's hear it, Peaches."

"I say if the winner draws himself, it's a wild card. He can call on himself, or the others."

"Fine by me." Randy passed the joint over to Ethan. It was nearly half gone.

Ethan felt lightheaded and very agreeable. "Okay."

"Great." Sam dropped the chip into the cup and turned to Ethan. "What's your biggest fantasy, Ethan? A sexual one. One you haven't done."

Ethan sipped at his beer, thinking. "I don't know. I mean—I have to think." He tapped his finger on the side of the bottle. *Fantasy. Fantasy. Sexual fantasy.* He began to panic, because he had no idea. For years his greatest longing was to have Nick for a long weekend. Now he had sex every night and an orgy on call. He was living the fantasy he hadn't even known he'd wanted. But that wasn't an answer. He wanted to have an answer. He frowned.

For no reason at all, he started to giggle. He giggled like a little girl, and the next thing he knew, Randy was too.

"You embarrassed, baby?" Randy asked, and they both started in again.

"No." Ethan wiped his eyes, because he was giggling so hard he was crying. "No, I just—I don't know. But I'm thinking. *Shh.*"

They giggled again, but this time he looked right at Randy, watching his body shake as he laughed, and hilarity turned on a dime and became a deep, consuming arousal. He breathed out, made himself focus. "I want to fuck you." He stared right at Randy. "In front of people. Total strangers."

Randy's eyes went dark, and he stopped giggling. He was still smiling, though, as he reached for the joint from the ashtray. "We'll put it on the to-do list." Taking another hit, he scooped up the cards.

The next board was 5 of hearts, king of spades, 2 of clubs, 7 of hearts, jack of diamonds, and Ethan grinned, because he had 7 of spades, jack of hearts. Sam had 2 of hearts, 3 of spades, and Randy had 9 of diamonds, 4 of clubs. But when he started to reach for the cup of chips, Randy quickly scooped them out of his hand.

"Oh, *no you don't.*" He almost leered, he was so victorious. "I have just won your stupid game. This hand, anyway. Fucking finally."

"But you don't have anything," Ethan complained. Then he giggled again.

Randy laughed too, but he also shook his head. "The fuck I don't. You see what I've got? You see it, Peaches? I've got skeet. Fucking Skeet has *skeet.*" He slapped his leg several times.

"What the hell?" Ethan asked, but Sam leaned forward and beamed.

"I get it—you have the 9, the 5, and 2 on the board, and you fill in with a 7 and 4 from your hand." Sam smiled at Ethan, who was still openly confused. "Skeet.

A 9, a 5 and a 2, and something in-between."

"That's a fucking weird hand," Ethan said, and laughed again.

Randy reached in and drew his own chip. He leered at Ethan. "Give me your fucking shirt, lover."

Ethan tried to be serious. "I get to decide what article of clothing." Standing, he kept his eyes on Randy as he undid the buckle of his belt, lust plainly written on his face as Ethan freed the catch.

Randy's countenance fell as Ethan pulled the belt out completely and tossed it aside.

"Fucking hell," Randy complained, then stopped as Ethan undid the button and the fly to his trousers.

"There you go," Randy whispered.

Ethan, who didn't feel like giggling anymore, stepped out of his pants, took a hit from the joint, and sat down.

Randy stared right at Ethan's crotch. "Let's stop playing and fuck."

"No," Sam said calmly, but Ethan thought maybe with a hint of wickedness. "I want to keep playing."

So they did.

Ethan lost track of time, of place, even of himself. At some point popcorn appeared, and damn if it wasn't the best popcorn he had ever had in his whole life. He wanted to make love to the bowl when it was gone, but settled for licking his fingers and running them along the inside, catching the salty butter on the rim.

He noticed Randy watched him whenever he did that.

Ethan was slightly drunk and very high. And horny. His erection was intermittent, which should have scared him, but he kept thinking, *Who cares?* He gleefully took off his jacket at Randy's order, then when he won and drew his own chip, removed his shirt. Sam only got called on when his chip was drawn—Randy always ordered Ethan to undress, and Ethan always went after Randy or himself, which was why Randy was also in nothing more than socks and underwear, begging for a chance to take the latter off too. When Ethan realized this, that it was in many ways a two-man game, he apologized.

"It's not a problem." Sam drifted between the half-naked men before him. "I'm beginning to understand the appeal of the voyeur to Mitch."

"I'm sorry he got called away longer, Sam. But we'll keep you company." Ethan realized he'd put his hand not just on Sam's thigh but practically on his cock, and he giggle-snorted. "Oops. Sorry."

Sam stopped his hand from withdrawing completely and caressed his palm before letting him go. "Stop apologizing, Ethan. Otherwise I might have to punish you."

Now Randy laughed, which made Ethan giggle again. God, this was fun.

"I want to fuck," Randy whined.

Sam wagged a finger at him. "Be a good boy and I might let you."

Randy frowned. "Who put you in charge, Peaches?"

Ethan giggled more.

Sam arched an eyebrow. "Okay, fine. Whoever can walk in a straight line from the kitchen to the bathroom gets to be in charge."

Ethan, who was having a hard time sitting up, threw up his hands in surrender. But Randy stood, hitched up his underwear and wandered toward the refrigerator in a drunken zigzag. He righted himself, drew a deep breath, and headed for the hallway, walking forward one slow, painful step at a time. When he listed left so hard he ran into the couch, he swayed, snorted then fell over sideways.

"I want to fuck him." Randy's cry was a plea and laugh at the same time. Upside down, his legs were spread and hanging over the back of the couch, and Ethan could see the tip of his cock peeking over the black band of his underwear. "Please, Peaches?"

Yes, Ethan thought. *Please, Peaches.*

Sam leaned his elbows on his knees and regarded Randy severely. "You haven't been a good boy."

Ethan giggled again. Or maybe he was still giggling from the last time. He couldn't tell.

Randy's laugh was dark. "Then you should *punish* me." He tugged at the waistband of his underwear, revealing a luscious portion of his groin, but not, alas, his penis. "Get the paddle, Sammy, and *punish* my bad ass."

The image of Randy bent over while being paddled by Sam filled Ethan's head, and he stopped giggling. He couldn't even breathe for a minute. *Yes. Punish him, Sam.*

Sam took hold of Randy's chin. "Be good, Randy, or you'll go to bed without any fucking at all."

Randy sobered—mostly. He touched Sam's hand in acquiescence. "Yes, sir." He stroked the hand. "But can we please stop playing the game? And play a different game? With sex in it?" He stroked again. "Please?"

Sam patted his cheek in a gesture that should have been almost paternal but was somehow arousing instead. "Sit up."

Randy did, sitting primly—if somewhat unsteadily—as he waited for his next instruction.

Sam looked at Ethan, then back at Randy. "You can kiss him. But just a kiss, or I'll punish you."

Randy almost growled. Stepping over the table, he knocked over an empty beer bottle and sent half the deck and the cup of chips onto the floor. He stared down at Ethan, a dopey, drunk-high look on his face.

Randy grabbed the waistband of his underwear, pushed it to the floor, straddled Ethan and pressed his naked body against Ethan's nearly naked one as he took his mouth in an open-mouthed, beer-and-cannabis-tainted kiss.

Ethan moaned, opened his mouth wide and drank him in.

The world was already spinning, but it left its axis and arced off into outer space when Randy stuck his tongue deep into Ethan's throat, drawing Ethan's own tongue into his mouth to suck on it. All the while he ground his cock into Ethan's stomach. Ethan moaned into his mouth and groped blindly for his ass, and

Randy pinched Ethan's nipple before pulling him out of his underwear. When he took their cocks together in his hand, Ethan shuddered and thrust up, and if he hadn't been so dazed by the marijuana, he would probably have come then and there.

Randy drew Ethan's hand up toward his own mouth. Ethan watched, dizzy and full of lust as Randy took the fingers deep inside.

"Hurry." He sucked again, letting his saliva run in thick strands down Ethan's fingers. "Put them in me, Slick. Fuck me, baby, before he comes back."

Ethan didn't ask questions, just slicked his fingers in Randy's mouth again, loving the look of that, the way Randy had, with the help of substances both legal and illegal, given himself more completely than Ethan had even known to wish for. For one second, he wished Randy trusted him enough to do it sober.

Then he gave the thought up and reached around Randy's waiting, willing body. Randy had himself open, spread, eager, and when Ethan pushed against his hole, Randy sucked him in. As Ethan pushed deeper, trying to be careful, Randy took his mouth in a kiss and moaned as he impaled himself. Shuddering, Ethan kissed him back and desperately tried to find a rhythm.

Someone pulled his fingers out and knocked them away. Ethan opened his eyes in time to see the look of dazed, eager anticipation on Randy's face before he placed his hands on the chair behind Ethan on either side of his shoulders, knees spread and straddling Ethan, head now pushed against Ethan's shoulder.

"Here it comes."

Behind Randy Sam stood poised with a wide wooden paddle in his hand. Ethan's eyes went wide.

Really?

Amazed, he watched the paddle swing down against the bare surface of Randy's exposed ass.

Randy cried out, rough and lusty, and it shook Ethan because these were more intense than the cries he made when they had sex. The paddle came down, and Randy shouted louder, burying himself harder against Ethan as the blows—there was no other word, Sam was striking *blows*—came faster and faster. Now Randy grunted and humped, and so did Ethan, because even though it was strange and scary and almost surreal, it was also the most fucking erotic thing he'd ever felt or seen.

Then all of a sudden it wasn't, because his shoulder was wet because Randy was sobbing.

When Sam stopped, however, Randy lashed out. "Don't *stop*." He was so raw and undone Ethan almost came undone along with him. Sam resumed, and it was weird for a moment, but then Randy started undulating again, gripping Ethan, kneading his biceps. Shutting his eyes, Ethan nuzzled Randy as he wept into Ethan's shoulder.

On some unspoken cue, or maybe because his arm was tired, Sam stopped, and this time Randy sagged against Ethan, who cradled him close.

Sam kissed the small of Randy's back, stroking him gently. "I'm going to go and get some lotion."

Randy nodded.

As Randy drew deep, ragged breaths, Ethan tried to figure out if that had actually happened or if this was some marijuana-induced hallucination. Then Randy kissed his neck, and Ethan took his face in his hands and kissed him back, long and deep.

"Sorry." Randy kept his eyes closed, and he looked exhausted. "It was a rough day in therapy."

"It's okay." Ethan nuzzled him. *I love you,* he thought, and then, as if the marijuana and alcohol were some sort of verbal chute, it came out of his mouth. "I love you, Randy."

"I love you too, baby." Randy's mouth sought his, then settled on his chin and sucked it a little. "Don't go, Ethan. Don't go."

That made Ethan open his eyes, and he was going to ask where the hell Randy thought he was going, and then he saw the pain on Randy's face. He couldn't say a word.

Randy stared at Ethan's chin, his fingers tracing his cheek. There were tears in his eyes again. "Don't go, Ethan. Please. Don't."

"Randy," Ethan whispered, but his throat was too full to say anything more.

Then Sam was back, and Ethan got a good look at Randy's ass and recoiled. It was as red as his chips.

"It's okay." Randy laughed, sorrow forgotten—God, but pot was weird—and winced as Sam applied cream. "I'm all nice and warm now."

Sam met Ethan's gaze as he worked. "I'm careful.

Mitch taught me. It really is okay. I know how to hurt him only in the right way." He smiled, half-wicked, half-shy. All Sam. "I can teach you later."

Ethan nodded. He couldn't look at Randy's ass, though, so he watched Randy's face instead, touching it, staring down into it. He tried to tell him, with his eyes, that he would never leave, not if he could help it, that he didn't know how he would ever leave this. Him. How he'd ever leave him.

It might have worked, if Randy's eyes hadn't been closed.

They stayed closed too. "Sorry," he slurred, as Sam finished with his ass. "Don't think I'm gonna get to fuck you, Slick."

Ethan kissed his temple in reply. Weird, how he'd been so horny, and still was, but sleep sounded good too.

Sam led them out of the living room and into his own bedroom—he stripped Ethan down the rest of the way and tucked him in beside Randy, where Ethan tried again to explain his feelings, but Randy just pushed his face down, and then Ethan saw the fat, pretty cock and forgot what he was going to say.

Ethan was never really sure if he came or not. He remembered a lot of kissing. A lot of mouths. Cocks and mouths and cocks in mouths. There were fingers in his ass at some point, and he remembered telling Sam, no thank you, he did not want to be spanked. He remembered tasting come, but he had no idea whose it was. There might have been food, but he might have just wished for it. The details were fuzzy. He was happy, though. He knew that.

He woke with an aching head and a chest that felt too heavy until he realized it was because Randy, his still-pinked ass bare to the air, was using Ethan's chest for a pillow.

Ethan's mouth also tasted like all kinds of hell.

Someone moved behind him, and he heard Sam say sleepily, "Here." An open bottle of water pressed into his hand, and Ethan drank greedily. Oh God, he felt like total shit.

"Go back to sleep," Sam murmured, wrapped his arms around Ethan's chest, and Ethan did.

CHAPTER TWENTY

"I'M SORRY." CARYLE leaned over Ethan's desk with grim resolution. "There's no way around it. We have plenty of small shows lined up, drag queens and kings and performers of all kinds. We have dancers and waitstaff and dealers, and that's great. But this is never going to work if we don't get a headliner."

Ethan tapped his pen against his ledger. They were three weeks from opening night, looking at Caryle's projections for the Butterfly event. They were dismal. "Would it help if we changed the name?"

"The name is actually the best thing you have going for you right now. I put some teaser flyers out in a variety of public places, and a lot of people picked them up. I think if you get a model on those, someone androgynous and beautiful, you'll really have their attention. But you need more than their attention. You need their bodies to come here on your opening night."

"We want them to *gamble*. That's where the money is here. That's where it's always been, and if this place is going to survive, where it needs to return. Back to the *tables* too, not those damn slots. They make me crazy. I want to see people at craps. I want to see them at roulette and at blackjack. Above all, I want to see them at poker. I want them in here spending their money. I want to make Bellagio nervous because they're losing players to us. I want this place to *work* again."

Caryle gave him a funny look. "I thought you just wanted to get a quick sale?"

Ethan paused, then pressed his lips together. "Yes. Well. Yes."

She pulled another paper out from the bottom of the stack. "I can get you more dancers, if we want a bigger show. I can get you more waitstaff too, who will do their jobs but be a sort of performance of their own. I think you want to keep the dealers professional, though—don't dress them up. I know the owner has visions of them tricked out in skimpy things, but you don't want people in charge of that much money distracted. Leave that for my people. Keeping in mind the spirit of the evening, I'm instructing them all to flirt generously with both sexes."

"Oh?" Ethan hadn't been expecting that.

"If you weren't already on a theme, I'd say go bacchanalian, but this actually might be better. 'Butterfly' is pretty innocuous. The associations are with beauty and light and love, but what it is at heart is transformation. So when the guests come in, I think we should offer them some additional transformations. Feather boas. Glitter paint for their faces. Masks. Little things they can accept or refuse, and lots of choices."

Ethan could see it. "Yes. That's perfect."

"If they're straight or gay or still trying to figure it

out, they can be whatever they want on this night. I can teach my people how to respond to that, how to flirt without making people uncomfortable. But however it happens, this place can be a safe zone. Well, and I'll get a lot of security too. Some will be obvious, some not so much. If anyone gets too fresh with anyone else, we can put an end to it discreetly. It will keep people in line but also free others. This can be the safe place."

Ethan carefully pulled himself down from the glitter-dusted vision she'd painted in his mind. "I think it's brilliant."

Caryle beamed. "Great." She tapped his stack of papers. "Get me a headliner, and I'll give you the most amazing Butterfly Nights you could ever dream of."

Ethan watched her go. Then he tilted slowly forward, bending at the waist so he could rest his forehead on the pile of papers in front of himself in quiet, terror-filled horror.

He could not get a headliner. He couldn't get a *side-liner*. Caryle wanted a star. A major act. Someone people would line up to see because they knew the name. Also, someone whose schedule was open enough they could drop into Vegas on absolutely no notice whatsoever, go to a washed-up casino, and get paid almost nothing at all.

Ethan banged his forehead a few times against the paper.

The phone rang, startling him. Sarah's extension flashed on the readout. "Ms. Reynolds." As he answered, he reached up to remove a Post-it which had stuck to his forehead. "How may I help you?"

"Mr. Ellison. I have Mr. Crabtree on the line."

Ethan sat up so fast he pulled the phone forward half a foot by the cord. "Put him through. Please. And thank you, Ms. Reynolds."

"Not at all, Mr. Ellison."

The line clicked. Ethan shut his eyes and held his breath until Crabtree's Santa chuckle rumbled in his ear. "Well, well, well. Ethan Ellison. How have you been?"

Ethan had spent many hours dreaming of what he would say to Crabtree—the dressing-down he would give him, the list of complaints, the contents of his spleen. More recently, he'd wanted to at least have him explain what his plan was, because he was sure there was one. Then he simply hoped there was one. All he knew was if Crabtree called, he could ask him questions, demand his help—*something*.

Which was why it was so bizarre all he could find to say was, "Fine. You?"

"I'm enjoying the fresh air of the mountains. Back up in your old stomping grounds, in fact."

"You're in Provo?"

"In American Fork. Near it, anyway. We have a lovely cabin here on Utah Lake. Absolutely beautiful. I have no idea how you ever left."

"We?" Ethan repeated.

"Some friends came with me."

There was an X-rated edge to the words. *Very* not American Fork.

"I hear there's to be a party at the casino? Something about butterflies?"

Ethan relaxed in his chair somewhat. "Butterfly Nights. Billy thinks if he makes a good show, he'll tempt your buyer himself. I tried to tell him I wasn't even sure you have one."

"Oh, I do, but I'm fairly sure he's safe from Billy. Still, the boy is free to try. Fair is fair."

Ethan doubted Crabtree played fair unless he fixed the outcome.

Crabtree continued. "I'm pleased about the statue. When Ms. Reynolds told me what you were up to, I saw to it personally you had all the help you needed."

"I did it in part to goad Randy. Though I think it could add a lot to the casino again."

"Yes, I heard about your *rub the demon's penis* idea. Clever. It will probably work too—at least to make the casino rich. Additionally, I'm charmed by your idea to take the casino back into the Golden Age of Vegas. I think my Billy would have loved it. This said, Mr. Ellison, you're missing several key elements to make the night a success. To start, you're going to need an entertainment act someone has actually heard of. Madonna impersonators will not bring in the kind of traffic you need."

"I know that, sir, but the problem—"

"I will get you an act, young man, so put the worry out of your head. But your *real* problem is you don't have the right game. A classy, high-stakes game to bring in real players with real money. You need to use one of those high-tech feeds to display the hole cards and get an audience. You'll want a feed out to pay-per-view too, and a good, high-quality leak so people can watch for free and spread the word about our casino. I'll take care of those things too. But advertise the game, son. And make damn sure you understand it is the *center* of everything you're doing. Every sequin, every feather, every toke that happens on the floor is all to support this game. Do you understand? Do you *understand* me, Ellison?"

Ethan had no fucking idea what he was talking about. "Are we talking about poker?"

"Of course we're talking about poker. A game in Billy's Room. Invite-only, but we put a glut of tickets on the black market, somebody reselling them off eBay. We make a big fuss over how they're illegal, and eBay takes them off, and then they get sold on the streets. That part I will also see to. But as far as you're concerned, the game tickets need to be legit, and you'll be checking them carefully at the door. You don't like that the tickets have gone out, and you suspect some sort of underground activity is organizing it. You won't say the word mob because people will think you're silly. But it's clear you're thinking this when the press talks to you."

"The press will talk to me?"

"Of course they will—you're new, you're exciting. You're also possibly crazy, and this whole thing looks as if it might come down around your ears any second. That's good theater. If you don't have CNN and E! camped out around you soon, I'll be disappointed."

"I take it you think I'm doing well, if you're finally showing up and getting yourself involved."

Crabtree laughed, and Ethan realized if Crabtree hadn't liked what he was doing, he'd have known by now. He wouldn't have had anybody follow him. He'd have had Ethan removed.

Ethan sat back in his chair, shaking a little. "Crabtree, do you know what happened to Evelyn Carter?"

There was a heavy pause. "That's a funny question for you to ask, young man."

"I've been reading about the past. About the mob gangs that used to rule Vegas. Or allegedly did. I know about the fifties mob, and the seventies-eighties mob. I know about Lansky's mob and then the Chicago Outfit. I know the Lansky mob was supposed to be the kinder, gentler one, and I know the Chicago Outfit had a reputation for being brutal. I know about Rosenthal and Billy, and I know about all the ones listed in the books and on websites. But—not Carter. He's this shadow, and then he just ends. They say in a hit, but—" He stopped, feeling foolish because of what he'd been thinking. "I don't know. Never mind, it doesn't matter. I'm just getting caught up in the story."

"What story is that?" Crabtree sounded mildly intrigued.

"I know Rosenthal went down because he was too addicted to fame. I assume Spilotro went down in the cornfield because he didn't get a job done. But I don't know about Evelyn Carter at all. I don't know if they killed him because he screwed up. I don't buy this stuff I read about him being caught up in the violence. I swear he was better than that." He paused, embarrassed. "I don't know. Just forget it. Probably I'm trying to make a romantic story where there isn't one."

There was a lengthy pause on Crabtree's end.

Ethan held his breath.

"I knew Carter." Crabtree chuckled, but it was a gentler laugh than Ethan had ever heard him give. "He'd have been touched to hear you read through the mess and thought that. Pleased. But I'm sorry to tell you, Ethan, most of what you've read *is* true. He was brutal, more than he needed to be. It cost him, one piece at a time, everything he held dear. Including me."

Why did this make Ethan so sad? "So they *did* kill him."

"No, son. He killed himself. He had nothing left. He couldn't even step foot in a casino anymore—they put his name in the Black Book. If he so much as walked in the front door of Herod's or anywhere, he committed a crime. He had a chip on his shoulder, that one. He had it all figured out how the world was supposed to work, and he kept waiting patiently for it to show up, and then, finally, he got impatient and took his revenge. Blew up everything around him, just because it wasn't doing what he wanted. He went crazy, really. Slowly. But people were starting to notice. If he hadn't killed himself, he'd have been taken care of."

"No." Ethan couldn't stop the pain from his voice.

"The seventies were a different time. Different outfit. Much as I loved him, he lost sight of the code. He forgot this was about making money, not settling scores. He got too caught up in the game, and forgot the real pot he played for. By the time he realized his mistake, it was too late. So he gave himself one last victory and took himself out before someone else could. And that, young man, is the story of Evelyn Carter."

Ethan stared down at his desk, remembering the faded pictures of the man from the internet. He also saw himself. Like Carter, he kept waiting for the big payout. Waiting for the moment things would go right. For the time when the wheel would come around to his number and give him what he deserved.

Except sometimes the wheel didn't come around. Because the wheel wasn't about you. The wheel wasn't about anyone. It was just a damn wheel. It was as Randy said—you had to get the best of it.

You had to go and be your own wheel.

"You still there, son?"

"Yes. Sorry." Ethan cleared his throat. "Thank you for telling me. I appreciate knowing the truth about him."

Crabtree cleared his throat. "The tournament will be handled through Ms. Reynolds. Four rounds, five hundred players, with first, second, and third prizes worth playing for, but the grand prize will be for ten million dollars."

Ethan nearly fell off his chair. "*Ten million dollars?*"

"Yes. It will have to come out of the assets, though buy-in will be twenty grand, so that will help a great deal. You'll be going up against the World Series of

Poker, by the way, so expect some pushback. But you'll also be drawing some of the losers away. It should work out quite well."

"Sure." *Ten million dollars.* Which he'd have to get from Billy. Fantastic.

"Before the tournament gets started we'll host a private game. Just one round for show, and this one truly will be invitation-only. Mine. Small table, big pot. You'll be at the table, Mr. Ellison, so keep practicing, and on more than your little computer game. Get yourself to Bellagio at least once a day. You've been neglecting your practice."

Had Crabtree been spying on him? Ethan snorted, quietly. Of course he had. "Is there anything else I should know?"

"If there is, I'll be sure to tell you. Give my love to the boys," he said, and hung up.

"THIS IS THE kill switch." Randy pointed to the red button beside the right handlebar of the motorcycle. "If you get into trouble, if you aren't sure the engine is totally off, and especially if you feel like you're falling over and are going to crash, *use the kill switch.*"

Sam flexed his fingers on the handlebars and nodded through the helmet. "Kill switch. Got it."

Randy hoped to hell he did. He'd shown Sam every YouTube video he could find about bike safety and what happened when you didn't follow it, though he tried to keep the danger vids to a minimum because he didn't want to freak him out. But now he was wondering if that had been a mistake. Maybe Peaches wasn't going to take this seriously.

Sam caught the look on Randy's face and touched his hand. "I'll be fine. I'm taking the course next week and getting my permit. I even made sure to sign up with Kari, the instructor who you said is also a dealer at Herod's, like we agreed. This is a trial run. Across an empty parking lot. Relax already."

"Fuck, Sam, there are so many ways to kill yourself on a bike." It wasn't that hot out, but Randy was sweating to death.

"You and Mitch *do* think you're my parents, don't you? Which if you consider what I do to the two of you in the bedroom is seriously fucked up, you know."

"I do *not* think of you as my son. Maybe as a brother-like figure in my more overprotective moments. But that doesn't mean we can't enjoy the occasional paddle. You're getting so good at it—it'd be a shame to waste such talent." He paused. "Wait—do to the *two* of us? What kinky stuff are you doing with the Old Man that you're not telling me about? Spill, Peaches."

Sam took off his helmet and leaned forward onto the gas tank. "We've gotten into fisting."

Randy let out a wicked growl. "Oh, baby. *Baby.* You have been holding *out.* And what, no equal opportunity? Because, honey, you need to know I am *very* good at that. And I'd be careful with you."

The look on Sam's face was almost evil. "It's not me getting fisted."

Randy stared. His jaw hung open. "No fucking way."

"You can't tell him I told. He'd be embarrassed. But he really likes it. I do too."

Mitch Tedsoe lets Sam fist him. Randy shook his head. "Jesus. He completely fucking trusts you, Sam. He swore to me he would never, ever let anybody do that to him. Ever."

Sam wiggled his fingers. "Little hands. That's the key. I can't take Mitch yet. I'm not sure I want to. But it's okay. That can be his thing."

Randy leaned on the handlebar and put his hand on Sam's thigh. "Peaches, as the owner of hands half the size of your husband's meat hooks, I would be *happy* to fist you in his stead."

Sam pressed two fingers against Randy's mouth. "You shouldn't be thinking about seducing me, Randy. From what I saw the other night with you and Ethan, I think you have your hands plenty full."

Randy tried to make his shrug casual. "Yeah, but who knows how long that's going to last? You and Mitch, now, I'm counting on you visiting me in the retirement home. Well, Mitch will be next door. You, sweet young thing, had better bring us contraband."

"I thought you and Ethan were serious. What happened? What did you do?"

"Why the hell are you assuming it's me? Anyway, nothing's happened. But you know it will. I'm being practical."

He fucking hated how much it hurt to admit that.

"You're being stupid. Randy—my God, the man is head over heels for you. You *both* are head over heels."

"Not everybody gets what you and Mitch have. I *never* get lucky. It's a ride, Peaches. It's a good ride, but it's going to end. I'm not going to pretend differently and get all chewed up."

"There's no kill switch on a heart."

Don't I fucking know it. "That's sweet, Peaches. We'll have them put it on the next Harley catalog cover."

Sam folded his arms and regarded Randy coolly. "If that's what you're telling yourself, even if you don't let him know this is how you view him, you're going to screw it up. Ethan loves you. I swear he does."

For now. "Sam, he's a fucking investment broker. Look at him at that casino. Crabtree knew what he was doing, plucking him up to run it. And when this game is done, he'll move on to something bigger. Better. Brighter. He's not going to stick around Vegas. He's sure as hell not going to shack up permanently with a prop player slash rig mechanic, I'll tell you that."

"He *adopted two cats* and *brought them to your house*. He clicker trained them so they wouldn't scratch your furniture and mess up your place. He goes to the *grocery store*. He's figured out what food you like just by studying the cupboards, and he knows to save one jar of peanut butter for you because you eat out of it with a spoon."

"He's considerate." Randy kicked at the dirt and watched the dust fly. "That's Slick for you. He's a nice, considerate guy."

"He *knows* you, sometimes better than I do. He loves you. I swear he does. Don't fuck it up."

"Are you about done? Because if we're going to cry about our feelings, I want to go home and get my blankie."

"Thank God Mitch wasn't such a dipshit about the two of us. *He* isn't scared I'm going to leave him."

Randy snorted. "Shit, he's fucking petrified of it. You're a lot younger than he is. I've seen his face when you guys are out, when you check out other guys even for playing around, and yes, he's scared. Like you're scared he's going to die on you. Everybody's fucking scared, Peaches. Everybody's scared of something."

"I face my fears. I go to therapy on my own now. I learned to drive a stick shift, and now I'm learning to ride a motorcycle. I go up to the Stratosphere tower with you whenever you ask. That night the two of you got high, I didn't even check my phone for a text. It was waiting for me when I woke up. I'm facing my fears. So is Mitch. And I think Ethan is too. What are *you* doing, Randy?"

"I'm giving you a goddamn motorcycle lesson, that's what I'm doing." Randy glared at the left handlebar. "That's the choke slider. Turn it, then kick the pedal back for first, two forward for second, and on up one at a time all the way to fifth gear."

Sam blinked at the downshift from deep conversation, fumbling around for the controls. "Wait—this? This here? The foot thing? Two what?"

"It's the same as the stick shift and clutch in a car, except you use your hand and your foot both."

But half an hour later when Sam came back around from his first successful lap, the question kept echoing in his head.

What are you doing, Randy?

He didn't have a fucking clue what he was doing. And any day now, it was going to bite him in the ass.

Enjoy the ride while it lasts. Just enjoy the ride.

IT WAS TWO weeks until Butterfly Nights, and Ethan still didn't know who their headlining act would be. Two weeks until the show poker game, and he knew he'd never be ready to take Crabtree on. He was losing it—not only his edge, but maybe even part of his mind. This was going to bite him in the ass. Hard.

It might even kill him.

Sam noticed his unease and tried to soothe him. He was only going to therapy once a week now, but he seemed more confident and less prone to a panic attack. He was as sunny as his nickname promised almost all the time. More and more it was Sam managing Ethan and Randy, and not simply in bedroom games. Which was probably why that day when Sam came into his office wearing his lime-green scrubs and a bright smile, Ethan looked at Sam with all the weariness and terror he felt and telegraphed, *Help me.*

Dropping his duffel in the corner, Sam hurried forward. "What happened? What's wrong?"

"I can't do this. I don't know why I ever thought I could. I don't know how to get out of it."

Sam put a hand on his shoulder and began to massage gently. "I got a text from Caryle. She's coming over with the costumes to show us. As soon as she gets a model, she says she's going to do a new round of advertising."

"We have no headliner. Just some lackluster buzz and some poker tournament I don't even fully understand but for which I am on the hook to Billy Junior." Ethan buried his hands in his hair. "I can't do this. *I can't do this.*"

Sam's hand tightened on his shoulder. "I need to hit the bathroom quick, and then we'll go downstairs and play some craps, okay?"

Ethan didn't want to play craps. He wanted to crawl into the secret closet and wall himself in. "Fine," he said instead.

Fifteen minutes later they were at the table to the left of the demon statue, Ethan staring into its unseeing golden eyes as Sam rolled the dice. It was weird, how some days the demon looked friendly and some days it looked sexy and sometimes it was the most menacing thing he'd ever seen. It was that now. It mocked him, leering tall as water poured from its nostrils, gleaming gold and glinting in the soft casino light.

Why had he ever thought he could run a casino? He had ten million dollars in the bank, all of it put there by a mob man. Sarah had pulled him aside the other day and coached him as to how to respond to that, should the Nevada Gaming Commission ask, and he was told to say a private investment he'd made had turned up surprisingly beneficial, which was why he'd quit his job. When Ethan had explained this wasn't true and could easily be proven, Sarah had simply replied the proof was being arranged, and not to worry. If the Gaming Commission wanted details, he was to send them to her and she would take care of it.

This wasn't even his game anymore. It never was. He was a fish all over again.

A group of college girls stood off to the side of the statue, giggling, reaching around the sprays of water to rub the exposed organ. Ethan watched them, noticing how they blushed when they first fumbled, but once they took the fat golden cock into their hands, their faces twisted into a quiet sort of triumph. When they walked away, they looked bolder and more confident. Sarah had given him a printout showing the guests who rubbed the demon dick stayed in the casino an average of two hours longer than the others, and they tended to spend at least half again as much money as their non-dick peers. They also won more, but because the house always wins, they collectively lost more too.

Was he rubbing a stupid golden phallus, thinking he was doing something wicked, giving himself a false sense of security, but he was really playing stooge for the house?

A hand on his back startled him, but when it slid down and around to his hip in a familiar way, he knew Randy was standing there even before he turned to face him. "Hey, Slick."

Ethan stared at him. *I can't do this, Randy,* he wanted to say, but couldn't, just looked at him, afraid if he spoke, the chaos inside him would come tumbling out.

Randy hooked his finger in a belt loop. "Come on, baby. I have something for you."

They started for the stairs. Ethan realized he'd abandoned Sam, but Randy shook his head and tugged again.

"Peaches is the one who called me. Come on, baby. Come on."

Now they're both coddling you.

Ethan stopped as they passed the demon statue and looked down at the gleaming cock. It already looked more polished than the rest of the statue, partly because the staff rubbed it too. They were buying it along with everyone else.

Swept up in a sudden gust of fury and terror, Ethan stormed across the casino, ignoring Randy's calls. He didn't know where he was headed until he got to the roulette table, but once he saw the spinning wheel, he pulled out a handful of chips, ordered change, and put fifty dollars down.

On black, and another stack on red.

"Slick, come on," Randy said, coming up beside him. "Don't do this. Don't aggravate yourself."

"I have perfect odds." Ethan glared at the wheel. "One of them has to win."

One of them had to lose too. But one would win. That would be enough.

Randy said nothing, but Ethan could feel his tension and his displeasure. Ethan was ready to launch into a justification for himself when he saw Randy wince. Returning his focus to the wheel, Ethan saw the little white ball bouncing happily in the double zero.

Green. It had landed on *green*.

"I fucking hate roulette," Randy murmured, but Ethan said nothing, just watched the dolly come down, feeling it hit the number like a punch in his gut. That wasn't even comedic. It was ridiculous. Only two numbers on the whole table were green. It wasn't *fair*.

"It isn't going to work." Terror, full of teeth and claws and golden demon leers, gripped Ethan. "It isn't going to work, and I'm not only going to look foolish in front of all of Las Vegas, they're going to *kill me*—"

Randy dragged him across the floor, this time not letting him stop for anything, not until they were inside the elevator and the doors were closed—and then he kissed Ethan hard on the mouth. At first Ethan stood there, still numb, and then he kissed back, hesitant, then desperate. There was no arousal, or if there was any, it was buried under fear, self-doubt, and a churning internal chaos he couldn't stop.

Eventually it got the better of him, and he drew back, gasping, his chest tight. "I'm so stupid."

"It's okay, Slick. It's okay."

Ethan shut his eyes. There was something wrong with him. Something really wrong.

The elevator doors opened, and Ethan slipped out of Randy's arms and stepped out. But when he would have gone into the safety of his office, Randy took him to a corner by the bathroom. "Let's stay here for now."

Ethan tried to move away. "I don't want anybody to see me like this."

"That's why we're staying here." He drew Ethan toward him. "Come on, baby. Stay here with me and put yourself together."

Ethan stared over his shoulder at his office door, which was still closed. "Who's in there? What's going on?"

"Leave it for now."

Ethan stormed to the door, throwing it open. The office was empty. "There's nobody here." He turned to Randy to glare at him, saw the other man's face and figured it out.

Bugged. His office was bugged.

Video too?

Red. Ethan literally saw red, the whole world reducing around his eyes, but he didn't feel angry. He felt hot and numb.

Randy took his hands, his face full of concern—and love—and led him away from the door, down the hall, and into a closet. He pulled on a light above their heads, a single bulb swinging on a chain, and it filled the room with dim, dusty light. When Randy led him to the floor, Ethan went in defeat into Randy's arms.

"I'm so stupid. So incredibly stupid."

Randy kissed his hair. "You just slowed down, baby. You said so yourself, you're fine until you slow down."

"Why are you putting up with me when all I do is

break down? I'm a farce. I'm ridiculous. Why aren't you making fun of me?"

"You aren't making a fool of yourself. You're amazing. You're fucking amazing. No one's telling you to stop because we're all too amazed. You're making this place work, and it's *good*. It's *great*. You aren't a fool. You're a god."

"But I don't know what it's *for*. I don't even know how it's happening. I don't know how to keep it going, either, and people are starting to notice, and they're going to find out. They're going to find out I'm making it up. They're going to laugh at me, and I deserve it. I'm betting on black. That's all I'm doing. Or black and red and it's going to come up green. How did it *do* that? It's stupid. *I'm* stupid."

Randy gripped his face. "You are *not stupid*."

"I am and you know it. That's why you haven't been saying anything. Because you know. Jesus Christ—I didn't know he had my office bugged, but *you* did. Why didn't you say? Are you laughing too?"

"Jesus fuck, *no*, Slick. Fucking hell—no, I am not laughing at you." Randy sank a little harder against Ethan. "I'm sorry. I'm sorry, I should have told you about the office. But you were flying too high. I thought telling you would be like making you slow down."

"Your house? Is it bugged?" Ethan thought of the X-rated plays that went on there on a regular basis.

"I fucking hope not. But maybe. Don't think about it. It doesn't matter."

"It matters, because I'm an *idiot*."

Randy grabbed his face and stared down into it. "You are not an idiot."

"I'm a big, stupid, *stupid* fucking idiot. Why the *hell* are you with me, Randy?"

He tried to look away, but Randy held his face, so he shut his eyes.

A soft, gentle kiss landed first against one of Ethan's eyes, then the other.

"I'm sorry." Now Randy sounded broken. "I shouldn't have introduced you to him. I should have been involved more, should have helped. I should have stopped this." He stroked the sides of Ethan's face, then sighed as he rested their foreheads together. "But you were flying, Ethan, and I got caught up in watching. I didn't stop you because I thought you had to know how good you were. I didn't think you needed me."

Ethan laughed, a bitter, strangled sound. Not need him? The thought was so ridiculous he couldn't even begin to address it. *I fucking need you, Randy. I need you. I love you. I love you, and I need you, so much it's probably bad. I love you more than I ever loved Nick, need you more than I needed him, and I'm scared, fucking scared, because I don't know how—I don't know what to do with that.*

How could he ever be the man Randy saw in him if he needed him so much? How could it ever be anything more than a lie? How could Randy love a lie?

How could Randy love him when he could barely love himself?

All this churned and bubbled inside him. How the

hell was he supposed to say that?

I need you, he tried to say, to keep it simple.

Except when he opened his mouth, something swept up and stopped it, and tears came out instead.

This drew him out of his swirl of despair when nothing else could, and he swiped angrily at them. "I never cried. I never cried for years, and now it's all I do."

Randy's laugh was wicked but rueful. "I know exactly what you mean. But don't, sweetheart. I know I shouldn't say that, but don't. I can't bear to see it. Because if you cry, I'll fall apart, and then I don't have anything left to impress you with, if I can't even be strong for you."

You'll always impress me, Randy, no matter what you do. You're always strong for me. You're strongest, actually, when you hold me like this and go all soft and tender. But he couldn't say this, either. He couldn't even say half of it. He buried his face in Randy's neck, curled his fingers around his shoulders, and held on. "I love you."

"I love you too, baby." Randy kissed his hair. "We've got to get out of this pit we fell into, Slick."

"If we leave the pit, we have to face the mess."

"What's messy, baby? Because I can't see it. Tell me so I can help."

"I'm Crabtree's stooge. He's laughing at me because I'm so stupid."

"He would never use his casino like that. It isn't his in name, but it's his in his heart. You might as well know. Crabtree and Billy Senior were lovers."

Ethan opened his eyes and blinked. What? *But what about Evelyn?*

"This place, Herod's—it's all he has left of Billy. His Billy. He wouldn't fuck with it. He's got some plan with it and you, and it's not that he's having a good time at your expense. If I thought for half a second he were pissing with you, I'd tear Nevada apart until I found him, and I'd take out his fucking teeth one at a time."

He's in Utah, Ethan almost said, then realized he couldn't trust that, either. He looked up at Randy instead. "Why? Why would you do that?"

Randy stared at him for a few seconds before taking Ethan's face in his hands and looking him straight in the eye, his dark, beautiful Randy eyes cutting holes through to the back of his head. "Because my name is not Nick Snow."

It was as if the "Hallelujah" chorus ran backward through Ethan's head. He had never known so many emotions at once in his life—joy, fear, disbelief, anger, sorrow, and love, beneath it all, love—so he shut his eyes.

Randy pulled Ethan to his feet and into the hall. "Come on."

As they walked, Randy's fingers brushed Ethan's hand, and he felt Nick's ring against his skin. Randy still wore it. Ethan noticed it at least once a day. He'd thought it was a reminder, either to Randy or to him. Some sort of warning not to get too close, to go too deep. But maybe that was wrong. All his thoughts seemed to be wrong, so this one must be too.

But he couldn't think for the life of him why Randy would be so attached to some other man's ring.

Outside the door to Ethan's office, Randy stopped. "I want to go in there, and I want to make love to you."

"You said the office was bugged."

"Oh, there's hidden video too, most likely." Randy grinned.

Ethan's blood began to hum.

Randy reached out and ran his hand down Ethan's neck. "I owe you a lap dance, for the fountain, and it occurred to me you might want to play out the fantasy you confessed the other night." Randy touched his fingers to Ethan's lips. "Show him, baby. Show him how strong you are. When life fucks you over, you don't slow down. You just keep going, keep moving, eyes peeled for the next opportunity, the next dance. Don't get bogged down in the endings or the parts where you know you're fucked even before you get there. Bluff, baby. Bluff until they all fold or until you start to believe it yourself. If you fail, get up and bluff again."

He ran his fingers down the line of Ethan's stubble then leaned forward to kiss the edge of his jaw before he whispered in his ear.

"Bluff him. But don't bluff me." He nipped at the lobe of Ethan's ear. "*Fuck* me."

Ethan stared at him a moment, swimming in that speech. Then he pushed Randy inside and against the door as it slammed closed, grinding them together as he took Randy's face in his hands.

When Randy pushed him onto the small sofa Sam had dragged out of storage, Ethan went, sinking into the vinyl and spreading his legs, his cock swelling as Randy began to dance before him. There was no music, but it didn't matter. Didn't matter at all, because it was Randy, and he was moving, graceful in a way only he could do. He could have been a pole dancer, the way he rotated his hips, so expertly, so smooth, so perfect, so professional. Knowing Randy, he likely *had* been a professional.

And he worries about me seeing him as not strong. How could I see him as anything but?

Hips still undulating to an unheard beat, Randy drew the hem of his T-shirt slowly up the sides of his body, over his nipples, over his shoulders. The fabric tangled in his arms, briefly obscuring his face as he exposed himself, as the shirt lifted higher and higher. Then it came away entirely as Randy stood, still dancing, still smiling, cool and easy and beautiful, still Randy, moving before him.

Don't slow down. Bluff.

Ethan still felt raw inside, but he kept his exterior cool, taking strength and security from Randy, replacing his veneer as his lover danced and stripped before him so expertly that there was no question—Randy had done this before.

Now he's doing it for me.

CHAPTER TWENTY-ONE

ETHAN KNEW THE body undulating before him so well he could almost paint it, but this was like seeing it for the first time, and he didn't know where to look because he was trying to see everything. Randy's thighs, so strong, not tanned like his torso, but defined and muscular. Thighs that hugged his beloved bike, that tensed when he crouched, that twisted with him when he maneuvered beneath an engine. Thighs he usually spread out over a chair, one leg extended to the side while he played poker.

Thighs which grazed Ethan's own now, which bore him, stabilized Randy as he leaned back, as one hand braced against the edge of the couch and the other slipped inside the waistband of his underwear to touch himself.

Ethan looked at Randy's chest, which was broad and thick with muscle. He took in Randy's belly, a tiny, tiny bit of paunch Ethan knew he was self-conscious about. The tiny bit of paunch Ethan loved to touch, to kiss, because it made Randy quiver and go soft.

As Randy positioned his arms behind his head, Ethan studied them—muscled arms, his prizes, which he showed off with shirts too tight and with sleeves barely there. He saw the black tattoo on his lover's shoulder—a spade, small and subtle. Ethan had kissed it. Licked it. Sucked it. Bitten it.

He took in Randy's floppy hair, greasy because he used too much gel. Sam was always after him for it, and Randy would yell at him then run his hands through his mop, making it worse. Dark, unruly hair matching the stubble on his jaw, the wildness of his big brown eyes.

Then there was Randy's mouth—thin, wide, hitching on the right side, the tiny scar that curled into the left. Tiny, but it was there. The cleft of his chin. The slope of his neck. The taut pebbles of his nipples.

Those nipples were inches from Ethan's face, moving, moving, moving, teasing him, brushing against his mouth before Randy stepped off the couch. Still swaying and dancing, he pushed his underwear down and stepped out of them. Bracing his hands on the wall behind Ethan's head, he knelt and began to dance again.

His cock was visible now too. His fat, long cock, rough and uncut like the rest of him. Thick and full of veins, it had been the source of hours of fascination for Ethan. He'd never touched an uncut penis before Randy, and Randy was happy to let him play with it at any and all times. It was a very erect cock now, and the head of Randy's penis pushed out through the sleeve of his foreskin, bulbous and pink and straining. Ethan liked best to grip it, to hold it tight and feel the skin shift under his hand, a membrane between himself and Randy's organ, a veil that never lifted—except for when the head came through, peeking out to wink its hello.

Mine. My Randy.

As if to make the claim for the benefit of their silent viewers, to let them know this cock, this man, this sensual creature was his, Ethan took the shaft in hand and drew it smartly into his mouth.

Randy pushed himself into Ethan's throat until Ethan grabbed those hips and forced him into his own rhythm. He held Randy's thighs, ran his hands up that stomach, to his chest, teasing those nipples, lingering there to pinch and roll them because he knew it made Randy go a little crazy. When Ethan pulled back from his lover's erection, Randy slid down Ethan's body, down his shirt, settling on the tent of Ethan's cock through his trousers, his naked body humping insistently against Ethan's clothes.

All Ethan's hesitation was gone, or at least no longer piloting the ship. He didn't understand how Randy could see him come so unglued and then so easily yield to him mere moments later, but that had been happening between them since they started.

Ethan undid his pants, and Randy, reading his mind, finished the job, taking Ethan's cock out and nesting it beside his own. It reminded Ethan of the other night, when they'd begun this way and ended with Sam paddling Randy while he crouched over Ethan. It made him want to press Randy into the couch and hump against him until they were both breathless and gasping, come spraying everywhere between them.

Gripping the sides of Randy's body, Ethan did just

that.

They needed better friction. Ethan fumbled with Sam's duffel, turning it inside out as he searched for lube, lotion, shaving cream—anything. He found a bottle of something that said NOMAD, expensive-looking and with a camel on it, but it was creamy, and he fumbled until he had a dollop of it in his hand.

"Fuck me, Ethan, *fuck me.*"

Ethan glanced briefly at the tube, something catching his eye, and then Randy stuck his tongue in Ethan's ear. Shivering, Ethan dove at his lover's mouth again. Their hands warred over their cocks until they were tugging them together, their chests rubbing hard and tight, nipples brushing nipples and hair and muscles. Ethan pressed their groins together, humping faster until he felt Randy ready to release—once he began, Ethan let himself go too. They collapsed, shuddering together, grinding in a sort of aftershock.

"Baby." Ethan kissed the nape of Randy's neck.

The door opened, and Ethan knew they should pull apart and be shocked, but he couldn't manage it—he was too spent. Then he saw who had come in, and he went still.

For a minute he thought he was hallucinating, because there in the doorway was something between a man and a woman and a bird. *Butterfly,* his brain corrected him, but it hardly mattered. This was like nothing he'd ever seen. Slight, rounded, beautiful, full of wings and sequins. Man? Woman? Angel? Insect? Beautiful and handsome, exotic and sexual and innocent all at once, eyes round and rimmed with dark lines and glitter, hair hidden by a headdress. Huge wings flanked either side of the skintight body suit.

"Oh." The butterfly glanced back out the door. "Don't go in. They're—You can't go in."

It was only then, when he recognized the voice, that Ethan figured it out. "Sam?"

Randy sat up too, reaching for his clothes but unhurriedly, though when he caught sight of Sam in the doorway, he stopped short. "Peaches?"

Sam came in and shut the door.

The young man Ethan had come to know and love was nowhere in this creature. No man or woman was, either. This had to be the costume Caryle had been speaking of.

It was fucking brilliant.

Sam seemed stunned, in some sort of shock, barely holding himself together. "Crabtree called. He has the headliners."

"Oh?" Ethan zipped himself discreetly, pretending his shirt and pants weren't sprayed with spunk. "Who is it? Wait—headliners? More than one?"

"One for each night. Some friend of his knows a whole bunch of performers, so we have someone for each night. He found three s-s-singers." Sam sank against the door. "They're all Australian. Because the friend is Australian."

Randy had climbed into his underwear and had his shirt over his head, but he watched Sam with concern. "Peaches, you okay?"

"Missy Higgins, some singer named Missy Higgins. She'll be the third night." Sam took a deep breath then let it out slowly. "And then Olivia Newton-John. She'll be the last night."

Ethan's eyebrows shot halfway up his forehead. "Sam—my God, that's *wonderful*." How the hell had Crabtree done that? Ethan had heard she wasn't even touring anymore.

Sam shook his head, and when he spoke, it was only in a whisper. "The first night—" His eyes were wild, almost crazy, full of wonder and hope and disbelief and utter, utter terror. He began to slide slowly down the door, a Technicolor butterfly melting slowly toward the floor. "The first night is Kylie."

Kylie: Sam's Kylie. Sam had given Ethan quite the education in the past few weeks about Kylie Minogue. She was on a level with Madonna everywhere but in the United States, and to many here too she was as big or bigger. Crabtree had scored *her*?

Randy laughed and went forward, still only half-dressed, to collect Sam off the floor, and Ethan took in the dazed wonder on the younger man's face and realized it didn't matter. However this had happened, it had happened. It was going to happen. Butterfly Nights was going to happen.

It was going to be fantastic. And worth every bit of pain and doubt and crazy it took to carry them there.

ETHAN HAD THOUGHT it'd be impossible to get *anyone*

on such short notice, so the idea that Crabtree had gotten anyone of any quality at all wasn't something he'd considered. He'd been seriously impressed by the inclusion of Olivia Newton-John. He'd almost gone to see her once a few years back when she'd been on tour and stopped in Provo, but it hadn't worked out. He'd wanted to go with Nick in fact—he couldn't remember, but he thought Nick had backed out at the last minute, and he hadn't wanted to go alone.

Now she was coming to "his" casino.

He still didn't understand how Crabtree had gotten Kylie. Even Billy seemed impressed.

"Kylie Minogue? Shit, she came through here a year ago, and the show sold out right away. You see video of that bird in concert? She is *hot*."

Ethan had not seen any videos of Kylie, and Sam was only too happy to supply them. When Ethan watched the beautiful woman glide across the stage in elaborate showgirl costumes, he had to admit it didn't get much more classic Vegas than that. She was amazing. She was stunning.

She was far, far too good for a place like Herod's.

"Crabtree knows her manager, I think," Randy confided as they sat at a poker table at Herod's two days before opening night, waiting for the dealer to break in a new deck. "Really, I'm not surprised. He knows everyone."

"But how did he get so many good performers on such short notice?"

"Bribes and called-in favors, I assume. The usual.

He likely got a list of possible candidates and started pulling strings. Though he knows about Sam and Kylie. That one was a gift, and probably cost Crabtree something big." He winked at Ethan, nudging him with his elbow. "Go on, Slick. You're the big blind."

Ethan tossed his chips into the pot, turning a ten-dollar chip over absently in his fingers, the glittering *Billy's!* logo flashing. When the betting came around to him again, he tossed his 3 and 2 offsuit into the muck, sat back, and let his mind wander.

The day before, Billy had announced he'd fired the vacationing casino manager and was making Ethan official. "I'll have the boys move your stuff down by morning." He thought it would look better, he'd said, to have Ethan there by the time the buyer showed up.

Then he'd winked at Ethan, and Ethan had to go play craps to calm down.

Moth to a flame, every now and again he stopped by the roulette table and bet on black. Sometimes he won, but never regularly, and overall, he lost money. It was, he decided, just a bad game—for the player. For the casino, it was a gold mine. People couldn't seem to resist the wheel, couldn't help themselves from betting on black and red and even and odd and their grandmother's birthday and their anniversary. People always thought they were due, that it was their turn.

Craps, now. Craps was still iffy, but it was a lot more fun, and he came out ahead more than he did behind. He found he did better if he took a lot of money to the table. He would lose two hundred dollars steadily over the period of ten minutes, then abruptly shoot up four. So long as he only bet what he could afford, it really was a game.

It was the same with Butterfly Nights. Now that half of Vegas was caught up in the intrigue and the mystery and the outrage of a tournament going up against the World Series of Poker—once they put in their ante, they got lost in the bluff same as everyone else. They placed their bets, someone rolled the dice, and they forgot they might lose everything they'd placed on the Pass Line, forgot the seven could come anytime at all.

Randy nudged Ethan's arm and brought him back to reality, as the hand had ended and Ethan had the button. He also had the ace of spades and king of spades: Big Slick, with a little something extra. He kept his cool as the flop came down 5 of spades, 6 of spades, 2 of spades. He drew the bettors in casually, like it didn't matter, because really, it didn't. He had nuts on this hand. He was going to win, especially after 9 of hearts and jack of clubs came down. Eventually the pot was so high it was obscene, and everyone folded, everyone but him and Randy.

Randy studied him, but Ethan looked at him blankly and waited for him to call. Because Ethan knew he would.

"All right, wise guy." Randy tossed in his chips. "Call. Let's see how your bad boys do with mine."

Randy laid down 3 of diamonds and 4 of diamonds. He had a straight.

Ethan laid down his cards, completing his high

flush, and blew Randy a kiss.

Randy grunted, but Ethan caught his grin too.

When they were alone, Ethan let his anxiety out, and Randy took it, spun it out and sent it away, making him laugh, making him moan. Home with Randy was an oasis and asylum—nothing made him feel stronger or more secure than curling up naked in bed beside him and falling asleep as the cats arranged themselves around them. It was a waiting time, and it felt safe. Good.

Then it was over, because the Butterfly Nights began.

OPENING NIGHT, RANDY decided, was a pretty clever gig, especially considering "night" began at noon.

Caryle had a huge black canvas tent set up over the sidewalk and all the open parking in the casino's lot. Once inside, guests were amazed by the twinkling light show and occasional glitter storm that tumbled over their heads. Even with the portable air-conditioning units she'd brought in, the place was still scalding, but nobody cared. It was cool in a much more important way, and it was exclusive—sort of. There was a steady business of forgery for the passes down the street in a back alley, and several people snuck in through a gap in the canvas. Caryle instructed the staff not to notice this.

Inside on the casino floor, Mandy—hired away for the night from the Golden Nugget—was doing a bang-up job as the floor manager. She kept the tables rolling and the waitstaff hopping, and she gave every guest a smile as they passed that assured them they were aces in her book. She also gave out a few special golden chips Caryle had devised as a promotion, which sent certain customers up to the VIP lounge. In reality, this was nothing more than a high-priced bar with butterfly lap dances available for fifty dollars. Nobody showed any skin, but everybody wanted one of those golden chips. There were even more counterfeit golden chips than there were fake VIP passes. By the time the fireworks went off at dusk and the general public was allowed in, there'd barely be room to move.

Ethan beamed as he and Randy watched from the bar. "It's so much better without the slots, don't you think?"

That had been Ethan's last, most daring move, one Billy had balked at hard. Every casino knew the slots were where the money was made these days, he argued. Ethan, bless him, had argued like Randy had never seen him argue but hoped to see him do many, many times in the future.

Billy had still looked ashen when they'd hauled the slots out, put more than two-thirds in storage and the rest in the old poker room in the back. The poker tables were now out front, right as you came in the door—all but Billy's Room, which remained exactly where it had always been, and where it stayed sealed, because Crabtree wasn't in town.

That would change, tonight—in under an hour, in fact.

"How's Sam?" Randy passed Ethan a bottle of water. Slick wasn't having anything to do with alcohol tonight.

Ethan sipped at it. "He's backstage, talking to Kylie."

"He didn't garble when he met her? That's good."

"He was polite, and she was charming. He kept saying he didn't want to bother her, but she just said no, he was no trouble at all, and got him talking. When I left, they were discussing the heart graffiti photos she apparently posts on Twitter."

"Any word on Mitch?"

"Possibly by the show tonight. Sam says he's being cagey, but he's past caring about that now."

Randy sipped at his Dirty Whiskey. "And you, Slick? You ready for your big game?"

Ethan looked a little stiff. "I wish I knew what he was planning. I don't want to look like a fool."

"I'm sure you'll be fine." Randy downed the last of his drink then nudged Ethan with his knee. "What do you need me for, baby? How can I help?"

Ethan nodded at the poker tables. "Mandy says people are starting to play, but the head dealer has several people singled out who don't know how to play but seem to want to. Could you run the beginners' table for a while? Build up their confidence so they move to the five-dollar tables?"

"Sure thing, Slick."

He started to rise, but Ethan caught his arm and brushed a kiss across his cheek before letting him go. "Thanks, Ace."

Then he was gone, off to check out more of his Butterfly Night.

The beginners' table had been Randy's idea, but Slick was the one who had expanded it into Poker 101. The newbies played for money, but just penny chips. For five dollars, you could have a shadow help you through your hand. For twenty dollars, you could participate in an open-hand game where an expert explained what the good plays were and how each hand should have proceeded according to convention. It was a popular table, and for the next hour it was Randy's.

Sure, a lot of the people were thick as posts, but they were nervous, and everyone expressed that in different ways. Randy enjoyed getting them all to relax, to begin to see their strengths and to find their feet in the game. None of them would be experts anytime soon, and some would never amount to anything. But they went to the five-dollar tables in droves every time he dismissed them from their round, and they didn't go as live ones. It felt good.

The best thing about working on the floor was that Randy got to see the flash mobs. That had been Caryle's brainchild. There would be shows on the stage every hour, amateur stuff that was heavy on drag queens and had a lot of *Cirque du Soleil* rip-offs, but it was still a free show. In the meantime, spontaneous shows would break out all around the casino floor. A song would play, and dancers would come out, and waitresses and players would dance. No dealers, because that was too confusing, but a lot of them started to wiggle along because it was fun. When Randy's shift was finally over, he was disappointed, because they were just starting "Xanadu".

Sam fell into step beside him as he headed off the floor. "I think your uncle would be proud of you."

Randy punched him lightly in the arm. "How was Ms. Minogue?"

Sam's expression turned rapturous. "She's so perfect. That was so sweet of her, to talk to me. I can't wait to see her perform. But I wish Mitch would get here."

"Go call him again. I'm sure he'll be here soon, but call him anyway."

Sam nodded. "Yeah. But I'm going to go upstairs. It's too loud in here, even with the slots gone."

Randy headed to the bar.

It was packed, which despite the fact this was good for Ethan, annoyed him. He liked having the River to himself, and he resented that there was only one stool left and that it was way down on the end. Sighing, he slid into the empty space and signaled Scully for a drink.

A man sat beside Randy, tucked as far in the corner as he could go. God, but the guy was a case. He wore a suit and tie, which on Slick looked really good, but on this guy just made him read like an uptight insurance salesman. *Cheap* tie. *Cheap* shirt. He should be directing the Presbyterian choir. He seemed scared too, though he was trying to cover it by appearing aloof. It wasn't working.

Randy, in a good mood but still ticked about the full bar, decided to fuck with him. He leaned over with a mildly leering grin. "Having a good time, buddy?"

The man recoiled, but Randy caught a flicker in his eye that was more than fear. *Oh-ho.* He had himself a closet case.

"It's fine." The man withdrew deeper into the shadows.

Randy dialed it down a bit and went for quiet charm instead. "Quite a crowd. Little bit of something for everyone here, I'm thinking. You here by yourself?" Randy glanced down at the man's lap and wasn't surprised to see a golden wedding band on his left hand. "Or is the wife with you?"

His diagnosis of closet case was confirmed when the man looked almost startled as he glanced down at his hand. *Yeah, you've got to remember to take the ring off if you're going to cruise, sweetheart.* Of course, it also helped to not be so damn scared you were about to fall off your stool.

"I'm by myself tonight," the man said.

Randy wanted to ask for his name, but he thought he'd send the poor thing into shock. He was cute, in a sorry sort of way. He was the cleanest of the cleanest cuts Randy had ever seen. After another scan of the man's outfit, Randy wondered if Presbyterian might be too generous. Possibly Baptist.

Or, God help the poor bastard, Mormon.

He ran his finger along Ethan's ring absently, and felt a surge of empathy. "You played any table games yet?"

The man's lips quirked in a nervous smile. "I—I

play a little poker. I guess that starts in a bit."

Randy motioned toward the main casino floor. "No, they're playing right now. You want to go? I'd sit down with you, if you're looking for company."

Fuck, that came out the wrong way. But the man just smiled gratefully. "Thank you—that's very kind. But I'm waiting for someone."

"Are you now? I see I shouldn't have let the grass grow under my feet."

It was nice, actually, to see the nervous man relax, to see him warm up under Randy's flattery. "No, sorry— it's—" He stopped, rubbed his mouth and shook his head. "Sorry. I don't—I don't ever do this."

"Let me help you through the niceties, then." Randy extended his hand. "Hi. I'm Randy. Nice to meet you."

Frowning, the man stared at Randy's hand. At his pinky.

At his ring. Slick's ring.

The music throbbed, the crowd roared, and the heat cooked, but for that moment, Randy heard nothing, and he'd never been colder in his life.

Crabtree came up behind him and patted him heartily on the shoulder. "Hello, Jansen. If you don't mind, I need to steal Mr. Snow here. He's due to start in the big game in fifteen minutes."

Nick. Nick Snow. This guy was Ethan's Nick.

Randy turned to Crabtree, wanting to ask him what the fuck this was about, but he found he couldn't. He had no rage, no fury, no nothing, just a cold fear. Hurt cut across him when he saw the distance on Crabtree's face, when he realized the old bastard had done this, had gone and found Nick and brought him here. Had let Randy sit here and make an ass of himself trying to make him feel welcome.

Snow kept staring at Randy's hand. "Where did you get that?"

Randy pulled the ring off his finger and laid it on the counter. "Best of luck in the game."

Then he turned around and got the fuck out of there.

CHAPTER TWENTY-TWO

E THAN WAS STANDING near the fountain when he saw Nick.

At first he thought he had to be hallucinating, but Crabtree's men were behind Nick, flanking him—herding him, Nick pale and terrified. Then he saw Ethan and lit up.

It all came back to Ethan in a great, warm rush.

Years. He'd had *years* with this man. Years of listening to his sorrows, joys, spending stolen moments which were, for the two of them, the highest of pleasures. No limos, no high rollers, no wild motorcycle rides across the Las Vegas Strip. They hadn't been that kind of couple.

He had enjoyed being Nick's secret, if he were honest. He'd enjoyed being his true partner, the one he came unglued for, the one he surrendered to. It had filled some sort of void within himself, the only rebellion he would allow in his ordered, careful life. With this man, he had flaunted the rules and strictures of society and found love. And it had been love. Ethan had cherished it. As he regarded his former lover, the demon fountain splashing behind him, the din of the casino surrounding them, he realized he still did and always would.

Ethan knew, too, this love was over.

Ethan turned to Crabtree. "I see you took your sweet time about coming back. What do you think?"

He felt Nick's surprise, his pain. *Yes. Yes, it does hurt, doesn't it? I am sorry for that. But you might love your next lover better, and maybe even your wife, if you learn what it feels like, if you can learn to live with the pain you're feeling now and still find a way to move on.*

Crabtree rocked on his heels and nodded as he surveyed the room. "Quite nice. Quite nice indeed. All the old ways brought back, and some of them improved." He frowned at Ethan. "But do all the dancers have to be so lithe, so genderless?"

"That is the idea." Ethan kept watching Nick out of the corner of his eye.

Crabtree turned to Nick. "Would you and Mr. Snow care for a moment to reconnect before the big game?"

"Game? You're putting Nick in your poker game? He doesn't even know how to play."

"I play a little," Nick said. Oh, he ached, Ethan knew. *See me,* he begged. Nick was being torn apart in pieces, right here on the floor. Ethan didn't like it.

He took a step closer to Crabtree. "This game ends now. Whatever you used to get Nick here, use it to get him home. This isn't his world, and it isn't his fight. It's abysmally low of you to include him at all."

"Ethan," Nick said quietly, desperately, swallowing his pride and all but pleading with him, right there in the open. "Please, Ethan—we need to talk."

"There's nothing to say. If you want to apologize, that would be welcome, but if you add one little rationale for why you did what you did, don't bother. What you did ended us, Nick, and you can't undo that. You could possibly rebuild friendship with a lot of time and work and effort, but not now. Not tonight. I have more important things to do right now."

Go home. Go home, be free, and live, Nick—take this pain and build yourself anew inside it, and find your own adventures. Find your own real life. Go in peace. Because despite it all, I do still love you enough to wish you that.

Nick withdrew, wounded, the last ties of the past snapping and falling away. Their true end, here before him. Letting that last regret go, Ethan started to turn away.

Then he caught a glimpse of something small and silver flashing in Nick's hand. "What is that?"

Nick opened his palm, showing him the circle of silver. "Your ring."

"It's not my ring. It's yours." He looked up at Nick's face in horror. "*Randy.* You got this from Randy. Where is he?"

"The man at the bar?" Nick closed his hand and withdrew it, anger and disbelief creeping into his expression. "You're with *him*? *You* gave my ring to *him*?"

No. He took it. He won it, fair and square after carefully adjusting the odds. And now he'd given it away.

Ethan turned to Crabtree. "Where is he?"

The gangster shrugged, but Ethan could also feel him watching carefully, reading every tell. "He left, I think. It doesn't matter."

Ethan wanted to shove Crabtree in the fountain. He wanted to grab the man by the collar and push his head under the water, to drown him, to kick him, to drive sharp objects into his throat, his heart, to fucking chop his penis off and stuff it in his mouth. Instead he pulled his wallet full of Crabtree's money, the keys to his office, his business cards, and a handful of loose chips from his pocket. Then he tossed them into the churning water.

Ethan pointed at Nick. "Send him home. Give him a good alibi too, for his wife. But get him out of here."

"Ethan!" Nick reached for him, but Crabtree stepped in and faced Ethan down, his gaze cold and unforgiving.

"Where do you think you're going? You have a casino to run and a game to play."

Ethan stared him boldly down. "I fold. I'm not playing any of your games, Crabtree, because you don't have the pot I want."

Was that a ghost of a smile around Crabtree's lips? "Oh, I think I do."

"No, you don't. Because it isn't yours to give." He scanned the crowd, but of course Randy was gone. He wouldn't be anywhere in the casino. He'd be out there, somewhere, letting Vegas nurse his wounds. He ran his hand over his mouth, fearing he was already too late.

Crabtree grabbed his arm. "This isn't a game you

get to quit."

Ethan shook him off. "Then you'll have to rub me out, mob man. But if you ever loved him at all, let me find him first."

He would never know how he found the strength to turn away from a gangster in his own casino and walk out, to stalk across the floor, leaving his former lover and the man who had openly threatened to kill him behind. All he knew in that moment was he needed to get out, to find Randy, that nothing else in the world was worth doing.

When Sam found Ethan, his armor cracked, and he melted a little in relief. "Do you know where he is?"

"I have a pretty good idea." Sam led him toward a side exit. "Come on. I rode Mitch's bike in today. I'll drive you."

RANDY STOOD AT the railing of the Stratosphere observation deck and looked out as dusk came over Sin City, trying not to let any of the tourists around him see as his heart broke into pieces that tumbled, one by one, over the edge.

Ethan would leave him eventually. He'd known that, known it ever since he picked the ring up off the roulette table, this couldn't last, because nothing did. But when Nick Snow—not a villain, not an asshole, just a quiet, ordinary man so plain he was almost mousy— had stood there, looking back at Randy, he'd realized he had screwed up. He'd looked at Nick Snow and realized he wanted Ethan forever.

Randy leaned forward on the rail so he could reach up with his hand and pinch the bridge of his nose.

How? How had he ended up here after all this time of trying not to, of working not to get involved? He hadn't hurt like this when Mitch left him, and he'd thought that was bad. Now he was so torn up inside he could hardly stand upright—and Slick was still here.

What the fuck was going to happen to him when Ethan was gone?

You'll go on. If he leaves you, you'll go on. You'll hurt, but you'll survive. You'll bleed awhile, and then you'll rebuild yourself—just like he did. Because you're strong too, Skeet. You're strong too.

There was pressure building at the back of Randy's eyes, a pressure pinching his nose wasn't going to stop. Fucking hell. He was not going to start fucking crying on the fucking observation deck. He fucking was not.

But he did cry. It was all this fucking therapy shit. All this digging up the past, all this *feeling*. He wanted to go back to where he was strong and cocky and piss-on-the-world, I-don't-need-it Randy Fucking Jansen, everybody's favorite bastard. This was what happened when you let yourself want stupid shit like having somebody forever. It was a fucking impossible bet. There weren't even any odds.

You never got anybody forever. He'd known since the day he'd come home from school and found out Uncle Gary was gone. Now he was losing again, because when Ethan left it would really fucking cut him open.

But there wasn't anything he could do to get away from it. Not anymore.

Randy stood at the railing, wind whipping up around him, the screams of the riders and the murmur of the tourists surrounding him, and he hurt. He tried to unpack it, but it wasn't tidy, this pain. There was no one person or place that caused it, no demon to exorcise, not by a single name. There was just pain, all thirty-some years of it, piled on in flakes and dust and bricks on top of itself. All the things which had hurt him he hadn't let get through, the Great Fucking Wall of Randy.

Randy opened his eyes, blinked out the wet and salt, and looked out onto the city and thought, fucking hell, jumping would be a lot easier than dealing with all that shit. Because he only had to jump once. This crap would come back, over and over and over and fucking over again.

But sometimes it wouldn't be crap.

He wasn't yet willing to say it might even be good most of the time. It was Slick's goddamn fucking wheel. Red, black, with some green thrown in to fuck you up. Or craps, where a seven could happen at any time. The odds were always going to favor the house, though. There was no getting around that.

But maybe, maybe if he wasn't hauling around this stupid wall, maybe if he could muck out some of this pain—maybe the game wouldn't be so bad. Maybe Ethan would be there to play awhile with him, and maybe not.

Maybe sometimes it would be fun to let fate play it out, to feel the rush when the wheel and the dice and the cards went your way, not because you were smart or clever or you knew how to bluff but because fate felt nice that day. Maybe it would be fun to show up with nothing and leave a king.

Or at least to have fun trying for it.

Randy laughed softly and wiped at his eyes. Well, he knew where to find the fucking therapist, didn't he? And this time Sam could go along and hold his hand for a change.

He could do this. He was going to love Slick as long as he was here. He would survive. Because, yeah. He was strong. That's how Uncle Gary had raised him.

Randy opened his eyes, looked out over the city, which was leaving the rosy glow of dusk and taking on the full mantle of night, and he tried out a smile.

"*Randy.*"

Ethan rushed onto the platform, his heart written all over his face. Randy wiped at his eyes as discreetly as he could.

"Hey, Slick. Aren't you supposed to be running a casino?"

Ethan crushed Randy desperately to his chest. "I thought you were going to jump."

The words, stupid as they were, were sweet and like a balm over the open wounds of Randy's heart. He kissed Ethan's cheek. "*You're* the drama queen, not me. Besides, they've got a rim for just that reason. By the time anybody got out there, security would be on their ass. No jumping at the Stratosphere."

Ethan trembled as he crushed Randy tighter. "I thought I'd be too late. I thought either you'd jump, or Sam would be wrong and you'd be somewhere else, somewhere I couldn't find you, and I couldn't stand it. I should have told you. I should have told you every time I thought it, and I kept dying over and over again in that fucking elevator, thinking I wouldn't get to."

"Slow down, baby. Easy, easy. I'm here. What is it you need to tell me?"

"That I love you."

Oh, Randy knew he was a *sap* because those words made him fly every time. "Baby, you've said that already. And I love you too."

"There's more. There's everything I feel when I look at you, everything that gets caught in my throat—I need to tell you, because it's more important than anything, more important than the fucking casino, than what Crabtree will do to me for leaving in the middle of his game. I need to tell you, Randy, that I—" He paused for breath, looked absolutely terrified for a moment, then rushed on. "I *need* you, Randy. I completely, utterly need you. Obviously I can physically live without you, and probably emotionally too, but I don't think it's a good idea. I keep trying to be strong without you, to show you, but it's not the same, and I don't want to try anymore."

Were they still standing on the deck, or had they floated up into the sky? Randy didn't dare look away from Ethan's beautiful, terrified face to check. "Ethan

Ellison, you *are* strong. You're strong in a way that has nothing to do with me."

"I don't care. I want to be strong with you—and I have to tell you, because I fucked it up in the limo—Randy, I don't *want* to go. I wanted to be strong because I didn't want to be dependent. I wanted you to see that you didn't have to carry me, that I wouldn't fuck up again and bet on black and get carried away by fantasy—but I can't. Not yet. Maybe never. But nothing in the world will ever be as good as life is with you."

He pulled his hands out of Randy's and closed them desperately around Randy's face.

"I don't want Nick. I don't want the casino. I don't want anything but you. I won't kill myself if you don't want me back forever, but I'm going to want you, Randy. Until I die."

In that moment, that beautiful, amazing moment, the round observation deck of the Stratosphere tower was not only a tower but a wheel, spinning and spinning on the bright blue ball of the earth, with odds that should make you run away. But this time—this *fucking time*—the ball didn't just land on black. It landed right on his goddamned fucking number.

Randy took the beautiful man in front of him into his arms, bent him backward over the rail, and kissed the living shit out of him.

When they broke apart finally, Randy grinned down at Ethan, who laughed breathlessly, bracing himself against the edge of the rail.

"That was *my* fantasy, you know." Randy pressed

his hips a little harder into Ethan's. "So, thanks."

Ethan tilted his head and gave him a funny look. "To have me run up here like an idiot and babble incoherently?"

"To have a big old hot, romantic kiss on the rail of the observation deck. I think about it every time I come up here, in fact." He sighed happily. "Except now I won't wish. I'll remember."

"Do you think there's any way to keep Crabtree from killing me for running out? Because I'm kind of wanting more than a few more hours with you."

Randy suspected this was the outcome Crabtree had hoped for all along. "I bet we can work something out." He took Ethan's hand, then lifted it and kissed it. "Come on. Let's go back."

Sam waited on the interior deck, but he came up to them, grinning, when they came through the doors. "Everything's okay?"

"Aces, Peaches." Randy slipped his arm around him too, a man on each side. "We're aces."

It was a nice ride down the elevator, with lots of snuggling, and Sam beamed as they wandered through the lobby shops. "Mitch should be here anytime now. He said he was just pulling into town and to watch for him at the casino."

Randy stopped when he realized Ethan wasn't standing next to him anymore. He was two shops back, staring into a window display with a funny expression on his face. "Hey, Slick—what are you doing?"

Face going pale, Ethan pointed to a display in the

window. "This is Sam's aftershave lotion."

Randy peered through the glass at the poster-sized image of Nomad—available in cologne, aftershave lotion, and bar soap. He remembered it from seeing it beside the sink, but he remembered, too, using it to aid some fantastically sexy friction in Ethan's office. "Yep. That's the stuff. I bought it right here for Sam. Thought it was appropriate, given the way he and Mitch wander all over, and also, it smelled nice. Felt even better."

Ethan didn't turn away from the poster. "Randy, do you know Crabtree's real name?"

"Nobody does."

Ethan would not move his focus from the window. "You said Crabtree had an affair with Billy Herod Senior. Is that all? Did he have an affair with anyone else?"

"What's going on, Slick? Talk to me. You're freaking me out."

"What about Evelyn Carter?"

"What does it matter if Crabtree fucked a dead money launderer? And what does it possibly have to do with shaving lotion?"

Ethan broke away from the window, looking confused. "Money launderer? I thought he was a hit man."

"You've been reading too much Wikipedia. Carter wasn't a hit man. He was the laundryman. He made money so clean you thought it just came off the press. Some people think he wasn't even a real person. I think he was real, though. But he never killed anybody as far as I know. Nobody on a big scale, anyway. *Crabtree* was the hit man. Keeps himself far to the back of the room, never gets in a group picture, meets you out back with a knife or a gun. I suppose it's possible he had a fling with Carter. But who cares?"

Ethan looked sick. "What about the money they say Carter hid before he died? Is that true?"

"Maybe. Why? What the fuck is this, Slick?"

"I don't think Evelyn Carter is dead. I think Crabtree gave me his money. It's the only thing that explains it. And if I'm right—" He swayed on his feet.

Randy caught him. "Baby, Carter is dead. And if he isn't, he's just an accountant. Crabtree isn't going to kill you. I don't know what he's going to do with the casino, but it has something to do with you. He likes you."

"I hope so." Ethan splayed his fingers on the glass.

Randy turned to the display. "What the *fuck* is it with this poster, Slick—"

But the word died in his throat as Randy saw the poster, the whole poster—the product, but the logo too. The name of the company, spelled out proudly and elegantly over the top of the bottle, over the entrance to the store, the store Randy had walked past and into many times.

Crabtree & Evelyn.

CHAPTER TWENTY-THREE

R ANDY PACED BACK and forth between the bikes in the Stratosphere parking garage, trying to get a grip on reality. "Crabtree cannot be Evelyn Carter. Carter is dead."

Sam shook his head. "If he could make dirty money disappear, how hard would an already obscure mobster's life be?"

Randy hated how much sense that made. "Crabtree has a lot of money. It could be his money he's been giving Ethan."

Ethan leaned against Randy's bike. He looked like he'd fall over without it. "You think Crabtree has twenty-five million dollars?"

Randy stopped short. "He's given you that much?"

"I thought it had to be wrong. I thought it was for something else. And Sarah kept telling me to send people to her who asked questions about where I was getting it. It's not all in my account, either. It's in investments and things all over the place, but they all come back to me. There's a book at her desk that explains how I got them—it's false, but it looks amazingly correct. It's even retroactive, as if I've been amassing this money for years."

Randy had to admit it added up. There was no reason Crabtree couldn't be Evelyn Carter. The timing even made sense—the time he died was when Billy went reclusive, and Crabtree had gone with him. For years he didn't touch the casino at all—probably waiting things out while Nevada rotated through several gaming commissioners. Probably Crabtree had grown the big ass beard then too, and put on the weight.

He never entered the casino from the front, and he spent as little time as possible on the floor. Because it was technically illegal for him to be there, if he was Evelyn Carter. But if Crabtree, the jolly old elf, just hung out in the shadows, who would look too closely at the mug shots?

"But *why*? Why is he giving you all this money?"

Ethan shook his head, his expression indicating he'd been asking himself the same question for some time and had given up finding the answer.

"Because he wants Ethan to buy the casino," Sam said.

Both Randy and Ethan turned to him.

Sam raised his eyebrows and cocked his head. "He's said all along he has a buyer. A buyer he never talks about, and who has never shown any official interest in the place. What he has done is get Billy to shift the assets around, to spruce the place up, and to let Ethan take full control because he thinks he's getting the better of his uncle."

"Hold on." Randy's head was spinning. "You're trying to tell me Crabtree *gave Ethan twenty-five million dollars*, which is weird enough all by itself, but then for fun decided to fuck him over for it?"

But as soon as the words were out of Randy's mouth, he remembered that first night, what Crabtree had said as they sat there on the couch watching Ethan play.

The only way aces go high after falling as hard as this one has is under extraordinary circumstances. And even then it isn't guaranteed.

For Crabtree the pot was someone to take over the casino for him, someone who could handle it and would do a good job. Someone who would care for it. Someone who would care for Billy Senior's greatest love—outside of Crabtree. This was all that was left of his Billy. Yes. It made sense he'd try to find someone to take care of it, someone he thought would treasure it in the same way.

Twenty-five million dollars. What a fucking blind.

Ethan looked thoughtful. "He's testing me. He's willing to give me two things near and dear to his heart, if he's decided I'm worthy. Now I just have to show up at this game and lay down my cards."

Two things? Randy frowned. "You get the casino and all his money?"

"No." Ethan met Randy's gaze, his expression soft. "The casino—and you."

Randy faltered. "He—he doesn't feel that way about me."

"He does. And so do I." Ethan pressed a kiss against

Randy's forehead. "What I don't understand is how he's going to get Billy's controlling shares. It must be part of this game, but it's not legal for Billy to toss in the deed. Is it?"

Sam pulled out his phone. "Well, it's probably moot anyway now. The game started half an hour ago."

"Oh, I suspect it's been delayed." Ethan took one of the helmets off the back of the bike and grinned at Randy. "Want to go play the game of your life, Ace?"

Randy snorted. "What makes you think Crabtree is going to let a jackass like me into Billy's Room?"

"Because I won't go in without you." Ethan strapped on his helmet, then waited for Randy to climb on in front of him and drive.

THE GAME HADN'T started without them, but as Randy predicted, Crabtree balked at having him play. "He doesn't have the ante for the game we're playing."

"Then I'll cover him," Ethan said, and he'd known Sam was right when he saw the flash of alarm in the gangster's eye.

The ante was one hundred thousand dollars, and it was all done under an honor system, apparently, because Crabtree simply handed out stacks of chips already ready for them in the room. Ethan noticed there were exactly enough and that none had been brought in extra for Randy. Crabtree had meant for Nick to be playing in the seat where Randy currently sat.

Crabtree had offered Ethan his revenge—money

back from what Nick had taken from him. Money Crabtree had likely assured Nick he'd get returned, and which he'd intended to rob him of on Ethan's behalf. But Nick wasn't here now.

Ethan was glad. He didn't have any interest in revenge or in the past. Just the future. And all he had to do was get there without running afoul of the law or Crabtree's knife.

Besides Crabtree, Ethan, and Randy, there were five other players—Billy Junior and a collection of men and women Ethan knew were the live ones in the show. He recognized Canada Cate beside him and smiled, and she returned the gesture before settling in to her seat. The chairs were buttery leather that would have made a cozy place for a nap, if they weren't pulled up to a table of high-stakes poker. The walls were rich mahogany paneling, floors lush tan carpet. A chandelier twinkled beautifully above the green felt of the table. Four cameras were poised above them, and two microphones drooped down.

Waitstaff of both genders slipped in and out of the room, though Ethan noticed they were not in the standard butterfly costume of the main floor. They were in more classically tailored uniforms—tasteful, but flattering. The men were also almost universally gifted with beards or at least hinted they were well-favored in body hair, and several were a little bit round.

"What's the pot, Crabtree?" Cate accepted an elegant umbrella drink from a waitress. Ethan thought he caught her giving a slow, seductive smile to the young lady, who returned the gesture warmly before moving on to the next gambler. Ethan *knew* he saw Cate admire the line of the waitress's neck beneath her upswept hair.

Crabtree patted his ample stomach. "A good question. Quite obviously the pot is at least eight hundred thousand. But I thought that number was a bit crass, so I've added an additional ante to make it an even million."

Everyone at the table nodded, satisfied but not exactly impressed. No one voiced this—except Billy.

"Come on, Crabbie." Billy gave his godfather a withering glance. "There's no way you brought us here for spare change."

Ethan doubted, no matter what happened, he could ever regard one million dollars as spare change.

"I did have one thought." Crabtree regarded his godson with a nasty twinkle in his eye. "I've heard a rumor Billy here is interested in selling his casino. As it so happens, everyone at this table except for me has expressed interest in investing."

Beside Ethan, Randy snorted.

Crabtree gave him a quelling glare. "*Most* everyone. Excepting Randy and Ethan, however, everyone else here is known to have interest and capital enough to buy, and as we can all see, this is a place with potential, thanks to Mr. Ellison's diligent efforts. I propose a game—the winner gets the pot, and he—or she—also gets the casino."

Billy stood up, white-faced. "You can't do that. It's *mine.*"

"The shares are yours—twenty-five percent out-right, twenty-six percent in assets in trust, which are yours to use but the transfer of which I control. If you agree to this game, I will transfer control to you. That's a total of fifty-one percent of the shares you would own. But to get control, you must play—and win—this game. Because your ante, boy, will be three percent of your shares."

Billy stilled.

Crabtree continued. "If you win, the money is yours, as are all the shares, and you may liquidate this place or sell it, whatever you like. If you lose, you will no longer own the controlling interest, and someone at this table will own the three percent you put in the pot. I suspect we could all enter in a gentlemen's—and ladies'—agreement that the winner will offer to buy you out to finish gaining the monopoly." Everyone around the table except for Randy and Ethan nodded. "There, you see? You can't lose, Billy, and if you do, it won't be much. It certainly looks as if you have the best of it, doesn't it?"

The wheels of greed revolved in Billy's eyes. "Who owns the other forty-nine percent?"

Crabtree motioned to a corner, and a man came forward with an open binder. "Here you are, the list of shareholders. Most of them aren't people, just entities and such. Of course, everyone here owns a share or two, at least, which you can see for yourself."

"Yes." Billy looked up at Ethan. "He does too."

Ethan managed not to blink and shrugged to cover

his astonishment. "I like Herod's, and I know investments. I thought this place was a good one."

Except several of the names on the ledger were for shell companies, part of his twenty-five million dollars and fabricated investment past. Ethan owned a great deal of Herod's already, it seemed.

Billy considered the ledger. Ethan could see him trying to find the catch.

Randy leaned forward. "This is all a fine plan, but if I win, I can't buy Billy out."

Crabtree had an answer for this too. "Yes, Randy and Ethan are something of a problem. So since it is Billy who risks the most, we will make Randy and Ethan part of his team. If either of them wins, they may offer to buy him out of his remaining shares." He laughed, and everyone else did too. "Or they will cede to Billy, who will get to keep his three percent and they keep the million-dollar pot. Is this agreed?"

Billy seemed pleased, but none of the other gamblers did. "That's a huge advantage," a round, red-faced man beside Crabtree said. "I won't stand for it."

Crabtree appeared troubled. "Hmm. I suppose Billy could put in a few percent more of his shares?"

"Fifteen," a sniveling, permanently unhappy-looking man said from Cate's right.

"Oh, that's too much." Cate shook her head. "I think five more would be acceptable."

"Ten," a man in a cowboy hat between Billy and Crabtree said.

"I'll do eight." Billy's eyes danced. "And no more.

And you'll all increase your ante. To double."

This was roundly approved by all. Crabtree smiled—wolfishly—at Ethan and Randy. "The boys can owe me."

Randy leaned forward. "No. We're staying in as we are." When the rest of the table protested, he waved a hand at them. "Come on. We're already screwed out of winning anything but the monetary pot. You all ante up and get double the chips. We'll enter in with what we have."

Ethan leaned over to whisper to him as the table erupted in argument. "Do you think that was smart?"

"None of this is smart. But they'll take it. They know I could kick everyone's ass here but Crabtree's for playing, and they know I taught you. But now they have a double chip advantage over both of us, so they'll agree. That, and they're all pot-blind now. And fuck, Billy's so on tilt it isn't even funny."

"What's on tilt again?"

"Letting your emotions lead, not your logic. It's a gift to play with someone on tilt, and Crabtree and his little performance has just wrapped up half this table in a big fucking bow. You're right, he's testing you. Because he wants to see if you can take it. He wants to see if you can handle this kind of heat." He squeezed Ethan's hand beneath the table. "You can, baby. If it's what you want."

Ethan didn't know yet exactly what he wanted, but he played along, watching as it unfolded as Randy predicted. Randy's terms were accepted, and then the lawyers descended, collecting signatures, offering copies, answering questions until everything was satisfactory to all parties. Then, finally, play began.

The cowboy hat went out first. Everyone else played tight, but he sashayed into each hand, always sure he could win, and he did—twenty percent of the time. Within the hour he was all-in. Crabtree descended on him, and he was out. The red-faced man followed soon after, falling prey to a trap set by Randy, and then, with a great deal of noise, Billy was gone. The sniveling, unhappy man went soon after, and then it was Crabtree, Randy, Ethan, and Cate.

What was more interesting than who was out and who was in was how the remaining chips were distributed. Cate was the current leader, but not by much. Crabtree was right behind her, and Ethan, to his shock, was just behind him. He had played tight the whole time, and as a result he had done little but amass chips one after the other. He'd never been ahead, and his won pots were usually small, but they were starting to add up.

Randy was well behind, and Ethan had figured out a long time ago his lover played only to protect Ethan's stack. Whenever Ethan made a bad mistake, Randy quickly outdid him and Ethan got his money back the next round. The oddest thing was, sometimes he thought Crabtree was doing the same thing, though not as well as Randy. Cate, however, played for real, and she took no prisoners. She aimed herself at Ethan, trying to draw him all-in, but Ethan wouldn't bite. So she turned her sights on Randy—which ultimately was what did her in.

Oh, it had been sweet to watch Randy play Canada Cate. It was the clash of the titans in skill, but what tripped Cate up was that Randy didn't want to win. He went from the tight, stealthy plays he'd used all night to abruptly erratic moves, and she was so distracted she never noticed that though Randy was losing, she was losing more, and it was all going to Ethan. Crabtree cut it off and swept her up, but by then the damage was done. Ethan, by a hair, was the chip leader. Randy was almost out. Cate, with a rueful smile, inclined her head and left the room.

Play turned ruthless as Ethan was caught between the other two men, Crabtree trying to win Randy's chips and Randy trying to funnel them to Ethan. It was the strangest kind of play, and it gave Ethan a headache trying to keep up—it wasn't about who won at all, it was about who lost and where and by how much and who picked up whose chips. He held on as best he could, and when it was over, he had managed to catch most of Randy's salvos. He was still ahead—but only by two thousand dollars.

One million and one thousand dollars. That was the total amount of the chips sitting in front of Ethan, and as this thought hit him, he felt it drag him like an anchor. *One million and one thousand dollars.* More money than he had ever had in his life, more money than he'd hoped to amass for a retirement package. Technically he had much more than this in the bank, but that was scattered about and all on paper. This was a stack of chips. This was sitting right in front of him.

Ethan slowed to a full stop. *I can't do this.*

Randy caught the look on his face and brushed a kiss across Ethan's lips. "You're always a high ace to me. No matter what happens. Just keep moving, Slick, and you'll be fine." He kissed him again, and then he was gone with the rest of them.

It was just Ethan and Crabtree.

And the cards.

Crabtree smiled, carnivorous and deadly, the man who could cut your heart right out of your chest and not so much as break a sweat. He'd give Ethan no quarter.

The problem was, Ethan knew he could never beat a man like this, not now and not ever. So he did the only thing he could do, what Randy, and even Crabtree, had taught him to do.

He bluffed.

He rubbed at his throat and looked around, feigning nervousness. It wasn't difficult.

"Need something to drink, boy?" Crabtree's tone suggested he'd be happy to offer hemlock.

Ethan nodded to the full water bottle beside him. "No. It's my hands. They're too dry from the cards." He reached into the pocket of his jacket which was hanging over the back of his chair and pretended to fumble until he was sure he could withdraw the object without his hands shaking like crazy. Uncapping the bottle, he squirted a small amount of the fragrant liquid on his hands.

He smoothed it around then recapped the bottle before setting it on the table so the CRABTREE & EVELYN label faced the gangster.

Crabtree continued to shuffle the cards. "My mother loved that brand. Her favorite was Evelyn Rose. That was where she got my name. And, of course, where I got the inspiration for the one I gave myself."

Ethan's gaze flickered to the cameras.

"They're on a feedback loop, and they will be until I say otherwise. No one's watching us right now. No one can hear us. I suppose I should point out no one will be allowed in. No one." He put the cards down. "So. What do we do now, Mr. Ellison?"

Ethan thought he might have a heart attack right then and there. "I thought we were going to play cards. Has that changed?"

Crabtree chuckled. "I like you, Ethan."

"That's good to hear," Ethan said, and he fucking meant it.

"I like your style, that you're confident but not cocky. I like how you seem to understand the stakes, the true stakes, but you don't let them intimidate you—not for long. I like that you have heart, that you take risks, and when they don't pan out, you pick yourself up and try again."

His smile faded, and he aimed a fat finger in warning at Ethan.

"But your self-doubt is going to kill you, if you don't get it under control. You can't rely on Randy to bolster you. You'll lose him, but not in a big dramatic moment like your little pansy from American Fork. It'll wear off piece by piece, and he'll do it for you every time, shaving off parts of himself until there's nothing left, not for him to live on, not for you to shore yourself up with. Get yourself under control, or you're going to be an even bigger fuckup than I was. You understand me, Ellison?"

Ethan felt oddly calm. "I understand you, Mr. Carter."

Crabtree glanced at the camera, made a motion with his finger then began to shuffle again. "Shall we play?"

He dealt the cards, two each.

Ethan left his on the table and watched Crabtree, who didn't look at his either.

"What would you do with this casino, Mr. Ellison, if you could afford to buy it?"

"I'd run it. I'd continue the theme of harking back to the glory days of Vegas, but I'd only continue doing that if it continued working. I would do a lot of research too. That's how I always operate with investments. I'm thorough. I'm meticulous. And I'm careful, as I'm sure you already know. If I were to err, it would be on the side of caution—unless, like this, the whole of the casino was on the line."

Crabtree kept his face unreadable. "And why would you do that?"

Even without a tell from his opponent, Ethan re-laxed. "Because I've come to love it, not as a business but as a place. Herod's gave me back my heart, possibly my soul. Being here, playing here, and working here has taught me more about life and the risks we take—that we *need* to take—than anything else I've done. If Herod's were mine, I would take the risks I needed to keep it. I wouldn't be anyone's man. I wouldn't be anyone's front. I would abide by the law. I would pay my taxes and, if I were doing well, I would invest in the community. Because I would make Las Vegas my home. That's what I would do, sir, if I could afford to buy this casino."

"And if you won," Crabtree added dryly.

"Yes."

Ethan waited.

Crabtree tapped his finger on the felt for a few more seconds. "What about the name? Would you change it?"

Ethan looked appalled. "Absolutely not. For heaven's sake, half the value of a place is in the branding, and I've just killed myself for a month stamping *Herod's* across the psyche of everyone I could reach."

Crabtree smiled, a bright, beaming grin, and Ethan felt like a veil lifted. The gangster, the trickster, the gruff old bastard and every one of his veneers fell away, and Ethan just saw a man to whom life had not always been fair. He saw a man who had tried to adjust the odds of life and lost a little more than he'd won even so. He saw a man who had bet on black and lost, a man who had retreated from the pain of it. A man who had tried to hide from that pain, had tried to mask it, but like Randy and Ethan, had never quite been able to hide completely.

Crabtree was an ace too. He was an ace, low so long he never thought he'd ever get up again. An ace, waiting for someone to give him a reason to rise.

Then it was gone. But it had been there, and Ethan had seen it. He knew he would never forget that Evelyn Crabtree Carter, not ever. Ethan wasn't playing just for himself, but for Randy, and Crabtree too.

Maybe he was playing for all the aces in the world, for every man and woman whom life had hit too hard, who needed one moment of wonder to believe again.

"Enough of this chatter." Crabtree peeked at his cards and tossed in his ante. "Let's play."

Ethan skimmed the ante off his stack as well and threw the chips gently into the center of the table. Crabtree had acted out of turn, but with the two of them, it hardly mattered for the blinds. The real game began now, and Ethan was the first to act. He could call, he could raise, or he could fold.

Without looking at his cards, Ethan pushed the whole lot of his million-plus dollars in chips into the center of the table.

He would never beat Crabtree in regular play. He might get lucky for a while, but he would never get enough of an advantage to truly come out ahead. And Crabtree wasn't going to give it to him, because he wanted to test him, to beat him up. He wanted to win the pot himself and then put conditions on it so he could maintain control—because he was going to give the casino to Ethan anyway. He couldn't own it, but if Crabtree was the one who gave the casino to Ethan, he would always be in charge. He would work hard to keep this advantage. Ethan did not, in any way, shape, or form, have the best of it by playing a regular game.

This move changed everything.

With Ethan all-in, Crabtree had two choices—he could fold or call. If he called, he would have to go all-in too, because Ethan had more chips than he did. Crabtree would win if he had the better hand—but Ethan would win if he didn't.

What mattered now was Crabtree did not have the best of it anymore. He couldn't read Ethan, because Ethan hadn't looked at his cards. There were endless variables yet, with the flop not down and with no one else in play. The only certainty was Crabtree's own hand. It had better be good, and he had better be lucky, if he called. If he folded, Ethan would only gain the ante. Not much would change.

Of course, if Crabtree folded this time, Ethan would do the same thing over again. And again. One way or another, this game was going to be left up to fate.

Ethan didn't care what Randy said. Fate owed him *big.*

His face carefully blank, Crabtree pushed all his chips into the center, reached for the deck and dealt the board, the flop, the turn, all the way to the river.

2 of spades, 10 of spades, 4 of clubs, 9 of spades, 6 of spades. Possible straight, possible flush. Several possible pairs, but no full houses, no four of a kind.

Ethan looked up at Crabtree and waited.

The gangster turned over his cards: king of clubs,

queen of clubs. Crabtree had high card.

Ethan flipped over his cards: 2 and a 3, offsuit.

He had a pair. Of 2s, but it was still a pair. And a pair beat high card.

He'd won.

Ethan stared out at the huge, huge pile of chips. Then he laughed. And laughed, and laughed, and laughed.

CHAPTER TWENTY-FOUR

RANDY ENJOYED WATCHING Billy and Ethan tussle over the sale of the casino.

The scene took place in Billy's office, which Randy enjoyed knowing would shortly be Ethan's. While Ethan spoke heatedly of deficits and improvements necessary and Billy essentially rolled over slowly under the intensity of Slick full steam, Randy sank into the sofa, dug the toes of his boots into the plush rug and began to catalog all the places and positions in which he was going to fuck the new owner. And, of course, be fucked in return.

Mitch showed up as Billy and Ethan finished up negotiations, holding a large box, and once Sam got done mobbing him, Mitch showed them what was inside—chips. Heavy, fucking beautiful casino chips of pristine color and satisfying weight, each one stamped, quite simply, with *Herod's*.

"I've been sitting on these bastards for a week." Mitch cast an irritated look at Crabtree. "The trailer is full of them, and new dice and cards too. I could've been home a long time ago, but he wouldn't let me come back."

Sam was pissed. "Why would he make you do that?"

"Because he said you needed some time without me to spread your wings." Mitch sighed. "And he was right. Sunshine, I don't know what you've been doing, but keep it up, and tell me if I get in the way of it again."

Sam's lips curved in a wicked smile. "I want my own bike. And by bike I mean motorcycle, not a ten-speed. I'm buying it with my own money, with my first paycheck. Something small and practical. But I want one."

Mitch drew Sam into his lap and kissed him. "Whatever you want, baby. Whatever you want."

Ethan, joining them at last, picked up a rack of chips, withdrew a hundred-dollar token and turned it idly in his fingers. "What's this?"

"My gift to the new owner of Herod's Poker Room and Casino." Crabtree lounged in the chair across from Randy, his pose casual, but he was nervous. It was hard, after all, to give your baby away, even when you knew the man taking her from you was perfect.

Ethan turned the chip over a few more times. "That was thoughtful, sir. Thank you." He tucked the chip into his pocket and glanced at his watch. "I think the concert is about to start, Sam. I'd hate for you to miss any of it."

They all went to watch together, sitting right in the front row, and Randy hardly saw anything on stage because he was too busy watching Sam. He watched, too, the way Mitch held his husband close, glad to be with him, and Randy enjoyed how right it was to see the two of them together, partnered, whole and happy.

When the performance stopped and Ethan took the stage, Randy knew what was coming, and he accepted his role in the lost bet with grace, or as much grace as he could manage in a pink feather boa, sequined underwear he pulled up over his jeans, a fuzzy yellow vest that made no sense at all, and the biggest fucking hat he'd ever seen. Actually, all things considered, it was a lot of fun. He danced like a fool on stage next to a pop princess who really was as kind and gracious and absolutely beautiful as Sam had billed her to be.

Then he was done, and he settled in to watch the rest of the show with Ethan.

Halfway through, Ethan led him out of the theater to the craps table.

"I want you to play with me." Ethan handed him a tray of chips. "I want you to play against the house, against fate, and I want you to have a good time while you do it."

Randy took the tray and grimaced down at the table. "That's a tall order."

He tried, though, for Slick, and he had to admit, it wasn't all bad. He did have to work not to tense up every time he rolled, bracing himself for the seven. He hated betting the Field or Hardways, and he refused point-blank to make a proposition bet. Still, it bit like hell when he rolled a seven at last. But he got over it, and yeah, it had been fun.

He'd even come out a little ahead, overall. That wasn't so bad.

"Your turn, Slick," he said, and stepped aside.

Ethan took his place at the end of the table, but it was weird because he seemed nervous. Probably residual nerves from the game and everything else. Randy thought it was sweet, and he ran a finger down his lover's arm, a quiet, soothing gesture. It didn't do much good, though.

Then fuck if Mitch and Sam didn't show up on the other side of the table, Sam eager, Mitch with a wicked grin.

Something was up.

"You're missing your show, Peaches," Randy said carefully, watching Sam's face.

"I need to be at this show right now." He nudged Ethan. "Go on. What are you waiting for?"

"I slowed down." Ethan was almost green now. "I have to stop doing that."

He threw.

Except what fell wasn't dice. Randy stared, his whole world going round and round as he stared down at the pair of shining gold rings.

Ethan looked ready to hurl, but he put on a bluff that probably fooled everybody else. "I didn't buy these with Crabtree's money, or anything from the casino. I did some investment work for Sam, and he gave me the money for them in trade. So these come from me, not from this." He turned to Randy again, full of terror, and love, and hope. "Would—would you marry me?"

Randy's heart soared. "You do know they call it Domestic Partnership for us gay boys, here in Nevada."

"I'm calling it a marriage." Ethan nudged Randy's boot with his sleek black loafer. "Come on, Ace. Stop dicking around and tell me yes or no."

"I am *never* going to stop dicking around. Especially with you."

The crowd gathered around them broke into snickers.

Randy looped his arms around Ethan's neck. "Yeah, Slick. I want a marriage with you. And a partnership, and whatever fucking else you want. I want you, Ethan Ellison."

"Well, you've got me, Randy Jansen."

Randy beamed, a grin running all the way down to his toes, cracking his heart open as the crowd cheered and whistled. He pressed his mouth to Ethan's and kissed him, opening all the way, letting the man he loved into his heart—all the way in, for better or for worse, for richer, for poorer, and all of that shit.

Forever.

ABOUT THE AUTHOR

Heidi Cullinan has always enjoyed a good love story, provided it has a happy ending. Proud to be from the first Midwestern state with full marriage equality, Heidi is a vocal advocate for LGBT rights. She writes positive-outcome romances for LGBT characters struggling against insurmountable odds because she believes there's no such thing as too much happy ever after. When Heidi isn't writing, she enjoys cooking, reading, playing with her cats, and watching anime, with or without her family. Find out more about Heidi at heidicullinan.com.

Did you enjoy this book?

If you did, please consider leaving a review online or recommending it to a friend. There's absolutely nothing that helps an author more than a reader's enthusiasm. Your word of mouth is greatly appreciated and helps me sell more books, which helps me write more books.

MORE BOOKS IN THE SPECIAL DELIVERY SERIES COMING SOON

SPECIAL DELIVERY

Sam knows he'll never find the excitement he craves in Middleton, Iowa. Then Sam meets Mitch, an independent, long-haul trucker. When Mitch offers to take him on a road trip west, Sam jumps at the chance. One minute Mitch is the star of Sam's X-rated fantasies, the next he's a perfect gentleman. And when they hit the Las Vegas city limit, Sam finds out why: Randy. Sam grapples with the meaning of friendship, letting go, growing up—even the meaning of love—because no matter how far he travels, eventually all roads lead home.

HOOCH AND CAKE

All Sam and Mitch want to do is get married, but between their busy schedules and the judgment of a small town, it's not as easy as it should be. Then their best friend Randy shows up, and the wedding that almost wasn't is about to become the wedding Iowa never even dreamed to see.

THE TWELVE DAYS OF RANDY

Randy and Ethan are ready to enjoy their first Christmas at home together, but when Crabtree ropes Randy into wily holiday antics, Ethan feels left out in the cold. When Herod's new owner discovers his husband only plays at being an imp to hide a Christmas spirit bigger and tackier than Las Vegas, Ethan vows to find a way to have his cake and eat it too. Especially if Randy's the one jumping out of the middle.

TOUGH LOVE

Chenco Ortiz harbors fierce dreams of being a drag star on a glittering stage, but when leatherman Steve Vance introduces him to the intoxicating world of sadomasochism, he finds strength in body and mind he's never dreamed to seek—strength enough maybe to save his tortured Papi too.

OTHER BOOKS BY HEIDI CULLINAN

There's a lot happening with my books right now! Sign up for my **release-announcement-only newsletter** on my website to be sure you don't miss a single release or re-release.

www.heidicullinan.com/newssignup

Want the inside scoop on upcoming releases, automatic delivery of all my titles in your preferred format, with option for signed paperbacks shipped worldwide? Consider joining my Patreon. You can learn more about it on my website.
www.patreon.com/heidicullinan

THE ROOSEVELT SERIES
Carry the Ocean
Shelter the Sea
Unleash the Earth (coming soon)
Shatter the Sky (coming soon)

LOVE LESSONS SERIES
Love Lessons (also available in German)
Frozen Heart
Fever Pitch (also available in German)
Lonely Hearts (also available in German)
Short Stay
Rebel Heart (coming fall 2017)

THE DANCING SERIES
Dance With Me
also available in French, Italian coming soon
Enjoy the Dance
Burn the Floor (coming soon)

MINNESOTA CHRISTMAS SERIES
Let It Snow
Sleigh Ride
Winter Wonderland
Santa Baby
More adventures in Logan, Minnesota, coming soon

CLOCKWORK LOVE SERIES
Clockwork Heart
Clockwork Pirate (coming soon)
Clockwork Princess (coming soon)

TUCKER SPRINGS SERIES
Second Hand (written with Marie Sexton) (available in French)
Dirty Laundry (available in French)
(more titles in this series by other authors)

SINGLE TITLES

Antisocial (coming summer 2017)

Nowhere Ranch (available in Italian)

Family Man (written with Marie Sexton)

A Private Gentleman

The Devil Will Do

Hero

Miles and the Magic Flute

NONFICTION

Your A Game: Winning Promo for Genre Fiction
(written with Damon Suede)

Many titles are also available in audio and more are in production. Check the listings wherever you purchase audiobooks to see which titles are available.